NEW BEGINNING

Also by Lukas Walker

Disarm

NEW BEGINNING

A THRILLER

LUKAS WALKER

This book is a work of fiction. Names, characters, organizations, places, and events are either products of the author's imagination or are used fictitiously. Any similarity to actual events or persons, living or dead, is entirely coincidental.

Copyright © 2024 by Lukas Walker

All rights reserved. No part of this book may be reproduced in any form without written permission from the author, except for brief quotations embodied in a book review.

First Edition November 2024

Cover Design and Interior Formatting by Books and Moods
Author Photograph by Chris Evan Photography

ISBN 979-8-218-51502-7 (paperback)
ISBN 979-8-218-51503-4 (ebook)

For Inquiries: LukasWalkerAuthor@gmail.com

For Camila
Thank you for going on this adventure with me.

Behind the ostensible government sits enthroned an invisible government owing no allegiance and acknowledging no responsibility to the people. To destroy this invisible government, to befoul the unholy alliance between corrupt business and corrupt politics is the first task of the statesmanship of the day.

—President Theodore Roosevelt, 1912

PROLOGUE

Lexington, Kentucky
June, 2023

CONGRESSMAN SETH WILSON felt like he had just closed his eyes when the alarm clock on his nightstand went off at 2:30 a.m. He hit snooze and rolled over as his wife Laura mumbled something and wrapped her arm over his chest. It had only been a couple of hours since he'd closed his laptop and snuck into bed, careful not to wake the woman of the house who routinely turned in by nine. With a baby and a full-time job as a nurse, she was a superhero—capable of doing anything—and that motivated Seth. Every day it did.

When he quit his law practice and went into politics, she had his back. When he lost that first election and found himself unemployed—she had his back. And when he ran again and won, she was right there beside him. Only this time she was nine months pregnant with their daughter Lizzy and just starting maternity leave. To say it had been a sacrifice would be an understatement. As one of the youngest members of Congress, representing Kentucky's 6th District, Seth worked around the clock for his constituents—serving on multiple House committees, drafting bills that would never see the light of day but created traction, and above all, trying to make a difference in a country that was spiraling out of control.

Seth lived in his office at the Capitol Complex when he was in Washington, D.C., sleeping on a pullout couch and showering at the gym in the basement. With the rising cost of rent, it was the most economical housing option in the city. Of course, they could probably afford an apartment in the nation's capitol if they got rid of their home in Kentucky, but that wasn't an option. Seth and Laura had both grown up in Lexington. They met each other on the swim team when they were seven, began dating in high school, nearly broke up but got back together in college, and were married shortly after they both graduated from the University of Kentucky.

A small city with roots in the horse industry, Lexington had rolling green hills, architecture dating back to the early nineteenth century, and a pleasant mix of Southern and Midwestern hospitality. It was an ideal place to raise a family—and raising a family was precisely what Seth and Laura planned on doing. It was also old-fashioned, but they were as old-fashioned as they came.

One-year-old Lizzy had yet to wake up. That would soon change, though, because she would hear her parents preparing for the day and immediately start screaming. The girl never wanted to be left out. Seth was on the House Committee on Energy and Commerce and had an early flight to D.C. for a final vote. After weeks of congressional hearings, he had barely been home since Easter. But it was all about to be over, and he was looking forward to some quality time with his family—and Laura was already making Fourth of July plans.

By the time Seth showered, shaved, and dressed, Laura had

fed Lizzy—whose screams filled the house the moment he turned on the shower—and brewed a fresh pot of Cherry Seed Coffee from the local Farmer's Market.

"Did you check in?" Laura asked as she poured her husband a heaping mug of the dark roast, followed by a dollop of half-and-half.

Seth frowned and reached into his pocket for his phone. "I did not."

With Lizzy on her hip, Laura poured herself a cup and joined him at the kitchen table.

"Let's hope there's an aisle seat," she said. "Remember what happened last time?"

"There will be." He finished checking in and put his phone away. "I've been back and forth on this all night. Still no idea if I'm doing the right thing."

"What's your gut tell you?"

"Nothing. That's the problem."

"Don't think about it anymore. You've done the work. You'll make the right call." She put her hand on his. "Even if it means upsetting a few people."

• • •

The Uber arrived a few minutes past four—it was a silver Toyota Prius—and Seth wheeled his carry-on out to the front porch of their three-bedroom brick home. He'd packed light. This was to be a short trip, and he would be home the following day.

Laura stood in the doorway holding Lizzy.

"I'll pick you up in the morning. We can get breakfast," she said.

"What about Liz?"

"My mother is coming over tonight. I think she can be persuaded to watch her."

Seth smiled. "It's a date."

He kissed his wife and daughter goodbye and climbed into the Prius.

Still too early to call it morning, the streets were empty. It was a short drive to the Bluegrass Airport—a cozy hub across the street from Keeneland race track—and Seth spent the five-minute commute flipping through his phone and reading the latest news reports surrounding the vote he would cast that afternoon.

It happened fast. As the car turned onto Man O' War Boulevard, heading northwest, the front driver's side tire blew, causing the vehicle to jolt then dip to the side as the wheel hit the pavement. The young Uber driver struggled to maintain control, and the car skidded to a stop on the side of the road.

"Are you okay?" he frantically asked his passenger.

"All good, buddy." Seth was startled, but he was fine.

"I don't know what happened."

"Your tire blew," Seth replied. He checked his watch. There was still time to make the flight. "You got a spare?"

"Yeah, I think so."

They both got out of the Prius and checked the trunk. Sure enough, there was a spare—one of those little guys that only gave you thirty miles before crapping out. The Uber driver couldn't have been more than twenty, and Seth could tell he'd never had a flat tire before, let alone knew how to change one. This further substantiated his belief that the new generation had lost out on important life skills due to an unhealthy reliance on technology and social media.

"You ever done this before?" Seth asked.

The boy shook his head as he went for his phone.

"Don't bother calling anyone. We'll change it ourselves."

The congressman liberated the spare and the jack from the trunk, then loosened the lug nuts that held the wheel in place. He explained each step of the process, hoping to teach the young man a life skill every adult should have. The driver stood behind the car watching and listening but still unconvinced he could ever do this on his own. Seth used the jack to lift the vehicle a foot into the air. He was about to remove the flat tire when a sudden burst of light illuminated the entire car. The Uber driver turned, his eyes widening in horror. Seth was hunched over the tire, his back to the road. He looked up.

Instantly blinded by headlights from an incoming semi-truck, Seth realized what was about to happen. But his body didn't have time to react. The front of the truck smashed into him at sixty-five miles per hour, amputating his legs at the torso and filtering them through the truck's undercarriage like a meat grinder. His upper body was thrown against the hood of the Prius, cracking his skull wide open and sending a splatter of blood and brain matter into the air. The little car and the big truck became one as the trucker slammed the air brakes and came to a smoke-filled stop in a grassy ditch beside the road.

CHAPTER 1

Port of Tianjin, China
170 Kilometers Southeast of Beijing

ONE WEEK AGO

The rain was relentless. Thousands of shipping containers stood like mountains amidst hundreds of cargo ships—some docked, others waiting patiently in the Bohai Bay. The largest port in Northern China, this was the center of the world's manufacturing and shipping industry where, every day, millions of consumer goods were transported to the United States. Chinese Communism was a unique hybrid of Marxist and democratic ideologies. On one hand, the State controlled every aspect of business, but unlike the once great Soviet Union, they managed to keep capitalism alive and well. And that's what made them dangerous.

Natalya Palmer took a taxi to the Jintang No. 4 Road and was dropped off at Tianjin Port Ro-Ro Terminal Company, where a medium-sized cargo ship had docked for the night. From the empty parking lot—easily the size of a football field—she could barely make out the ship, and the ocean was nothing but darkness behind it. The only light that perforated the wet air came from the parking lot's antique metal-halide lamps and the distant glow from the city of Tianjin behind her.

She checked the time on her phone: five minutes till one.

Should be anytime.

At the edge of the parking lot, a hundred yards from the ship, there were blocks of shipping containers stacked in pairs of twos and threes. She checked one of them, and sure enough, it was unlocked. Ineptitude was everywhere, even in China. She hid inside, lit a cigarette, and waited.

Natalya was in her late thirties with an athletic figure, green eyes, and short blond hair, though its true color was a chestnut brown. She was beautiful by anyone's standards, an attribute she had utilized on more than one occasion. It had been nearly a year since her CIA cover in Russia was blown and she was thrust into an impossible mission to thwart a nuclear attack on the U.S. She had joined forces with a team of CIA contractors to neutralize the threat and save the world from plummeting into a third world war.

However, unbeknownst to them—and the CIA—she was working as an FBI operative within a gray counterintelligence group code named *Woodhaven*, with one directive: investigate the activities of the New World Order. Referred to as the NWO, this deep state organization—believed to be controlled by the Chinese Communist Party, or CCP—had spent the better part of the twentieth century building a global network intent on creating a "one-government world." They had orchestrated the nuclear attack, and the fight to stop them had only just begun.

Best suited for clandestine operations, Natalya had gone dark after her last mission and was assigned a new cover. For the past eleven months her only connection to Woodhaven had been updates, orders, and intel—all through encrypted messages—to and from her handler, FBI Special Agent Adam Conner. Her new identity was a punk-rock emo chick living in Beijing who could write code faster than any other programmer in China. A bit of an exaggeration—and it was all bullshit—but that pitch had gotten her in the door at TZH, one of China's largest telecommunication technology companies whose success, like most businesses, was grounded in their ties to the CCP.

Natalya's resume—along with her passport—said she was born in China to English teachers who had both died during the COVID-19 pandemic in 2020. As a naturalized citizen and proud supporter of the CCP—*fuck America*—she had passed her government evaluation and started as a Junior User Experience Programmer at TZH. To prepare for her latest role, she spent three months studying programming languages like C++, Python, and JavaScript. It was brutal, but she had mastered the basics well enough to keep her cover intact for the last eight months.

Adam Conner believed the NWO's next move would be in the technology sector. China was cracking down on companies disloyal to the party—separating themselves from Silicon Valley and building their own state-controlled arsenal of Apples and Facebooks. Natalya's directive was to keep an ear to the ground. So far she had learned nothing. But like their U.S. counterparts, the Chinese tech community was small, and though she worked at TZH, she soon found herself grabbing after-work drinks with programmers from other companies like Alibaba, ByteDance, and WeChat. Mostly, she got better at her job.

Then, two days ago, she overheard a programmer friend discussing a new AI chip developed by Semiconductor Manufacturing International Corporation, or SMIC, the largest microchip manufacturer in mainland China. Headquartered in Shanghai, with a plant in Beijing, SMIC was controlled by the People's Liberation Army—the CCP's armed forces—and was prohibited from selling to American companies by the United States Department of Defense.

Semiconductor chips are integrated circuits that power all electronic devices—phones, laptops, TVs, even automobiles—and are one of China's largest exports. AI chips are a more advanced version. They're able to process enormous amounts of data, solve complex computations, and are essential for developing artificial intelligence systems. However, SMIC's new AI chip was different; according to Natalya's friend, it was more powerful than any other chip on the market and had the ability to power AI systems like never seen before. That was enough to spark Natalya's interest. A little digging revealed that a shipment of AI chips was being delivered to the Tianjin Port Ro-Ro Terminal Company at one o'clock in the morning. The fact that it was happening at night was suspicious and made her wonder who the buyer was.

At precisely 1:00 a.m., a box truck pulled into the parking lot and headed toward the ship. Natalya crushed her cigarette as she stepped outside the container and used the hood on her coat to shield herself from the rain. The weather made it easier to stay hidden, but it also made it difficult to make out the faces of the men who exited the truck. There were two of them, both Chinese and dressed in green military uniforms and armed with QBZ-95s—5.8x42mm round standard issue rifles for the People's Liberation Army. They stood beside the truck and waited—in the rain.

Goddamn communists do whatever they're told.

A light appeared from inside of the cargo ship. Then out of the rain came a man holding an umbrella and flanked by what looked like two mercenaries—military types with black tactical uniforms and AK-47s. All three of them were Middle Eastern. The Chinese soldiers greeted them—it was too far away for Natalya to hear what they were saying, but it sounded like Mandarin—and then went to the back of the truck and opened the door. One of the Middle Eastern mercenaries helped them unload two large wooden crates onto two dollies. Natalya removed a Canon PowerShot camera from her jacket and used the optical zoom to get a better view. SMIC was clearly printed in red on top of each crate. They were large enough to hold hundreds, if not thousands, of chips, and USA was stamped in bold lettering on the sides.

An illegal purchase.

Natalya took pictures of the crates and the men carrying them toward the ship, trying her best to capture the face of the man with the umbrella—more than likely the buyer. She caught a break when he stopped and turned. She snapped the photo just in time for him to join the others as they disappeared from view. Returning to the container, she closed the door to hide any light from the camera's LCD screen and zoomed in on the picture she'd just taken. Her eyes widened, and she let out a gasp as she stared at the face of the buyer. She knew who he was. Conner needed to be alerted as soon as possible.

CHAPTER 2

Geneva, Switzerland

Chris Harding couldn't take his eyes off the mountains towering above the city. Geneva was the center of financial and cultural influence in the world with architecture dating back to the Middle Ages. The urban sprawl was a plethora of ancient buildings and gardens, Renaissance homes, and Gothic castles and fortresses, all beneath the peaks of the Swiss Alps. Once a part of the Holy Roman Empire, the city was now an international hub for banking and diplomacy. It was home to the Red Cross and the United Nations' European headquarters. It was the center of peace in the world. And Chris was there to kidnap someone.

Dressed in Levi's and a baseball cap, he looked like any other tourist. But hidden beneath his Grunt Style T-shirt was a Beretta M9 handgun, a Buck 119 Special Pro tactical knife, and two 15-round magazines. At forty-one years old with broad shoulders and the frame of a man who used to go to the gym, he had spent more than a decade in the U.S. Army's Special Forces, leading missions in Iraq and Afghanistan and cultivating the tradecraft of a deadly fighting machine. After an honorable discharge due to a knee injury, he worked as a private military contractor for the CIA. But the consequences of his chosen profession were hard to stomach. Years of PTSD had destroyed his marriage, separated him from his only daughter, and left him but a shell of a man. Then came Roland Anderson and the team he now called family.

Roland was the group leader—a former CIA analyst who, despite graduating from Harvard, twice, had lost his career because of internal politics. In his forties, he was a nerd who dreamed of being James Bond. But he was smart—truly the brains of the operation.

Then there was George Hartman. Chris's childhood friend, who had found himself caught up in the last mission, was an All-American conspiracy theorist from Eastern Kentucky. He didn't trust the government and had spent most of his life learning how to protect himself from them. He could handle a weapon—owned more than most European countries—and was an accomplished hacker and whiz on the dark web.

He was engaged to thirty-six-year-old Tricia Perkins. A voluptuous and opinionated Black woman from New York City, she had once been Roland's assistant but had since become the team's defacto leader; that meant she kept the boys in line. She knew how to manage tactical operations, investigate intel, and was the glue that held the team together.

The final member was another vet—former Marine and proud Texan, Terry Harper. He and Chris had always hated each other, but after Terry rescued Chris's family from a corrupt CIA hitman, they became like brothers.

Eleven months ago, Roland owned a private military contracting company called Anderson Security. When he was hired by the CIA to stop a Russian nuclear attack on the United States, he assembled the "Anderson" team—a renegade group of scoundrels: Chris, Terry, Tricia, and George. They teamed up with undercover spy Natalya Palmer and went on to expose an international conspiracy by the New World Order to create a one-world government. But that success put their families in danger. In order to protect those they loved they joined Woodhaven, the FBI's gray counterintelligence group led by FBI Special Agent Adam Conner, and were offered new identities along with a chance to continue the work they had started. The official story was that they had died in an explosion in Los Angeles, but in reality, they were on a mission to uncover the next NWO plot against America. Their fake identities shielded them in some respects, but if they were ever caught, the FBI would deny their existence. This reality created a special bond among the "Anderson" team. Separated from friends and family, they were essentially ghosts in their own country—it was now them against the world.

The sun was shining, and the air was filled with the sound of cars and scooters racing through the crowded streets, occasionally honking their horns and avoiding the steady flow of foot traffic. George and Tricia were stationed at the nearby Hotel d'Angleterre, and Roland and Terry were parked a couple of blocks from Chris inside a Mercedes Sprinter Crew van they had rented at the airport. Roland came through Chris's Nano earpiece, diverting his attention from the Swiss Alps back to reality.

"Chris, what's your location?"

"Francois Bonivard or something—I'm in front of a church, Holy Trinity Church."

At the hotel, an elegant building from the 1870s overlooking Lake Geneva, Tricia plugged in the location on her laptop. "Got it," she said. "Target will reach you in approximately two minutes."

"Copy that," said Chris.

The target was sixty-year-old Swiss banker, Mikael Gerber. He spent most of his career managing offshore accounts for global commerce but had recently transitioned into cryptocurrency, which meant his clients were anything but savory. Arms dealers, organized crime syndicates, and charity groups funding terrorist organizations like Hamas, Hezbollah, and ISIS all knew him by name.

Cryptocurrency had risen in popularity over the past decade. This new digital currency—coins built in an unregulated form, without underlining assets, and void of government interference—had caused a ripple from Wall Street to London to Beijing. Pimple-faced kids were making millions from what traditionalists labeled "fake money." The SEC had tried to stop it but soon gave up, and suddenly investment bankers were buying up shares of Bitcoin and Ethereum as fast as humanly possible, creating ETFs and funding startups with ICOs—the crypto version of an IPO—and paving the way for global criminal organizations to finance their operations.

The NWO had been a difficult adversary. Other than a holding company registered in Denver, Colorado on May 9, 1945, there was no proof they even existed. The company was spread out like a web with hundreds of shell companies and offshore accounts connected to politicians and businessmen from all over the world, including the current president of the United States. But it was all conjecture, and since the chemical attack on Los Angeles the year before, there had not been a single world event that could be tied to a "New World Order." That was until a new blockchain platform emerged in the summer of 2023.

George had discovered it while listening in on a dark-web chat room. This new cryptocurrency was called HX5 and was not available on platforms like Coinbase or Robinhood. Instead, it was only accessible through a dark web crypto brokerage and was being used exclusively by criminals to pay for their activities. Further investigation led George to the owner of that brokerage, a wealthy banker in Geneva named Mikael Gerber. The theory was that the NWO was using HX5 to fund their international operations, and Gerber was their broker.

After weeks of surveillance, it was time to make their move. It was impossible to access a digital coin transaction history unless you were the hosting platform—in this case, Gerber's brokerage. Since only Gerber could access those transactions, the Anderson team would have to schedule a time to meet him in person. In other words, kidnap him. They had flown in on a chartered Gulfstream G550, turned the hotel into their base of operations, and prepared to abduct and coerce the Swiss banker into giving them access to his wallet—permanently destroying his professional reputation in the criminal world and quite possibly signing his death sentence.

Gerber exited a silver Mercedes S500 and joined the midday foot traffic, heading toward a baroque-style office building a block south of Chris's location. The banker was a large man with a thick head of silver hair neatly combed to the side. His charcoal suit was well tailored, his black crocodile-printed Dolce & Gabbana dress shoes were polished, and his gold Rolex matched the pinky ring on his right hand.

"Eyes on the target," Chris said.

"Copy that," said Roland. "We're thirty seconds out."

"Don't screw up," Terry said as he cranked up the van and merged into traffic.

"Don't crash the van," Chris replied.

"I'm giving you a mental middle finger, Harding."

"Shut up and focus, boys," Tricia ordered through the radio.

Chris pretended to take pictures of the Holy Trinity Church with his phone. As a student of history, he marveled at the Renaissance basilica in front of him and wished he was a real tourist who could go inside. As Gerber passed him on his way to the office building, Chris snapped another shot and followed, keeping a distance of three to four people between them.

They stopped at a red light.

"Ten seconds," Roland said through the radio.

The light turned green, and they joined a sea of pedestrians crossing the street. The Mercedes Sprinter Crew came around the corner and parked a few yards in front of them. Chris increased his pace until he was directly behind his target.

Replacing his hat with a black ski mask, he unholstered his Beretta and grabbed the banker's arm as he whispered in his ear, "Mr. Gerber, I need you to come with me." He pressed the gun against his back. "Make a sound, and you're dead."

The banker froze but didn't seem concerned.

"Whatever you say," he replied in a thick Swiss accent.

Chris tapped the side of the van. The door slid open, and he forced Gerber inside. Roland was waiting for them in the backseat. Terry was behind the wheel. Both were wearing ski masks.

"Asset is in custody. We're en route," Terry said as he eased into traffic.

Chris kept the Beretta on Gerber, whose eyes were fixated on his.

"We're not going to hurt you," Chris said. "We just need something you have. Once we get it, you'll be on your way."

Gerber smiled. "I understand."

He went for his pocket. Chris tightened his grip on the gun.

"I'm only reaching for my phone," the banker said, continuing the movement and retrieving a Samsung Galaxy from his jacket pocket.

"Three minutes out," Terry said into the radio.

Gerber ignored him. He focused on Chris and said, "My phone's GPS is connected to my office. If I do not follow my daily routine *exactly*, an alarm goes off and my private security detail is alerted. They are the best in the world and can find me anywhere."

"Assuming you have your phone with you," Chris replied.

"Never assume anything, young man." He pulled up his left sleeve, revealing a small scar on his wrist. "This microchip acts as my own personal GPS tracker. It is so exact, so precise, that the slightest deviation from my daily routine will alert my security team." He smiled. "They'll be on you before you know it. So whatever it is you want from me, you had better ask now."

Chris glanced at Roland, who shook his head. They needed to wait until they were in a secure location. Chris was about to say something to the banker when they all felt a sudden jolt to the left. Terry had made a hard right into an alley.

"We got company," he said.

Gerber laughed as his captors realized they were being followed by a black Range Rover with tinted windows.

At the hotel, George and Tricia were watching the events in real-time from a hacked satellite video feed. Tricia looked up the Range Rover's license plate on her MacBook Pro. It was registered to the same private security company they had on Gerber's file. Skilled mercenaries from Syria who protected some of the most dangerous men in the world, and of course, corrupt Swiss bankers.

"Y'all need to lose those assholes," George said.

"You think?" Roland replied.

Terry exited the alley onto a main thoroughfare only to slam the brakes as he hit a sea of bumper-to-bumper traffic. The Range Rover was directly behind them. Originally, the plan was to interrogate the banker at the hotel, but they couldn't risk an altercation with his security detail. It was time to improvise.

"I need you to open the digital wallet on your phone," Chris said.

Gerber's eyes lit up as he realized what they were after. "I see, I see. But of course."

He unlocked the Samsung, opened his crypto wallet, and began the two-part authentication process—an eye scan followed by a password. He then received a second password—changed every few seconds—and was granted access. He handed over the phone. Chris took it and stared at the screen. Not what he expected. The wallet was empty.

Gerber could see the disappointment in his captor's eyes. "You think you're the first to try and steal from me?"

"Where is your transaction history stored?"

"You obviously do not understand how cryptocurrency works."

Roland said, "As the only broker for HX5, you are required to maintain a history of every coin bought and sold. That's what we need."

The banker looked at the other masked man, then back to the one holding the gun.

"Now," Chris ordered.

Back at the hotel, George and Tricia saw two black metallic Mercedes G-Class SUVs weaving in and out of traffic.

"Two G-wagons coming in hot," Tricia said.

"Roger that," Terry replied. He turned to the backseat. "Wrap it up, guys."

Chris pressed the gun to Gerber's forehead. "Transaction history, or I pull the trigger."

"Trish, a little help, please?" Terry said.

She was already on it. "Make a left on Rue de Fribourg."

Terry did as he was told, nearly colliding with a young man on a bicycle as he turned onto a narrow cobblestone street lined with retail shops and cafés. He checked his rearview mirror. The Range Rover was right behind them, followed closely by the two G-wagons.

The window rolled down on the passenger side of the first G-wagon, and a man leaned out holding a MAC-10 submachine gun. He opened fire on the Ranger Rover, filling it with a burst of .45 ACP rounds. The driver was killed instantly, causing the SUV to crash into a patio café, ripping through tables, people, and finally the front door.

"Shit," George said as he watched the events unfold on Tricia's monitor.

Terry and Roland were armed with Glock 17s, Chris had his Beretta, and they each had two extra magazines, but that was it—no match for fully automatic gunfire.

Terry made a hard left at the end of the block, nearly tipping the van sideways. He regained control but was immediately met by the second G-wagon pulling up beside them. The backseat window came down and another MAC-10 appeared.

"Incoming!" Terry yelled.

Everyone ducked as the submachine gun opened fire, sending a hail of bullets through the van. The shooting stopped just in time for the second G-wagon—the one that shot up the Range Rover—to pull up beside them on the driver's side. A window came down and a grenade launcher showed its ugly head.

Terry saw it first. "*Fucking A!* Trish, I need an exit ASAP!"

"I'm working on it."

"Oh my God," Roland gasped, his eyes locked on the large caliber weapon.

Tricia scanned the map. "There's a parking structure three blocks away." She zoomed in on the satellite image of the building. "The entrance has a clearance of nine feet. You'll make it; the G-wagons won't."

Terry turned the steering wheel left and side-swiped the SUV. He then floored the gas, redlining the sprinter van's engine and accelerating through the narrow street, dodging cars, Vespas, and screaming pedestrians.

Gerber was starting to panic.

"Those men are not part of my security team," he said in a shaky voice.

"What are you talking about?" Chris said.

The banker was breathing heavily. He clutched his chest. "I feel a pain."

"You're fine. Who are these guys?"

More heavy breathing. Then, "My guys don't shoot until I'm safe. They would never hurt all these people."

"I doubt that, pal."

"No, it's true." He struggled to pull something from his pocket. "There are things I've done, people who have paid me." More labored breathing. "I never should have taken their money." He squeezed a flash drive into Chris's hand.

Terry managed to add space between them and the G-wagons just as they began their assault. The grenade launcher was discharged—sending a 40mm grenade in their direction. It missed its target and hit a row of parked cars. A loud explosion followed as a ball of fire and black smoke shot into the air. More rifles came into view—two HK MP5 submachine guns and an AK-47—and opened fire on the van. People screamed and ran for cover. Some made it. Some did not. The G-wagon expelled another grenade. This one landed inside a building. Fire exploded from the windows and sent glass and debris into the street.

Chris ignored the chaos that surrounded him and continued his interrogation.

"What do you know about NWO Holdings?"

The banker didn't respond. He was still struggling to breathe, holding his chest. Chris hoped it was just a panic attack and not a heart attack.

"You brokered a transaction for NWO Holdings. What was it for?"

Gerber found his breath. "I should never have taken their money. They would come for me, that was certain." He stared up at Chris, finding his eyes, and said, "I work for—"

A bullet entered the van and hit Gerber in the temple. It exited the back of his head, taking fragments of his scalp and brain matter with it, and sending a burst of blood into the air—much of which landed on Chris's face and the flash drive in his hand.

Terry saw the parking structure a block away on the right and made a hard turn inside. Tricia was correct about the clearance, and the sprinter van entered without incident. But the G-wagon on their tail wasn't paying attention to clearance requirements. The upper half of the top-heavy SUV slammed into the concrete roof, bringing the Mercedes to a complete stop.

The Anderson team rallied at the win. Tricia's resourcefulness had bought them some time. Gerber was dead, but at least they had his cell phone and the mysterious flash drive. Hopefully that was enough. It was time to ditch the vehicle.

"On foot," Chris said.

Roland and Terry agreed. They all exited the sprinter van with their pistols drawn. By now their assailants had done the same and were entering the garage on foot. There were at least eight of them, Middle Eastern men dressed in black and armed with MP5s and AK-47s.

The Anderson team followed Tricia's directions and headed for the far side of the garage where a stairwell and exit would be. Just as they turned the corner and spotted the door, the mercenaries opened fire behind them.

Chris felt a bullet whiz past him—one side-step, and he would have been dead. He ignored his mortality and returned fire, letting off four rounds in quick succession. He hit one guy in the leg but missed the others. Terry followed up with a burst of shots and landed a couple in the chest, but the bastards were wearing vests and kept coming. Roland had a difficult time running and shooting at the same time. Regardless of what his occupation had become over the past year, the Harvard man was still a thinker, not a killer.

They made it to the stairwell, which was exposed to the outside by steel bars, revealing a blue sky shrouded by gray smoke from the grenade-induced explosions. Sirens echoed through the city. Chris took a final shot at the mercenaries before leaving the garage. He emptied his magazine, and this time he a landed kill shot, penetrating the man's forehead and thrusting his body to the ground. Chris ejected the empty mag and inserted a new one as he followed Terry and Roland into the stairwell.

They emerged from the parking structure to find the street

filled with police cruisers, EMT vehicles, and Swiss military personnel. The carnage was horrific—people helping their wounded loved ones and mourning those who had died. Chris, Roland, and Terry disappeared into the crowd, trying not to think about the geopolitical ramifications of the day's events in what would surely be labeled a "mass shooting" and "terrorist" attack by the media.

The mercenaries did not follow them into the stairwell, having realized their target was not one of them. They returned to the sprinter van where they found Gerber's dead body in the backseat. The leader looked through his pockets, searching for something.

He looked up at his men, a grim look on his face.

"It's gone," he said in Farsi.

CHAPTER 3

Port of Tianjin, China

NATALYA OPENED THREEMA on her phone—a message encryption app—and sent the photos to Adam Conner. It was mid-afternoon in D.C., and she hoped he would respond quickly. Putting her gear away, she stepped outside the container to see if the men had returned from the ship. She peered around the corner just in time to see the truck drive away. The Middle Eastern men were nowhere to be seen. It was raining harder than before, and she realized finding a taxi at this hour—at this location—would be difficult. But she needed to get back to her apartment and run a background check on the man she had photographed. She would have to walk it.

...

Feng Chen watched as the woman exited the Port of Tianjin parking lot and made her way on foot down Jintang No. 4 Road. Having turned off his engine and lights, his Honda Civic appeared to be parked on the side of the road, barely noticeable in the heavy rain. He pressed a pair of binoculars against his thick-rimmed glasses and confirmed her identity: Natalya Palmer. It would take her at least twenty minutes to reach the main street and catch the bus that would transport her to Beijing. There was no sense following her. He already knew where she was going. That she had been at the port on this particular evening confirmed the suspicions he'd had for the past several weeks.

Chen worked for the Chinese Ministry of State Security as a senior intelligence officer. A clandestine organization much like the CIA, they focused their attention on individuals who posed a threat to the Chinese Communist Party. And Chen was nothing short of a loyal communist. His parents' suffering during China's economic decline in the 1970s had made him determined to build a better life for his own children. He was good at his job because he was disciplined. And it was the little things. The perfectly pressed suits, the shined shoes, a strict adherence to the rules—and his hat. He loved his hat. His father's fedora had been with him since the beginning. It was a constant reminder of the work he was doing.

He called his two subordinates, Qianfan and Fenua, and told them to meet him at Natalya's apartment. He then fired up the engine and aimed the Honda toward Beijing. Home to more than twenty-one million people, it was the largest metropolitan area in China. Thousands of skyscrapers filled the cityscape, and in the middle of it all was the Forbidden City, a reminder of Imperial China's glorious history. A reminder of what it could be once more.

• • •

Natalya was no fool. She had seen Chen's economy car parked when she walked by. There were other vehicles on the road that night, but she had seen this one before—outside her apartment, outside her office—and knew someone was watching her. Until tonight this had not been cause for concern. The Chinese were untrusting of those not "racially pure," even looking down on Chinese nationalists from other ethnic groups, and surveillance was to be expected. However, with her discovery of the AI chip transaction, she knew this was more than typical government prying. If someone was indeed following her, it only solidified her suspicions that something devious was at play. She just hoped she had enough intel to make her efforts worthwhile. This would be her last night in the apartment she had called home for the better part of a year. Tomorrow she would go dark.

The bus picked her up at the entrance to the Port of Tianjin. The Civic was nowhere to be seen. Of course, that didn't mean it wasn't there. Maybe she was paranoid.

Always trust your gut.

She paid the driver and leaned back on the hard plastic seat. Public transportation never felt so good. She was soaking wet and dreaming of a shower. But the night was nowhere close to being over, and someone was following her.

• • •

Chen watched Natalya enter the lobby of her high-rise apartment building in the Xicheng District of Beijing. Constructed in the mid-'90s, it had probably been a fine place to live at one time. However, decades of decline had transformed it into nothing but an affordable place to sleep. *At least it has a view*, Chen thought. Qianfan and Fenua stood beside him wearing matching black suits. He motioned for them to follow him.

They took the stairs to avoid running into Natalya on their way up. They needed this to be a surprise. If she was who he thought she was, she already knew of his existence. She'd also be armed and dangerous. Chen was always cautious, even when he was certain of the outcome.

Natalya's apartment on the seventy-fifth floor was a long way up. Chen was the oldest, and yet the younger men—both in their twenties—were the ones out of breath when they finally reached their destination.

Discipline.

They arrived at apartment number 7510 and Fenua knocked on the door. Nothing. He knocked again, this time harder. Still nothing. Chen nodded and Qianfan kicked it in, the lock breaking through the rotting frame and releasing the door. Qianfan and Fenua entered with their QSZ-92 pistols drawn. Chen followed them into the apartment to find Natalya sitting by the window. She was facing them with a lit cigarette in one hand and a SIG Sauer P226 in the other.

Chen could see in her eyes that she recognized him. His intuition had been correct. A part of him was happy, but he was also concerned because he now had confirmation that she was part of the American spy ring he had been working tirelessly to destroy: Woodhaven.

"You know why I'm here," he said. His English was flawless.

Natalya stared back in stony silence.

Chen removed a black-and-white photograph from his jacket pocket and aimed it at her so she could see. It was an image of Chris Harding and Roland Anderson having drinks at Islamorada Brewery and Distillery in the Florida Keys.

"I have no idea who you are," she lied.

"Your name is Natalya Palmer. And you are a spy."

"Then arrest me."

"All in good time." He pointed at the photograph. "What can you tell me about these men? And don't say you don't know them.

We both know that's not true."

Natalya's grip tightened on the SIG.

"Come now, don't do that," said Chen. "We both want what's best for our countries, so let's not make this more difficult than it has to be. My men will leave, you'll put down your weapon, and you and I will have a civilized conversation."

Natalya considered her options. A communist could never be trusted, but then again, what choice did she have? She had yet to hear from Conner even though it had been nearly an hour since she sent him the photographs. Hopefully, they would suffice if she found herself locked away in a Chinese prison. As always, the FBI would not claim her if she was caught.

"Okay," she said, setting her pistol on the floor and kicking it toward Chen.

He smiled. "Thank you." Then to his men he said, "*Zài wàimiàn děngdào shíjiān dàole.*"

Wait outside until it's time.

Natalya understood perfectly.

Qianfan and Fenua did as they were told, closing the door behind them. Chen removed a pack of Chunghwas from his jacket and took a cigarette from the bright red box.

"Mind if I join you?" he said as he lit one and breathed in the rich tobacco. "I'm surprised a woman like you smokes."

She crushed her cigarette and stood up. "What do you want from me?"

"Information."

"I'm just a programmer."

"Yes, yes, I know—at TZH. You've been there for six months and have received excellent marks. Impressive. Especially since you only began coding nine months ago."

He took a long drag from his cigarette and waited for her response.

She resisted blushing, her entire cover blown. "What do you want to know?"

"Finally you admit to knowing something."

"Why haven't you killed me yet?"

Ask questions—maintain control of the conversation.

"A very astute question, Ms. Palmer." He took a step toward her. She stood her ground. He said, "Woodhaven is investigating the Chinese government, and it's my job to ensure nothing harmful to this country leaves this country. At this very moment, I have agents watching Mr. Harding and Mr. Anderson as well as their esteemed associates. A single phone call and their cover is blown."

"Seems their cover is already blown, Mr. Chen."

He smiled. "I like you. I really do. A part of me doesn't want this to happen."

"Want what to happen?" She was nervous, but she sure as hell wasn't going to show it.

"Earlier this evening you took photographs of a transaction. What do you know about the product that was delivered to the Port of Tianjin?"

Natalya decided to play ball. Perhaps she could learn something. "A new semiconductor chip capable of powering next-generation AI."

"Yes, we know all about that. What you Americans don't realize is that China believes in capitalism. It's what makes an economy thrive. You look at us as evil for our socialistic views. But that could not be further from the truth. Our strength lies in our ability to take care of our own. The AI chip industry is the future. This transaction is nothing more than capitalism."

"The United States Department of Defense has forbid the purchase of products manufactured by SMIC. What happened tonight was illegal."

Chen laughed as he took another drag from his cigarette. He watched the gray smoke fill the air, then looked Natalya directly in the eyes and said, "What did you send your handler?"

His voice had changed, becoming dark and cold.

"What does it matter?" Natalya replied, meeting his gaze. "If what you say is true, then I'm simply proving China's love for their own."

Chen smiled. He had reached the end of his smoke. The beautiful spy stood still as he stepped around her and snubbed out the cigarette butt in a plastic ashtray beside her chair. Regardless of what he was about to do, he would never leave a mess in someone else's home, even if they were an enemy of the state.

He tipped his hat to her and said, "Thank you for your time, Ms. Palmer. If I were you, I would leave this country as quickly as possible. You have found nothing, and your need to gather intel is no longer relevant."

She watched in silence as he exited the apartment. As soon as he was gone, she grabbed her phone and sent a secure Threema message to Conner.

Woodhaven is compromised. I repeat, compromised. Notify Anderson team ASAP.

•••

Chen took the elevator this time. As he passed through the lobby and the security guard asleep at his desk, he noticed the rain had finally stopped, leaving the city shrouded in a thick, wet fog. He crossed the street. Qianfan and Fenua were waiting for him beside his Honda.

In Mandarin he said, "You know what to do."

They nodded and proceeded to their Nio ET7 sedan that was parked down the street. Fenua removed a compact explosive detonator from the backseat. He stared at the red button on top for a moment before looking at his partner.

I don't think I can do this.

Qianfan saw his hesitation and grabbed the detonator.

"*Wéi rénmín fúwù*," he said as he pressed the red button.

To serve the people.

The explosion was colossal, and Natalya's one-hundred-story apartment building burst into flames. Every soul inside was either disintegrated on impact, burned to a crisp, or empaled by the concrete and glass that shot through the air with such velocity that debris landed dozens of yards from the detonation site.

As Chen watched the bomb go off, he took out his phone and made a call. The voice that answered was American, and he spoke in English.

"Agent Palmer has been terminated," Chen said. "But she learned more than we anticipated, and I believe she has already informed Special Agent Adam Conner. The time has come to exterminate Woodhaven."

CHAPTER 4

Washington, D.C.

24 HOURS AGO

NEWS OF THE mass shooting in Geneva made national headlines, and though officials had no leads on who was responsible, Adam Conner knew it was the Anderson team. Roland had debriefed him less than an hour after it happened and explained where things went south. Someone else was after Mikael Gerber. Conner was furious, but Roland reminded him that their identities were still intact. They'd also made an incredible discovery.

Conner inserted the banker's flash drive and opened the encrypted file on the desktop computer in his corner office at FBI Headquarters on Pennsylvania Avenue. As Director of National Security Operations at the FBI, he oversaw hundreds of agents across the country with one mandate: find and secure any potential threats to national security. But his most important role was not listed on the bureau's website, nor was its existence known to anyone other than the FBI director himself. Conner supervised Woodhaven directly. Had since its inception in 2017.

General Al Kempe, Chairman of the Joint Chiefs of Staff, had for many years suspected there was an elite group of politicians and businessmen—the Deep State—controlling America's financial and political institutions. He tasked Conner with forming an investigative team to look into it. The name "Woodhaven" came from the location of their first meeting in Palm Desert, California: the Woodhaven Country Club. Away from the capital's prying eyes, Kempe had spent a weekend with Conner and FBI Director Aden Smith—who retired in 2018, making way for the current director, Steven House—and outlined the clandestine operation's directive: find out who is pulling the strings and stop them.

None of this could be on the books. It was a secret known only to Kempe, Conner, and the incumbent FBI director. The years had proven fruitful. They learned of an organization called the New World Order that had existed since the end of World War II and was allegedly responsible for large-scale world events ever since—the assassination of President Kennedy in 1963, Nixon's doing away with the gold standard in 1971, the Iran hostage crisis in '79, 9/11. And of course, it all boiled down to one goal: create a one-world government without countries or borders—communism on crack.

Recruiting the Anderson team had originated out of necessity; they simply knew too much. But they had proven themselves to be competent operators when they uncovered a corrupt weapons manufacturer attempting to start a war with Russia in order to receive billions in defense contracts from the U.S. Department of Defense. The quantum computer that created the nuclear threat in 2022 had been the work of the NWO, and the Anderson team had stopped it. They were now on a global mission to find out the NWO's next move, while Conner's top spy, Natalya Palmer, was undercover in China—the most powerful communist country in the world. But so far, Woodhaven's efforts had hit nothing but walls, and Conner was finding it increasingly difficult to justify the expense. The colossal loss of life in Switzerland, though not directly caused by his team, was still a result of their operation. It would be the final straw unless the information on Gerber's flash drive proved useful.

Conner stared at his screen and tried to process what he was seeing. Typically a broker would work with multiple clients, constituting multiple transactions from multiple parties. In the case of a corrupt Swiss banker, there would be arms dealers, terrorists, and human traffickers—all buying and selling products and services banned in most countries. But this was different. There was only one transaction. And the buyer was NWO Holdings.

• • •

FBI Director Steven House's office took up more than a thousand square feet of the top floor of FBI Headquarters. The blue carpeting and traditional mahogany furniture, combined with a massive oil painting of J. Edgar Hoover, reeked of U.S. government power. Large windows provided a wash of sunlight as well as breathtaking views of the White House. The director was behind his desk, flanked by two American flags, when Conner entered.

"It's a goddam shit show," said House.

Conner took a seat in front of him. "I agree."

"Woodhaven has become nothing short of a liability. Zero credible intel and a ridiculous amount of taxpayer dollars spent." He turned his computer screen toward Conner and pointed at a BBC news report of the Geneva shooting. "And now this!"

"I know, a tragic loss of life."

"In fucking Switzerland of all places. Those peaceful socialist-loving cunts are going to have a heyday. NATO still thinks we were in the wrong for how we handled Russia last year—entering a sovereign nation and killing dozens of people—and this," he poked the screen with his finger, "will not go over well."

"I agree. But for the record, my team *was* ambushed."

"Be that as it may, I'm going to get shit on by the president. And with Al Kempe retiring last month, there's no one else to shield me." He leaned back in his chair. "You know, I never wanted this. I inherited it."

House's feelings about Woodhaven did not come as a surprise to Conner. The FBI director was a politician, not a spymaster, and he believed the FBI's sole function was intelligence. With social unrest at the forefront of the country's minds, House had fallen prey to the swamp of D.C.—dark halls filled with corrupt state legislators and money-hungry lobbyists in tailored suits—and was systematically transforming the FBI into a civil rights enforcement agency. To that end, he had little need for operators—less for former military personnel—and had spent the past five years since his promotion to director slashing every ground ops program the bureau had. And he was right. With Kempe out of the picture, Woodhaven was dead in the water. It was time to share the news.

"We have new intel."

"Unless it's concrete proof that the NWO, if they even exist, is responsible for an immediate threat to this country, I don't want to hear it. I'm going before the oversight committee tomorrow, and I will be informing them that, as of this week, all gray intelligence operations led by the FBI will cease to exist. Let the fucking CIA do their job."

Conner handed him the flash drive. "You'll want to see this first."

NEW BEGINNING

House eyed him suspiciously as he inserted the USB drive into his computer, his director credentials giving him the necessary security clearance to access the file. His face went blank when he saw what was on the screen.

CHAPTER 5

Dulles International Airport was the largest airport in Washington, D.C. It was built in 1962, and its main terminal featured a combination of glass and concrete mid-century architecture. Dulles represented the "face of home" whenever Chris returned from overseas. For most of his military career, he had flown commercial, but in his current role as a secret FBI operative, he flew private, which meant arriving at the Dulles Jet Center located just north of the main terminal.

What happened in Geneva was devastating. Sixteen people were killed and dozens more were injured. This weighed heavily on the Anderson team as they took a black GMC Suburban to the Woodhaven safe house. Their search for information, aimed at saving lives, had inadvertently caused the death of innocent men, women, and children. Chris took it the hardest. His history overseas and the PTSD that had permanently developed inside his war-weathered mind caused him to blame himself for the tactical shortcomings of the mission. There was also the fact that traffic footage would eventually be reviewed, and the moment when Chris forced Gerber into the backseat of the van would trigger facial recognition, matching his face with his old identity prior to

NEW BEGINNING

Woodhaven.

He was supposed to be dead. So was Roland, Terry, Tricia, and George. The FBI had released their names as part of the casualties from the bioterrorism attack on Los Angeles the year before. This could be fixed—new identities formed and information suppressed—but innocent lives lost could not.

The familiar sights of Virginia brought back memories. Chris's ex-wife, Jessica, and his daughter, Claire, had recently moved to Phoenix from their home in Falls Church to be closer to Jessica's mother, whose health had deteriorated over the past year. The move made sense for them. Jessica's new husband, Damon, worked remotely as the Senior Vice President of Finance at Allstate and could live anywhere, making a six-figure income from non-stop Zoom meetings. Falls Church and Chris's old life there was now history—a moment in time.

"Don't let it get to you."

Chris snapped out of his daydream and glanced at Roland in the seat beside him.

"I'm good," he said.

"You don't look good. What's on your mind?"

The former soldier didn't respond because he didn't know. Perhaps it was nostalgia. That would pass. Maybe it was the guilt of having failed as a father and husband that haunted him. He was also concerned about why their intercontinental flight had been rerouted mid-Atlantic and changed course for Washington when they typically debriefed via video conference call with Conner from their safe house in the Florida Keys. Something wasn't right.

The Suburban turned onto a tree-lined street in the historic neighborhood of Georgetown and stopped in front of a three-story brick townhouse. The Anderson team piled out of the SUV and entered through the front door using a key code Roland had received from Conner. Inside they found a living room outfitted with comfortable but conservative furnishings and an original stone fireplace. There were two leather couches facing an oak coffee table and an armchair in the corner that appeared to be more for show than comfort. There was also a wet bar built into the wall—a modern addition to the nineteenth-century home—with bottles of liquor piled on top and a beer fridge at the bottom.

The middle-aged Woodhaven leader was leaning against the mantel holding a glass of Bombay Sapphire on ice. No time was wasted on pleasantries; he got straight to the point.

"Mikael Gerber's crypto brokerage shows a single transaction—a week ago—between NWO Holdings and a Chinese semiconductor chip manufacturer called SMIC for a shipment of AI chips."

Everyone took a seat around the coffee table facing Adam Conner.

"SMIC is prohibited by the United States Department of Defense from doing business with American companies," said Roland.

"Correct. The value of the purchase is consistent with Chinese microchips—roughly forty thousand dollars per chip. Eight million for the entire order. But it was paid for with HX5. As you know, HX5 is a new cryptocurrency with a market cap of one billion dollars and is used primarily by criminals and terrorists."

"NWO falls into that category," Terry said.

"Yes, and doing business with prohibited Chinese companies is very much a concern. In fact, it's inline with our profile on the NWO."

Chris lit a Camel cigarette. "So what's the problem? Why are we debriefing here? Is it because of what happened in Geneva?"

"That's a lot of questions, Chris," Tricia scolded.

"I'd like to know. We got what we came for—solid intel on the NWO's next play."

He inhaled the cigarette deeply, then let out the smoke slowly.

Conner understood Chris's position and his response was gentle, like a professor explaining a complex math problem to a student. "The director doesn't see it that way."

"Adam House is an asshole," said Terry.

George nodded in agreement.

"He has a different approach," replied Conner. "But the point is, he's given us one week to turn this new intel into actionable results."

"What the hell does that mean?" Terry asked.

"It means we go into Witness Protection," Tricia said.

"They're shutting us down," added Roland.

"Fucking A," said George.

Chris flicked ashes into a glass ashtray on the coffee table. "Explain yourself, Conner."

"Woodhaven requires significant funding, and there are questions regarding its necessity. The CIA has resources already allocated for investigating national security risks, and the FBI director is getting pressure from Congress to tighten the purse strings on unnecessary programs. This is an opportunity to show your worth. Find out what the AI chips are being used for and if they constitute a national security risk."

Roland's mind was already at work. "To do that, we need to figure out who their point-of-contact is—who's picking up the goods."

Tricia was way ahead of the Harvard man. "When is the order

scheduled to ship?"

"We don't know," Conner said. "I'll see what I can find out from our asset in Beijing."

Chris knew exactly who the "asset" was—a woman from the past—and took a long hit from his cigarette, contemplating the situation.

Conner continued. "There's something else."

He removed an iPad from a leather briefcase satchel beside the fireplace, opened the photo app, and placed the tablet on the coffee table. The faces of two Middle Eastern men appeared on the screen.

"Bashir Mahmoud and Adham Mostafa," he said. "Iranian mercenaries. They operate extensively throughout Europe and are responsible for the Brussels bombings in 2016, the Manchester Arena bombing in 2017, and most recently, the 2020 Hanau shootings in Germany. They have ties to Hamas, al-Qaeda, Hezbollah, the Taliban—practically every Islamic terrorist cell in the world. They've worked for the Bratva in Russia and have been linked to multiple cartels in Mexico. Their MO is transporting illegal merchandise, including people, and carrying out high-profile assassinations. Based on facial recognition from traffic cameras in Geneva, I believe they could be the men who followed you."

"They wanted Gerber dead," Roland said.

"Covering their tracks," Chris added.

Conner nodded. "This is the first time we've been able to connect the NWO to an actual transaction. Makes sense why they'd eliminate the only guy who could tie them to it. Keep the iPad. It's got Mahmoud's and Mostafa's files on it."

There was silence all around as the team processed their orders. They had seven days to find out why the NWO had purchased

AI chips from a Chinese company—who wasn't legally supposed to sell them in the U.S.—and why the broker responsible for the transaction had been targeted by two Iranian mercenaries. Failure meant the dissolution of Woodhaven and the life they'd all come to know.

...

Chris grabbed an IPA from the beer fridge and stepped outside the townhouse for another cigarette. He was still jet-lagged, and although it was nearly three o'clock in the morning, sleep was out of the question. They had eight hours before they flew back home to Florida, and he was going to spend it drinking IPAs, smoking—and thinking. He had managed to find a sense of peace within himself over the last twelve months. The work helped, but it was his new family that put his anxiety at bay. They had become a close-knit group—underdogs out to save the world like grown-up characters from *The Goonies*. What would happen if they failed and were forced to separate, plummeted into witness protection? He had no idea how he would take it. Without a purpose. Without a family. A man alone.

Terry joined him on the front stoop, a Coors Light in his hand.

"What a shit show," he said.

"Isn't it always?"

"You'd think, for once, the government would get their act together."

"If they did, we'd be out of a job."

"You got that right."

Chris was drinking a 21st Amendment West Coast IPA, in a glass. Full of flavor, it was strong—seven percent ABV—and went down smooth with an earthy kick of hops at the end. He eyed Terry's domestic beer. It came in a can and had less than five percent alcohol.

"That shit's beer-water, man," he said.

"American as apple pie, though."

"One of these days I'll get you to drink a real beer."

"Hops don't make it real."

"At least you'll stay hydrated."

"Yeah, yeah, with all the beer-water I'm drinking. I get it. Don't quit your day job, Harding." Another swig of his Coors. Then, "There's something I gotta talk to you about."

"What's up?"

"I'm getting out."

"What does that mean?"

"It means I'm tired."

"Aren't we all?"

"I'm serious, dude. I'm tired of this shit. I want a normal life. Hell, that's what we were over there fighting for, right? I just thought it would end one day. Thought I'd come home."

Chris was silent. He understood *exactly* what the former Marine was trying to say.

"I'm not gonna leave y'all hanging or anything. But I gotta follow my own path. After we complete this mission, I'm out."

"Witness Protection?"

"A new life, brother."

Chris stared into the eyes of a man he'd once despised, grown to respect, and now considered a brother. He would hate to see him go, but he understood. Perhaps a part of him was envious of his friend's newfound inner peace and his desire to give it all up, to live again.

"A new beginning," Chris responded.

Terry finished the last drop of his beer and smiled. "I like that."

A burp followed and Chris realized his glass was nearly depleted as well. A grin spread across his face as an idea popped into his head.

"That wet bar inside is full of top-shelf booze. I think I saw a bottle of Macallan 30 in there. What do you say we get shit-faced on Uncle Sam's dime?"

CHAPTER 6

South Florida

The Anderson team landed at Miami International Airport at 10:32 a.m. Flying commercial was an adjustment for all of them, having recently discovered the joys of private air travel. Who would have thought skipping TSA or a beer fridge inside the cabin—well, that was mainly for Chris—followed by a quick exit from the plane directly to a waiting SUV would be so rewarding? Sadly, they arrived this time like everyone else. After waiting for their luggage and checked handguns at baggage claim, they caught an Uber to Islamorada. The blue Dodge mini-van that picked them up took the FL-836 W, passed the suburbs of Miami—palm trees and lakes as far as the eye could see—and left the downtown skyline behind them. Once they hit the Ronald Reagan Turnpike, it was a smooth hour to the Florida Keys.

It was 1:35 p.m. when they arrived at their house in Islamorada, a tropical village known for its white sand, pale-blue waters, and year-round sport fishing and scuba diving. There was a brewery—the Islamorada Brewery and Distillery, where Chris and Roland had their nightly beers—and a few small restaurants, but that was about it. This was a place to escape the rest of the world. A place to disappear. The perfect home for a group of spies investigating an enigmatic evil bent on taking over the world. Their blue-stucco ranch was located on a sand-caked avenue between the Atlantic Ocean and the Overseas Highway that traveled from the tip of Florida to Key West—the southernmost part of the United States and a mere ninety miles from the island country of Cuba.

Everyone dropped their luggage and got straight to work. Their "war room" wasn't a room but rather a man cave with two beer fridges and three couches facing a 65-inch TV where Roland could make his weekly presentations and George and Terry could watch football. George's computer setup and Tricia's desk were side-by-side against the wall. The space received plenty of Florida sunshine thanks to a picture window looking out on a courtyard in the middle of the five-bedroom, five-bathroom home. Built right after World War II and remodeled by the FBI in 2021, it featured a state-of-the-art security system and a weapons safe outfitted with an assortment of pistols and assault rifles.

Finding Mahmoud and Mostafa was not an easy task. But George, a lifelong conspiracy theorist and self-proclaimed Libertarian, was a pro when it came to navigating the dark web and finding those who didn't want to be found. Add Tricia to the mix, who could easily have been a successful detective in another life, and you had yourself an investigative team second to none.

While George and Tricia searched for information, Roland took Terry and Chris outside to the courtyard. Chris smoked a cigarette and Terry chewed on his wintergreen Skoal dip.

Roland said, "I know we're under the clock, but I wanted to talk to you guys about Trish and George. They were supposed to get married after we got back from Geneva."

"Terrible luck," said Terry, spitting out a wad of tobacco juice.

Roland grimaced. "You're disgusting."

Terry's response was a shit-eating grin and another spit of the brown liquid.

"They caught a bad hand," Chris said.

"Look on the bright side—we may all be taking some time off," Terry said.

"It won't come to that," Roland replied.

"I don't think you can know that," Chris said.

"Have we ever failed a challenge before?"

"Yes, we have."

"Not counting Russia. Look guys, Conner knows our value."

"Doesn't matter," said Terry. "Politicians lose interest fast. And let's face it, is the NWO really a threat? Sometimes it feels like we're just chasing a ghost."

"What about these AI chips? And the Iranians?" Chris said. "There's something going on there."

"It's probably some rich asshole in Dubai playing with daddy's money."

Chris looked at Roland. "What do you think?"

"I think we do our best to finish the mission. If it turns out to be nothing then—"

"We're out of a job," said Terry.

"That is a possibility."

"And is that so bad?"

Roland shrugged. "I like to think we're doing some good. Even though we helped get a bunch of people killed yesterday."

"Another reason to retire."

"Yeah, I guess." The Harvard man cleared his throat. "Anyway, what I wanted to say was, I think we should go out tonight."

"Are you serious?" Chris said. "Harvard man wants to hit the town on a school night."

"Nothing crazy; we just go to the brewery. It's been a rough couple days, and I think we all need a night off to clear our heads. Besides, Trish and George deserve a celebration."

Chris was impressed. Although Roland had evolved over the past year—nightly beers and a more tempered personality—he was still the same old Harvard man. A prude until the end who never allowed living to get in the way of work.

"Let's do it," Chris said, extinguishing his cigarette in a plastic smoker's receptacle. "Maybe I can persuade George to drink an IPA."

CHAPTER 7

*FBI Headquarters
Washington, D.C.*

ADAM CONNER WAS in a staff meeting when he noticed Natalya's encrypted text message. After scanning its contents, he ducked out early and went straight to his office, a nondescript space with pastel walls, cheap carpeting, and standard bureau furnishings. He called his agent on a KryptAll secure mobile phone. There was no answer. Not an immediate cause for worry; she was in the field and would respond when she could. Sipping his third coffee of the day, he scrolled through the message again, this time clicking on each photo one by one. There were two Chinese military-types handing over wooden crates to what appeared to be three Middle Eastern men. Both crates had SMIC clearly printed on top and USA stamped on the side. That got Conner's attention—*the NWO transaction*. Anticipating a visual of the buyer, he swiped to the next picture. He nearly jumped out of his seat when he saw it. Flanked by two armed mercenaries was none other than Adham Mostafa.

It was the middle of the night in Beijing. Conner would probably have to wait until morning before hearing back from Natalya, but it was mid-afternoon in Florida and her intel would be useful to the Anderson team. He called Roland.

The Harvard man picked up on the second ring. "This is Roland."

"One of our operatives just photographed Adham Mostafa receiving an illegal shipment from SMIC. I'm sending it to you now."

Roland, having just returned to the war room after his talk with Chris and Terry, opened Threema and waited for the message to arrive. When it did, he clicked on the grainy photo, instantly recognizing the face of Adham Mostafa.

"Who took these?" he asked.

Conner thought about lying but opted for transparency. "Agent Palmer."

There had been zero contact between Natalya Palmer and Roland's team since the events of last year, and he had hoped Chris would never think of her again. The combat veteran and the spy had carried on a brief, but passionate, romance and Roland was concerned she would cloud his judgment.

"When was this?" he replied, ignoring the part about Natalya.

"A few moments ago—have George look into all authorized shipments coming out of the Port of Tianjin in the past twelve hours. Find out where that cargo ship is headed. I don't believe in coincidences. We can safely assume those crates are filled with the AI chips purchased by NWO Holdings and that Adham Mostafa is under their employ."

Conner disconnected the call and sent an email to FBI Director House, requesting an emergency meeting. The director's executive assistant put him on the schedule for nine o'clock the following morning.

• • •

Conner left the J. Edgar Hoover Building a few minutes past six, heading toward his one-bedroom apartment in Georgetown. The cobblestone streets and eighteenth-century townhomes reeked of American history—the stomping grounds of the Founding Fathers—but Conner lived in one of the few modern buildings, constructed to attract the younger generation. He chose the luxury high-rise because he was divorced and secretly wanted to find a younger woman to date him. Of course, it was all helpless. Nevertheless, he would regularly find himself at the bars nearby, hoping and praying for someone to notice him.

As usual, he stopped for dinner at one of the local spots. This time it was Martin's Tavern on Wisconsin Avenue. After a hearty meal, six pints of beer, zero luck with the ladies, and still no word from Natalya, he called it a night. It was after nine when he arrived drunk at the glass tower he called home. The apartment was small, but it had floor-to-ceiling windows that displayed a breathtaking view of the nation's capital. He kept the lights off, allowing the glow of the city to illuminate the living room, and grabbed a bottle of Samuel Adams from the fridge before dropping to the couch.

He tried Natalya's phone again. The number was disconnected. *What the hell is going on?*

He took out his iPhone and opened the Threema app to see if the alerts had been silenced. Like all messaging applications, Threema sent alerts when new text messages were received. Perhaps Natalya had ditched her encrypted phone and responded through text on another device.

There were no messages. Threema needed an update and had been inactive all afternoon. Conner initiated the update, left the smartphone on the cushion beside him, and turned on the TV, falling asleep almost immediately. He was awakened by the vibrating phone as a delayed message was transmitted through the newly updated Threema app.

> **Woodhaven is compromised. I repeat, compromised. Notify Anderson team ASAP.**

Conner's grogginess disappeared as he read the message.
Shit, fuck—call Roland.

He scrambled to locate the saved number. That's when he felt it. Cold steel against the back of his head. He'd been around long enough to recognize the muzzle of a semiautomatic handgun and in that split-second realized his life was about to end. He never heard it, but the suppressed SIG P226 made a cracking sound as it sent a projectile through his brain and a splash of blood over the black leather couch.

CHAPTER 8

Islamorada, Florida Keys

Everyone was in the war room when Roland briefed them on the intel from Conner, courtesy of Natalya Palmer. The last time Chris had seen Natalya was in California, and he was reminded of the night he first met her inside an abandoned Russian farmhouse at the start of their mission to disarm the quantum computer that controlled Russia's entire arsenal of nuclear warheads. She had betrayed his trust, only to save his life in the end—along with the lives of the entire team—and revealed herself as an undercover agent for Woodhaven. Would he ever see her again? One could never know in this game.

Tricia ran the MarineTraffic app on her laptop and was able to find the destination for Ro-Ro Terminal Company's ship out of Tianjin: Port of Los Angeles.

"The ship is scheduled to arrive in Long Beach in twenty-three days," she said.

"Why wouldn't they just use an air freight?" Terry asked. "Hell of a lot faster."

"I don't know."

NEW BEGINNING

"The Port of Los Angeles allows them to bypass customs. It's an illegal shipment and would be difficult to smuggle through LAX," Roland explained.

Terry nodded. "Makes sense."

"We're waiting on additional intel from Palmer," Roland continued, decidedly referring to her formally. "We'll have a more solid course of action tomorrow. But I think this is enough to get the director off our backs for a while."

"Since we have nothing else to do tonight, maybe it's time we get a head start on the evening," said Chris.

George perked up. "What's happening this evening?"

• • •

Caleb Webb used the telescopic sight on his M24 sniper rifle to watch the Anderson team inside their war room. The picture window provided him a perfect view from his rooftop hiding spot across the street. It was a vacant Airbnb with a flat roof—an ideal location to watch, to wait. He checked his phone, confirming his orders. Nothing had changed. The directive was to terminate everyone. Caleb was in his thirties, spent way too much time at the gym, and had mastered the art of killing for a living. He grew up in San Diego and then partied his way through college at UC Santa Barbara before enlisting in the United States Marine Corps. Four years later, he was recruited as a CIA contractor. He never asked questions, a quality that had kept him steadily employed for the past eight years. As a hired assassin, he traveled the globe, permanently eliminating individuals the United States government deemed "a clear and present danger." But he knew what he was: a tool with which to wield geopolitical control over an increasingly volatile world.

There was movement inside. He followed his targets as they exited the house and walked as a group down the street. There was a brewery at the corner where the road intersected with the Overseas Highway, and they were all holding cans of beer. This was to be a night of drinking, which meant they would be gone for at least a couple of hours. He had time.

* * *

Happy Hour was in full swing at the Islamorada Brewery and Distillery. The tropical themed bar made their own beer and vodka, grilled up hamburgers and fries, and had a patio filled with picnic tables painted green, yellow, and blue. The Anderson team were regulars, and the bartenders knew them well. Roland and Chris drank IPAs—this time it was the Floridays American. Roland had only recently become a hop-drinking man, having graduated from hard seltzers and baby beers. George and Terry preferred their Miller and Coors over the "fancy shit" Chris and the Harvard man consumed. However, at the brewery, they typically opted for the Go Fish lager—light and crisp, just how they liked it. Tricia despised the taste of beer and always ordered the Perfect Key Lime Pie Martini with house vodka. They found a spot outside—a stroke of luck considering how busy it was—and took over an entire picnic table near the outdoor beer shack. Easy access to more liquidation.

Chris and George were soon ready for round two and joined the line at the beer shack behind two bearded bikers. They had grown up together, slinging fists and cheap bourbon, but had drifted apart over the years. Their childhood friendship had been renewed, once more slinging fists and booze like the good old days, only now they were working for the federal government on top secret missions across the globe.

"Congrats, man," Chris said.

George grinned. "Hard to believe isn't it?"

"I still don't get what Trish sees in you."

"Me neither—I pinch my ass every day, wondering if I'm dreaming. But then she pinches it too, and I know it's real."

"I don't want to picture that."

"When you gonna find you a girl?"

"I'm a lone wolf, brother."

"Bullshit."

"I'm not built for relationships."

"Everyone is built for relationships."

"You're as ugly as they come, and you found someone. So I guess that's true."

"Course it's true."

Chris shuffled his feet. "I don't have much to offer a woman. Besides, I've got you guys. And I've got beer. What more could a guy ask for?"

"Dude, that's depressing. And you're wrong. You got a lot to offer." He paused. Then, "What happened with Jess and Natalya, those things don't define you." He pointed to Chris's chest. "It's what's in there that counts, ole boy."

"Still reading that Kindle, huh?"

"Every night."

"Self-help books?"

George raised his middle finger.

"Right—only guns and cars."

"Damn straight."

While Chris and George were waiting in line, Roland was having a heart-to-heart with Tricia. She had been with him ever since he left the CIA and started Anderson Security, even sticking by his side when the business nearly failed. A ride-or-die until the end, she was more than a former assistant-turned-spy-partner; she was family. And Roland was scared of what life would be like if she retired from Woodhaven. After all, she was their "mother," their leader—keeping a group of men in check, or "mentally challenged assholes" as she liked to call them. Marriage was a new chapter, and Roland knew all too well what new chapters meant.

"I'm not leaving, Roland," Tricia said. The Harvard man was being emotional, and she had to stop that nonsense.

"I know."

"He doesn't," Terry said.

"You loving little man," Tricia purred. "I appreciate the sentiment."

Roland blushed. "I'm truly happy for you. Not what I'd expected, but you two make a lovely couple."

"Weird isn't it?" she replied.

"Well, you know what they say. Opposites attract."

"This doesn't change our commitment to the team."

Terry felt a twinge of guilt. He had yet to tell anyone but Chris he was leaving and wondered how the others were going to take it. He ignored the concern, finishing off the last of his lager instead.

Chris and George returned, holding fresh beers and trays of shot glasses filled to the brim with an assortment of spirits.

"Shots? Really?" Roland exclaimed.

George placed his tray of booze on the table. "Hell, yeah. It's my bachelor party." He took a gulp of beer. "Just without the strippers."

Tricia raised an eyebrow. "No strippers tonight, boys. Why don't you single men go find some nice girls to talk to? And I'll enjoy the rest of the evening with my future husband."

"Worst bachelor party, ever," Terry said.

"Let's take shots," Chris said. "We got vodka and rum. Choose your poison."

They each took a glass.

"To George and Tricia," Chris said.

"George and Tricia," Terry and Roland echoed in unison.

• • •

It was almost midnight when Chris climbed into bed. He was too tired—too drunk—to bother with his nightly ritual of showering before sleep. He would do it in the morning after a quick swim in the ocean. The house was dark, the rest of the team having already turned in for the night. He powered on his Magicteam Sound Machine—white noise to block out the sound of silence—and stared up at the ceiling, his head spinning from too many IPAs and shots of rum. No luck with the ladies that night, even with Tricia pointing out the ones each man should talk to. Terry struck out twice, Roland chickened out three times, and Chris didn't even bother trying. It had been a great night, nevertheless, and Chris couldn't help but smile thinking about the renegade group of people he now shared his life with.

He had to pee.

Wearing only boxers and a white T-shirt, he stumbled through the darkness to the bathroom. He supported himself with the wall as he filled the toilet with a steady stream of clear urine—all that IPA down the drain, literally.

Now he was thirsty.

He made it to the kitchen, moonlight filtering through the sliding door that looked out on the courtyard. It was a clear night, and he could see the palm trees swaying in the breeze. He opened the refrigerator, took out a bottle of water, and was about to close the door when a ball of fire abruptly swept through the room. An explosion followed, the velocity of the blast throwing him to the floor. Fire was everywhere. And it was loud, like a train hurdling toward him.

Another explosion further away, then screams.

What the hell just happened?

He picked himself up and was immediately met with a wall of black smoke. Coughing, he covered his mouth and made for what was left of the sliding door, which had been blown out, filling the living room with shards of glass. He got outside to the courtyard and breathed in the fresh air. Catching his breath, and realizing he was now perfectly sober, he took in his surroundings. He remembered the others asleep in their beds. There was no time to call 911. They would all be dead by the time the fire department arrived.

It's up to you to rescue them.

He searched for an area untouched by flames and smoke and found only one: the war room. He kicked in the door and forced himself inside. Thankfully the fire had yet to overrun that part of the house. He reached the hallway and made for the first bedroom, the master suite.

"George! Trish!"

There was no reply.

"Fuck."

He was about to open their door when part of the ceiling came crashing down. He dodged the debris just in time. Smoke and drywall dust permeated the air. It was hard to see, hard to breathe.

Keep going.

He kicked in George and Tricia's door. A ball of fire exploded into his face, hurling him backward to the floor. The bedroom was consumed with flames. Unable to process what that meant, he picked himself up and continued on to the next room.

"Roland!" he screamed, his voice hoarse from inhaling so much smoke.

There was no response.

He felt lightheaded, and the heat was unbearable. More smoke filled the room. More fire. Each breath more labored than the last. He needed fresh air, or he was going to black out. He staggered down the hallway, searching for an exit. It felt like a tunnel—his vision blurred, his head pounding from lack of oxygen. Primal fear began to set in.

Not expecting this, not prepared.
This has to be a dream. Has to be.
And then—
Everything went dark.

CHAPTER 9

Greenwood Enterprises
Fairfax, Virginia

DAN GREENWOOD WAS more than a private military contractor. He was a fixer, with clients ranging from Fortune 500 companies to tech startups. Born in the port city of Guangzhou in the Guangdong Province of China, Greenwood immigrated to the United States with his parents when he was only three years old. The family soon adopted the name "Greenwood" to help them assimilate into their middle-class Baltimore, Maryland neighborhood. His strict Chinese upbringing pushed him to excel in school, and he eventually earned a BA from Johns Hopkins University. He worked hard, determined to achieve a lifestyle his father only dreamed about.

His company, Greenwood Enterprises, operated a front business that provided tactical training. The compound resembled a military base with nearly a hundred employees ranging from former military operatives to administrative staff, training civilians and law enforcement agencies in self-defense, hostage rescue, and the tradecraft of tactical warfare. There were classrooms outfitted

NEW BEGINNING

with virtual reality training modules, deep-dive swimming pools, a state-of-the-art gym, and an outdoor firing range. They also provided armed security for political figures, ambassadors, and foreign dignitaries. These were the guys Uncle Sam called when they needed unsanctioned black ops missions completed in days, under the radar, and without error.

But his bread-and-butter was contracted assassinations of "High-Value Individuals"—or HVIs—for the Central Intelligence Agency. He had served his country proudly in Afghanistan as a Marine but became jaded with the political whims of old men in ivory towers handing down orders without comprehension of the consequences. He realized that there were no good guys or bad guys, just eight billion people trying to survive. After a stint as a CIA contractor, he went into business for himself and quickly built a reputation as a man who got things done no matter the cost. Highly lucrative and highly illegal, eliminating HVIs had made him rich—a large colonial house in Washington, D.C., a tropical spread in West Palm Beach, and a penthouse in Manhattan. But this job was his largest payday yet. And his client was not the CIA.

Greenwood stared out the window of his office, which was on the top floor of a six-story building at the center of the expansive property. It was three o'clock in the morning and the compound was deserted, surrounded by miles of empty Virginia countryside. He opened the Proton VPN application on his iPad and swiped to open the encrypted email he had just received from his operative in Florida. Caleb Webb had first proved himself on the battlefields of Afghanistan. Greenwood took an instant liking to the young soldier, eventually recruiting and training him to become one of his top assassins.

The report included video footage of the explosion. Caleb had cut the house's gas line and timed the detonation perfectly. By the time Islamorada's fire department arrived, the 3,400-square-foot ranch was consumed by flames. No one could have survived that. Even the firemen were unable to venture inside. Satisfied with the outcome, Greenwood swiped the message away. Both contracts had been successful. Adam Conner's death would be ruled a home invasion, and Chris Harding, Roland Anderson, Tricia Perkins, and George Hartman had all perished in an accidental explosion stemming from a gas leak.

It was time to start his day. After changing into a pair of shorts, a T-shirt, and running shoes, he grabbed a bottle of water from the mini-fridge and began his morning workout—a five-mile run followed by weight training at the onsite gym. He relished those early hours of the morning while the rest of the country was fast asleep. It gave him a chance to free the demons that occupied his mind. The sun was on the horizon when he finished, and his employees were beginning to arrive for the day, along with the customers who paid top dollar for military-grade tactical firearm training.

Greenwood checked his watch. It was a few minutes past six. His client would be awake and ready for a debrief. Drenched in sweat, his muscles bulging from the workout, he returned to his office and used a KryptAll phone to make the call.

• • •

FBI Headquarters
Washington, D.C.

Steven House disconnected his call with Dan Greenwood and took a moment to process the news, gazing out the window of his office at the sun peaking over the top of the White House. It should never have come to this. But the future of a great nation sometimes required unsavory events to take place, and Woodhaven had become a liability. He had been tasked with eliminating every threat to the cause—had been appointed FBI director for that very purpose. He believed he could do it politically—convincing Congress that operations like Woodhaven were unnecessary, even Un-American—and he would have succeeded had it not been for Geneva. If only he had known about the operation beforehand, he never would have let it happen. But now they were too close to the truth, too close to destroying everything. There was no other option.

The FBI director was ready to be finished with the whole thing. He took a seat behind his desk and made another call on the KryptAll phone in his hand. The unmistakable voice of Feng Chen, senior intelligence officer with the Chinese Ministry of State Security, came on the line. House informed him that the contracts on Woodhaven had been successful.

"You have done well," Chen said.

Condescending prick, go fuck yourself.

"And Palmer?" House replied.

"As I stated before, she is no longer alive on this earth."

"Then that concludes our business."

"Yes, it is no longer wise for us to communicate. But I look forward to the future of our two countries."

With that, Chen disconnected the call.

The director leaned back in his seat and let out a sigh of relief. But there was more work yet to be done. Politicking, swimming the swamp, and preparing for the next phase of the plan.

• • •

House arrived at the 10:00 a.m. oversight committee meeting to find the wood-paneled conference room already full. The attorney general and director of national intelligence were seated at the head of the table, flanked by a team of lawyers and ODNI staffers. At the other end were two well-known members of the House of Representatives: Albert Lowe, representing New York's 10th Congressional District, and Robin Valencia from California's 30th District. The purpose of the oversight committee meeting was to approve the FBI's budget for the next quarter and to ensure that it was acting in the country's best interest, but as House learned years before, its true purpose was to gain political alliances.

After going through several talking points, the conversation turned to the FBI's use of gray ops, both domestically and overseas.

Valencia began. "With the United States' negative image globally regarding the use of military force and the president's push for international peace and partnership, we believe the less—how do I put it, spying is the only word coming to mind—the better."

"Specifically with China," Lowe added.

"I couldn't agree more," said House. "That's why we've trimmed the fat. All of our gray intelligence operations, both at home and abroad, have been dissolved, effective immediately."

"Music to my ears," Valencia replied.

"The president's administration has the bureau's full support, and going forward, we will let the CIA actually do some real intelligence work. After all, that is what the American people are paying them for, right?"

That got laughs all around, causing a smile to break across House's face. Woodhaven was no more, and his political situation was finally looking up.

NEW BEGINNING

• • •

Chris opened his eyes. Everything was a blur. Nothing but white lights. He thought he might be dead but then saw figures wearing what looked like scrubs leaning over him and talking loudly. At least it seemed to be loud, but he couldn't tell. Everything was muffled. His eyes began to adjust, and he realized the bright lights were coming from the fluorescent bulbs that lined the creamy-white ceiling. He was lying on a gurney and moving fast. Nurses, that's what they were, were rushing him down a long hallway. Then the pain returned. Throbbing, aching pain that pulsated through his entire body. He couldn't move. But he could breathe. And then he realized he was wearing an oxygen mask.

The gurney slammed through double doors and entered a large room. More nurses—or doctors, he couldn't tell—were everywhere, talking excessively, asking him questions that he couldn't answer because he couldn't speak. He thought he heard something about severe burns and smoke inhalation. That made sense. His last memory was standing outside Roland's bedroom calling out his name. Had the others gotten out? He didn't know. His thoughts were interrupted by a figure in scrubs removing the oxygen mask and saying something about anesthesia. Another mask went over his mouth, and he felt himself dozing off.

Yup, definitely being put under.

His last thought before darkness took hold of him.

CHAPTER 10

New York City

6 MONTHS LATER

For Alena Moore, nothing beat Christmastime in the city. It reminded her of an old movie with Cary Grant and was one of the reasons why she had always dreamed of living in Manhattan. At thirty-three, she had finally made it. While her classmates partied through college, she studied, and while her friends got married in their twenties, she worked—day and night, always hustling. Alena always knew she wanted to be an investigative journalist. It fit her old-fashioned values and preferences, not just because she loved print—a dying media by the time she got there—but because she valued the "truth," something few in television cared much for. Eventually, she planned to ditch her MacBook Air for a portable typewriter, write adventure novels, and become the female version of Ernest Hemingway, whose visceral reporting of World War II had inspired her to put pen to paper in the first place.

She was only five-foot-three, with dark brown hair that matched her eyes, but she was fierce. Never backed down from a fight. Her moderate politics angered many, though few could argue her dedication to finding the truth no matter what side of the aisle it came from. She had burned just as many Republicans as she had Democrats. And she wasn't interested in working online at some blog no one read. No, she wanted to write for the largest newspaper in the world, the CNN of print—the *New York Times*.

She took a sip of her Venti Starbucks coffee—light cream, no sugar—and made her way through the sea of pedestrian commuters to her office at the New York Times Building on Eighth Avenue. Today was a good day. After three months of research, interviews, and countless drafts—lots of beer at night and coffee in the morning—she had finally completed her latest piece. And today she had an approval meeting with her editor, Henry Dunlap. If he signed off, her story would go to print and she would be one step closer to ditching the news desk altogether, allowing her to focus on investigative reporting full-time—perhaps her own column, a book deal, a syndicated talk show. The possibilities were endless.

Alena entered the glassy skyscraper and waved at the security guard. He'd been there since the fifty-two-story building opened in 2007. The newspaper took up the bottom half of the building, and the newsroom was on the fourth floor. She passed through the lobby and squeezed into a crowded elevator, nearly spilling her coffee in the process.

Her desk in the bullpen was chaotic. Past boyfriends would say she was "messy," but she preferred the term "absent-minded" and refused to change. Her cubicle neighbor, Bradley, poked his head over the four-foot wall that divided their workspaces.

"Henry's been asking for you all morning," he said in his usual whiny voice laced with a distinct Brooklyn accent. "You should probably go in there."

She hated him. "Thank you, Bradley."

But he wasn't ready to go and stared at her through his gigantic glasses—she was convinced the prescription was negative eight—those beady little eyes darting around her desk. She ignored him and turned on her desktop computer. As it powered up, she sipped her coffee and scrolled through her inbox on her iPhone. Sure enough, Dunlap had sent an email at eight o'clock sharp asking to see her first thing. She took one final sip of coffee and got up.

As she walked away, Bradley said, "What did you do this time?"

She ignored him and climbed the staircase to the editors' offices on the floor above. It was an open floor plan that allowed management to look down on the reporters below—their minions, as some would say. Alena's nerves were on fire. Anticipation, excitement—this was it. Years of hard work and sacrifice were about to pay off. She had finally written a story compelling enough to propel her career to the next level.

"I can't print this," Dunlap said as soon as Alena entered his office and closed the door behind her.

"You always say that, and then I convince you otherwise, and it's a success every time."

Henry Dunlap was nearly sixty, kept his gray hair short, and always wore khakis and starched dress shirts. He had kind eyes and was one of the few editors at the *Times* who truly cared about the work—and the staff. He had been the one to hire Alena as a reporter and had championed her all the way to her first investigative piece two years prior. He was fair, but he was tough. Journalistic integrity was strictly enforced.

"It's good work," he said. "But I can't run it."

Alena plopped into a chair facing his desk and crossed her

arms. "Explain."

"For starters, your sources—"

"What about them?"

"You don't have any."

"People are scared to go on the record."

"That's just it; you're alleging that a congressman was murdered because he was about to vote 'yes' on a Nysta ban in the United States."

"He was."

"This isn't an opinion piece. This is news. If you can't prove it, we can't print it. You know that, Alena."

Nysta was one of the largest social media platforms in the world, competing against Facebook, Instagram, and X head-to-head in active users, having reached 1.6 billion worldwide since launching in 2022. One could post texts, photos, and videos, as well as reposts from other social media platforms. What made it unique was its proprietary algorithm that enabled a user to reach millions of people with a single post, eliminating the need to build a massive following. Instead of "followers" there were "groups" like "People who love Harry Potter" or "Small businesses in St. Louis." It had revolutionized the way people connected.

But it was a Chinese-owned company, and there were concerns in Washington that the app was sharing users' data with the Chinese Communist Party. For many in Congress, Nysta was a threat to national security. Eight months ago, a bill was brought before the House requiring Nysta's parent company, SMIC, to sell the app in order for it to continue operating within the United States. Nysta CEO and founder Andrew Chew went before the House Committee on Energy and Commerce to make his case for the app he had built out of his garage. He wanted to be transparent, and his way of doing that was to suggest all data be managed domestically by the largest cybersecurity firm in America: Auspex Technology. It was an arrangement that would virtually guarantee zero data interference from the Chinese government.

The biggest issue was that many in Congress simply did not understand social media. In fact, Chew was called upon multiple times to explain *"exactly what it is Nysta does"* and *"why the hell do we even need an app like this?"* The media ate it up, and during the weeks-long hearings, the entire country was bombarded with pundits discussing Nysta's pros and cons, the ethics of user data sharing, and whether China was secretly trying to steal America's cat photos. But Chew performed well, convincing much of the committee to vote in his favor. All except one.

From the beginning, Seth Wilson, a young congressman from Kentucky, had strongly advocated banning Nysta in the United States altogether. He believed the app posed a significant threat to the American people—specifically children—and there was nothing Chew could say to change his mind. Being a Southern gentleman, he had graciously met with the opposition, many of them lobbyists for big tech, but he was firm. He would vote against Nysta operating in the United States, regardless of who managed their user data. Wilson became the tie-breaker. But on the day he was scheduled to cast his vote, he was killed in an auto accident a few miles from his home in Lexington.

"I have a witness at the scene," Alena said. "The Uber driver, he saw the entire thing."

"Yes, the trucker who plowed into him. It's all public knowledge. We even did a report on it when it happened back in June."

"I know, but what about the truck driver? He wasn't scheduled to drive that day. In fact, there's no record he was even the one operating the truck."

"Did you speak to him personally?"

"Yes."

"And?"

"He hung up on me five times, blocked my numbers, slammed the door in my face—"

"Then you haven't proven a thing."

"People are scared. What Nysta is doing—it's a coordinated attack on the United States."

"You're the only one who thinks that. Your hypothesis that Chew duped Congress and is now running a data factory for the Chinese Communist Party is absurd."

Alena leaned back in her seat and glared at Dunlap. "Is this about Blake?"

Blake Schwartz was the Gen-Z trust fund baby who had just inherited a majority stake in the *New York Times*. He was a spoilt brat who had no idea how the newspaper business worked, less how real life worked. He spent most of his time online updating his Instagram stories, expressing concern for the latest social trends on X, and posting videos of his Manhattan penthouse on Nysta. What sparked fear among the senior editors was that he believed print media was dead—a relic of corporate greed, intolerance, and a bygone era that needed to be forgotten. Even so, the twerp was oddly smart. He attracted the best advertisers and persuaded them to spend massive ad dollars in return for positive media exposure. One of those advertisers was Auspex Technology.

"I can't keep having this argument."

"I mean, it's pretty obvious. Our biggest client is Auspex Technology, and I guess it looks kinda bad on them if the data they're supposed to protect is all part of a diabolical plan to steal American information—which is a lot if you think about it, like every aspect of our lives put on Nysta and sent to China."

"Dear lord, Alena—let it go. I know you've worked hard on this, but it's not there. I don't think it ever will be. Write the stories I give you, or you're back at the news desk full-time."

"You wouldn't."

"I can't keep covering for you if you bring me nothing."

"Give me two more weeks," she blurted out without thinking.

"No."

She weighed her options. It was all or nothing.

"How about one week? If I can't convince you, I'll drop it and," she struggled to get the words out, "do that piece on the future of sustainable energy within the auto industry."

Dunlap stared at her, thinking. Then, "Fine! But two weeks, that's it, and I want a solid source that confirms your theory. After that, I never want to hear another negative thing about Nysta. My daughter loves it."

"You got it, boss."

As she got up to leave, Dunlap said, "And just so you know, I don't give a shit what Blake thinks. We write the truth here—regardless of who our advertisers are."

CHAPTER 11

NOTHING IS MORE frustrating for a writer than a mandatory rewrite of finished work. Alena's instincts told her she was on to something big, perhaps a comprehensive series of articles detailing the cyber war she saw emerging between China and the rest of the world—specifically, the United States. But deep down she knew Dunlap was right. Her sources were weak. She begrudgingly spent the rest of the morning, into the afternoon, scrolling through notes, early drafts, and interviews—every source—searching for something she may have overlooked. Nothing caught her eye. She needed a drink.

Beer Authority was a gastropub above a Chase bank directly across the street from the New York Times Building. Alena was kind of a regular there, skipping out of the office for an afternoon beer, a couple beef sliders, and a chance to clear her mind—and write. Today was no exception. Her usual spot was one of the circular tables near the bar. She ordered a Firestone Mind Haze IPA and opened her laptop.

Within minutes she was on Facebook.

She admired the older writers who were able to distance themselves from outside distractions while they worked. But she was a product of her generation and liked to distract her mind for a few moments before switching gears and tackling whatever problem she was working through. Today was figuring out where the hell to begin again. She knew that Nysta received the same type of user data as other social media platforms. Photos and videos, contact information, IP addresses, and metadata—search history and shopping preferences. This was all standard operating procedure, used to create user profiles for targeted marketing campaigns that could be packaged and sold to online retailers.

None of this was a concern. China rarely did business with the average American consumer directly. Instead, they opted to provide investment capital and global manufacturing services. The issue was Nysta's second form of revenue: verified profiles. Much like the blue checkmark on X, these red emblems verified that the user was who they said they were. But Nysta went a step further. Verified profiles were given unlimited access to "groups," whereas free accounts could only join five at a time. For the negligible price of $4.99 per month, anyone could reach anyone. Still not the issue. The issue was the credit cards. To pay for this premium service, a user was required to have a valid Visa or Mastercard on file. Most people thought nothing of it. After all, saving forms of payment on websites had become as common as breathing, and now Nysta—a Chinese-owned company—had access to a hundred-and-fifty million American credit cards.

Alena's Firestone Mind Haze arrived, and she ordered two beef sliders and a side of fries to go with it. She sipped the foam off the top of the glass and followed up with a gulp of the New England-style IPA. It was hoppy, but fresh, almost sweet. She wasn't a creature of habit—liked to try every IPA she could find—and Beer Authority had a rotating tap. This one was good. She would probably order a second one.

She scrolled through her Facebook feed, staring at pictures of people she used to know, many of whom were now married with kids. Not only had she given up on the party life, she had given up on the dating life as well. Her career always took first place, and most relationships fizzled out within a few weeks. Still, she was young; she had time, even though the number of quality men was dwindling—casualties of marriage—as she moved deeper into her thirties. She was about to get back to work when a notification pinged, and a Facebook message appeared at the top right corner of the screen. Her first instinct was to click out of it. But then she noticed who it was from. It was Amy Dotson.

Amy was one of Alena's oldest friends going all the way back to middle school and the other A in the "Double-As" as they used to call themselves. They had both transferred to the same school at the same time and were quickly labeled "emo-punk nerds" in a school dominated by preppy kids in polo shirts and khakis. And they were smart, only taking AP classes while ogling the guys who would not give them the time of day. Alena smiled as she remembered them sitting outside, lighting up Marlboro Light cigarettes and blowing smoke in the direction of the cheerleaders. Then there was the time they skipped school for all-you-can-eat pancakes at the local diner only to get caught and spend the rest of the week in detention. But times changed. Careers had to be forged. They drifted apart after high school and had not spoken in over ten years; they weren't even friends on Facebook. Alena knew she was partly to blame. A double major had kept her too busy, even for her oldest and dearest friend.

The message was brief.

> **Alena, it's Amy. I know it's been a while, but I don't know who else to call. 415-859-1986.**

Alena stared at the screen, unsure what to think. The message was concerning, but at the same time, Amy had always been dramatic. Alena clicked on her profile and scrolled through posts and pictures, searching for clues. Nothing out of the ordinary. She decided to try LinkedIn. A quick search produced several names with the correct Amy being at the very top.

Oh my God.

Alena felt goosebumps forming on the back of her neck as she read her estranged friend's job title: Senior Platform Engineer at Nysta. What were the odds? It had to be a coincidence. But what if it wasn't? She went back to Amy's message. *I don't know who else to call.*

She was in trouble. Alena picked up her phone, took a deep breath, and dialed the number listed in the message.

CHAPTER 12

Nysta Headquarters
Palo Alto, California

Amy Dotson sat inside her silver Tesla, staring at the incoming call from "Alena Moore" on her iPhone 15. She hadn't expected a response so quick, or at all, and she realized her decision to become a whistleblower and destroy her entire career would be official if she pressed the green button on the phone and answered the call from her oldest friend. Her car was parked at her designated spot in the six-level parking structure beneath the office. Located just a few miles from the Google campus, Nysta was everything a tech startup should be. A towering glass structure in the shape of a giant N designed by the same architect as the Walt Disney Concert Hall in Los Angeles. This was the heart of Silicon Valley—headquarters for the world's largest technology companies where electric cars and over-paid nerds roamed free.

Amy was a petite Chinese American with dark hair and hazel eyes. Born in Austin, Texas to immigrant parents, she grew up in a family that valued education above all. She had always loved the arts—at one point wanted to be a dancer—but her father insisted she study computer science. Sixth grade saw her enter all AP classes, and even though she had straight As and happy folks, she was miserable. That was until she met Alena.

Alena was a free spirit who said and did as she pleased. Amy admired her and, deep down, wanted to be just like her. It was tough when Alena went off to NYU and Amy was accepted at UCLA. They drifted apart and now—more than a decade later—were about to speak again. *If only under better circumstances*, Amy thought.

She pressed the green button.

"Hey."

"Hey," Alena replied.

"It's been a long time."

"Yeah, it's crazy."

Amy paused.

This is awkward.

"How are you?" Alena asked.

"Been better." That was the truth.

"I know I should have kept in touch. I just—you know me, always on the grind. I feel like an asshole."

"No, no, I could have called you too. Don't worry about it."

Amy had the call connected to her car but was holding the phone in her hand. It began to shake. She could still back out, still forget what she had seen and move on. Maybe she was crazy, and this was all a misunderstanding.

"I don't know how to say this, but I reached out because I, I'm not sure—"

"What's wrong, Amy?"

She could still hang up. What a way to reconnect with an old friend. But she was resolved. It was the right thing to do, and Alena was the only person she could trust.

"I know you're a journalist. And we go way back. You wouldn't judge me."

"What's going on?"

"So uh, I work at Nysta."

"I know."

"Of course you do. It's a great job—came at the right time after I got laid off last year."

"You were at Netflix, right?"

"Yeah, and I always wanted to work in social, and the people here are amazing. The pay is *ridiculous*—I love it here."

"Okay?"

"I don't want to do this over the phone. If I flew to New York, could we meet?"

The sliders arrived at Alena's table at Beer Authority. She smiled and thanked the waiter with her eyes. "Right, of course." She wasn't expecting a meet-up. "I'm pretty swamped at work right now. Deadlines, you know, but—"

"Don't worry about it."

Alena realized she was doing it again—pushing her friends away.

"You know what? *Yes*, you should come to New York. We'll get drunk. It'll be just like the old days. Except now we don't need fake IDs to buy beer."

The joke lightened the mood. Amy smiled. "Don't remind me how old we are."

"I'm still two months younger than you, bitch."

Amy laughed. "Okay, I'll text you when I get there."

"You sure you don't wanna tell me what's going on? You seem anxious."

Amy looked around the parking garage at the rows of Teslas plugged into the EV charging stations installed in every spot. Anyone could be listening. Maybe through her iPhone. Maybe they hacked her car and were watching her at this very moment, documenting the entire conversation. It was best to do this in person. Best to be brief.

"I found something at work that I shouldn't have, and I think it's a big deal."

"What do you mean?"

"My job is to troubleshoot application updates. I won't get into the technical side of it, but it's essentially proofreading the update's line of code."

"Okay?"

"We have an update scheduled to drop next week. This morning, I found something that wasn't supposed to be there."

"Like what?"

Amy thought she saw someone watching her from around the corner of the garage.

Stop it, you're being paranoid.

"Amy?"

"There was an inconsistency in the code. I reported it to my supervisor, and less than ten minutes later, the director of human resources called me into her office—said I was making false accusations against the company."

"HR is a joke."

"Tell me about it. They made me sign an NDA about the update."

"That's weird. Wouldn't your regular NDA cover that?"

"It would."

"Did you sign it?"

"I had to. They wouldn't let me return to work until I did. I'm really freaking out here because I know they're lying to me, and I know there's something going on. I'm scared for my job, but I don't want to be involved in something illegal."

Alena could sense the fear in Amy's voice. "Why call me? Sounds like you need a lawyer." She immediately regretted how that came out. It was her typical apathetic response to anything that didn't involve *her*. She believed Amy, but at the same time, she didn't. Amy had always been a drama queen with a wild imagination. Alena was also thinking about her story. Here it was she had hit a concrete wall and then, out of the blue, came a desperate call from an old friend who just happened to work for the company she was investigating.

Coincidence? Probably. Just focus on your friend.

"There's not much I can do if you won't tell me what you saw in the update."

"It's best I do it in person. I'll be in New York tomorrow. I have it all saved on a flash drive. I'll show you everything"

"So much for that NDA," Alena teased.

"If it's what I think it is, someone needs to stop them. And you're the only person I can trust."

CHAPTER 13

Rush hour on I-80 was well underway by the time Amy crossed the Oakland Bay Bridge heading into downtown San Francisco. She used her time in stalled traffic to check flights, quickly finding a red-eye leaving at 1:00 a.m. She purchased the ticket and tried to relax as she stared out at the sea of cars in front of her. There was no way to know if she was making the right decision or not. Regardless, she had left the office early, was taking a long weekend, and would soon be thousands of miles away. Traffic began to move again, and she was jolted forward by honking from the car behind her.

She lived in a luxury high-rise on Pine Street in the historic financial district, a few blocks from the San Francisco Ferry Terminal and Pier 1—home to her favorite restaurant, La Mar Cocina Peruana. The two-bedroom apartment with epic views of the Bay and Treasure Island was not far from Chinatown, which her mother loved and she hated. It was also safe. Even with the city's rising homeless epidemic, she had never once had an incident.

Her dog, Miley, was nipping at the door when she arrived. Only eight months old, the blond-haired female Pomeranian was already full-grown and potty trained. Outside of work, caring for

Miley was her only activity—her whole world. And that little dog loved her, could not wait for her to get home each night, and was excited—perhaps a bit surprised—that she was home so early.

"Hi, baby," Amy said as she closed the door behind her.

Miley climbed up her leg and smiled, tung hanging out.

"Glad to see momma, huh?"

Her bowl was empty.

"Let's get you some food."

Miley knew what that meant and dashed across the hardwood floor to the two pink bowls with her name on them. Amy poured a generous serving of organic dog food into the first one and refilled the water from a bottle of spring water in the second one.

She needed to walk her, but first she wanted to save the information she had stolen from the office. Her remote workstation was where the dining room table should have been. She sat down at the white desk, opened her work laptop, and inserted two flash drives. She stared at the folder labeled *Nysta Update* on the home screen. This was it. The moment of truth. She took a deep breath and copied the file to both drives. One went into her purse, and the other was sealed inside a manila envelope. She scribbled an address on the front and pressed a stamp to the top right corner.

By now, Miley had finished her early dinner, drank her water, and was ready to go outside. She stood at Amy's feet and gazed longingly at her as if to say, *"Please take me outside so I can pee."*

It was December so the days where shorter, and although it was only a few minutes past five, the sun was already dipping below the horizon. The skyscrapers surrounding the apartment building blocked the light as the blue haze of evening began its descent upon the city. Amy grabbed the envelope, put on a coat—the Bay Area was chilly this time of year—and connected Miley's pink leash.

The little dog jumped for joy as her and her mother made their way down the hallway to the elevator. Once they reached the ground floor, Amy dropped the envelope in the mailbox. She smiled at the security guard stationed in the lobby. His name was Sam, and he was a nice guy, a skinny Hispanic kid from Sacramento who was working his way through college and always made a point to smile at Amy when she came through the lobby to walk Miley. It was the only time she left the building on foot.

"Miley is getting bigger," Sam observed.

"I think this is as big as she'll get."

He leaned down to pet her. She let him. "Hey there, Miley, how's your day going?"

She barked an answer and licked his hand. He laughed. "I'm having a good day too."

"How's school?" Amy asked.

"It's good. I have finals next week, which sucks."

"Then Christmas break."

"Thank God."

"Going to see your folks?"

"Sure am—can't wait. What about you?"

"Actually, I'm headed out of town for the weekend." She regretted telling him—not sure why—but decided to move on before he asked where. "Have a good night, Sam."

"You too."

Amy and Miley exited the building and started off down the sidewalk. Walks typically lasted about fifteen minutes, with Miley peeing and pooping twice, waiting patiently for her mother to pick up her excrement in the pink doggy bags she carried with her before moving on. On weekends, they ventured down to the pier or to nearby Sue Bierman Park, but that was too far for a weekday.

Besides, Amy needed to pack.

They did a full circle—three city blocks—before heading back to the apartment. Amy was looking at her phone. Miley was sniffing the ground.

"You got any change?"

The voice came from behind her.

Amy turned.

It was a homeless man wearing tattered blue khakis and an old, red winter coat. His long hair and beard were tangled, and his entire body was covered in dirt.

"I'm sorry, no," Amy replied, pulling Miley toward her and quickening her pace. Her apartment was the next building—just a few more yards.

She walked faster. But she could smell him, feel him.

He was following her.

This wasn't the first time Amy had been accosted by a homeless man. As long as she ignored them and continued walking, they would lose interest and wonder off like zombies.

She made it to her building, could see Sam through the glass doors. That's when she felt it. From behind, a knife entered her back, producing a sharp pain that spread through her entire body like an electrical shock.

The smell of the homeless man beside her, his dirty body pressed against her's.

Cold, unforgiving steel inside her body.

Before she could process what had happened, she felt another sharp pain in her back, then another to her side, and another, then another, and another—

She screamed and let go of the leash as she fell to the ground, blood pouring out of her side. Miley barked, but the homeless man kicked her little body, tossing it against the side of the building. She yelped a couple of times, then went limp. Amy tried to call for help, but the words wouldn't come out. The world lost its focus. She thought she saw Sam running toward her, the sound of people yelling in the distance. And then everything went dark.

CHAPTER 14

New York City

"What do you mean, she never boarded?" Alena wanted to toss the phone across the room, better yet, strangle the moron on the other end of the line.

"I'm sorry, ma'am, we have no record of her being on the flight," said the woman on the phone. She had a strong Indian accent and was absolutely void of emotion. She was a robot.

"Please check again—Amy Dotson. D-O-T-S-O-N."

There was a pause. Then, "We have no record of her on—"

"I know—no record of her on the plane. My question is, did she have a ticket?"

"Yes, there was a ticket."

"Thank you," Alena said while thinking, *you're an idiot*. "Now, did she transfer her flight itinerary, or just not show up?"

"I'm sorry, ma'am, we have no record of—"

Waste of time. Click.

Alena was pacing her living room, thinking. The apartment was small—no more than six hundred square feet, which was typical for a $4,000-a-month one-bedroom pad in the Upper West

Side of Manhattan—but it was cozy with exposed brick walls and a cherry tree outside the living room window. She kept it neat. Lots of flowers. Paintings on the walls. And most importantly, her mahogany and oak writing desk. A gift from her parents when she graduated college, the vintage French nineteenth-century-style pedestal desk had seen her through grad school, internships, and those early lean years when writing was all she had.

Amy had sent a text with her itinerary the night before. Alena hadn't heard from her since. Amy's flight was supposed to land at LaGuardia Airport in Queens at 10:25 a.m., which meant she would arrive at Alena's apartment by taxi around noon, one o'clock at the latest. She never did. Nor did she respond to Alena's calls and texts. At first, Alena wondered if her old friend had backed out at the last minute and was now too embarrassed to take her calls. It would not be the first time Amy had cried wolf.

But could something have happened to her? After all, she had found something in the Nysta update that concerned her, was chastised by HR for speaking up, and had been audibly shaken on the phone. What if Alena's hypothesis—that Nysta was funneling data to China—could be substantiated by what Amy discovered? If so, perhaps the same people who killed the congressman from Kentucky were behind this.

Stop it, you've read too many spy novels.

But she was an investigative journalist and was going to find out exactly what happened.

A quick Google search produced Amy's address and the telephone number for the building. She called, and after a few rings, a young man answered.

"Heritage," he said.

"Hi, yes, I'm looking for an Amy Dotson."

"Is she a resident?"

"Yes."

"I'm sorry, we can't disclose our residents' personal information."

"Not even their names?"

"No."

"I understand, but she's a friend of mine, and I know she lives there. I just need to know if she's okay."

"Why wouldn't she be okay?"

"That's what I'm trying to find out. Could you do a wellness check for me?"

There was a pause. She knew he was thinking. He sounded young, and stupid. Of course, everyone she talked to right now was stupid. He came back on the line.

"Okay, I can check. What was her name again?"

"Amy Dotson."

"Right. Hold."

She heard the phone hit the counter. He was oblivious to the functions of a "hold" button. She waited for what felt like an eternity before the young man returned.

"I uh…" He sounded flustered, concerned. "I have terrible news."

CHAPTER 15

Palisade, Colorado

CHRIS HARDING WAS already awake when his alarm went off at 4:00 a.m. He had finally decided to take advantage of the chronic insomnia that had plagued him for so many years. He washed his face, threw on a pair of sweats and a T-shirt, and dropped to the floor—a hundred push-ups, twenty pull-ups, and fifty crunches. He downed a glass of water, put on a pair of Nikes and an old hoodie, and walked out the door.

The ten-degree morning hit him like a brick, the cold air filling his lungs as he went down the stairs to the sidewalk below, but the beard that covered his face kept him warm. His studio apartment was above a local barbershop in the downtown area of Palisade, a village adjacent to the Colorado River between Grand Junction and Aspen—barely a dot on the map—a throwback to small-town Americana. It was the dead of winter, though, and the town maintained a steady flow of snow that was never really given a chance to thaw.

Chris began with a steady jog down the deserted sidewalk before increasing his pace to a brisk run. Running cleared his head,

NEW BEGINNING

helped him focus, and after months of the same morning routine—covering all two square miles of downtown, twice—he was in the best shape of his life. He had cut down on the cigarettes—less than half a pack a day—and quit drinking alcohol, replacing beer with large quantities of coffee and green tea. It had been six months since the explosion, and his near-death experience had forged a desire to take care of his body. But the reason he quit drinking ran much deeper than a forty-one-year-old's sense of mortality. That summer night in Florida had changed his life forever. Everything he had grown to love, every bit of normal he had managed to create in his life had been taken away—instantly.

The doctors had told him he suffered from short-term memory loss due to a lack of oxygen to the brain. It was a form of traumatic brain injury and he spent the next two weeks lying in a hospital bed, staring out the window, and wondering who the hell he was. It reminded him of *The Bourne Identity*, and he wondered if he was a spy. Ironically he *was* a spy, a real-life version of Jason Bourne, and the only reason he was still alive was because he didn't know his name. The hospital was unable to verify his identity. Had it, he was certain he would have been killed in his sleep by the same people who murdered Roland, Tricia, George, and Terry—in their beds, at night, without warning.

His memory had returned in pieces, slowly, over time. First his name, then his bank account information, and finally what happened. But the one thing that never left him was his sense of survival. This was a guy who flew his team out of Russia in an old airplane and then crash-landed while being shot at. Who kept on fighting even when the odds were stacked against him. Resilience was in his blood even if his mind got in the way sometimes. When he returned to the house in Islamorada he found nothing but two walls and a concrete foundation. Seeing it had been difficult. But it cleared up the fog that still surrounded that dreadful night. The last night he got drunk. Never again would he let himself be inhibited by an outside substance.

Records indicated everyone had died in the house, including Chris. And Adam Connor's death-by-burglary had made national news. It was clear someone had betrayed them, and the list of potential suspects was short. There were only a handful of people still alive who knew of Woodhaven's existence: FBI Director Steven House, retired General and co-founder of Woodhaven Al Kempe, former FBI Director and co-founder of Woodhaven Aden Smith, and super-spy Natalya Palmer, who was undercover in China at the time of the attack. Any one of them could have ordered the hit. But why?

Chris thought of his ex-wife, Jessica, and his ten-year-old daughter, Claire. If he went after those responsible for murdering his closest friends, he would be putting them in danger. Their safety relied on him staying "dead." It was time to become a true ghost, to disappear into the night and let evil lie. He drained the team's $50,000 slush fund account, bought himself a new driver's license and social security card, and hit the road. Palisade had been an accident, a stop along the way to nowhere. He met a cool guy with a Harley Davison and a beard named Frank Boone, who owned the local brewery, Susie Brews—named after his wife—and a studio apartment downtown. It just so happened that Frank needed a new bartender as well as a new tenant, and he decided Chris was a perfect candidate for both.

• • •

Chris handed two pints of dark wheat ale to a young couple waiting at the bar. They thanked him and carried their beers to a nearby table. Susie Brews was housed inside an old warehouse with polished concrete floors and stainless-steel fermentation tanks in the back beside a small kitchen that cooked up the best BBQ in Colorado. The indoor dining room and bar were situated in the front. A covered patio provided outdoor seating along with an additional bar, only open during the summer months. It was a happening place on the weekends. However, during the day it was nothing but locals and road-trippers on their way to the ski resorts in Vail and Aspen.

Susie Boone joined Chris behind the bar.

"How was your run?" she asked.

In her late thirties, Susie had jet-black hair and tattoo-covered arms. She was Frank's wife but was also the master brewer and knew more about beer than any other person Chris had ever met.

"It was good, cold," he replied.

"Nobody gets up that early to run outside. You're crazy."

"So I've been told."

"I know you're off tomorrow but any chance you could work? Rick called in sick again."

"Bastard."

"I'm starting to wonder if he's just slow-quitting."

"Nah, he's just lazy. But yeah, I can cover."

She laughed. "Thank you, Dale—always saving the day."

Chris's new identity was Dale Finer, and he had only recently gotten used to the name.

Susie started to leave, then remembered something. "There's a snowstorm coming through tonight. Supposed to last all weekend."

"Yeah, I heard about that."

"Bar will probably be slow so—"

"I'll close early and hit the road before it gets dark."

During snowstorms, the people of Palisade who owned 4x4 trucks would traverse Interstate 70 and help stranded travelers unprepared for Colorado's inclement weather. Chris still had the 2022 Ford F-150 the FBI bought him—with new plates and registration, of course—and Frank had given him an old police scanner so he could track emergency calls during the storms. His services had already been utilized twice since the winter season began in late November.

"What did we do before you arrived?" Susie said with a smile.

The bell rang and two plates of BBQ and fries arrived in the window behind the bar. Susie returned to brewing, and Chris delivered the food. With no other customers to serve, he headed outside for a cigarette.

As he inhaled the smoke from his Camel Blue and scrolled through the news on his prepaid smartphone, he thought about his new life in Palisade. These were good people. He liked feeling useful, feeling needed. Susie and Frank treated him like family, introducing him to their friends and inviting him to weekly game nights at their house. Susie had even tried setting him up with a couple of local women. They were nice enough, but Chris wasn't ready to start dating again. Jessica still had a piece of his heart, and Natalya had destroyed what was left. Besides, a ghost hiding from his past was not an ideal romantic partner.

CHAPTER 16

New York City

"I apologize for the wait, Alena," said Special Agent James Duff.

He was a tall guy in his mid-forties who wore designer suits and had a golden retriever named Riggs, after Martin Riggs from *Lethal Weapon*. A former analyst at Goldman Sachs, he was assigned to the FBI's White-Collar Crime Program and had met Alena several months prior when she was doing research for her article on Nysta.

"It's okay. Thanks for seeing me," Alena said.

She was sitting in a terribly uncomfortable chair in the lobby of the FBI's New York field office, within a towering skyscraper at 26 Federal Plaza.

"You don't have to be so professional." He smiled. "It wasn't always so."

"Yeah, let's not talk about that."

"I can't help it. You never returned my calls. I started to wonder if you were just using me for my position."

"No, I was using you for sex."

"I guess that's better."

"Can we talk?"

"Right, let's uh—let's take a walk. My office is small, and I could use some fresh air."

They exited the lobby and headed toward Thomas Paine Park across the street. Nestled between every major federal building in the city and the financial district, the park would typically have been bustling with activity—vendors selling coffee and hot-dogs, corporate stooges taking their state-imposed fifteen-minute breaks, and local residents walking their dogs—but it was December and Alena and Duff had plenty of privacy as they strolled along the sidewalk.

"I'm sorry to hear about your friend. I hope she pulls through," Duff said.

"She's still in a coma. It doesn't look good."

"Never give up hope."

"Thanks." Alena wasn't looking for a TED talk; she was on a mission. "Did you get a chance to read what I sent you?"

"I did. It was, uh, very interesting."

"What does that mean?"

"It means you're a good writer. Have you ever thought about writing a novel?"

"Focus, James."

"Sorry. From what I can tell, Amy was attacked by an unhoused man. Police arrested him a few hours later, and he confessed to the whole thing."

"You mean a homeless person?"

Duff frowned. "They're called 'unhoused,' Alena."

"I always forget you're from California."

"But I'm a New Yorker now. You wanna get dinner later?"

Alena stopped walking and faced him. "Really?"

"Sorry."

"So no connection at all between Amy getting stabbed and her whistleblowing about the Nysta update?"

"It's a stretch, at best. Tech companies don't hire hitmen. That's only in the movies. Plus, you don't even know what was in the update. For all you know, your friend was mistaken—saw something that wasn't there. She wouldn't even tell you what it was."

"What I do know is that my friend was brutally attacked with a knife and is now in a coma—hours, mind you, after confiding in me that something was wrong at Nysta. You didn't hear the desperation in her voice. She was scared for her life."

"I get that, I really do. But like I said, you don't know what she saw."

"I would have had she not been attacked. It's a cover up, plain and simple."

"Is this about your story?"

"You're an asshole."

He took a deep breath. "Alena, you need more proof. I know your editor won't publish without it. And if you want my help opening a case, I need proof as well."

"That's why I'm flying to San Francisco tomorrow. Amy said she saved everything. That means it's on a flash drive somewhere. And I'm going to find it."

Duff was at a loss for words. She was ferocious—never gave up. She was amazing.

"You wanna grab coffee?" he asked.

Her eyes flared. *Seriously?*

"As friends," he conceded.

"Fine, as friends. I'll call you when I get back from California."

With that, she was gone. He watched her cross the street, raising her arm in the air as a sort of dismissive waive. It was disappointing, but he would help her because it might allow him the chance to see her again. Their few nights together had been amazing, even made him delete his Hinge profile—only to immediately reactivate it after she ghosted him. He watched her turn the corner and disappear from view.

Unbeknownst to him, someone else was watching her as well.

It was a young man in a navy blue suit sitting on a bench drinking a cup of coffee while pretending to scroll on his phone. He had been there for the entire conversation between Alena and the special agent. He heard everything. As he watched Duff cross the street and climb the steps to the FBI building, he stopped scrolling on his phone and made a call.

CHAPTER 17

Denver, Colorado

ALENA'S FLIGHT FROM LaGuardia to San Francisco experienced turbulence as they crossed into Colorado, and the captain was forced to land the plane at Denver International Airport, where all flights were stranded until further notice. Alena found herself huddled in the terminal along with hundreds of people watching the monitors and waiting for a new flight out. Screaming babies and "Jingle Bell Rock" on loop gave her a headache, so she escaped to a bar for a drink. Usually it would be beer, but today she was stressed and needed something stronger. She ordered an Old Fashioned with Woodford Reserve and stared out the giant windows at the snow-capped mountains and the howling wind trying its best to break through the glass—an angry winter wonderland.

As she sipped her drink, she checked the weather report on her phone. A winter storm was moving through the area with an average snowfall of thirty-five inches and a daytime high of ten degrees—negative two at night. Ski resorts in Aspen and Vail were shut down and, despite recommendations to stay off the road, Interstate 70 appeared to be at a standstill. The storm wasn't letting up any time soon. She might have to spend the night at the airport. Amy was in a coma at UCSF Medical Center in San Francisco. Time was not on her side. Alena downed the bourbon and motioned for the bartender.

"Check please."

Everyone else had the same idea, and the car rental agencies were as packed as the terminal. Alena anticipated this and spent her commute on the shuttle to the rental car garage checking the rental agencies' online reservations. The only thing available was a red Chevrolet Spark. Not the best vehicle for a snowstorm, but it would have to do. After an hour in line, she paid the fee and collected her keys.

• • •

Caleb Webb watched the attendant hand Alena a set of keys. He watched as she flung her luggage into the backseat of the red Chevrolet Spark. As she headed for the exit, Caleb fired up his Sting-Gray Jeep Wrangler Rubicon 4x4 and followed. He had been tailing her ever since she left LaGuardia, and his orders were simple. Make sure she never reached San Francisco.

CHAPTER 18

The thirteen-hundred-mile journey from Denver to the Bay Area required Alena to take I-70 west toward Grand Junction, then Interstate 80 through Utah and Nevada, where she would finally reach her destination after eighteen-plus hours of driving. It would probably take longer because of the storm. But as soon as she entered the Rocky Mountains, she realized she had made a mistake. The stretch of interstate traversing the Rockies was known as the "Vail Pass" and was one of the most dangerous roads to navigate during a winter storm. Extreme weather conditions created a bottleneck of traffic as thousands of vehicles inched their way through the snow and ice. Darkness took over, the temperature dropping below zero, and Alena found herself in an endless sea of red taillights snaking their way into the fog of night.

"What the hell was I thinking?" she asked herself in a low voice.

Her phone had service—that was a relief. It was Colorado, after all, and she anticipated competent clearing of the roads to get things moving. She had a full tank, but no reserves, so she shut off the engine periodically to conserve gas. When her tank hit the halfway mark—after two hours of standstill—she began to panic.

The closest gas station was forty miles away in some small town called Palisade. At this rate, it was doubtful she would make it.

The Google Maps app gave an alternate route. If she could inch forward just a few yards, she could take the next exit and work her way around the stoppage. She decided to take her chances and moved the car onto the shoulder, passing the vehicles in front of her. The semi-trucks had pressed the snow into little mountains of ice, and her compact car got stuck more than once. But she made it. The exit was just ahead. Hopefully, this road would be drivable. It wasn't.

As soon as she turned off the interstate, the ice slush transformed into fresh layers of snow. Her wheels started spinning, the car turning in different directions.

Shit—no, no, no!

She hit the gas. More spinning. She reversed the car, then slammed the gear back into drive. The Chevy Spark found solid ground beneath the snow this time and jolted forward.

She let out a sigh of relief.

As she continued slowly down the two-lane highway, she saw headlights to her left from the vehicles still stuck on the interstate. She had outsmarted all of them.

Focus on the road ahead.

She traveled deeper into the mountains, and the interstate disappeared. The winding road became a steep incline covered in snow and ice with a hundred-foot drop to her left. She pumped her brakes and held the steering wheel as tightly as she could. Her tires were only inches from the edge of the cliff. One wrong move and she'd go off the edge.

Focus, focus.

And then it happened.

NEW BEGINNING

She hit a patch of ice, and the Chevy spun to the side. The hood of the car was now facing the edge of the cliff.

"Shit!"

She froze, scared to move.

What do I do now?

The car began sliding forward, inching closer and closer to the edge.

She slammed the brakes, but nothing happened.

She braced herself.

The car went off the side of the road.

Freefalling.

It happened too fast for her to think.

Then—

She landed headfirst in a pile of snow on a hillside—another cliff, really—several yards below the highway.

• • •

Chris was heading up the mountain, having avoided I-70, when he saw Alena's car go off the road. The winding two-lane highways that populated the Vail Pass were unsafe even during the summer months—winter storms made them nearly undrivable—but his truck managed to keep traction, thanks to snow tires and four-wheel drive. It was still dangerous, though, and he kept a slow, steady pace to avoid getting stuck himself. He had finished his shift at the brewery, then spent the past two hours cruising through the storm and listening in on his police scanner for reports of accidents.

"You'll get there before the EMTs or AAA," Frank Boone had said when he gave him the scanner.

Chris put the truck in park, grabbed his gloves, and climbed out. He was wearing a North Face winter coat and a pair of Sorel Caribou boots. Both kept him warm as he stomped through the snow to the spot where the vehicle had slid off the road. The track marks were fresh, and he could see the car below the ridge, planted bumper-first in a pile of snow.

"Hello?" he called out.

There was no response.

Shit.

He steadied himself with his hands as he climbed over the edge and slid down the side of the cliff, using the heel of his boot as a break, digging into the snow as he descended the ridge. He stopped himself with a hanging tree limb, then climbed toward the driver's side of the car.

Alena had heard the faint sound of someone yelling, but she was frozen in panic, unable to move or speak. The engine had stopped running. Nothing was spewing from the top, but she had no idea what to do next. She would never admitted it, but she was scared to death.

Chris's pounding on the window startled her. She jolted and turned. Then screamed.

"It's okay," he said. "I'm here to help you."

Their eyes met. Chris tried to ignore the fact that she was absolutely beautiful. Right now he needed to get her out of the car before it continued its journey down the side of the mountain.

To Alena, he looked like a lumberjack, or some type of outdoor madman, with his massive beard and piercing blue eyes.

She unlocked the door, and Chris pulled it open.

"We gotta get you up to the road," he said.

"It happened so fast."

"It always does."

"Who are you?"

"Just someone trying to help."

She eyed him suspiciously. It was doubtful a rapist would risk his own life to save someone dangling from the side of a mountain. "I need to get my stuff," she said.

"No time for that, ma'am."

Before she could protest, he reached inside and grasped her upper arm. He pulled her from the car and steadied them both against the side of the cliff. She immediately felt the effects of the weather. Her lightweight jacket was not designed for it. The temperature was well below zero, and Chris could see she was freezing. He decided to rough it and removed his thick winter coat and draped it over her shoulders.

She smiled. "Thank you."

He said nothing and started back up the cliff, reaching for her hand. Instead of taking it, she brushed past him to the back door of the car.

"What are you doing?"

"I have to get my stuff."

"You're kidding."

She ignored him and continued pulling at the frozen handle. The door was half buried in snow, making it nearly impossible for her to open it. Chris sighed. He would have to help her. He did so—only needing one arm—and together they got it open. Out came a roller carry-on and a large purse that could easily double as a handbag. Chris was going to have to carry all of it. He almost regretted helping her.

Up the ridge they went. Chris holding a suitcase, a giant purse, and the hands of a woman who had just driven off the side of a cliff. The snow began falling harder, but they managed to make it to the road without incident.

"What about my car?" Alena asked.

"You'll have to leave it there until the storm passes," Chris replied. He pointed to the F-150 parked a few yards away. "I'll take you to the nearest hotel."

She nodded and followed him to the truck, all the while wondering who the hell he was, why he was out in the storm, and why he had helped her. She was nervous but thankful someone had come along, even though he might still turn out to be a serial killer and she would never be seen or heard from again.

Chris tossed the luggage into the extended cab seat and slammed the door shut. A pair of headlights lit up the night. Another vehicle was traveling toward them. Chris realized they were blocking the road and waved at the driver to stop. All he needed now was for some idiot to come sliding down the pass and wreck his truck. Thankfully the other vehicle slowed down and came to a stop a couple of yards in front of them. It was a Sting-Gray Jeep Rubicon. The engine remained on, and the driver did not get out.

Alena had a thing for details—it was what made her a great journalist—and she knew she had seen that Jeep before. At the rental car garage back in Denver.

What a small world.

Chris called out, "Hey, buddy, I'm moving this thing. Just give me a second." He turned to Alena. "Let's get going."

She nodded and climbed into the truck. Chris opened the driver's side door—

Muzzle flashes lit up the night sky as two 5.56x45mm sourced rounds exploded from the direction of the Jeep, decimating the F-150's side mirror and missing Chris's head by an inch.

A man exited the Jeep with an M4 carbine aimed directly at them.

He opened fire.

CHAPTER 19

Muscle memory kicked in, and Chris dove inside the truck.

"Get down!" he screamed at Alena.

She ducked below the dash panel as a hail of bullets ripped through the truck. The sound was deafening. She had never heard a gun fired in real life, let alone in her direction.

Chris went for the glove box and removed his Beretta M9. No time to check the chamber; he knew it was loaded. He extended the pistol out the window and let off four shots. The other gunman paused for a second, not expecting return fire. Seizing the opportunity, Chris leaned out of the truck and fired eight more rounds at the assailant. It had been six months since he had shot a gun; combine that with heavy snow and darkness, it wasn't surprising that he missed. With only three bullets left in the magazine, he ducked back inside the cab and waited.

Caleb kept his rifle aimed forward and slowly walked toward the truck.

Who the hell is this guy, he thought.

He had only been assigned one target. The woman. Her armed companion complicated things. But the guy only had three more shots left; had he possessed a spare magazine, he would have continued to shoot. Taking him out was going to be easy.

Chris's old reflexes were kicking into fourth gear. He knew the gunman was a pro. And he knew he had counted his shots. All was quiet. Chris could hear the crunching of the man's boots against the snow. When he was certain the assailant was no more than two yards from the front of the truck, he made his move. Diving out of the cab, Chris emptied what was left of his magazine midair and hit the snow with his left shoulder. He didn't miss this time. Both shots landed in Caleb's chest, dropping him to the ground as blood peppered the air.

Alena heard the crack of Chris's pistol and the thud of Caleb's body against snow.

Chris jumped to his feet and approached the man riling in his own blood on the ground. He kicked the M4 away and leaned down. Caleb was still breathing, but it was labored. He choked as blood spilled out of his mouth. One of the bullets had punctured a lung, which meant he had only minutes left to live.

"Who the fuck are you?" Chris demanded.

Caleb looked up at him. Those eyes. He'd seen them before. He choked as recognition sunk in. "Harding?" he gasped. "You were supposed to be dead."

Not what Chris expected to hear. He grabbed him by the shirt. "Who are you?"

The death rattle in Caleb's lungs had begun. He struggled to breathe; it was even harder for him to speak. "How did you survive the explosion?"

Chris's eyes narrowed. "How do you know about that?"

The assassin opened his mouth to respond but coughed up blood instead. His breathing slowed, then his eyes glazed over, still open. His soul had left him.

Chris nearly fell over as he stepped back.

Was this the man responsible for murdering his entire team?

Alena climbed out of the truck and slowly walked toward Chris and Caleb's lifeless body. She had seen death in pictures and videos but had never witnessed it firsthand.

"Is he?" she asked.

"Yes," Chris replied matter-of-factly.

He opened the dead man's jacket and removed a wallet. Inside was a Virginia driver's license for a man named Caleb Webb with a Washington, D.C. address. Chris stuffed the ID in his pocket and continued searching the corpse for more clues. What he found next was concerning. A small body cam attached to Caleb's flannel shirt. Chris shut it off and stood up.

"Shit," he said, staring down at the body.

"What is it?" Alena asked.

He ignored her question and instead crossed toward her, stopping inches from her face.

"Who the hell are you?"

She stepped back. "Check your space, dude. I could say the same about you. You just killed that guy."

"Yeah."

"And you're okay with it."

"Better him than us."

She couldn't respond. He had a valid point, but that still didn't give him the right to murder a man in cold blood. Self-defense meant wounding then calling the police for help.

"Why was he trying to kill you?" Chris asked, his tone less abrasive.

"I have no idea."

He stared at her blankly, deciding whether to believe her or not.

"Are you a cop or something?" she asked.

"No."

"Then what are you doing out here in the storm?"

"Helping idiots like you."

She fumed. "I'm not an idiot, mister. I'm a reporter. For the *New York Times*? Perhaps you've heard of it?"

"I've heard of it. Don't read it though."

"Figures. Trigger-happy people like you are the reason why we have mass shootings."

She was still wearing his coat, but that didn't stop her from crossing her arms and glaring at him.

"You talk too much. Look—I live nearby, and a few of us come out during storms to help people. I saw you go off the side of the road."

Her tone softened. "Thank you for that."

"Yeah."

Now she felt bad. "What's your name?"

"Dale."

"What are you, some kind of bro? No last name, just Dale?"

He frowned. "Dale Finer."

"Well, thank you for saving me and murdering a stranger, Dale Finer."

"And you?"

"What about me?"

"Do you have a name?"

"It's Alena Moore."

He nodded but didn't say anything.

"Now that we know each other," she said, "what happens next?"

"I take you to a hotel. And then I go home."

"What about this," her eyes darted to the corpse, "dead guy?"

"What about him?"

"We have to call the cops."

"Can't do that."

"Why not? You murdered—"

"He's a professional. And whatever you did, you do not want the police involved."

"A professional, 'what?' And I didn't do anything."

"Cut the crap, lady. You did something. Otherwise, you wouldn't have a paid assassin on your tail armed with an M4 assault rifle and," he removed the body cam from Caleb's shirt and showed it to her, "a body cam recording everything."

"Wait, hold on. Assassin? Like a hitman? I don't know—how do you know that? And what do you mean, 'body cam?' Like is he a cop?"

"He's not a cop. It doesn't matter; what matters is that you need to stop doing whatever it is you're doing and get as far away from that man as possible." He realized how dramatic he sounded and followed up with, "You'll be fine."

But she wouldn't. Paid assassins went where the money was. They had no affiliation with their targets, and whoever hired Caleb Webb wouldn't stop until she was dead. Things were now complicated for Chris as well. Not only did Caleb recognize him, but he knew about the explosion in Islamorada. Was he responsible? If not, was his employer? The body cam had recorded the entire confrontation between Chris and Caleb, which meant whoever hired Caleb now knew Chris was alive and well in Colorado. If there was a connection, his cover was blown.

"Will they send someone else?" Alena asked.

"It's possible." It was a certainty.

"What do I do?"

Chris had spent the last six months living a peaceful life, detached from the violence of his past, and had come to terms with being a civilian. But in an instant, he had been sucked right back into the life he left behind. He felt like Michael Corleone in *The Godfather: Part III*. If his cover was indeed blown, he needed to become a ghost again—and fast, before the innocent people of Palisade fell victim to his past.

He went to the Jeep. There was a thermos of coffee in the cupholder and a burner phone in the console. Chris flipped open the burner and scrolled through the most recent texts and calls. They were all to a single number with a Virginia area code. He put it down and checked the glove compartment. There was a Hertz car registration card, a rental receipt, and—exactly what he was looking for: Caleb's personal cell phone. It was turned off, of course, and would need a password for access, but it was something. He pocketed the two phones and returned to Alena, who was staring at Caleb's dead body.

"Don't look at him," Chris said.

He took a photo of the corpse with his own phone, then headed toward the truck.

"Let's get going," he said.

Alena snapped out of her trance and followed him.

Chris tried to ignore the bullet holes and busted side mirror. The engine and tires were both intact. That's what mattered. He pressed the start button, turned the heater on full blast, and drove away from the scene.

• • •

The F-150 plowed through the incoming snow, the windshield

wipers on high-speed mode and the four-wheel drive working overtime to combat the accumulated snow on the road. Once Chris had thawed his frozen body, he decided it was time to question the reporter sitting quietly in the passenger seat and staring out the window into the cold darkness.

"I need to know what you're involved in," he said. "No bullshit. You're a reporter—is this about a story you're working on?"

Alena hesitated, unsure if she could trust this bearded mountain man with questionable moral character. But right now she had no choice. "I'm on my way to California to see a friend in the hospital. She's my source."

"Source for what?"

"A story I'm doing on Nysta."

"What's that?"

"You're kidding. The social media app?"

"Never heard of it."

She almost laughed. "Why am I not surprised?"

"Is it like Facebook?"

"Something like that."

"I don't do social media."

This guy really was a mountain man. "They've been under close scrutiny for how they handle user data," Alena explained.

"Don't all those things take your data?"

"They do. But Nysta is the only one owned by the Chinese. It's a communist-controlled social media platform with billions of users worldwide, and that's concerning because cyber warfare is the future."

"I've heard that. What does this have to do with you?"

"Six months ago, Congress required them to hand over data management to an American company, Auspex Technology."

"I've heard of them—largest cybersecurity firm in the country. They have extensive contracts with the federal government, including the CIA."

Never heard of Nysta but knows about CIA contracts, thought Alena. *Who is this guy?*

"Correct. But I believe Nysta still has something up their sleeve. While most in Congress favored Nysta's continued operation—contingent upon Auspex hosting user data on their servers, of course—there were still some opposed to it entirely. The day before the House voted on whether or not to allow Nysta to continue operations, a congressman from Kentucky was killed in a car accident—while on his way to vote *against* Auspex handling data management."

"That was all over the news."

Alena nodded. "But I believe he was silenced."

"Why?"

"That's what I'm trying to figure out."

"Seems like a stretch to me."

"Well, yesterday, an engineer at Nysta—who happens to be my oldest friend—contacted me out of the blue. She discovered inconsistencies in the code for the app's latest update, which is scheduled to drop next week. What she saw scared her to death. Wouldn't even tell me what it was over the phone. She planned to fly to New York to see me in person. She never made it."

The pain was evident in Alena's eyes.

"What happened?" Chris responded softly.

"She was attacked—stabbed—outside her apartment a couple of hours after we spoke."

"And you think Nysta is responsible?"

"I know they are."

"Did you call the police?"

"FBI—I have a contact in their New York office."

"What did they say?"

"That I was crazy, but if I found proof they would look into it."

"Is there proof?"

"My friend saved everything to a flash drive."

There it was. Chris sped up and made a hard right turn onto a two-lane highway parallel with the interstate—a sea of red and white lights cutting through the snow and fog.

"Who did you speak to at the FBI?"

"Just a friend," Alena said. "He's more of an acquaintance, really—helped me with a story in the past." She left out the part where she ghosted him after two dates.

"Anyone else?"

"No."

Chris did not believe in coincidences. The man lying dead in the snow on a mountain pass was hired to kill Alena after she spoke to someone at the FBI regarding "confidential information" saved on a flash drive. Based on Caleb's home address, Chris surmised he was a federal contractor—that meant CIA, FBI. Like every major country in the world, and despite being illegal, the United States carried out targeted assassinations. The same politicians who approved murder-for-hire were the same ones toting more gun control. It was hypocrisy at its finest. The assassin's connection to Woodhaven was still unknown, but Chris was certain that whoever hired Caleb was now coming after both Alena *and* him.

He looked at the beautiful journalist beside him—her big brown eyes waiting for a response, hoping it would make her feel better, would take away the fear that permeated her mind. Chris wasn't one for bullshit; what you see is what you get. He had to tell her the truth.

"The way I see it, you have two choices," he said. "One, you go into hiding. Which of course won't work because they will find you, and they will kill you."

Alene's eyes widened. "You're joking."

"No."

"What's the other option?"

"You finish what you started. Find your friend, get the flash drive, finish your article, and expose the truth—which is exactly what these people don't want. So you're still dead."

"You're a real positive person, aren't you?"

He shrugged.

"Just drop me at the nearest hotel, please."

"You got it."

But there were no hotels. Because of the storm, every Holiday Inn, Hampton Inn, and dingy Motel 6 between them and Palisade was booked solid. Chris stopped the truck at a Love's gas station near a strip of fast food restaurants.

"I've got a couch you can crash on," he said. "But you're gone in the morning."

"I don't know you."

"Fine, I'll drop you at the Holiday Inn. You can sleep in the lobby."

She considered her situation. It was late, it was cold, and someone had just tried to kill her. She had no idea what to do next, and the only person who could help her was a bearded madman who just might murder her in her sleep. She was all out of options.

CHAPTER 20

Chris parked the truck in the alley behind his apartment and led the way up the stairs to the 400-square-foot studio he called home—which suddenly felt smaller than usual, claustrophobic even. Alena was not impressed. The sandalwood carpet was ancient, so was the furniture, and the vintage appliances were from the late 1970s. At least there was a fresh coat of paint on the walls. And the entire place was tidy and clean.

He's poor, but he's not a slob.

"I could use a beer," she said.

"I don't drink anymore."

Of course he didn't. "Water is fine."

Chris removed two glasses from a cabinet above the sink and filled them with spring water from a bottle on the counter.

"There's a pizza in the freezer if you're hungry," he said, handing her a glass.

"I'm okay."

Alena sat on a gray couch beside the front door and sipped her water. Surveying the apartment, she saw a kitchen table with two chairs, a twin bed, and a small television across from where she was sitting. A collection of DVDs were neatly stacked beneath the TV.

John Wayne, Humphrey Bogart, Sylvester Stallone, Clint Eastwood—old-school action films starring old-school action stars.

"It's cozy," she said.

"It's a shithole. But it works for now. I'm going to put on some tea. Want some?"

"Sure."

She waited as he boiled the water, filled two mugs, and dropped in pouches of green tea. He carried the steaming beverages to the "living area" and placed them on a battered coffee table, then took a seat beside her and lit a cigarette.

"Those things are bad for you," she said.

"Trying to quit." He released the smoke from his lungs and leaned back.

They sat quietly for a moment, neither sure what to say next.

Alena broke the silence. "Did you know that guy?"

"No."

"He seemed to know you."

Chris shrugged.

"He's not the first person you've killed, is he?"

"No," Chris replied. "Crash here tonight, but you need to be—"

"Gone in the morning, got it. Do you have a bathroom I can use?"

"Yeah, it's right back there," he said, pointing to an open door behind the TV.

"Thank you."

She disappeared through the door, closing it behind her. Chris extinguished his cigarette in an ashtray on the coffee table and lit another. Smoke engulfed his face as he contemplated the situation he had found himself in. Running was an option, but it would be more difficult now that someone at the FBI knew he was alive.

There was no telling who had betrayed him and his team. Or what their motivations were. Even if he could disappear again, Jessica and Claire would be in danger. Sacrificing his own life was always a last resort, but perhaps it was time to track down those responsible for murdering his team in their sleep. The question was, could he trust Alena? She was in danger, that was a certainty—wouldn't last the week on her own—and he was the only person who could help her.

"Look, I know you don't want me here." Alena had returned from the bathroom and was standing beside the TV. "And I don't blame you," she said. "I'm going to go."

"Sit down," he replied.

"I'm good."

"I'm going to help you."

"How? According to you, I'm screwed no matter what I do."

"I'll make sure you get to California—unharmed. All I ask in return is to speak to your friend."

"She's in a coma."

"Then let me see what's on the flash drive."

Alena sat down slowly, considering the offer.

"I don't need your help," she said.

"Without me, you'll be dead within twenty-four hours." Off her startled and angered reaction, he added, "I know how the people that are after you think."

"How?"

"Because I used to be one of them."

That caught her off guard. She regretted taking a seat. "You killed people for a living?"

"No, not exactly. Well, sometimes. But only when I had to."

"How do I know you won't try and kill me?"

"You don't."

"That makes me feel much better."

Of course she didn't trust him. *He* wouldn't trust him.

"My real name is Chris Harding. I believe there's a connection between my past occupation and the man who tried to kill you."

She had known "Dale" wasn't his real name. He had too much facial hair and bottled-up anger for a name like that. "What did you do?"

"Pissed off some dangerous people."

"The same ones who are after me?"

"I don't know. That's why I need to see what's on your friend's flash drive."

Alena nodded. She couldn't decide whether he was helping her or using her—or both. But he had already saved her life, twice. And she believed him when he said her life was in danger. Perhaps trusting him was her only option.

"It's a deal," she said. "But screw me over," she aimed her finger at him, "and I kill you."

"Noted."

"When do we start?"

Chris took a final drag of his cigarette and crushed it in the ashtray. "First, I need a beer."

CHAPTER 21

Washington, D.C.

Dan Greenwood had built his business on the promise that contracts would be carried out efficiently and without error. This was accomplished by hiring the best talent in the world. Caleb Webb was just that—a competent assassin who always delivered. So when he failed to check in and evaded multiple attempts at communication, Greenwood became concerned. Having left the office for the day, he was enjoying an evening at home watching the Patriots play the Rams while sipping Woodford Reserve on the rocks. He kept the game on the TV and went to his home office in the front of the house—an area typically designated as the living room.

He turned on his desktop computer, logged in to the TOR Network, and accessed the security portal. Every operation was monitored by a compact body cam outfitted with a GPS tracking device. In the case of comms failure, the operative's last known location could be accessed along with POV video footage of the event. Greenwood clicked on Caleb's profile and scrolled through the grainy footage that appeared on the screen, fast-forwarding past the Denver International Airport, Alena at baggage claim,

Alena leaving the rental car garage, hours of traffic on I-70. He stopped and hit play when Caleb exited the Jeep with his rifle.

Greenwood watched as Caleb fired two shots at what appeared to be a full-sized truck. But instead of walking toward the truck and finishing the job, the assassin ducked back inside the Jeep as another shooter fired shots in his direction.

What the fuck? Who the hell is shooting?

The footage swung into the air and landed on the dark sky above, the image losing much of its focus as snow landed on the lens.

Shit.

Caleb was hit.

A man with a beard entered the frame and stared down into the camera. Those eyes—fierce and angry. Greenwood recognized the man but could not place him.

"*Who the fuck are you?*" the bearded man demanded.

"*Harding? You were supposed to be dead.*"

Greenwood froze. It was impossible.

"*Who are you?*"

"*How did you survive the explosion?*"

"*How do you know about that?*"

"*Is he?*" a woman asked.

"*Yes.*"

Muffled sounds, then a hand covered the lens and the feed went dead.

Greenwood leaned back in the chair, his mind racing. Six months ago, he had been paid handsomely for the contract—carried out by Caleb—that sent Chris Harding and his associates to the afterlife. Was he the only one alive? Was he still operational? What the hell was he doing in Colorado with Alena Moore? Was there a connection? Were they working together? So many questions, and he knew the FBI director would ask all of them.

But one did not get to Greenwood's position without having contingencies in place. There were now two contracts that required execution, and after that, he needed confirmation that the rest of Woodhaven was permanently in the grave. He removed the encrypted cell phone from his desk and called the only man he could trust to get the job done.

Chris Harding and Alena Moore would both soon be dead.

CHAPTER 22

Nysta Headquarters
Palo Alto, California

Nysta CEO Andrew Chew was living the American dream. But he had a problem. One of his senior programmers had expressed concern over their latest update: Nysta 2.3. Her supervisor had contacted HR, who in turn called Chew's office. The social media startup had an open-door policy and prided itself in having the best Human Resources team in Silicon Valley. However, this was no ordinary complaint, and Amy Dotson's allegations would have dire consequences if leaked. She was a liability that needed to be contained. But Chew was also concerned about how she learned what she did in the first place—the update's code was supposed to have been hidden, unnoticeable to anyone other than the one who built it. How much did Ms. Dotson know?

Chew was born in China and came to the United States for college, where he earned a bachelor's degree in computer science from Stanford University. He had intended to return home and work for his father, but upon graduation was offered a job simply too good to pass up. It was during his tenure as a user experience programmer at Apple that he got the idea for what would one day become Nysta. After developing the algorithm in his apartment—in the evenings and on weekends—he quit his job and began the search for venture capital funding. He was confident his idea would sell. It did not. Unable to stomach the realities of entrepreneurship, he turned to his father, whose connections put him in contact with one of the largest companies in China: SMIC. They backed Nysta—in exchange for sixty percent equity—and within two years, Chew was one of the wealthiest men in the world. He became an American citizen and leading innovator beside the two men who inspired him the most: Steve Jobs and Elon Musk. But beneath all the accolades, Chew never forgot those responsible for his success. They would never allow him to.

His office was surrounded by glass, overlooking a sea of communal desks and colorful booths where staff could grab coffee and healthy snacks while plugged into their laptops. The campus was expansive and most senior executives were in a different building, but Chew preferred to be where the action was. He began his career as a programmer, and a room filled with humming computers and tennis shoe-clad tech-nerds made him feel right at home. Outside communication came through his twenty-two-year-old executive assistant. He refused to speak on the phone—preferred text messaging—and left running the company to his Chief Operating Officer, Barry Allen. He never exercised, found sex to be a waste of time, and only ate to sustain himself—preferring smoothies and supplements.

Chew wanted to meet with Amy Dotson as soon as she returned to work. Only she never did. When he learned that she was in a coma after being assaulted outside her apartment, he was relieved. Concerned, but relieved. However, he wanted confirmation that the matter was fully contained. He ordered Barry Allen into his office. His second-in-command arrived a few minutes later wearing a dark blue suit and a purple tie. In contrast to Chew's trim figure and casual uniform of jeans and polo shirts, Allen—well into his fifties—was overweight, bald, and had spent his entire career politicking his way to the top echelons of corporate America.

"Who else knows about this?" Chew asked.

"Other than you and me, just Amy's supervisor and Pankti from HR," Allen replied. "But they're only privy to the broad strokes. Evidently, Amy told them very little."

"Enough to cause alarm. We should send flowers."

"I don't think that's a good idea."

"She's in the hospital, Barry."

"And that's none of our concern. The update drops in a matter of days, and you know as well as I do what will happen to both of us if anything goes wrong."

Chew was about to respond, but Allen cut him off. "And I mean, *anything*."

"I know, I know," Chew said. "It's just—we had something to do with this, didn't we?"

"I took care of it."

Chew knew he did. "I hate this." He stared out the window at the staffers hard at work below. "I built this company from the ground up. And I did it because I wanted to bring the world together in a new way. I wanted to build something—not destroy lives. And it seems like destroying lives is exactly what we're doing."

"I understand how you feel, Andrew. I really do. But sometimes you have to dance with the one who brought you. And this is what they want."

"Ugh, this is so triggering."

CHAPTER 23

Susie Brews
Palisade, Colorado

CHRIS UNLOCKED THE door and turned off the alarm. Alena followed him inside as he flipped on the lights and headed for the bar.

"What'll you have?" he asked, taking down two bar stools and motioning for her to sit.

"I could go for an IPA."

At least she has good taste in beer.

He removed two frosted pint glasses from a fridge behind the bar and poured them both a Land of Cowboys IPA. A popular ale among the locals, it was one of the few taps available year-round. The West Coast-style IPA was a full-bodied brew named after the western landscape that surrounded Palisade—specifically the Arches National Park, a hundred and twenty miles west in Moab, Utah. Chris placed the beers on the bar and sat down beside Alena. She noticed him staring intently at the golden glass of goodness.

"How long has it been?" she asked.

He took a sip. The hops hit his tongue, and the bitterness filled his mouth. It went down smooth, and he smiled, admiring the glass. "Too long."

"You're weird." She tried her beer. "It's not bad. Seven percent?"

"Six-point-eight. You need at least six, otherwise you end up with no flavor. More than seven, and the taste of alcohol is overpowering—in my opinion."

"Didn't know you were a connoisseur."

He shrugged. "I just like beer."

They drank for a moment in silence, both contemplating their new realities. Even though he had sworn off drinking, the beer helped curb Chris's old anxiety that was threatening to rear its ugly head. Alena's entire world had been thrown upside down, and she found herself unprepared to process the day's events—or the bearded stranger beside her.

"We leave in the morning," Chris said, breaking the silence.

"It's already morning."

"When the sun comes up," he clarified.

"What about my car?"

"Leave it. We'll take the truck."

"I didn't get the rental car insurance coverage."

"Least of your worries right now."

She nodded. For once she agreed with him.

"It's a fifteen-hour drive to San Francisco," she said, changing the subject.

"We should take the southern route. Don't want to get stuck in another snowstorm." He pulled up Google Maps on his phone. "I'm thinking we go through Vegas."

"Why not Interstate Fifty through Reno?"

"Because Reno got a fresh layer of snow a couple days ago, and there's more coming. We need to stay south."

"You know best." Her voice reeked of sarcasm.

"Sure do."

Chris's glass was empty, so he leaned over the bar and refilled it with a Double IPA from the tap called Mount Garfield, named after the cretaceous-sandstone-capped mountain overlooking the town of Palisade.

"Should you have another one?" Alena said.

He glared at her. *Really?*

"You're right, not my place. Actually, you know what? I'll have another one too."

He poured her a glass of the Mount Garfield.

"Oh, that's strong," she said, tasting the double-hopped brew.

Chris was about to educate her on the differences between regular and double IPAs when the front door swung open. Frank Boone appeared in the doorway, his imposing figure filling the entire frame. He was in his late fifties, covered in tattoos—arms the size of tree trunks—and his wrinkled face still evinced traces of the chisel-jawed man of his youth. He had always reminded Chris of Mel Gibson.

"Shit, what time is it?" Frank asked as he flipped over another stool and took a seat beside Chris.

"Late—want a beer?"

"Dumb question, Chris." He smiled at Alena. "Who's your friend?"

"Alena Moore, *New York Times*," she said, extending her hand.

Chris went behind the bar to get Frank's drink—a "Hitler's Hell" German-style Doppelbock—and filled a tulip glass with the dark brown lager.

Frank smiled. "Big city gal—nice to meet you. I'm Frank Boone, Susie Brews." He looked at Chris. "So this is what you do when the bar is closed."

"It's not like that," Chris replied, handing him the beer.

"I don't care, but Susie will. She's gonna be pissed. But don't worry, I'm not gonna tell her." He took a healthy quaff of Hitler's Hell, then looked at Alena. "Susie is my wife. She's the boss." Back to Chris. "I'm just glad to see you drinking again." Another swig of beer, then back at Alena. "This son of a bitch wouldn't touch a drop, and I always say, *never trust a man—*"

"Who doesn't drink," said Alena.

Frank laughed. "Damn straight." His tone darkened. "So, Chris—can we trust you?"

"Now *that's* a dumb question, Frank."

"Is it?" He locked eyes with the former soldier. "Ed called me about a half hour ago. He's working out on I-70 tonight."

Ed Farber was the local sheriff and one of Frank's best friends. Chris knew where Frank was going with this but waited for him to finish, slowly sipping his Double IPA.

"Hell of a night," Frank continued. "Ed found two abandoned vehicles on a two-lane highway just off the interstate. Well, one was parked. The other looked like it took a nosedive over the cliff."

Alena shot Chris a glance. *What the hell?* He ignored her.

"It was pretty bad out there," Chris said.

"Yeah, but the thing is, he found something else." Frank waited for Chris to respond. When he didn't, Frank said, "It was concerning, at least for Palisade."

"What did he find?" Chris said, holding Frank's gaze.

"I was hoping you could tell me."

"What are you trying to say, Frank?"

The older man laughed. "I'm kidding. How the heck would you know?"

"We wouldn't," Alena said.

"Of course not."

There was an awkward silence, then Chris said, "Cut the crap, Frank. What did Ed find?"

Frank took another sip of beer. "A dead guy. Shot in the chest. Most likely from a handgun. But he had an M4 beside him—quite a few shell casings too."

Frank was an expert on guns. In fact, he was a fanatic. Chris was careful with his response. The less his friend knew, the better. After everything they had done for him, the last thing Chris wanted to do was put the Boones in danger. "They have any idea what happened?"

"We'll know more when Ed gets here. But you were out there tonight. See anything?"

"No."

"I saw your truck in the parking lot. I know bullet holes when I see them."

Alena shot Chris a glance. *He knows.*

So much for keeping the incident under wraps for the night. It had already become a crime scene, and whoever was after them would know their location sooner than later.

CHAPTER 24

*Dulles International Airport
Virginia*

Erick Webb crossed the rain-drenched airfield toward the waiting Gulfstream G650. The temperature was well below freezing, but that wasn't a concern. Less than an hour ago, he had received a call from Dan Greenwood informing him that his identical twin brother, Caleb Webb, was dead—murdered by a rouge spy and former Army Special Forces operative. Erick was two minutes older than Caleb. That made him the eldest, the protector. A role he'd dutifully carried out since they were children. Their relationship went beyond blood, though. They were brothers in arms, Marines who never came home from war—soldiers who never stopped fighting.

They had the same tactical training and military background, but while Caleb had always been the stoic one—keeping his emotions in check—Erick wore his heart on his sleeve. That made him more prone to violent outbursts. He was a brutal, passionate assassin who enjoyed his work, enjoyed inflicting pain. And tonight he was out for blood. This was more than simply fulfilling a contract.

This was revenge.

He boarded the aircraft and took a seat in the cabin. Anticipating a quick trip, he had packed light—a duffel bag filled with weapons and the clothes on his back: black jeans, tactical boots, a flannel shirt, and a black Down jacket. Once the Gulfstream was en route, he opened the Kill Package Greenwood had sent him and inspected the photographs of Chris Harding and Alena Moore. But it was Chris's face he focused on. He zoomed in on the picture, locking eyes with the man who had murdered his brother. This was his next victim. And he would enjoy the killing he was being paid handsomely to perform.

CHAPTER 25

Palisade, Colorado

"I knew your name wasn't Dale," said Frank. "You've got too much facial hair."

While draining Susie Brew's tap dry, Chris and Alena had told him everything. That was, everything Alena knew to be true. But Frank was no idiot.

"Every man has a past," he said. "And that's fine by me. I understand why you didn't tell me."

"I don't want to jam you and Susie up," Chris replied.

"Nah, we're good. I got my demons too. Don't for one minute think you're the first son of a bitch to escape to Palisade." He finished the last of his beer and stood up. "But we gotta get going. Ed will be here soon, and I don't think you two should be here."

"Agreed," Chris said.

"Go back to the apartment. I'll get rid of Ed and be over as soon as I can." He checked his watch. "Sun is up in three hours. You should be out of town by then. What are you packing?"

Chris removed the Beretta from the back of his jeans. "Got two extra mags, but this is it."

"Shit, okay, I got some goodies you can take."

"We'll be fine."

"I'm no fool, Chris. I may not know the whole story, but I know enough to tell you you're going to need a little more firing power than a 9mm handgun has to offer."

• • •

Alena watched Chris pack and wondered if she had made the right decision. But time was of the essence. This was no longer just about her career—Dunlap would not give her another extension—this was about her life. Her only chance at survival was learning what Amy discovered, and that was only possible with the help of a bearded stranger who could drink four IPAs after killing a man in cold blood.

As promised, Frank arrived an hour later with two hardshell weapons cases. One contained a SIG Sauer MPX K submachine gun with a 4.5-inch barrel and an EOTech sight—not something one buys at a California gun show. Alena's eyes nearly came out of their sockets.

"Holy shit, that's an MPX," Chris said, smiling. "I've heard about those."

"Yeah," said Frank. "And here's what makes this one cool." He pointed to the SilencerCo Hybrid 46M suppressor safely secured in foam beside the gun. "With this bad boy, it'll sound like a goddam bee-bee gun."

"Always be silent."

Frank opened the second case. It was a short-barreled rifle, calibered in .300 Blackout, with a custom military-green matte finish. Alena thought it looked entirely too violent to be in the car with them on the way to California but said nothing.

"What the hell is that?" Chris asked.

Though trained to kill, he had never been much of a gun enthusiast, sticking with the weapons he used in the Army. That meant his faithful Beretta M9. Or when a rifle was necessary, and available, an M4 carbine.

"This is the SIG MCX-SPEAR LT 300 BLK," Frank said. "Nine-inch barrel. Built out with a folding stock, an EOTech HWS XPS2 optic, and a SilencerCo suppressor—this baby will blow the fuck out of your target. And it's great for suppressing and close-quarter combat. Always be silent."

The final gift came in a smaller case. A handgun.

"The P226," Frank said. "I know you're a Beretta guy, but you should at least give this one a try. Better recoil on follow-up shots. And it's reliable to a fault."

Chris had shot the SIG P226 many times. However, when he joined the Army in 2002, the Beretta was still the pistol of choice, and he had learned to love the legendary handgun even though its reliability was rated significantly lower than the SIG Sauer's.

"That's what they tell me," he said. "But this little guy's been through hell and back. I'd feel naked without it."

"I understand. I've got an old 1911 that jams up about every time I fire it. But I wouldn't trade that gal for the world. Still, take the P226 just in case. Good to have a backup. And you know, new ain't always bad."

Chris took the weapons and thanked Frank for everything. He had been a good friend, taking him in, giving him a place to stay, a job—no questions asked. Chris always found it odd when complete strangers reached out in kindness, selflessly giving without expectation. He knew Frank had a history too—equally stoic like himself—and he was thankful to have called him a friend.

That last handshake was firm, and Frank looked Chris in the eyes and said, "Good luck, brother. Take care of whatever you need to do, and if your path brings you back, you're always welcome."

He knew he would probably never see Chris Harding again.

CHAPTER 26

Chris and Alena hit the road just as the sun broke over the horizon, revealing a landscape still covered in snow. They filled the truck's twenty-six-gallon tank at a gas station beside the 70 on-ramp and stocked up on water and protein bars. The interstate had cleared up significantly since the night before, and the plan was to push through to Nevada, where they would stop for the night before crossing into California. Alena's cell phone was traceable, so Chris made her destroy it. She objected at first but understood why it had to be done. After backing up her data to the cloud, she reluctantly crushed her brand-new iPhone 15 and deposited it in a trash can at the gas station. Chris gave her a burner phone from his stash to maintain secure comms in case they were separated.

As soon as they merged onto the interstate, Chris lit a cigarette and cracked the window, allowing the smoke to filter outside.

"Do you really have to smoke?" Alena grumbled between fake coughs.

"Sure do."

He turned up the radio and Tim McGraw's "If I Was a Cowboy" blasted through the speakers. Alena leaned her head against the back of her seat. It was going to be a long drive.

A few miles west of Palisade was the larger town of Grand Junction. Roughly forty miles from the Utah border, it was a vista of open space and endless mountains caked in snow. However, as soon as they entered Utah, the mountains were replaced with burnt-orange rocky peaks, and the canopy of snow became nothing more than patches of white beneath a crisp, blue western sky. They were in the land of cowboys, and it reminded Chris of the old western movies he had once watched with Jessica and Claire on Saturday nights.

"What's the plan when we get there?" Alena asked.

"I don't know yet," Chris replied, lighting a fresh cigarette and brushing the thoughts of his family out of his mind.

"So you have no plan at all?"

"I'm not much of a planner—more of a doer."

Great, one of those guys who probably never finished high school and is proud of it.

"Okay, well, I'd like to go see Amy at the hospital."

"Amy?"

Alena frowned. "My friend?"

"Right. But you said she's in a coma."

"Yeah, a coma—she's not dead."

"The flash drive won't be there."

"Obviously. But her mother will be."

"So?"

"She might know where it is."

"Why would she know?"

Alena shrugged. "I don't know. Doesn't matter. She barely talks to me anyway. Hates me, actually."

"I can see why."

"You're an asshole."

"We'll figure it out," Chris said. "Where do you think Amy left the flash drive?"

"I have no idea. That's why we go to the hospital first."

"Not her apartment?"

"I don't have a key."

"Don't worry about that."

"So you're a burglar too? You just break laws as you see fit?"

"Pretty much."

"Well, I doubt it's at her apartment. Whoever did this would've gone through her things, don't you think?"

"That's true. Okay, we'll go to the hospital." Chris sped up and changed lanes, passing a semi-truck before returning to cruising speed in the right lane. "She works at Nysta, right?"

"Programmer."

He nodded but said nothing.

"You think someone at the company is working with the FBI?" Alena asked.

Chris ignored the question. "What do you know about Nysta's senior leadership?"

There was no hesitation in her response. She had spent months researching every aspect the startup's major players.

"Andrew Chew is their CEO. He's brilliant—born in China, educated in the U.S.—but he's your typical tech bro genius."

"What does that mean?"

"It means he's book smart, but he's soft."

"So he's a pussy."

"No, he's a tech bro. And it's not okay to say that."

"Say what?"

This guy is a human resources nightmare, Alena thought.

"Never mind," she said. "He built the app and is happier behind a computer—not really management material. He leaves that to his Chief Operations Officer, Barry Allen. Now that guy is scary. A real corporate bulldog. When Chew went before Congress, he was fighting to save his company. They were going to shut him down altogether."

"So he was motivated by money, something he built," Chris said.

Okay, not a complete neanderthal.

"Exactly. And Chew is very outspoken about his love for this country and his desire to fulfill the American dream."

"Aren't we all?" Chris snuffed out his cigarette and lit another. "What about the Nysta update? You mentioned 'inconsistencies'—what kind?"

"I have no idea."

"But you have a theory."

"I think the update connects Nysta with Auspex."

"How so?"

"It was Nysta who suggested a partnership with Auspex in the first place. What if Auspex is in on it?"

"As in, they're sending information to China?"

"You got it. Auspex has the capability to engage in unchecked cyber warfare by funneling sensitive American information without fear of being caught by the NSA. The deal with Congress was all part of the plan. And the update is the magic bullet."

"That's a bold theory," Chris replied tentatively.

"Well, I don't know if *that's* their plan. But something is happening. I know it in my gut."

Chris nodded. He was a firm believer in following one's gut, a discipline that had saved his life on more than one occasion.

"And," Alena continued, "the congressman from Kentucky

died conveniently the day he was expected to vote against the deal."

"You think he was silenced."

"After last night, I *know* he was."

Chris found her annoying. She talked too much. Was too opinionated. But she was smart, and if her theory was correct, it made sense why her and Amy's lives were in danger. He needed to find out who put the contract on them and if there was a connection with Woodhaven. Based on Alena's hypothesis, it could be anyone at Nysta or Auspex. He was certain the man he killed the night before worked for either the CIA or the FBI. Alena had already spoken to the FBI. So that put them at the top. But how widespread was it? A single person? The entire bureau? And what was their motivation?

There's a connection, just find it.

"Who owns Nysta?" he said.

"SMIC," she replied. "They're the largest semiconductor chip manufacturer in mainland China. Headquartered in Shanghai."

Okay, not a coincidence.

The recognition in his eyes betrayed his thoughts.

"You know it?" Alena asked.

Chris tightened his grip on the steering wheel as he remembered his last Woodhaven debriefing after Geneva.

"*Mikael Gerber's crypto brokerage shows a single transaction—a week ago—between NWO Holdings and a Chinese semiconductor chip manufacturer called SMIC for a shipment of AI chips,*" Adam Conner had said.

That was six months ago. The same time frame as the Nysta congressional hearings. There it was—the connection.

"Yeah, I know it."

CHAPTER 27

Grand Junction, Colorado

Erick Webb's Gulfstream touched down at Grand Junction Regional Airport at seven o'clock in the morning. Stepping out of the aircraft, he was instantly hit with the crisp Colorado air, still well below freezing despite the sun, bouncing light off the snow that lingered on the ground. Erick put on his Oakley sunglasses as he crossed the runway to the black GMC Yukon waiting for him on the airfield.

It was typically a fifteen-minute drive to Palisade, but Erick made it in less than ten. Greenwood had emailed him the last coordinates for Alena Moore's cell phone. The sleepy town was deserted, and Erick found parking on the street directly in front of his destination, a downtown apartment above a barbershop. It was doubtful anyone would be home. The former Army Special Forces operative who lived there would know better than to stick around. But it was a starting point on Erick's mission to seek revenge on the man who killed his brother.

As a precaution, he chambered his SIG P226, keeping it ready at his side as he walked up the stairs to the apartment. The door was locked, so he holstered his gun as he picked the lock then grasped the weapon with two hands and entered. He moved through the dark apartment with stealth, clearing the entire space—every room, every closet. And it didn't take long. The studio apartment was unimpressively small. Once he was confident no one was home, he re-holstered his SIG and returned to the living room. He was about to flip on a light when he heard a voice coming from the front door.

"Put your fucking hands in the air!"

Erick froze.

"Okay," he said, raising his hands over his head.

"Now turn around, slowly."

Erick did as he was told and found himself face-to-face with a large, angry man in his fifties and the barrel of an AR-15.

"I don't have time for this," Erick said.

"Well, you're gonna make time," Frank replied. "Otherwise I'm gonna blow a fucking hole inside you so big I could take a shit through it."

"Mighty big talk for an old man."

"I know who you are."

Erick's eyes narrowed as he inched forward, attempting to close the gap between them.

Frank tightened his grip on the rifle. "You take another step and—"

It was instant. The SIG came out of Erick's holster, and a 124-grain bullet left the barrel and landed in Frank's chest. Before he could react, another one entered his right shoulder, followed by another just below his neck. Erick finished the execution with a final shot to the chest that knocked Frank back outside the doorway to the porch. He dropped the AR and clutched his throat as blood poured out. He choked. His eyes widened.

Fucking A, this cocksucker just killed me.

His last thought as he collapsed to the ground, dead on impact.

The assassin stepped toward the dead man, avoiding the pool of blood accumulating around him, and yanked his iPhone and wallet from his jeans. He checked the driver's license, memorized the address, then pulled Frank's head back and used his eyes—still open—to unlock the phone. The Safari app revealed a recent search history: information about Nysta and directions to San Francisco. Erick returned the wallet to Frank's back pocket and put the cell phone in his own pocket as he headed down the stairs.

• • •

Changing kegs was Susie's least favorite part of the job. She preferred the creative process of brewing the beer—perfecting the blend of flavors until a batch was ready to reveal to the public. She had spent her twenties working as a bartender in Denver, serving up whiskey and cheap domestic beer to drunk bikers. It wasn't what she had envisioned for her life—a mundane occupation at best—but it was where she met Frank. When they got married, he pushed her to pursue a career she loved. And that was making beer. Something she had been doing for years inside the bathtub of her one-bedroom apartment.

She hadn't seen her husband the night before—he was invariably drinking with his cop buddies—and the snowstorm had essentially stopped business. But today would be busy because she was launching a new IPA. It was supper hoppy, but malty, and it was dark and brooding, just like her husband. She planned to call it "The Frank" and was excited to see what the customers would think of it.

NEW BEGINNING

Susie finished filling the kegs and was behind the bar testing the taps when she heard the front door. Still three hours before they opened for lunch, it startled her, and she realized she had forgotten to lock the door when she arrived. But it didn't matter. She didn't even bother turning around. After all, she knew most of the regulars. It was probably Joe or Ed, still drunk from last night with Frank, stopping by for a morning pick-me-up.

"Not open yet, guys," she said as she pulled a rack of glasses from the dishwasher.

Susie heard footsteps on the concrete floor—then nothing.

She set the rack on the backbar and turned around. The man in front of her was wearing a black Down jacket and a flannel shirt. His eyes were dark, and he was staring at her—motionless. She had never seen him before.

"Did you hear me? We're closed, dude. Come back at eleven."

"Are you Susie Boone?" Erick Webb asked.

"Yeah, why?"

The handgun appeared from a holster hidden beneath his jacket. She saw it as if in slow motion and raised her hands in front of her, a futile attempt to prevent what was coming next.

Erick aimed the pistol at her face.

"No, no!" she screamed.

He pulled the trigger.

CHAPTER 28

Interstate 70 East
Utah-Nevada Border

By the time Chris and Alena reached southwest Utah, the snow had disappeared completely, and an hour into Nevada, the landscape became pure desert with midday temperatures topping at sixty-five degrees. The open space was magnificent. Chris had never driven coast-to-coast before, and he marveled at how the landscape morphed into a world once inhabited by cowboys and Indians—gunslingers and natives trying to survive in the harsh Wild West.

While Chris guzzled coffee, chain-smoked, and admired the scenery, Alena went through her notes. The burner phone didn't have a hotspot, so she was unable to connect her laptop to the internet. She couldn't recall the last time she had gone more than an hour off the grid, and the isolation was driving her nuts. Their first stop at a Love's in Nevada would allow her the chance to finally check her email.

Chris pulled into the gas station and parked in front of the pump nearest the exit.

"I'd hit the bathroom if I were you," he said as he climbed out of the truck.

"Thanks, dad," Alena replied.

She grabbed her computer bag and went inside. Chris paid for the gas with a prepaid debit card—it was easier than carrying cash—and stared out across the open desert while he filled the tank.

Alena was more concerned with checking her email than relieving herself. Finding a Subway inside, she opened her laptop on one of the many tables scattered throughout and connected to the fast food restaurant's complimentary Wi-Fi.

"Finally," she said as the icon on the top right corner of her computer screen indicated the device was online.

Chris returned the nozzle to the fuel dispenser and headed inside to use the restroom and grab another cup of coffee. On his way, he noticed a black SUV pull into the station and park at a pump across from the F-150. Chris continued through the door and removed his sunglasses. He stood behind a newspaper rack and watched the SUV. No one got out, and the engine was still running. He remembered he was unarmed. That his weapons were in the truck.

Find Alena.

His eyes darted around the store—clocking each exit, the clerk behind the desk, an elderly couple buying hats, an old trucker filling a sixty-four-ounce cup of soda. She was nowhere to be seen. Back outside. The SUV was still there. Back to the store.

Where the hell are you?

Finally, he spotted her—inside the Subway, eyes glued to her computer screen. He made a beeline for the table, slamming the laptop shut upon arrival.

"What is wrong with you?" She glared up at him.

"We have to get out of here. And you can't be online."

"I'm just checking my email."

"They can trace your location."

"Fine."

She took her sweet time returning the MacBook to her bag.

"Hurry up," Chris said impatiently.

"Why are you rushing me?"

"Because we need to go."

He was jittery, tapping his foot and glancing around the room.

"What happened? Something happened," she said. Then, seeing the anxiety in his eyes, "Is somebody—"

"I don't know, but we're not taking any chances. Can we please go?"

She nodded, speeding up the process and standing up. Chris led the way back to the front of the Love's store and peered out the glass sliding doors. The black SUV was still parked beside the pump. The driver was still inside.

"Go out the back door and wait there," Chris said. "I'll bring the truck around."

"Okay."

She didn't move.

"Now!"

She nearly jumped. "I'm going."

As Alena made for the back, Chris put on his sunglasses and passed through the sliding doors. Eying the SUV with his peripherals, he crossed the parking lot to the passenger side of his truck. He opened the door and removed the SIG Sauer from the glove box. He would have preferred the Beretta, but Frank's gift was easier to reach. Careful to conceal the weapon, he racked the slide and chambered a round, then stuffed the gun in the back of his jeans and walked around the truck toward the SUV.

The windows were tinted, but he could see the outline of someone in the driver's seat. The engine was still running. As Chris got closer, he put his hand on his hip. Ready. The engine cut off, and someone climbed out of the cab. The former commando stopped and waited. Around the corner of the vehicle came a large man in his thirties, wearing a tattered camo ball cap and a jean jacket. His matching blue jeans were dirty, and his cowboy boots clicked on the concrete as he approached.

"You got a problem, man?" he asked.

An assassin would have already driven off, or engaged.

"No, sorry, dude," Chris replied. "Thought you were someone else."

The man grunted. "Better check yourself, buddy. That's a fighting stance you got there."

Chris was silent. The man waited for a moment, debating whether or not to make a scene. He decided against it and turned and walked toward the store, disappearing inside. Chris let out a sigh of relief and returned to the truck.

He drove around to the back of the building where Alena was waiting for him.

"Is everything okay?" she asked, jumping inside the cab.

"Yeah." He lit a cigarette. "False alarm."

CHAPTER 29

Palisade, Colorado

SHERIFF ED FARBER arrived at Susie Brews shortly before noon. He was one of three police officers in town, having joined the force ten years prior after more than a decade as a hard-knuckled Chicago PD detective. Like others before him, he came to Palisade to escape the stress of city life. The town reminded him of Mayberry, and he looked at himself as a kind of Andy Griffith—drinking with the locals, helping cats out of trees, and keeping the high school kids out of trouble. There was the occasional theft, which was usually perpetrated by someone passing through, but never had he seen a murder—not in Palisade, anyway.

The crime scene was brutal. One of the regulars had happened upon Susie and immediately called 911. Farber went inside first, followed by his two deputies, Harrison and Martinez—both in their twenties and both born and raised in Palisade.

The concrete floor was covered in blood and shattered glass with Susie slumped against the backbar, her head leaning on her left shoulder—eyes still open. The bullet wound was filled with coagulated blood that had oozed out and left a stream from her forehead to her mouth.

"Shit," Farber said, looking way.

The two deputies peered over his shoulder.

"Oh my God," said Martinez.

Harrison was silent as he stared at the corpse in disbelief.

"Okay," Farber said, regaining his composure. "We need to secure the scene. Then we call the Sheriff's Department. They'll have a ballistics team out here, and we can get to work."

The others nodded. Palisade did not have the resources to handle a murder case. Nearby Grand Junction did, but they would refer them to the Colorado Sheriff's Department anyway since it was out of their jurisdiction.

Farber stepped outside. He had to call Frank. He took a moment to formulate what to say to his best friend before pressing the green button on his cell phone. It went straight to voicemail. He was about to leave a message when Harrison came running out of the bar.

"Sheriff, we got another one!"

...

Frank's murder was even more grizzly than his wife's. His body was riddled with four bullet holes, and he was lying in a pool of blood. His eyes were open, too, but they exhibited a fear that Farber had only seen a few times in his career. The victim was not expecting to die when he did. Farber stared down at his best friend, anger welling up inside.

Harrison came up the stairs behind him, having left Martinez at the brewery to await the ballistics team. He saw the body.

"Oh shit," he said, recoiling in horror. "What the hell is going on?"

Farber ignored him. He carefully stepped over the corpse and tried the front door. It was locked. Rather than pick the lock, he drew his Glock 22 and kicked the door in. Using the pistol as a guide, he checked the entire apartment. Not only was it clear, but there were no visible signs of forced entry. Clothes were missing from the bedroom and toiletries from the bathroom in a way that indicated the occupant had packed and left in a hurry. Farber returned to the front door where the young deputy was waiting.

"We have our suspect," Farber announced.

"Who?"

The sheriff's eyes narrowed.

"Dale Finer," he said. "Put out an APB for that son of a bitch."

CHAPTER 30

Barstow, California

INTERSTATE 15 CUTS directly through Barstow, a historic small town in the Mojave Desert dating back to the 1800s and once a major stop along Route 66. A plethora of auto parts and mechanic shops line Main Street beside gas stations, fast food restaurants, and cheap motels. The streets are wide and the landscape flat, giving visibility to the mountains in the distance. With the sun having dropped below the horizon, and neither having slept in over twenty-four hours, Chris and Alena decided Barstow was the perfect midway point to stop for the night.

They chose a place called the Best Motel, across the street from a vacant building that had probably once been a Kmart. The L-shaped motel was painted red and yellow to match its desert surroundings. There was no pool, just a single palm tree, and half of the sign out front was missing. Chris assumed it was built in the 1950s and had perhaps been a popular destination during Route 66's heyday but had gone into disarray as the decades went by. It was no longer "the best," but it was the type of establishment that took cash and didn't ask questions.

Chris parked the truck in front of a small office near the front of the motel. When they went inside it felt like they were entering a time capsule. There were four lime-green vinyl-accented waiting chairs from the 1960s separated by an old-fashioned gum machine and a coffee table with a stack of old magazines on top. Wood paneling adorned the walls, ashtrays that resembled lamps were in each corner, and the entire office smelled of tobacco, old coffee, and mint gum. Behind the desk was a man with three teeth and a shit-eating grin. He had long, greasy hair tucked behind an old baseball cap, a Nascar T-shirt, and sores covering his gaunt face. Alena quickly realized he was the epitome of a desert town meth-head. She had read about them but never seen one.

The meth-head heard them enter and looked up from the auto magazine he was reading.

"What can I do ya for?"

"We need a room for the night," Chris said.

Alena nudged his shoulder.

"Two rooms," he said.

The meth-head didn't miss a beat. "Fifty-five per night, each—check out is at eleven."

"And we'll be paying in cash," Chris said.

"Not a problem, I'll just need to see some sorta ID."

"We'd rather not," Alena said.

"Lady, I gotta have an ID. Rules, ya know."

"We get it," said Chris. "Thing is, I don't want my wife to know I'm here. Get what I'm saying?"

The meth-head gave him a blank look. Then he got it and smiled. "Right, right." Then he was confused again. "Why two rooms?"

"Look," Alena said. "I'm married too. We're trying to play it smart."

"Right."

Another long pause as he tried to process what she said.

Chris was growing impatient. "Forget it." He turned to leave. "We'll go somewhere else."

"Hold on." The meth-head smiled. "I understand. I'm with ya. Gotta keep the wife happy."

"Exactly," Chris said.

"I love my husband," Alena added.

The meth-head shook his head. "Love, it's what makes this world go around." He winked at Chris. "Your secret is safe with me."

With that, he ran two cards through a little machine.

"Last two on the top floor," he said, handing them to Chris.

"Thanks, man. I owe you one."

"Well, if you're offering, you could always take a few pictures."

"Bye!" Alena said.

She snatched one of the cards out of Chris's hand and marched toward the door.

• • •

The room was musty, and Chris considered sleeping in the truck. Orange carpeting and a thirty-year-old TV accented the pastel bedcover and mattress that dipped in the middle from decades of use. Chris had picked up a six-pack of Goose Island IPA at a gas station, the only IPA they had. He popped open a bottle and took a swig—leaving the rest in the mini-fridge, which he was surprised even existed, and worked. Now that he was back on the drinking bandwagon, he would have preferred his 21st Amendment West Coast IPA, but the Goose was a solid substitute.

He stepped outside the room and lit a cigarette. The Mojave could reach eighty during the day but dropped to a cool fifty degrees at night. From the balcony, he could see the interstate's red and white lights snaking through the darkness. It was an eerie place, the desert, but he loved it. It represented endless possibilities, an endless road to freedom, and the life he yearned for but could never seem to achieve. Life's choices dictate the future, and for the first time in months, he allowed himself to wallow in those choices. Choices he feared would soon catch up to him.

"I guess we had the same idea."

He turned to see Alena standing in the doorway to her room, which was right next to his.

"Want a beer?" he offered.

She shrugged. "What do you have?"

Chris disappeared inside his room, returning a few seconds later with an opened bottle.

"Barstow has a limited supply of craft beer," he said, handing it to her.

"Goose Island." She took a sip. "My first IPA."

"Mine too."

"I guess that's one thing we have in common."

"I guess."

He leaned against the railing, staring out at the desert, and took a long, slow drag from his cigarette.

"We're in deep shit, aren't we?" Alena said, leaning against the railing beside him.

He laughed. "You could say that."

"I'm not some delicate flower. I'm tough. It's just…I've never seen a dead person before. In the flesh, that is. I've seen them on TV—obviously not the same thing."

"It never gets easier."

"You've seen quite a few, huh?"

"Dead people?"

"Yeah."

"More than most I suppose."

She considered his response. Then, "Where did you serve?"

"What do you mean?"

"I had a boyfriend in college who was in the Marines. You military guys have a way about you."

"That's a generalization."

"You're also really good at killing people."

"I've had practice," he replied with a smirk.

"Haha, funny—but seriously, how does this whole thing end?"

"You want my honest opinion?" he said, facing her.

"It would be nice."

"We're fucked."

"Great."

"They put out a contract on you. That's illegal, which means it's off the books. It also means we can't trust anyone—not the police, not the CIA, definitely not the FBI."

"So there's no one we can report this to."

"Nope."

"Except the media. Public perception is everything and cancel culture works. I'm a journalist. I could blow this whole thing wide open."

"That's why they're after you, Alena. You're a threat. Until we know who's behind this, your life is in danger. And my cover is blown."

Shouldn't have said that last part.

"You're cover?" Alena asked.

"Forget about it."

"No, I'd like to know who I'm dealing with."

"We're not going there."

"I think we should."

He shook his head.

"I'm glad you're helping me," she pushed. "But how do I know you're not one of them? How do I know you're not just with me for information and then plan to kill me after you get what you need?"

"Jeez, you think too much."

"You don't think *enough*," she shot back.

He flicked his cigarette off the balcony. "Look—I'm helping you because I don't want other people to get hurt. Okay? You included. But my priority is to keep my family safe, and I can't tell you everything because I don't know you. What I can tell you is that I've dealt with these types of people before, and they don't mess around. I need to find out what's going on or some people very close to me, including those in Palisade, are going to get hurt."

"I'm sorry," she responded, feeling guilty for not trusting him.

"It's fine."

"Thank you for helping me. I don't mean to be a pain."

"You're not a pain."

Their eyes met, and for the first time, Chris realized how beautiful she was—fiery as hell, but a knockout nevertheless.

He pushed those thoughts out of his mind and said, "Here's what's going to happen. Tomorrow, we go to the hospital and check on your friend—see if she can tell us anything. If not, we go to her apartment—try and find that flash drive."

"And then?"

"We'll cross that bridge when we get there."

She nodded.

NEW BEGINNING

By now both bottles of beer were empty.

"We should get some shuteye," Chris said.

"Yeah."

• • •

Chris and Alena checked out as soon as the sun came up the following morning. Chris inspected the truck's tire pressure while Alena dropped the keycards in the office. The meth-head was still there—he must have worked the graveyard shift—and he smiled at Alena as she entered and handed him the two keycards and Chris's prepaid debit card.

"Have a good time?" he asked, swiping the Visa.

"Yeah, it was great. Can we speed this up?"

"Yes, ma'am," he replied. He returned the debit card. "Let me get your receipt."

Before she could object, he disappeared into the back, reappearing thirty seconds later with a receipt printed on continuous-form computer paper from an old '90s pin-fed printer. She hadn't seen one of those since she was in middle school.

"Thanks," she said, taking the receipt and heading for the door.

She glanced up at the tiny TV hanging from the wall. The volume was down, so she hadn't noticed it when she came in. It was a local news channel, and there was a photo of Chris on the top right corner of the screen above an anchor who looked like a used car salesman. The blood drained from her face. She didn't need the volume turned up to understand what the newscaster was saying. The captions told her everything she needed to know. Dale Finer, a.k.a Chris Harding, was wanted for the murder of Frank and Susie Boone.

She glanced back at the meth-head. He was oblivious, reading a Playboy magazine and picking his nose. She pushed open the glass door and speed-walked to the truck. Chris had just finished checking the tires—taking a few PSIs out of each one to accommodate the change in temperature—and was about to climb into the cab.

"We have a problem," Alena said, her voice quivering.

CHAPTER 31

Chris stepped on the gas and accelerated at full speed, hitting the on-ramp and merging into traffic on Interstate 15. He was furious, his hands grasping the steering wheel as tight as he could. It was all his fault. He should never have gotten so close to Frank and Susie. His mind was racing—all the possibilities, all the choices he could have made in the past flooding to the forefront of his mind and clouding all sense of reason. He had survived the explosion in Florida—him, the biggest degenerate of the entire group—and now that stroke of undeserved luck had caused two innocent people to die. He might as well have pulled the trigger himself.

The engine roared and the RPMs hit the red as he passed eighty-five miles per hour, then ninety, then a hundred. Alena held onto the seat and stared at Chris. He was reacting exactly as she would, but it was strange because he was always so composed.

"It's not your fault," she said.

He didn't reply.

She tried again. "They obviously sent someone else." She thought about it. Then, "How did they know about Frank and Susie though?"

Chris nearly lost control of the wheel as he grabbed his pack of Camels from the dash, lit one, and took a drag. Smoked filled the cab.

"Please open a window," Alena said.

He did as he was told.

"Should you pull over?"

"No, I'm fine. I'm just—fuck!" He bit his finger in a desperate attempt to suppress the rage building inside him. "They sent someone else after us. Tracked your phone more than likely. Frank must have shown up. He never could stay out of a fight. Goddamnit, Frank! Whoever it was decided to frame me for their murders so the police would put out an APB."

What he said made sense. Alena stayed silent, unsure how to respond.

"We just need to get to San Francisco without getting pulled over," Chris said, calming himself down with a plan of action.

"Do you have like a fake license plate or something?"

"This one's fake, but it's registered to Dale."

"That won't help."

"Bullet holes won't either. We need another route—something off the interstate."

Highway Patrol loved those long stretches of interstate between cities, and Chris knew it was only a matter of time before someone clocked his F-150.

"I'll need internet for that," Alena said.

"I have a hotspot in the glove box."

"You're kidding me. You've had Wi-Fi all this time?"

Chris shrugged. "It's only for emergencies."

Out came the hotspot—a little box the size of a cell phone—and a USB-C cable. Alena connected her laptop to the device. And for the first time in what felt like forever, she was online. While she searched Google Maps for non-freeway routes to Northern California, Chris turned on his police scanner.

"Really?" Alena said.

"Frank."

Her face went somber. "He's a good guy."

"Was." Chris tried not to think about it. "We can use this to avoid the police. I'm not about to shoot a cop, no matter what the situation is. If we get pulled over, we tell them everything."

"Is that smart?"

"No, so let's not let it happen. Any luck with directions?"

"Looks like we're coming up on Kramer Junction. It's just a gas station, but there's a two-lane highway—the 395. We can take that."

"Perfect."

"It's going to add a few hours."

"Better than getting pulled over."

She nodded. "Then take Exit 179."

"Roger that."

• • •

After killing Frank and Susie, Erick hit the road. He knew Chris would take the southern route—that's what he would do—so he set the Yukon on a route that took him through Utah to Interstate 15 in Nevada and finally into California. Perhaps he could catch up with them on the way. He had seen the F-150 from his brother's body cam but not the plate number. No matter—they were both heading for the same place.

The day was uneventful. Open country filled with snow that quickly turned into a desert with rock formations and golden mountains on the horizon. It was dark when he crossed the border into California. He needed a pick-me-up to get him through the night, so he stopped off at a diner on the side of the freeway. The restaurant was nearly empty and smelled of fried bacon and eggs. It was one of those old-timey joints that had once been the mainstay for cross-country meals but had since been replaced by McDonald's and Denny's.

He found himself a booth beside the window and opened his laptop—time to catch up on the APB and see if there were any hits on Chris and Alena.

A waitress in a burgundy apron stopped by his table.

"Can I get you anything to eat?" she asked.

"Just coffee, thanks."

"Suit yourself."

She returned a moment later with a steaming mug of coffee and a container of cream.

"Black is fine," he said as she set the items on the table.

She nodded and took back the creamer. Then, "Sure I can't get you anything else?"

"I'm sure."

"Okay, but I have to tell you, we have the best French toast west of the Mississippi."

"I'll keep that in mind."

She left him to it but returned every twenty minutes to refill his coffee and offer him another meal that was "the best kept secret west of the Mississippi" and a subtle grunt when he demurred. However, once it hit midnight, he realized he was hungry and finally agreed to one of her suggestions: homemade apple pie.

Erick planned to drive straight through to San Fransisco. The APB had proven useless as had Frank's cell phone. The guy really loved guns—what good that did him. But based on what Erick knew about Chris Harding, he expected him and Alena to elude authorities and make it to San Francisco the following day. Amy Dotson's hospital would be their first stop. And he would be waiting for them. He squared the bill with the waitress and left the diner. Loaded up on caffeine, he hit the road, pointing his Yukon toward the open desert.

CHAPTER 32

UCSF Medical Center
San Francisco, California

It was dark when Chris and Alena arrived at the hospital—located a couple of blocks from the water in Mission Bay, just south of downtown. Chris parked the truck in a parking structure adjacent to the main building and grabbed his Beretta from the backseat.

"We make this quick," he said, stuffing the pistol in the back of his jeans. "We have no idea who might be watching her."

Normally, Alena would have scoffed at him carrying a concealed weapon into a hospital, but these were unique circumstances, and she was actually relieved he would be armed.

"Same could be said about you," she replied, referring to the fact that he was wanted for murder, his face already making the rounds on local television stations.

He frowned. "Let's get this over with."

Chris hated hospitals. Always had. And this one was no different. As one of the top medical facilities in the city and part of the UCSF campus, it was incredibly busy with doctors, nurses, and techs all rushing around in matching scrubs, plus an endless supply of sick people. As they passed through the lobby toward the elevator bays, Chris wondered why the walls were always so green and the lights were always so bright—so stark—as if they'd been bathed in bleach. It reminded him of the weeks he spent in a lonely hospital bed after the explosion. He made sure to count the number of security guards on duty. There were two in the lobby; more would be watching from a windowless control room somewhere deep inside the building.

Amy was in the ICU, which was on the fifth floor. Chris and Alena exited the elevator and stopped at a desk in front of a pair of double-acting doors leading to a long hallway filled with patient rooms and a sea of mint-green gowns and scrubs. Chris clocked another security guard leaning against a counter and chatting up a pretty nurse. Two security cameras watched them from the corner of the ceiling. Hopefully, they were manned by minimum-wage wannabe cops in poorly fitted blue uniforms rather than law enforcement officers or FBI agents.

The nurse behind the desk was a petite Asian woman in her twenties with her dark hair pulled back in a ponytail. She smiled at Chris and Alena as they approached.

"Can I help you?" she asked.

"We're looking for Amy Dotson," Alena said.

"Are you family?"

"No, but—"

"I'm sorry, I can't divulge information about patients unless it's to immediate family."

"Yeah, if I didn't know she was here. But I do—she's a friend, and I'd like to see her."

"I'm sorry."

Alena leaned forward, fuming. "You're sorry? *You're sorry?*"

"Ma'am, I'm going to need you to back up."

"Or what?"

Chris touched Alena's shoulder, and she leaned back.

He smiled at the woman behind the desk. "What my wife means is, she's very upset about Ms. Dotson. They are best friends, and we've flown across the country to see her. Is there any way you can help us?"

The woman softened. "Normally, yes—but her file is restricted." She paused. "There aren't that many rooms, though." She smiled at Chris.

"Thank you," he said, getting the hint.

"Thank you," Alena said.

The nurse glared back.

Chris escorted Alena through the double-acting doors into the ICU.

"Wife? Really?" Alena whispered.

"Yeah, I don't know where that came from."

• • •

Erick's Yukon was parked in the UCSF Medical Center garage, and his laptop was connected to the hospital's security camera feed. The stakeout had been brutal—he'd been there for nearly three hours—but he kept himself fueled with a steady intake of Cliff bars and coffee. Finally, he saw them. Chris and Alena making their way through the lobby, disappearing into an elevator, and then reemerging several seconds later on the fifth-floor ICU.

The assassin closed his laptop and turned off the engine. He attached a suppressor to his SIG P226, racked the slide, and stuffed the weapon inside his inner coat pocket as he exited the vehicle.

The sliding doors opened, and Erick entered the hospital lobby, his eyes filled with a lethal combination of excitement and rage. This was no ordinary hit; this was revenge.

CHAPTER 33

Amy's room was a corner suite at the end of the ICU hallway. She was connected to a plethora of tubes and a computer that monitored her heart rate, breathing, and pulse—quietly beeping each time her heart pumped blood through her veins. Her mother was seated in a chair beside her reading something on her phone.

Chris and Alena stopped outside the door and looked in. He could sense her hesitation.

"Are you okay?" he asked.

"Yeah—I'm fine." She wasn't.

Daiyu Dotson never liked Alena—hated her, actually—and would be less than thrilled to see her appear out of the past at a time like this. Though only sixty years old, she carried herself like a woman ten years her senior, her hazel eyes betraying a mistrust for the world around her. She wore jeans, a blouse, and a black sweater that matched her neatly styled short hair.

Did she get her hair done before coming here? "I can't do this," Alena said.

"Of course you can."

"She hates me." Alena shook her head. "No, this is going to be a disaster. Let's just go to the apartment. You were right."

She turned to leave, but Chris stopped her.

"Don't you want to see Amy?"

"Yes, but—"

"Remember." Chris pointed at Daiyu. "Her daughter is the one connected to all those tubes. She's having a worse day than you are." He thought about his own daughter and how he would feel in Daiyu's situation. "Go easy on her."

Alena nodded. "You're right."

Taking a deep breath, she opened the door and went inside.

Chris stayed put. It was a delicate situation in there, and he wasn't comfortable joining the reunion just yet. Besides, he was concerned with their environment—too many variables. Whoever killed Frank and Susie could be anywhere. Chris leaned against the baby-blue wall and scanned the hallway: doctors and nurses wheeling patients in and out of rooms, visitors clamoring to see their loved ones—any one of them could be an assassin waiting to strike.

• • •

Daiyu's eyes darkened when she saw Alena step into the room. It wasn't just darkness in her eyes, though; it was surprise mixed with a dreaded sense of relief that there was some sort of normality to this awful situation—a situation that didn't even feel real. Alena could hear the sound of Amy's breathing machine as it mechanically pushed air in and out of her lungs—it sounded like Darth Vader, and it broke her heart. She felt guilty knowing she was there for a story, not her old friend's wellbeing—a friend she had pushed away for the very career that now brought them together once more.

"Mrs. Dotson, how are you?"

"Not good, Alena," Daiyu snapped. "What are you doing here?"

"I heard what happened. I'm so sorry."

"Why are you sorry? You didn't do this to her."

"No, but it's just—" Alena leaned over the bed, staring at Amy. "I had to come."

Daiyu raised an eyebrow. "Why are you pretending to be concerned?"

"I'm not," Alena stammered.

"What did you get her involved with?" Daiyu replied, standing up.

"I can't talk about it."

"I'm her mother; you have to talk about it."

For a second, Alena felt like she was back in high school as she cowered in front of an older woman no more than five feet tall. "I need a key to Amy's apartment," she replied timidly.

"Why?"

"She has information."

Daiyu raised another eyebrow. "What's going on, Alena?"

Might as well tell her. "Amy got involved with something at work. It's what got her in this mess to begin with. And to fix it, I need to know everything she knew. She was supposed to fly to New York, but then…" Alena remembered her friend was in a coma and saw the pain in her mother's eyes. "I know you don't like me, and let's be honest, I don't like you either. But we both love Amy, and she got hurt because she saw something she shouldn't have. I'm trying to figure out what it was."

"How are you going to do that?" Daiyu replied without missing a beat.

"Amy told me she saved everything on a flash drive. She didn't want to talk about it over the phone."

There was a long pause. Daiyu looked at her daughter, tears forming in her eyes. She caught herself and returned to her usual hardened exterior. Then she looked back at Alena. Slowly her suspicion turned to concern.

Daiyu leaned forward and whispered in Alena's ear. "I have the flash drive, Alena."

Not the response Alena was expecting. Before she could reply, Chris poked his head inside the room.

"We have to go," he said.

"What happened?" Alena asked.

Chris shut the door behind him as he entered. "I got a bad feeling." He had seen a man in a hoodie exit the elevator, look his way, then duck down the opposite end of the hallway. "It's probably nothing, but I don't want to take any chances." He smiled at Daiyu. "Good evening, ma'am."

The older woman seemed to already know what was going on. Her eyes locked on Chris, examining his grizzled features. Could he be trusted? He looked like a cross between a mountain man and a truck driver.

"There's more going on here than you know," she said.

"What do you mean?" Alena asked.

"Not here—not now," Daiyu replied. She opened her purse and took out a notebook and a pen, then scribbled something on the page, ripped it out, and pressed the small piece of paper into Alena's hand. "Meet me here tonight," she whispered. "I'll give you the flash drive. And I'll explain everything."

CHAPTER 34

Chris and Alena left Amy's room, heading toward the elevators with Chris on full alert, sweeping the hallway with his eyes as they walked. That little voice inside him was screaming like a madman to get out. And he was never wrong. Alena's mind was racing, too. Not only had she seen her oldest friend connected to a million tubes, she had learned that Daiyu knew something. But how much did she know? There were a million answers to her questions, and she was going through all of them all at once. Chris was more tense than usual, causing her stomach to cluster into knots as she power-walked to keep up with him.

They passed the nurse's station and the Asian woman who had helped them before and were about to enter the elevator bay when a man came around the corner of the hallway in front of them, blocking their path. Chris immediately recognized him as the man who attacked them in Colorado. The man he'd already killed. *There's no way.*

"Shit," Chris said.

Alena hadn't noticed him at first, but now she did, and her eyes widened in disbelief as she stared at the man she'd last seen lying dead in the snow.

Erick started toward them, his face void of emotion, his stance determined. Chris took Alena by the arm and marched them both back the way they came, continuing through the ICU, passing Amy's room. Alena glanced back. Erick was following them, slowly, calculated, as if they were animals and he was on the hunt. She tried to quicken their pace, and Chris happily obliged. There was a door with a glowing green exit sign above it. *Perfect*. Chris pushed it open and led Alena into a stairwell with exposed cement blocks and a steel staircase.

Down they went, their footsteps echoing through the stairwell. They were on the fifth floor so it wouldn't take long to reach ground level. They heard the door above them open and slam shut, then footsteps pounding behind them. Chris didn't bother looking back; he knew who it was. He removed the Beretta M9 from the back of his jeans as they sprinted down the stairs.

The steps behind them grew faster.

They went faster.

He was gaining on them.

Fucking A, Chris thought. He yanked back the slide on the pistol and turned around. He was instantly face-to-face with Erick and the barrel of a SIG P226. Alena continued down the stairs until she reached the first floor, where she stopped and waited.

Without hesitating, Chris dived to the side of the stairs, dropping down to the platform below. At the same time, Erick fired twice. The bullets landed in the concrete behind Chris's head, barely avoiding contact. Even suppressed, the sound of gunfire was deafening, and its echo reverberated throughout the chamber as well as the surrounding floors. Chris hadn't planned on a gunfight inside the hospital—too much attention—but now he had no choice. He returned fire, releasing three unsuppressed—and loud—rounds at his attacker.

Erick ducked, avoiding the lead tearing through the stairwell.

More shots were fired—back and forth, neither man hitting his mark. Police would arrive anytime, and Chris didn't want to be there when they did. The way he saw it, he had two options. Fight or flight. He chose the less responsible of the two and sprinted up the stairs and tackled Erick. Both men dropped their weapons as they tumbled back down the stairs to the landing below.

Erick was younger, and he was in better shape. He flipped Chris around and planted a firm punch in the face. The blow nearly sent Chris into darkness. Powering through the resulting brain fog, he attempted a side hook response, but Erick blocked it with his forearm. Chris slipped in his leg and tried to pin the other man down in a jiu-jitsu triangle choke. It was unsuccessful. Three more punches—one to the rib, the stomach, to the side of the head—then Erick grabbed him by the neck. Chris tried to break free, but the assassin was too strong and his grip only tightened, restricting Chris's airflow. He struggled to breathe. *Panic.* His eyes darted around the landing, searching for his gun. There it was. It was too far away to reach.

Erick's weapon was closer, and he used his free hand—the one not choking the life out of Chris—to grab his SIG.

"This is for my brother," he growled, pointing the gun at Chris's head.

"Fuck you!" said a voice from behind them.

Before Erick could process that someone was screaming at him, Alena's foot landed between his legs. She had heard the gunshots and the struggle that followed. Fear is paralyzing, but the human body's response to danger can surprise even those unaccustomed to violent altercations. If Chris lost the fight, Alena knew she was next. She had to intervene.

Intense pain radiated from Erick's groin causing him to loosen his grip around Chris's neck. The former commando took advantage of the moment and broke free of his assailant's grasp, knocking the SIG from his hand. Chris was now able to reach the Beretta. Gun in hand, he jumped to his feet and sent a 9mm round into Erick's shoulder.

The assassin was still recovering from the blunt-force attack on his scrotum when the bullet from Chris's M9 landed in his scapula just below the clavicle bone. The gunshot would have caused most men to faint, but not Erick; an extreme pain threshold, combined with a rush of adrenaline, enabled him to continue forward. He raised his right leg and sent a side-kick that knocked Chris's pistol back to the floor. Unarmed once more, Chris was forced into another fistfight with a man whose skills were quickly proving superior to his. The assassin followed up the kick with another, nearly sending Chris back to the ground. More hits to the face. Chris struggled to maintain consciousness, doing his best to raise his arms in defense.

Alena watched in horror as Chris took hit after hit. But Erick couldn't last forever; he knew that. The wound in his shoulder had weakened his right arm. It was time to switch to lower body once more. A low kick nearly snapped Chris's kneecap, sending him back against the wall.

Stay in the fight, Chris told himself.

His next jab was blocked. Erick followed with four strikes to the face. Chris took them but earned himself two cuts and a pool of blood beneath the skin of his left eye.

He'd had enough.

Using all the energy he could muster, he pushed Erick back

and dived for his Beretta. This put him in a kneeling position a couple of feet from his opponent. It was time for the old tried-and-true. He grabbed Erick's balls, and he squeezed. The assassin let out an agonizing scream. But Chris wasn't finished. He turned the testicles like he was turning on a faucet. The hitman's screams turned to high-pitched shrieks—like a caged dog in heat. Chris released the now severely damaged groin and pistol-whipped his opponent across the jaw with the butt of his gun, a force that sent him tumbling to the landing floor. Chris stood up and pressed the Beretta against Erick's forehead. He was about to pull the trigger and end the son of a bitch for good when the stairwell door directly above them opened. Two SFPD officers wearing SWAT gear and armed with M4 rifles stormed through the open doorway.

"Drop it!" one of them ordered.

At first, Chris ignored the officer, his grip only tightening on the Beretta. As much as he wanted to pull that trigger, he knew it would be the last thing he ever did.

"Drop the *fucking* gun!"

Chris slowly lowered his weapon and placed it on the ground before kicking it away.

"Hands in the air!"

Chris did as he was told. The officer barking orders kept his M4 on him while his partner knelt down to check on Erick—who, as far as Chris was concerned, was milking the situation and overplaying his gunshot wound. He was the victim, Chris the perpetrator, and as soon as they recognized him, Chris would be charged with Frank and Susie's murder—Alena as an accessory. Erick would go free, and they'd be killed in prison within twenty-four hours.

It was now or never.

CHAPTER 35

Chris could see Alena cowering on the landing, a floor below him, directly in front of an exit doorway. More police officers flooded the stairwell above him. His trusted Beretta that had been with him for more than ten years was too far to reach. He would have to leave it.

It was a split decision.

Using the railing to propel his body forward, Chris dived down the stairwell with such velocity that it took the cops by surprise, and they didn't immediately shoot.

"*Go!*" Chris yelled to Alena as he sprinted passed her toward the exit.

They made it through the door just in time. As it shut behind them, they heard the sound of semiautomatic gunfire erupting through the stairwell.

Still running, Chris attempted to catch his bearings and calibrate their location. They were in the hospital parking garage, which meant they needed to exit the building—an impossibility with the amount of police that would have already surrounded the hospital—and make it back to the truck inside the public parking structure across the street.

It was Alena who realized where they actually were.

"This is the same garage we parked in," she said.

"No, we parked across the street."

"We *are* across the street."

He stopped running and looked around. "Are you sure?"

"You might have a concussion. Yes, I'm sure. You see that?" She pointed to the yellow number painted on the concrete pillar beside them. "We parked one level up."

Chris nodded—disregarding her visual prowess—and they both sprinted up the ramp just as five police officers entered the garage behind them with their guns drawn.

"Stop!" one of them ordered.

Chris and Alena ignored the command and turned the corner. The officers opened fire, then followed, screaming into their radios for backup.

Chris unlocked the truck with his fob as he and Alena approached. They both jumped inside, and Chris pressed the start button, firing up the 5.0L V8 engine. A bullet took out the passenger side mirror. Both mirrors were now destroyed, but there was no time to pout—eight SFPD officers surrounded them with their rifles drawn, spraying the garage with lead. Alena covered her ears, attempting to block out the deafening sound of gunfire. Chris pressed the gas, and the tires squealed against the polished concrete floor as they leaped out of the parking spot and made a hard left around the corner, straining a suspension not built for tactical driving and nearly tipping the truck over.

The exit was blocked by a boom barrier.

"Did you validate parking?" Alena asked.

"No."

Chris plowed straight through the boom barrier.

"Validated," he said, making a hard right onto the street in front of the hospital.

They were immediately met by dozens of police vehicles and uniformed officers with their guns drawn. Chris floored the gas and crashed into two cruisers. The officers standing nearby ducked for cover, while others opened fire on the rogue F-150.

Chris cleared the blockage and turned onto a major thoroughfare with a light rail metro track cutting through the median. To their right were high-rise office buildings and luxury apartments, and to their left was the San Francisco Bay. Blue lights appeared behind them. Chris increased his speed, weaving through traffic, and nearly collided with two electric cars driven by tech industry talent acquisition specialists. More cruisers turned onto the street behind them.

"We're never going to make it," Chris said.

The sirens grew louder. One cruiser was now only three cars behind them.

Think, Chris, think.

He saw a metro train approaching in the rearview mirror. It gave him an idea.

All right, that could work.

He slowed down, waiting as the train got closer—which also narrowed the gap between them and the army of law enforcement officers on their tail.

"What are you doing?" Alena screamed.

Chris ignored her, his eyes fixated on the train. A black-and-white hit their bumper.

Another came up to their right side.

"*Chris!*"

It was time.

He made a left turn onto the median *and* the tracks. He opened the throttle, pushing the engine to its max, and tightened his grip on the steering wheel as they bounced over the tracks.

Alena screamed. The train laid on its horn, and—

The F-150 made it across the tracks to the opposite lane, a rush of wind nearly tipping the truck over as it missed the oncoming train by a fraction of an inch. Chris slammed the steering wheel to the left and executed a hard U-turn. They were now heading back the way they came, only now, the police were blocked by the train.

"Get us out of here," Chris said.

Though her stomach was in her throat, Alena was already on it. Fumbling for her laptop, she connected to the hotspot, opened Chrome, and went to Google Maps.

"Where are we going?" she asked, trying to make sense of the endless grid that was San Francisco.

"Anywhere but here."

The train went by, allowing the police to continue pursuit. Sirens and flashing lights appeared once more in their rearview mirror.

"Make a left at the light," Alena said.

The light was red, but Chris ignored it and made the turn without stopping. They crossed the intersection—there was lots of honking and middle fingers from incoming traffic—and entered downtown, which was a maze of skyscrapers jam-packed with pedestrians and electric vehicles. They were stuck. Then came a loud thumping sound overhead. Chris looked out the window to see a police chopper hovering above them.

"Shit," he said. "Is there a parking structure nearby?"

"Four more blocks," Alena replied.

The full-sized truck was too large to weave in and out of traffic, so Chris forced his way through, knocking the mirrors off a Toyota Prius and a Tesla as he passed and then rear-ending a Subaru. The street transitioned to a steep hill, and the skyscrapers were replaced by Victorian-era architecture and ornately decorated buildings painted floral blues and whites. The Ford's V8 engine came in handy, allowing them to effortlessly cruise up the incline, leaving the police department's Dodge sedans in the dust.

Alena pointed to the next intersection. "There."

Chris turned into the garage. Another boom barrier blocked their path.

Goddam paid parking everywhere.

He took the ticket and waited for what felt like an eternity as the barrier went up. He thought about ramming it like he did the last one, but if he did, the police would notice it and their new hideout would be blown. Finally, the barrier went up. They drove to the lowest level of the six-level garage and parked beside a concrete pillar. Chris leaned his head against the back of the seat and let out a sigh of relief. As the adrenaline subsided, he began to feel the throbbing pain from his wounds. Alena noticed them too—specifically the large gash above his right eye. It was caked in dried blood.

"That doesn't look good," she said. "It needs to be cleaned. Do you have a—"

"In the glove box, but it's okay, I'm fine."

She ignored him. The first aid kit was where it was supposed to be. Inside it she found gauze, Band-Aids, and disinfectant wipes, the last of which she removed from the plastic container. She tore open the wipe and leaned toward Chris. He flinched.

"Hold still," she said.

She cleaned the dried blood from his forehead, then applied

two more wipes, ensuring the wound was thoroughly disinfected. Her touch felt soft on Chris's skin, and it tingled—not like the peroxide seeping into the cut, but like a warm cup of tea on a cold day. He thought about breaking a smile but didn't.

Alena wondered why she suddenly felt the urge to take care of him. She'd never been much on taking care of other people, let alone a man whose past was a mystery and who had killed someone in front of her without even breaking a sweat. If those weren't red flags, what were?

"You need stitches," she said.

"I'll be okay."

She tossed the used wipes into the side compartment on the door. "Now what?"

"Give me a second."

Chris grabbed a pack of Camels from the center console. He removed a cigarette from the box, lit one with his Bic lighter, and took a long drag, allowing the nicotine to fill every crevice of his lungs. Finally, he was relaxed. Now he could think.

"We're gonna stay here for a while," he said. "Until it gets dark, at least." He turned and faced Alena. "Then we get that flash drive and get the hell out of town."

CHAPTER 36

The Marriott Palace Hotel in downtown San Francisco was nothing short of extraordinary. Built in 1875, the Gilded Age architecture represented luxury at its finest—marble pillars, crystal chandeliers, and ornate woodwork in addition to ensuite hardwood floors and stunning views of both the skyline and the Golden Gate Bridge, made it one of the premier hotels in the city. Daiyu stayed there whenever she visited Amy, and even though this wasn't a typical visit and she was mentally preparing to bury her only daughter—doctors were recommending her pull the plug—she refused to change her routine. She began each day with a morning walk through Union Square into Chinatown, then back to the hotel on one of the historic cable cars.

She had stayed with her daughter until visiting hours were over, instructing the nurse to notify her if there were any changes to Amy's condition. Daiyu knew there wouldn't be. She was a realist, but she was also a mother and still hoped for a miracle. Alena and the bearded man showing up at the hospital had been unexpected, but Daiyu was thankful someone else had taken an interest in what happened to Amy. The flash drive had been shipped overnight to her house in Texas, arriving shortly after she heard the news of

NEW BEGINNING

Amy's attack. An hour later she was on a flight to San Francisco.

The contents of the drive had concerned her, of course, but it also confirmed her fears about the man Amy worked for: Andrew Chew. Like many Chinese Americans, Daiyu and Amy's father, Wèiguó, had left the communist regime of their homeland for the American dream. But their new life came at a cost. For decades, government officials in Beijing had harassed and intimidated Chinese expats in America by threatening family back home. Wèiguó's parents were elderly and at risk of losing their state-funded apartment, so it wasn't a surprise when he and Daiyu were contacted by "Chinese spies" at their Austin home. They navigated the situation as best they could, but it wasn't easy.

When Wèiguó was killed in a car accident—a drunk driver hit him head-on while he was driving home from work—Daiyu was left to raise their daughter alone. Perhaps that was what hardened her. Perhaps that was why she didn't trust Amy's American friends, like Alena. And perhaps that was what had pushed mother and daughter into a reluctantly codependent relationship. Finances had never been an issue. Wèiguó's business partner saw to it that his friend's wife and daughter were taken care of.

Daiyu had been concerned when Amy received an offer to work at Nysta. She knew the history of the company, but more than that, she understood how Andrew Chew had financed his groundbreaking tech startup. SMIC was controlled by the Chinese Communist Party—everyone in China knew that, and every Chinese American immigrant knew what that meant. Chew would be forced to do the bidding of a vile regime that hated the United States almost as much as it hated its own people.

But Amy was determined to work there. She told her mother it was the opportunity of a lifetime—bigger and better than Facebook or X. Hell, it was the new frontier in social media, and she would be at the forefront of innovative technology. Daiyu's concerns were solidified when she received the flash drive. She knew in her gut Amy was attacked because of that information; that was just how the Chinese did things. It was intimidation. It was, *stop this or we will kill you and your entire family.*

So Daiyu returned to her hotel room—the presidential suite, decorated like a Parisian mansion—and waited for Alena and Chris to arrive. Talking to them was a risk, but it was her only viable option—the only thing she could do to make her daughter's sacrifice worth it.

• • •

Chris and Alena entered the Marriott Palace Hotel lobby a few minutes past 7:00 p.m. They had waited inside the parking structure for two hours. The F-150 was filled with bullet holes and no longer safe to use—its license plate had also been recorded by multiple traffic cameras—so they took a cable car to the address Daiyu had given Alena. She wasn't at all surprised by the opulence. The Dotsons had always demanded the finest things in life, even during tragic circumstances. The front desk attendant, an attractive woman with a distinctively British accent, had been instructed to give Chris and Alena access to Daiyu's room. They took the elevator to the top floor. When they arrived at the presidential suite, the door opened before they had a chance to knock.

Daiyu inspected the hallway behind them as she ushered them inside. Chris and Alena took a seat on a blue sofa opposite two matching chairs and a glass coffee table. Daiyu settled into one of the chairs and removed a flash drive from her pocket.

She placed it on the table. "Amy was always thorough. Got that from her father. She sent this to me. I assume she kept the other copy to give to you." Daiyu paused to compose herself, determined to remain the strong woman she'd always been. "My daughter is going to die because of what's on here, isn't she?"

Alena glanced at Chris, then back at Daiyu. "She's not going to die."

"Don't be naïve, Alena. Of course she will die. Doctors know it, I know it; you should know it too. Now why do you care?"

"She was my friend."

"But you have an article to write, yes?"

"Yes, but—"

"This is all very dangerous. It would be wise for you to let it go."

"Do you know what's on the drive?" Alena replied.

"I do not. There is a password." She paused. "Chinese Americans are hard working people, Alena. We came here for a better life. Unfortunately, our homeland does not always approve, and success can make one a target. Nysta's CEO, Andrew Chew, was bought and paid for by the Chinese Communist Party, and they have spies everywhere—even in law enforcement. I know this because Amy's father was one of them."

Holy shit. Talk about family secrets. This revelation took Alena by surprise, and she wasn't sure how to respond. The only thing that came out was, "*What?*"

"He had no choice. It was the only way to protect our family back home. It's what they do; they threaten, they intimidate, and they always win." Daiyu's eyes finally gave in and filled with tears. "He died in a car accident, but I always knew it was a lie. He refused to relay information to his handler in Beijing. Told them he was through. They killed him for it."

Chris leaned forward. "What kind of information?"

"He was a partner at a very important accounting firm with very important clients."

"Corporate espionage."

She nodded. There was a solemn pause. Then, "When Amy told me she took a job at Nysta, I was concerned. What if she gets pulled into the same thing?"

She broke. Tears flooded her face.

In a futile attempt at consoling her, Chris said, "This has nothing to do with your husband's work. Andrew Chew and the people he works for are responsible, no one else."

Daiyu smiled, the first Alena had ever seen. "Then whatever is on that flash drive should not be ignored. What will you do with it?"

Alena said, "I'm going to expose those responsible. Words are powerful."

Chris knew this wasn't true. Alena already had a price on her head, and publishing an article in the *New York Times* would only exasperate the situation. Whatever they were trying to hide was big enough to warrant a death squad, and there was a connection between this and his team's assassination, he was certain. He kept his thoughts to himself.

"Do you know the name of your husband's handler?" he asked.

Daiyu locked eyes with the former soldier. She could see that he was a man of action, a man who had seen and done the unfathomable. But could she trust him?

"Feng Chen," she said. "That's all I know. They communicated on the dark web. Never by phone."

"Was he located in the U.S.?"

"That I do not know." Then, addressing Chris and Alena together—her tone serious once more and void of emotion and feeling—she said, "Take the drive, but you must be careful."

Her advice was redundant; they both knew it. The trail of blood behind them was proof. But Alena understood that, in her own way, Daiyu was being a mother.

"We'll be careful," Alena said. "But what about you? Eventually they're going to figure out that you had the flash drive."

"We have never liked each other—we both know it. But you mustn't worry about me. Without my daughter, I have nothing. And I have nothing to fear. I will happily leave this life to be with my daughter and husband. But you two—you must be careful. Something is coming, and those responsible will stop at nothing to make sure it comes to pass."

• • •

Chris took a much-needed sip from a giant goblet-shaped glass filled with 21st Amendment West Coast IPA. Across the street from Daiyu's hotel was a small bar called the House of Shields. The neon sign out front was shaped like a sword, and the inside had a medieval theme and dark mahogany booths. Alena had ordered the 21st Amendment as well, and she liked it, though she preferred her IPAs less malty and more mosaic and floral in tones. Nevertheless, she was equally in need of a stiff drink, and the beer hit the spot. With liquid courage in front of them, it was finally the moment of truth. It was time to rip off the Band-Aid.

"Let's do it," Chris said.

Alena nodded. She took another sip of courage, then removed her MacBook from her bag and inserted the flash drive into the laptop's USB-C port.

"Shit, I forgot," Alena said, looking up from the screen. "Password protected."

"Amy *is* thorough. Any idea what it is?"

"No clue—let me think."

"No pressure," Chris replied, sipping his beer.

"None at all, just our lives hanging in the balance."

"At least we have beer."

"There is that." She rolled her eyes. "Beer doesn't fix everything, though."

"In my experience, it does."

She typed in a password. It didn't work. "What experience is that?"

"You know, killing people."

"I guess a beer tastes pretty good after taking a life." She tried another password. Still no luck. "Shit."

"Everything we just went through, and now we can't even open the damn thing."

"Shut up, I got it."

She took another sip of IPA, then typed in: TheAmericanDream2023. Like magic, the drive opened, revealing a folder labeled *Nysta Update*.

"Wall-a," she said, celebrating with another taste of IPA.

"See?" Chris replied. "Beer fixes everything."

She moved the laptop around so that they both could see the contents of the folder, a series of screenshots. She opened the first one. It was a string of code.

"I guess it never occurred to me that neither of us know a single thing about code," Chris said, staring at the numbers and symbols populating the screen.

"Speak for yourself. You probably freak out when it's time to update your iPhone."

"I hate computers."

Alena ignored him and turned the laptop back in front of her. She read through the sequence of code, deciphering it as best she could. It appeared to be a software update for the Nysta app—the one Amy had mentioned on the phone. Alena only had an elementary understanding of computer science, but from what she could tell, it was JavaScript and it was—

"Oh my God," she gasped.

"You figured it out?"

"Yeah."

"And?"

"It's not good."

"Be more specific, please."

Alena was still staring at her screen in disbelief. "This is a software update that will enable Nysta to collect their users' financial data—bank accounts, crypto wallets, pensions, investment portfolios. For all intents and purposes, it's a virus programmed to take everything." She looked up at Chris, color draining from her face. "There are nearly two billion global users—over a hundred million in the U.S.—and Nysta will have full access to every single one of their life's savings the moment this update is installed on their phones. And it's scheduled to drop in less than a week."

CHAPTER 37

THERE WASN'T ENOUGH beer in the world to actually fix the problem, but that didn't stop Chris and Alena from ordering another round from the House of Shields waitress, an attractive brunette covered in tattoos. Chris was no financial wizard, but he understood the gravity of the situation. If Nysta were planning a cyberattack of this magnitude, it would have a devastating effect on the global economy, essentially eroding the Dollar and sending the U.S., and the world, into a depression. Alena explained how the Federal Reserve would be forced to print more money, further exasperating the problem with inflation. Increased interest rates would stifle new business growth, which in turn would lead to layoffs and a rise in unemployment not seen since the Great Depression. But that wasn't the worst of it.

"If China is behind this—and I think we can both agree they are—then they will have economic superiority," Alena said. "They'll be the most powerful nation in the world."

Chris nodded. "Not to mention their relationship with Russia and Iran."

"My gut was right. I mean, I never expected something this big." She pointed to the computer. "But this is the proof I need to take down Nysta."

Chris frowned. "It's not exactly proof, though. We don't know if they plan to do this."

"Why else would they collect all that data?"

"I don't know. All I'm saying is that we're speculating here. It's not enough to pull a Ronan Farrow."

She was shocked. "How do you know about Ronan? You've read his work?"

Ronan Farrow was an investigative reporter who took down some of the biggest names in Hollywood with his groundbreaking article in *The New Yorker* exposing ramped sexual harassment within the film industry elite.

"I'm literate," Chris said as he took another sip of beer. "But you're also forgetting something else."

"Yes, I know. There's an assassin after me."

"After *us*," he corrected her. "Someone in the FBI is working with China to make this happen. They'll stop at nothing to keep this intel from seeing the light of day."

She slumped back against the booth. He was right. Her brief moment of excitement was over and reality sunk in. The information she'd been searching for was the very thing that would get her killed. "What do we do?"

Chris had no idea. He knew they needed to figure out who ordered the contract on Amy and Alena. Was there a connection to Woodhaven? His gut told him there was. If so, this would require more resources than they had—too many players involved, not enough information.

Wait, that was it—more information.

"Is there a way to stop the update?" he asked.

Alena shrugged. "I'm sure there is. I wouldn't know how."

"Who would?"

"Someone at Nysta. Maybe the guy who built it?"

"Then we need to have a conversation with Andrew Chew."

"How are we going to do that?"

"We go to his house."

"Of course, we just break in. And do what? Force him to tell us everything?"

"Yeah."

"You're crazy."

Chris finished his beer and motioned for the waitress, who nodded and made a beeline for the bar to get them another round.

It was time to tell Alena everything. Chris took a deep breath and said, "I need to know I can trust you."

"After what we've just been through?" she scoffed. "Of course you can trust me."

"What I'm about to tell you is classified."

"Okay?"

"You knowing about it could put you in danger."

"I think we're past that."

Two more beers arrived. Chris thanked the waitress and took a sip of the IPA. "Last year, I was involved in a covert CIA operation to take out Russian nuclear missiles—"

"Oh my God, that was you?"

"Yes."

"You died, right? Yeah, you did. I knew I recognized your name."

He glared at her.

"Sorry, keep going."

"Obviously I didn't die. I was recruited by the FBI to join a secret group."

NEW BEGINNING

"What kind of secret group?"

"The kind you don't know exists—in the gray."

"Like *The Gray Man*?"

"The movie?"

"No, the book."

"There's a book?"

"Never mind. Continue."

Chris frowned. "Anyway, our job was to investigate a deep state organization known as the New World Order—or NWO."

"I've heard of that conspiracy theory."

"Stop interrupting."

"Sorry."

"Six months ago—after a year of dead-ends—we discovered a crypto wallet with a transaction between the NWO and Chinese semiconductor chip manufacturer, SMIC, for a shipment of AI chips."

"Wait."

"The same company that owns a majority share in Nysta."

"Whoah," Alena said, unsure how else to respond.

"Yup, and those AI chips were delivered to Iranian terrorist, Adham Mostafa. His partner, Bashir Mahmoud, murdered the Swiss banker responsible for brokering the deal, but not before we secured a flash drive implicating Mostafa and Mahmoud *and* the NWO—who we believed they were working for."

"The terrorist attack in Geneva," Alena said. "I saw the news coverage. It was horrific. You were there?"

Chris nodded. "After Geneva, we were tasked with finding and apprehending Adham Mostafa and Bashir Mahmoud. But before we were able to, my entire team was killed in an explosion at our safe house in Florida. The same night, our handler was murdered at his home in D.C. We weren't on the FBI's payroll, so any trace of our existence was destroyed. We learned too much, and someone wanted us silenced."

Alena knew Chris had a past, but she wasn't expecting this. He was a spy—a real-life James Bond—not unlike the men who were after them.

"Who tried to silence you?" she asked.

"That I don't know. Someone at the FBI was involved, I think. FBI Director Steven House comes to mind. But there's no way to know for sure."

"You think the director of the FBI attacked a covert FBI team?"

"I don't know. Those things do happen."

"Assassinations are illegal."

"Only if you get caught. Perhaps he was working with the NWO, or perhaps he wasn't involved at all." Chris took a sip of beer. "I have no idea how or why I survived. But I was afraid that whoever came after us would go after my family if they knew I was still alive. So I went dark, and well, that's where you met me."

"I'm sorry, that's a lot to go through."

Chris shrugged. "It is what it is. My gut tells me there's a connection between this Nysta update and the Iranian terrorists and the NWO. I think my team was killed by the same people who are trying to kill you."

Alena was afraid before; she was terrified now.

"There's more," Chris continued. "The guy who came after us at the hospital? He looks exactly like the man I killed in Colorado."

"I saw that too. You think he survived?"

"Fuck no. It's his brother. There was something about both of them. I couldn't put my finger on it. But today I made the connection. They're twins—assassins-for-hire, Caleb and Erick Webb."

"How do you know it's them?"

"There aren't many twins who kill people for a living."

"That's a good point."

"I think the man at the hospital today was Erick."

"How can you tell?"

"Because Erick is the more deadly of the two."

"And you killed his brother."

"Which explains why he was so angry."

"Who do they work for?"

"The most corrupt private military contractor in America: Greenwood Enterprises."

"I've heard of them. They provide tactical training for police agencies all over the country. You say they're secretly carrying out targeted killings on American citizens?"

"I can't prove it, but yeah."

Alena thought for a moment. Then, "Is there anyone alive you trust that you could call?" She realized how insensitive she sounded. "I'm sorry, didn't mean it like that."

"It's true. Most people I know and trust are dead." Chris took a deep breath, trying not to think about it. "There is one person, though. Pretty sure he's still alive. Don't know if I can trust him."

"Who is he?"

"The man who got me into all this in the first place."

"You never thought to call him before?"

"I did. But there was someone powerful enough to take out my entire team without us even suspecting we were in danger. Going after them wasn't worth the risk to the few people left in this world that I care about. I make that phone call, and I'm no longer dead."

Alena considered what Chris was saying. He was a tormented

soul, continually dealt a bad hand, who now just wanted to forget his past and start over. Meeting her had destroyed any hope of that.

"You should have just let me die," she said.

"What are you talking about?"

"In the storm—you shouldn't have gotten involved. Now they know you're alive. And your family is in danger, all because of me."

"It's not like that."

"It's exactly like that. I can do this alone, Chris." Her voice was soft, understanding. She didn't want to do it alone—she was scared to death—but she knew someone had to. "I shouldn't have gotten you involved in all this. Just give me this guy's number, and I'll call him myself."

Chris finished the beer, then looked her in the eyes. Those big brown eyes. "I'm seeing this through." His voice was firm and decisive. "We stick together until we know who's behind all this. Until the threat is neutralized. Now—Amy's mother claimed Chinese spies put pressure on Andrew Chew. I think it's time we pay him a little visit."

• • •

Erick entered the Marriott Palace Hotel and took the elevator to the presidential suite. After calling Greenwood, a representative from the FBI had arrived—shortly after "taking him into their custody"—and delivered Erick to a safe house in San Francisco's Mission District. Another look at his Kill Package had confirmed the address for Daiyu's hotel. Erick exited the elevator and removed his SIG. Keeping the suppressed weapon to his side, he proceeded to the suite at the end of the hall and knocked.

A few seconds later, Daiyu opened the door. Erick's eyes were dark and cold, and she could see into his soul—the soul of a killer. But she was expecting him, and there was no fear; she was ready. Erick was taken aback by this, and he hesitated. Then, remembering who he was and why he was there, he aimed the pistol at her forehead and pulled the trigger.

CHAPTER 38

Boca Raton, Florida

A<small>L</small> K<small>EMPE</small> <small>RECEIVED</small> a text message from an unknown number at his ocean-side vacation home. The retired general and former Chairman of the Joint Chiefs of Staff had begun his long career in 1980 when he graduated from West Point. Following a three-year assignment at the Special Forces training facility in Fort Bragg, North Carolina, he was tasked with administering special operations training for the Iraqi Army during the Iran-Iraq War. In a conflict spanning eight years, the United States had sided with the Ba'athist Iraq government—providing weapons, dual-use technologies, and tactical training—in their mutual fight against post-Revolutionary Iran.

It was during this war between terrorists that Kempe found his stride. As a military attaché to the CIA, including a year in Baghdad assisting in the sale of weapons to the Iraqi Armed Forces, he was introduced to the world of espionage and relationships that hastened his rise in the United States Army ranks, making Lieutenant General by the time he was thirty in 1988. Three marriages and four wars later, Kempe had built a unique resume.

NEW BEGINNING

Publicly, he was a highly decorated general who commanded six divisions during the Invasion of Panama, the Persian Gulf War, and the War in Afghanistan. But privately, he maintained strong ties with U.S. intelligence agencies, collaborating with the CIA and the FBI to further anti-terrorism operations, both domestic and abroad. Woodhaven was one such collaboration, established to fight threats beyond Islamic extremism—a deep state organization called the New World Order. Finally, in 2012, after thirty-two years of service, Kempe was appointed Chairman of the Joint Chiefs of Staff by President Barack Obama.

At sixty-five, his body had aged. Years of Diet Cokes, bourbon, and red meat—all while fighting wars from behind a desk—had taken its toll. His thick, rounded features and thinning white hair helped him blend in with the Boca Raton locals. Another retired government worker living out his golden years in style.

The sun had set, and he was enjoying a Cuban cigar and a Woodford Reserve over ice on his back patio, just a few yards from the ocean. The sound of waves crashing against the shore. The cool breeze against his Hawaiian sports shirt. Retirement was treating him well.

He read the message once more, sipping his bourbon and thinking. Finally, he got up and went inside. The landline was there for one reason. The remote possibility that he would have a national security emergency and need a secure line. He dialed the number from the text and waited.

It rang three times. Then, "Hello?"

Kempe instantly recognized the voice of Chris Harding.

"Harding, is that you?"

"How are you, General?"

Chris was outside the House of Shields smoking a cigarette.

"I'm hanging in there," Kempe replied. "How the hell are you still alive?"

"It's a long story."

Kempe replenished his bourbon from a small bar built into the wall. "Where are you?"

"I'm afraid I can't tell you that."

"I'm retired, kid, so don't waste my time. Why are you calling me?"

There was a long pause.

"I need your help," Chris finally said.

CHAPTER 39

Metro Parking Garage
San Francisco, California

It was hard to say goodbye to the Ford F-150, but there was no way Chris and Alena were getting out of the city in it. It was riddled with bullet holes, had been recorded on multiple traffic cameras, and its license plate was on the APB registry. Unwanted police attention was all but guaranteed. They needed a new vehicle, and fast. They found it in a silver 2002 Toyota Corolla parked on the next level up. Chris picked the lock, and they loaded their bags and his guns into the backseat. Chris then removed the panel below the steering wheel and hot-wired the starter. The engine with 200,000 miles on it fired right up, proof that Toyotas never die.

Interstate 80 took them over the Oakland Bay Bridge, through Treasure Island, and into the city of Oakland—the San Francisco skyline behind them, casting a yellow glow across the bay.

"So you think this Al Kempe is going to help us?" Alena asked.

"He's the former Chairman of the Joint Chiefs of Staff and the only person outside the FBI who knows I'm still alive."

"Other than me," Alena teased.

"Other than you," Chris replied. "We bring him actionable intel—proof of a national security threat—"

"We already have that on the flash drive."

"We need confirmation from a pro. That's where Andrew Chew comes in. We get him to admit to the attack, or at least who he works for. Kempe has connections in the intelligence community and in D.C. Hopefully he'll be able to shed some light on what's going on."

"I'd like to think it's all over after that. But it's not, is it?"

"Not even close. If this thing is connected to the NWO, there's no telling how far up the food chain it goes. Until we know more, we may have to go dark. Completely off the grid."

"I thought you might say that. What about my article?"

"When this is all over, you'll be the one to expose the truth. I promise. But not until we neutralize those responsible for putting our lives in danger."

"You're going to kill more people, aren't you?"

"Alena, if you want to stay alive, we have to do things my way."

She nodded and looked out the window. Her entire life had been thrown upside down. But she was oddly okay with it. Her eyes darted back to Chris. There was something about him she was beginning to like.

• • •

A few miles away, inside the Marriott Palace Hotel, Erick was seated on the blue couch in Daiyu's hotel suite—her dead body was on the floor beside the door, a pool of blood beneath her head—staring at a text message on his burner phone. The address on the screen had come from Greenwood, but the intel originated from an unknown source, well above Erick's pay grade. He plugged the address into the Google Maps app on his smartphone. The location wasn't far, just across the bridge in Oakland at the home of Nysta CEO and founder Andrew Chew.

Erick memorized the address, deleted the message, and smiled. He wouldn't underestimate his opponent again. This time the element of surprise would be his, and Chris Harding and Alena Moore would not last the night.

CHAPTER 40

Andrew Chew lived in a Mediterranean-style home on Sea View Avenue in Piedmont, a few miles east of Oakland. It was one of the most affluent neighborhoods in the Bay Area with homes that dated back to the 1930s. Chew had a full staff to take care of the property, but he was obsessed with privacy—ironic since he ran a social media platform—and they were required to leave before he got home from work each night.

Chris and Alena arrived shortly before 3:00 a.m. and parked the Corolla a block down the street. The house would be empty except for Chew. Easy in and out.

"We don't have much time," Chris said. "The neighborhood courtesy patrol won't like seeing a Toyota parked in front of a five-million-dollar house."

"You should have stollen a nicer car."

"I don't know how to hot-wire a Tesla."

"If you're going to be a criminal, you need to learn. EV is the future."

"I'll keep that in mind."

"What about security? Won't Chew have an alarm?" Alena asked.

"Yeah, but we'll disable it."

"You know how to do that?"

"Maybe you should stay here. Pretend to be sleeping in your car."

"Fuck you."

"All right, let's go."

They exited the car and crossed the street toward Chew's off-white stucco home. The house was dark, but the steps leading to the front door were illuminated by two lamps on top of a cream-colored wall that separated the front yard from the sidewalk. Chris picked the lock with a lock pick kit, conveniently stored in his coat pocket. His ability to effortlessly break the law never ceased to amaze Alena.

Once inside, Chris opened the security box on the wall beside the door. A delay had been activated, giving them only sixty seconds before the alarm went off. Most security systems are relatively easy to disengage if you know what you're doing. Chris did. He disarmed the alarm with only five seconds to spare and motioned for Alena to follow him. The dark-stained hardwood floors matched the furniture, and the walls were baby blue with a glossy white trim. Everything was clean and tidy. It was like no one lived there.

They climbed the staircase that was directly in front of the foyer, taking their time. Slowly inching their way to the top. The upstairs opened into a long hallway with rooms on either side.

"Last door on the left," Alena whispered.

She had looked over the floorpan on Zillow during the drive over.

Chris nodded and started down the hallway with Alena following close behind. They reached the last room on the left, and

Chris carefully turned the handle and slowly opened the door. The bedroom was scarcely furnished. Just a king size bed against the wall and a desk in front of two windows that looked out at the street. Moonlight cast a glow across the white carpet. Chew was fast asleep and snoring like a freight train, blissfully unaware of the intruders entering his space. Chris removed the SIG Sauer P226 with the SilencerCo suppressor Frank had given him from the back of his jeans and pointed it at Chew's head, pressing the tip of the suppressor against his temple. Alena stood behind Chris, reminding herself why they were breaking into this man's home.

Chew's eyes opened, and he felt the cold steel on his skin. His eyes met Chris's—a dark figure with a full beard staring down at him. He jumped up. Was about to scream when the intruder put his finger to his lips, silently informing him not to utter a sound. Chew nodded and froze in place, halfway sitting up and halfway leaning against his pillow.

"We're not here to hurt you," Chris said quietly.

"What do you want?" Chew replied, the words cracking as they left his mouth.

"I need information about the Nysta update."

• • •

Alena's laptop was open on Chew's bedroom desk. He was seated in front of it, still in his blue-checkered pajamas, with Chris and Alena hovering over him—the SIG still out and ready. Alena's phone was on the desk as well, recording the entire conversation. The tech genius stared at the images on the screen; he knew exactly what they were.

"This is not what you think it is," Chew said.

"Enlighten us, then," Alena replied.

Chris had anticipated leading the interrogation but decided to keep his mouth shut and see what Alena could get out of this rich asshole.

"You wouldn't understand," Chew said.

Alena's eyes narrowed. "Try me."

"Well, for starters, this is not an accurate representation of what a software update even is. There are a multitude of parts, like constructing a building—you have to look at the entire picture." He pointed at the screen. "This is just one of those parts."

"So stealing users' bank account information is 'just one of those parts'?"

"That's not what this is."

Chris pressed the gun against the back of Chew's head. "Stop lying."

"I'm not! This is standard information pulled from every site in the world. Yes, we sell the data, and yes, some people have an issue with it. But that's just how the internet works. It's marketing. It's business. "

"If what you're saying is true, then why was Amy Dotson attacked?" Alena asked.

"I don't know who that is."

"I find that hard to believe."

"Not my problem," Chew said impertinently.

"It is your problem, pal." Chris grabbed him by the throat, turned him around so that he was facing him, and pressed the gun against the side of his head. "Ms. Dotson was nearly killed hours after reporting her concerns about your 'software' update to HR. She was so scared when she left the office that she made two copies of this flash drive. Why would she do that?"

"I—I don't know. I swear I don't know. This is way below what

I deal with."

Both men stared at each other, sizing one another up. One was a hardened warrior, the other a spoiled Silicon Valley businessman. Alena broke the silence.

"How long have you been working for the Chinese Communist Party?" she asked.

Not what Chew expected to hear. "I don't know what you're talking about," he lied.

Chris was losing his patience. "I'm giving you one more chance before I put a bullet in your head."

Fear returned to Chew; this wasn't the world he lived in. "Fine. Fine! Can you just put that thing away? I don't like guns. They make me nervous."

Chris reluctantly lowered the pistol and stepped back, giving the man-child his space.

"Okay, yes, there *is* something going on with the update," Chew said. "But it's not what you think. We don't store information; we just collect it."

"Who has access to it?" Alena asked.

"I don't know."

"Not good enough," Chris said, returning the SIG to Chew's head. "You're lying."

"They'll kill me, man."

"What do you think I'll do…*man*?"

"I'm not the one in charge. I know it looks that way, but I just take orders."

Chew was sweating bullets and shaking. A wet spot appeared in the groin of his pajamas.

"Get yourself together," Chris said.

Chew took a deep breath. Then, "Everything is stored in a central database. Once the update goes through, Nysta will not have access to it. Whatever happens to users' personal information—it's out of my hands."

"Who runs the database?" Alena asked.

"Auspex Technology," Chew said. "They ordered the updated. Told us to build a virus. If you want to blame someone, blame them."

Chris's head snapped back at the mention of Auspex. He looked at Alena. The same company Congress approved to manage Nysta's data—to keep it out of Chinese hands—was the one stealing it.

She returned his gaze, verbalizing what they both already knew. "The largest data management company in the United States—responsible for network security across the country, including the CIA—has commissioned a virus that will steal *everything* from millions of Americans. The biggest cyber heist in history. Talk about corporations screwing the middle class. After this, there won't be a middle class."

Chris turned to Chew. "You know this for sure?"

The tech bro nodded. "This was always the plan when they received the contract from Congress. My job was to present the idea of Auspex hosting Nysta data on their servers, then build the update at an appropriate time. That's all I know." Tears formed in his eyes. "I had no choice. They threatened my family, my business. Everything I've worked for. And look—we don't know what they plan to do with this. It's all money, man."

"You got that right." Chris knew all too well what large corporations in bed with corrupt governments were capable of.

"How do we stop it?" Alena said.

Chew hesitated.

"Answer the fucking question," Chris said.

"I can't."

"I really don't feel like cleaning brain matter off this carpet," Chris replied.

"You can't do this."

Chris was finished talking. He lowered the SIG and pulled the trigger. Suppressed gunfire erupted as the bullet entered Chew's foot, splitting it in half and severing his big toe. He fell from his chair, screaming in agony.

"Next one goes in your head," Chris said. "Now answer the question."

Alena stood silently, her hand over her mouth. Chris's eyes were dark and cold. He had become an interrogator, and reason was no longer a tool.

"Help me! I'm going to bleed out!" Chew screamed.

Alena decided to tolerate the violence. "After you give us what we need to know."

Chris glanced at her, nodding his approval. She looked away in shame.

"Okay, okay," Chew said through tears. "I can stop it. But they'll kill me."

"What the hell do you think I'll do?" Chris said.

"Look, the update has been built and approved by Android and Apple app stores. That means the source code for the update has already been transferred to Auspex's central database."

"In English."

"The source code, it's the original code used to build the application. In this case, the update. And it controls everything. Whoever has that code would still be able to launch the update even if I stopped it from our end."

"What about the code on this flash drive? Would that work?" Alena asked.

"Source code means original—that's just a copy, nothing more than a duplicate. The whole point of Auspex handling data was to handicap us. We build it; they control it. It's that simple. The only thing I can do at this point is hit the little green button and approve the update's launch on the day it's scheduled. After that, it's on every user's phone or tablet the next time they connect to the internet—which means pretty much instantly."

"How long do we have?" Chris asked.

Alena knew the answer. She said, "Four days and four hours."

"Please help me. I'm losing blood," Chew pleaded.

Chris glanced down at him. The white carpet was now a rich burgundy, and Chew's face was growing pale. A few more minutes and he'd be useless.

"Okay," Chris said. "But I have one more question. Who do you work for?"

Chew breathed heavy as his pulse weakened. "I don't know."

"Yes, you do."

"I'm telling the…" His voice trailed off.

Chris grabbed him by the shirt and smacked him across the face.

Chew blinked. "You hit me."

"Your employer," Chris said.

"*I don't know!*"

"Bullshit!"

"They keep everyone in the dark."

"Who's *they*?" Alena asked.

"The people in charge."

Chris pressed the gun against Chew's wound. He screamed in

pain.

"Is that necessary?" Alena said.

Chris ignored her. His eyes locked on Chew's. "Who's calling the shots? I know you know, and I know you're scared of them. But right now, I'm the one you should be scared of."

Chew nodded, trying to suppress the desire to cry. "It was at a fundraiser in Dallas where I met Jean Mackler, Auspex Technology's CEO. We were getting heat for being a Chinese-owned social media app, and he had a solution. They handle domestic data management. I keep my company."

"Win-win," said Chris.

"I said no. Mackler has a reputation for pushing out his partners, and I still had visions of making it on my own. But then my investors approached me."

"SMIC," Chris said.

Chew nodded. "I never should have taken their money."

Chris's tone softened. "Tell me."

"One of their vice presidents came to my office. Told me this would keep Nysta operational. That I would be compensated for everything. He set up the entire thing—the deal with Congress, Auspex Technology's contract."

"Is he the one who threatened your family?" Alena asked.

Chew nodded. "It wasn't about the money. You have to believe me. I'm just a victim. That's how these guys work. They fund you, and then they own you. I haven't seen the man who came to my office since that day. But I know what will happen if I don't comply." He looked at Alena. "That's why they hurt your friend. She knew too much."

Chris stood up. They had more than enough information to bring to Kempe. He stopped the recording on the phone and leaned forward, looking Chew in the eyes.

"You have a first aid kit anywhere?"

"Bathroom."

Chris returned the SIG to the back of his jeans, then used both hands to help Chew stand.

"I'm going to fix you up, but you say nothing of this visit. Understand me?"

"I—I understand."

"If you don't, he'll kill you," Alena added.

Chris nearly choked in surprise at her words. It was almost funny—the woman who hated violence—but before he could smile at her and confirm her threat, the window shattered and a bullet landed in the wall behind them, missing his head by an inch. It was followed by the familiar cracking sound of a suppressed M4 as more shots entered the room in rapid succession.

CHAPTER 41

Erick focused the M4 carbine's mounted sight on the upstairs window of Chew's house and squeezed the trigger, each shot echoing through the quiet suburban street. There were two targets—if Chew got in the way there would be a third. Erick had failed once; he would not fail again. Nothing was going to stand between him and his revenge.

Inside, Chris instinctively dropped the CEO in his arms and dived toward Alena, hurling them both to the floor just in time for another onslaught of gunfire. Chew was not so lucky. Four rounds ripped into his chest and torso, passing through his body and knocking him to the floor. One punctured his lung, causing him to choke up blood as he writhed on the carpet, now covered with shattered glass and chunks of drywall.

SIG in hand, Chris crawled toward the now open window and peered out. More bullets erupted past his head, forcing him back inside.

"Shit."

He had no idea where the shooter was coming from. Not a sniper—if he were, they would already be dead. Chris aimed his pistol out the window and let off four shots, hoping to hit something. He didn't, and the shooter continued his attack, transforming the bedroom into a war zone—the bed riddled with bullets, cotton and drywall dust floating in the hazy air. Alena clung to the carpeting. She looked at Chew. His eyes were open, but he was not breathing.

Then the shooting stopped. Everything was calm, eerily so, and Chris knew whoever was outside was about to enter the house.

"We gotta move," he said.

He started for the door, still crawling on the floor. Alena followed, then stopped.

"The laptop," she said.

"Get it."

She reached up and grabbed the MacBook from the desk, then dropped back to the carpet and followed Chris. As soon as they entered the hallway, Chris stood up. He motioned for Alena to do the same. Then, SIG guiding the way, he carefully walked toward the staircase. Alena went behind him, clutching the laptop to her chest. With a two-handed grip and his finger on the trigger, Chris pointed the gun around the corner and aimed it down the staircase. No one was there, but the attacker could easily be waiting for them below, hidden from sight and ready to kill them as they descended the staircase. Chris used his right hand to motion for Alena to enter one of the guest bedrooms on the right. She nodded and slipped into the room. Chris followed, closing the door behind them but leaving it cracked to give him a visual of the hallway.

It felt like an eternity, but in reality, it was only seconds before they heard footsteps approaching the top of the staircase. Chris tightened his grip on the pistol, beads of sweat dripping down his forehead. He was a pro, had ended more human life than he cared to remember, but he was still scared. It was okay to be scared; in fact, it was preferred. One of his instructors back at the Kennedy Special Warfare Center in Fort Liberty, North Carolina had once told him: *"Fear makes a man vulnerable, and vulnerability pushes the human spirit to go beyond what it believes it's capable of."* Chris had found this to be true, and every time he ended up in a "sticky" situation, he would recite that quote in his head until his confidence returned.

Alena was shell-shocked—unable to process the amount of carnage she'd witnessed over the past two days and unable to fathom how she would ever make it out alive. She stared at the bear of a man in front of her—holding a gun, eyes ablaze—and hoped he would send whoever was after them straight to hell.

A dark figure appeared at the top of the stairs. Chris could make out the M4 rifle guiding the assassin through the darkness. This was his moment. He had the "higher ground." He raised the P226 toward the crack in the doorway and prepared for the shot. He would only get one. And even though lack of practice and training had robbed him of his marksmanship skills, he planned on hitting his target. The woman behind him was counting on it, and he'd be damned if he let her down. Target in focus. Finger on the trigger. He squeezed.

Three shots.

The figure dropped to the ground.

Without hesitating, the former Special Forces operative approached the person lying on the carpet, instantly recognizing him as the man who attacked them at the hospital. The brother of the man he killed in Colorado. The government-contracted assassin, Erick Webb.

Chris wasn't taking chances and fired two more rounds into the man. The body bounced as bullets slammed into his chest cavities.

"Let's go," Chris said.

Alena came out of the room. She stepped over the body.

"Is he—"

"Hurry!"

They needed to get out of the house before the police arrived. Wealthy neighborhoods rarely allowed people to fire automatic rifles into the night—especially in California where much of the population believed only criminals deserved to own guns. Alena followed the bearded warrior down the stairs, his gun guiding the way.

As soon as they reached the first floor, Chris checked the living room on the right and the hallway on the left for additional intruders. It was clear, and he motioned for Alena to follow him toward the front door. But as soon as his hand touched the handle, a bullet slammed into the wood beside him. He recoiled, pushing Alena back in the process, then aimed his weapon in the direction of the shot and fired three times. He dived to the right as more rounds flew past him and into the wall. That son of a bitch wasn't dead. Chris realized he must have been wearing body armor, and the rounds had only briefly knocked him unconscious.

Chris emptied his magazine in the direction of the shooter, then grabbed the spare in his back pocket and performed a tactical reload. He used a two-handed grip and inched his way around the banister. Alena was pinned against the hallway wall behind him.

The shooting stopped. The gunman was reloading as well. Chris put his left finger to his lips, instructing Alena to stay quiet. Then they waited. His right finger on the trigger. Ready.

They didn't have to wait long. Erick slid down the banister holding the M4 with one arm, steadying himself with the other.

The fully automatic rifle went off in succession, spraying the room with lead. Alena ducked as the bullets decimated the wall behind her. Gunpowder, drywall debris, and shell casings filled the air. Chris didn't have time to shoot back. Instead, he grabbed Erick's arm, forcing the rifle away, and yanked him over the banister to the hardwood floor. The assassin landed on top of Chris, causing him to drop his SIG. The handgun slid down the hallway, just out of reach. Chris swiftly landed a punch, but Erick countered with a firm blow to his head, followed by a front chokehold.

Chris struggled to break free, but the younger man was stronger. Unable to breathe, he gasped for air. Everything around him became a blur, and his head felt like it was about to explode. The hand pressed harder, forcing him in and out of consciousness. The smell of sweat and body odor filled his senses, then even that began to fade away. Goddammit, he wished he was younger. He struggled to find his knife. It was in its holster in his front pocket, and his attacker was on top of him, pressing against the very spot he needed to reach.

Erick used his free hand to bring up his own P226. Chris's vision was out of focus, but he knew what a gun looked like coming toward him. He thwarted the incoming weapon, clasping Erick's wrist and pushing the gun away from his face.

The barrel inched closer.

Fuck, this guy is strong.

As a last valiant survival effort, Chris wrapped his right leg around Erick's and twisted the kneecap. Erick winced in pain but stopped the leg from going further in the wrong direction. This action inadvertently caused him to relax his right arm, and the diversion was exactly what Chris needed to push the gun out of his face and use all of his upper body strength to flip Erick around and pin him on the floor. In the same motion, he pulled back Erick's hand to the point the wrist was about to crack, causing him to release his grip on the pistol entirely. The gun fell to the floor, but Erick countered with a series of side hooks, pummeling Chris's head.

More punches. More struggle. Then—

Out came Erick's Ka-Bar Bowie knife. The seven-inch steel blade went for Chris's shoulder—exactly where his heart was. Erick gripped the leather handle and pressed down. Chris stopped the forward thrust just as he felt the tip of the blade against his skin. He could finally breathe again, but the wind was still out of him, and it took everything he had to keep the knife from entering his chest cavity and piercing his heart.

Erick was now inches away from his target, his sweat dripping on Chris's face. His eyes were blazing with anger and hate. It was time to avenge his brother, and he could almost taste the blood that was about to be shed.

"I'm going to kill you, Harding," Erick said through clenched teeth.

Chris didn't have the energy to respond and instead focused on the knife piercing his skin, a fraction of an inch from destroying his heart. Alena was still pinned to the wall, scared to death, frozen in place—unsure what to do. She wanted to help, but her body couldn't move. Chris was struggling, and it dawned on her that he might not make it; he might not survive this one. The other man was significantly better trained—bigger, stronger, and younger—but most of all, he was angry. And he wasn't finished.

"And then I'm going to skin that bitch like a cow."

Somehow that last comment gave Chris the inner strength he needed.

Erick continued. "This is for my brother, you fucking—"

In one swift motion, Chris used his free hand to flip the knife around so that the blade was pointed at Erick's neck. It landed in his throat, and the force of his own weight pushed the blade through the trachea to the brain stem and out the back of his neck.

He choked on the last part of *fucking*, and his eyes widened. That brief moment before everything goes black, when one knows they are about to leave this world. Erick didn't have long to ponder this—or fully comprehend the fact that Chris had killed him just like he had killed his brother—before his soul left and his being was filled with darkness.

Chris pushed the limp body off and breathed a sigh of relief, relaxing his muscles as he came down from the adrenaline high of killing a man with a knife—the most intimate way to extinguish another human being.

Alena dropped to his side.

"Are you okay?"

"Yeah," he groaned. "Just need a second."

Alena glanced at Erick and the knife stuck through his neck. It was leaking blood all over the hardwood floor. She wanted to vomit.

"We gotta go," Chris said. He was still catching his breath.

Alena helped him stand up.

"My gun," he said.

Unbelievable, this guy. During the fight, the P226 had landed in the living room. Alena reluctantly got it for him, and he held onto it like a child holds a pacifier. Pistol in one hand, he turned his attention to the bloody corpse beside him.

"What are you doing?" Alena said.

"It's gotta be here."

He reached inside Erick's coat pocket. Sure enough, the burner phone was there. He extracted it and stuffed it in his own pocket. Then he tried to stand up and nearly fell over, would have if Alena hadn't steadied him.

"We have to get you to a hospital," she said, grabbing him by the shoulder.

"No, I'm good. I'll walk it off."

Alena frowned but said nothing. She helped Chris to the door, opening it with her left hand while propping him up with her right. As soon as the door opened, they were met with flashing red and blue lights and a sea of unmarked sedans and SUVs. Only it wasn't the police; it was the FBI.

Chris dropped his pistol and put his hands in the air as FBI agents stormed the front of the house. Alena did the same, but held onto her laptop. Chris counted at least twenty agents. Most of them were dressed in plain clothes and armed with either M4s or HK MP5s. They had on bulletproof vests and American flag baseball caps—just like the ones he had—and they all had beards. These guys were former military, the FBI's muscle, and it was doubtful they had any idea who Chris was, only that he was a threat. The rest of the agents were your average G-men in black suits, starched white dress shirts, and high-and-tight haircuts—zero facial hair. One of them, a hulk of a guy—nearly seven feet tall—approached them with a stern look on his face. His tie looked like it was strangling him, and he barely fit into the suit. His arms were the size of tree trunks.

"Chris Harding and Alena Moore, you are both under arrest for the murders of Andrew Chew, Frank Boone, and Susie Boone, and for conspiring to commit espionage." He pointed to the laptop. "I'm gonna need that, ma'am."

Alena was reluctant, but Chris gave her the go-ahead with a

nod, and she handed it over.

"And the flash drive," the agent said.

Alena's eyes flared with disgust as she removed the flash drive from her pocket. Everything they'd gone through, and now she was handing it over to the very people who had tried to kill them. The agent snatched it out of her hand, grunted, and walked away. Four other agents in suits handcuffed them and led them to a black GMC Yukon.

As they were stuffed into the backseat, Chris whispered to Alena, "They knew Chew was dead before they even went inside."

The door slammed shut behind them.

CHAPTER 42

*Dulles International Airport
Virginia*

The sunrise cast a blueish-orange glow across the snow- and ice-seared airstrip. Dan Greenwood arrived at Dulles International Airport in his 2023 Corvette Stingray and parked the red sports car in front of a private aircraft hangar. He had on a black leather jacket, matching black T-shirt and boots, and a pair of lived-in blue jeans. He packed light—a backpack and a Glock G21—everything else he needed would be on the ground. He boarded the Gulfstream that was waiting for him and took a seat in one of the cabin's plush leather seats.

The FBI raid on Andrew Chew's house was unexpected, but it made sense. House now had a viable reason to detain Harding and the reporter—evidence created by Greenwood's men—and had gone behind the private military contractor's back and used federal agents to make the arrest. Caleb and Erick Webb had proven useless, both dying at the hands of the very man they were contracted to kill.

If you want something done right, you do it yourself.

Once the jet reached cruising altitude, Greenwood called House. He wanted answers. The secure line rang several times before the FBI director picked up.

"This had better be good," House barked. He was just getting into the office and was still working his way through his morning Venti Starbucks Caffè Latte.

"What the hell happened in Oakland?"

"That's a very good question. Your man failed to deliver."

"You call me next time. A federal arrest is public. Someone might ask questions."

"Don't put this on me. I hired you because of your reputation as the best. That reputation turned out to be an exaggeration. So I took matters into my own hands."

Greenwood imagined pummeling the FBI director's head over and over again. But he kept his cool and replied, "What do you need me to do?"

"I need you to destroy that goddamn flash drive and finish the job I hired you to do. Harding and the reporter are being held at a secure location—literally locked in a room with no weapons. Think you can handle that?"

"It might help if I had a better understanding of what all this is about."

"Above your pay grade. Do the fucking job, or I'll find someone else who can."

"Roger that," Greenwood replied. *You piece of shit.*

He disconnected the call and stared out the window. Only clouds and sunlight as far as the eye could see. It was time to do what he did best.

CHAPTER 43

FBI Field Office
San Francisco, California

The FBI's field office was located near Union Square within a daunting glass-and-steel structure that looked more like a futuristic prison than a federal building. Chris knew it would be impossible to escape from, but he was relieved to be heading there. The alternative—some random house where they'd be killed upon arrival, like a mob hit—was worse. Still, his heart sank knowing he had let Alena down. His own family would be safe; he'd actually die this time, and any trace of his existence would dissolve into ancient history. Alena was equally upset. She was going to die. Her story would never see the light of day, and everything they'd gone through was for nothing.

They arrived as the sun broke the horizon. The Yukon pulled into an underground garage guarded by security cameras that were controlled by a team of FBI agents from somewhere inside the building. The SUV went down five levels and parked beside a row of similar-looking government fleet vehicles. The concrete jungle beneath the earth reminded Chris of the summer before. The summer he spent in Russia disarming a quantum computer that controlled Russia's entire arsenal of nuclear warheads.

The two agents in the front seat climbed out, and as Chris waited for them to open the backdoors, he glanced at Alena. It was a look that said, *I'm sorry*, and at the same time, he reached out—the best he could while being handcuffed—and squeezed her fingers. She squeezed back and smiled. He had done his best, and for that, she was thankful. Perhaps he wasn't just a bearded madman after all. Their brief moment was halted when the agents opened the doors and pulled them both out of the vehicle.

They were led through the parking garage to a single door. Both agents had their sidearms drawn, cautious to a fault and probably upset that they had been stuck transporting the prisoners. Chris laughed inside at the incompetence of the federal government. They couldn't even supply these men with enough backup to properly transport two *highly dangerous criminals*.

The agents scanned their badges and stared up at the security cameras. They were granted access and through the doorway they went. A stark off-white hallway with green tiled floors came next. At the end of the hallway was another door. Another security confirmation from the cameras, another hallway, around a corner—Chris was keeping track of their direction—and finally, they stopped in front of a thick steel door. One of the agents typed in a code on a keypad connected to the handle. Chris couldn't see, but he heard six beeps—a six-digit code—and the door swung open.

Chris and Alena were pushed inside, and the door was slammed shut behind them. The sound of the automatic bolt lock was startling, not shocking. The room was small. It had gray carpet and a small table with four plastic chairs around it—very similar to the last FBI holding cell Chris had been in, only this one was newer and didn't smell like mold and cigarettes. Speaking of cigarettes, he could use one, but the goddam smokes were back in the stolen Toyota.

"Those assholes could have at least taken these things off," Alena complained, pulling at the handcuffs. "They hurt."

Chris didn't respond. He was exhausted. The adrenaline rush from the night before had subsided, and his body was now dealing with the repercussions of intense hand-to-hand combat with a much younger man. He took a seat in one of the plastic chairs. It felt like heaven.

Alena dropped to the chair beside him. She was terrified, and talking was what she did when she was afraid.

"What happens next?" she asked.

"We wait," Chris replied.

"For how long? Are they going to kill us? If they *were* going to kill us, wouldn't they have done it already? Or are they taking us to some supermax prison in the middle of nowhere?"

"I don't know."

She imagined what it would feel like to die. She had come close many times over the past couple of days, but now it actually felt real—her life was about to come to an end.

Unless, she thought. "Do you have a plan?"

"No."

"Why are you so quiet?" Then it dawned on her. "You've been in this situation before."

He finally looked at her. His eyes were tired, but they confirmed her suspicion.

Perhaps there was hope. *He's done this before, and he's still alive.*

"What happened last time?"

Chris stared at the handcuffs, remembering his conversation

with FBI Special Agent Adam Conner—the man who recruited him for Woodhaven, now dead, murdered in his own home.

"I was given a choice," Chris said quietly.

Nysta and Auspex were in bed with China. The FBI was involved. These were facts. Was the cyberattack real? Or had they stumbled upon a federal investigation and this was all a mistake? That's what happened last time. The FBI turned out to be the good guys. Perhaps this was no different. *That's wishful thinking*, he told himself.

"What kind of choice?" Alena asked.

Before Chris could respond, the deadlock on the door turned. Alena shot him a look of desperation, hoping for reassurance. He was unable to give it to her.

The door opened, and a woman appeared in the doorway. She was alone. Chris gasped. She was the last person he expected to see. She was wearing a black suit and a white blouse that still managed to show off her perfect breasts. Her hair and makeup were different, but her green eyes were the same.

"Hi, Chris," Natalya Palmer said as she entered the room and closed the door behind her.

CHAPTER 44

"When you didn't make contact, I assumed you were dead," Chris said, standing up.

"Never make assumptions," Natalya said. "However you're only partially incorrect. *Officially*, I am dead."

Alena was confused. "You two know each other?"

"A little bit," Natalya said, breaking a smile. "And you are Alena Moore from the *New York Times*."

"Who are you?"

"Alena, this is Natalya Palmer. We worked together," Chris explained.

"Worked together—yeah, I know what that means," Alena replied, eyeing Natalya.

"Al Kempe sent me to get you both out," Natalya said. "We don't have much time."

"I'm not going anywhere with you," Alena said.

"That's your choice, but you will die if you stay here."

"We can trust her," Chris said. He wasn't entirely sure they could.

Alena hesitated but relented. The bearded man had kept her alive this long.

"Okay," she said. "But not without my laptop, and—"

"I already have the flash drive," Natalya said. "You're going to have to get a new laptop."

"My entire life is on that computer."

"Then stay put. Like I said—your choice."

Alena fumed. "*Fine!*"

"Glad you're coming. All right, plan is simple: You're my prisoners. Make it believable."

She opened the door and led them—still handcuffed—down the hallway the way they had come earlier with the FBI agents. Chris eyed the security cameras and wondered how Natalya had acquired an ID with security clearance. When they arrived at the door to the parking structure, Natalya veered right into a stairwell. They went up a single flight of stairs and then through a door leading to another level of the parking structure. It was filled with Ford Mustangs and GMC Yukons, all black and sporting "Government Exempt" license plates. Natalya picked one of the sports cars nearest the door and unlocked it with a key fob. She forced Chris and Alena into the backseat, guiding their heads like a cop would during an arrest. She then got behind the wheel, pressed the start button—the V8 engine rumbled as it fired up—and hit the gas. The tires squealed as the vehicle spun around the corners up to the ground level, where it exited into the morning sunshine.

The ride was bumpy—Mustangs aren't known for comfortable backseats—and Natalya was not taking them on a joy ride. She weaved in and out of traffic, dodging San Fransisco commuters in their Teslas and electric scooters. Once they put some distance between them and the FBI building, Natalya tossed a pair of keys into the backseat.

"You can get out of those cuffs now."

NEW BEGINNING

Chris caught the keys mid-air, freed himself, and then did the same for Alena.

"There's a brand new SIG P226-XFIVE LEGION behind the passenger seat," Natalya said. "I know you love your Beretta, but this is the best I could do in a pinch. Personally, I think it's an upgrade."

Chris retrieved the black Pelican case and removed the 9mm pistol from its foam interior. He checked the magazine, found it full, and reinserted it, admiring the beautiful craftsmanship of the SIG Sauer handgun.

"It'll do just fine," he said, stuffing the weapon into the side of his jeans.

Watching Natalya drive reminded Chris of the first time they met. She had picked him and his team up in the middle of the night and driven them to Moscow. It was the start of the mission that forever changed his life—made him a ghost and permanently separated him from his life and family.

"Last thing I heard, you were undercover in Beijing," he said. "Where have you been the past six months?"

"Surviving," Natalya replied.

Back to that night, six months ago, in her apartment in the capital city of the People's Republic of China. She recounted how she had discovered the AI chips purchased by Adham Mostafa, how her cover was compromised, and her encounter with Feng Chen.

"Feng Chen?" Alena said. She shot Chris a confused look.

"Yes," Natalya confirmed, making a hard right turn that nearly threw Alena into Chris's lap. "Chinese Ministry of State Security—he'd been following me for weeks, at least."

She explained how he had detailed information on Woodhaven—specifically the safe house in Islamorada—and that she had tried to warn Adam Conner.

"It was too late," she said.

After Chen left, she knew she was done for. It wouldn't be a firing squad or a black ops attack; it would be something the press could label an "accident." That's when it clicked. They were going to kill her with a bomb. The only way to survive an explosion inside a building is—

"You pulled an Indiana Jones," Chris said.

"What?"

"When he hides inside the fridge to escape the nuclear explosion in the desert."

"I don't remember that."

"It's from the 2008 movie."

"Heard it was awful. Haven't seen it. But yes, I hid inside the fridge."

"That actually works?" Alena asked.

"Barely—I blacked out. When I came to, the fridge was halfway out the side of the building, and everything was on fire." She raised her blouse, revealing third-degree burn scars on her side. "Anyway, that wasn't the worst of it. Getting out of China was impossible, so I got an old contact to stow me away on a cargo ship. Twenty days in a cargo container with nothing but beef jerky and protein bars. Not a fun time."

She merged onto the 101 freeway heading south. Chris wasn't ready to recount his own near-death experience, but Natalya's story was reassuring. Perhaps she could be trusted.

"What did Kempe tell you?" he asked.

"Everything you told him."

"There's been some developments."

"Hold that thought. There's a chartered plane waiting for us at the Palo Alto Airport. Kempe wants a full debrief once we're in the air."

"Where are we going?" Alena asked.

Natalya ignored her. "Chris, there's something else you need to know." She removed an iPad from her purse on the passenger seat and passed it back to him. "You and I weren't the only ones to survive the Woodhaven hit."

He swiped up on the tablet. His eyes widened in disbelief when he saw what was on the screen.

Impossible.

"When was this taken?"

"Yesterday," Natalya replied. "The police weren't the only ones looking for you after your APB."

Chris stared at the grainy photograph of a truck driving through what appeared to be the downtown area of a small town. There were three people inside: Roland Anderson, Tricia Perkins, and George Hartman.

He looked up at Alena and said, "We're going to Eastern Kentucky."

CHAPTER 45

Greenwood arrived in San Francisco and took a rented car to the FBI field office, where he was taken to the evidence vault to pick up the flash drive the nearly seven-foot-tall agent had extracted from Alena. Whatever was on it was worth a multi-million dollar contract on Amy Dotson and Alena Moore. But the only item in evidence was Moore's MacBook Air—the flash drive was nowhere to be found.

Greenwood handed the laptop back to the agent in charge of evidence.

"There's no flash drive."

The man shrugged. "I know. Someone already picked it up."

"What do you mean, 'someone already picked it up?' I'm supposed to pick it up."

"I don't know what to tell you."

"Could you tell me who it was?"

The agent sighed—he wasn't getting paid enough for this—and hit a few buttons on his ten-year-old desktop computer.

"An *Agent N* checked it out ninety-two minutes ago."

"N?"

"Yeah, that's all it says. Authorized by the director himself, though."

"You don't remember who it was?"

"I was on lunch."

Greenwood stared at the middle-aged man before him. He smelled of Burger King and body odor and wore a cheap suit that draped over his flabby frame like a poncho.

"You're a moron."

• • •

A young FBI agent fresh out of Quantico escorted Greenwood to the holding cell where Chris and Alena had been detained. Leaving the kid standing in the hallway, he entered alone. The room was void of security cameras to allow for more "inventive" forms of interrogation, something Greenwood planned to take full advantage of. Neither were leaving that cell alive.

The room was empty. Just plastic chairs and a table. Hoping he'd been sent to the wrong cell, he exited, leaving the door open.

"It's empty."

"Uh..." the young agent stammered.

"Are you retarded?"

"I don't think so."

"Then tell me this is the correct cell."

"Uh, yes, sir, it is."

Something was terribly wrong.

"I need to see your security camera footage *right now*."

• • •

The security office was a dark room filled with dozens of computers, and the blue glow from the screens illuminated the pale-faced guards who spent their days watching security cameras and monitoring every square foot of the building. The young agent led Greenwood to the watch commander at the front of the office. He looked up from his coffee and donuts as they approached. A big man he was—fat was the best word for it—and Greenwood wondered how he ever made it through the Farm.

"I need to see your evidence vault and level D security footage for the past three hours," Greenwood said.

The watch commander looked him up and down. "I'll need authorization for that."

Greenwood laughed as he unholstered his Glock and pointed it at the fat man's head.

"You've been authorized."

Thirty seconds later, Greenwood was staring at the footage on the commander's own computer. The evidence vault video was conveniently "unavailable" so he begrudgingly settled for the level D footage. A beautiful woman entered the frame, unlocked the door with a badge, and went inside. After two minutes she reemerged, this time with Chris and Alena in tow. Greenwood shook his head at the incompetence—in typical government fashion, not a single one of those morons in the security office had noticed the prisoners' escape.

He slowed the video and stopped on the woman, using the control to zoom in on her face. It was grainy, but he knew he recognized her. He pulled up an archived email on his phone—the Woodhaven Kill Package—and scanned through the file, finally stopping on a photograph of Natalya Palmer. He held the phone up to the computer monitor for a comparison. It was an exact match. Chris Harding was not the only one to survive.

CHAPTER 46

The Palo Alto Airport was little more than a parking lot for aircraft rentals and chartered planes. No major airlines operated on-site. Natalya drove directly onto the airstrip and parked the Mustang beside an impressive white and blue Gulfstream G650 that was fueled up and ready to go. Chris and Alena got out of the car and followed Natalya up the ramp to the jet. Alena was taking each new experience in stride. She had written about contract killers, government plots, and private jets filled with spies but never dreamed she would end up a part of it all. The inside of the Gulfstream was nothing short of luxury. There were six cream-colored leather seats with wood trim, a TV mounted on the wall, and a kitchen and bedroom behind the main cabin. Natalya explained that the aircraft was leased by a chartered aviation firm called Maritime Inc., which Kempe owned a majority interest in. It was outfitted with the latest cybersecurity technology, making it the perfect "safe house" in the air.

The pilot was a former Agency man named Jack O'Brien. He was in his late sixties and had a mane of white hair protruding from a Boston Red Sox ball cap. He was a close friend of Kempe's going back to Iraq in the 1980s, further insuring that conversations aboard the aircraft would remain private.

As soon as they were wheels up, Natalya connected an iPad to a USB port on her chair's armrest, and a few seconds later, Al Kempe appeared on the mounted TV—through a secured conference call—in front of a backdrop of palm trees and white sand, wearing a colorful Hawaiian shirt and a straw hat. Natalya positioned the iPad so that he could see.

"You look homeless," the general said, eyeing Chris's untamed beard.

"Says the man on vacation."

"Retirement." He paused to light a cigar, then said, "Until you called, we thought Natalya was the only one to survive."

"Do you have confirmation that my team is still alive?"

"Not a hundred percent, but our intel is strong. The photograph Natalya showed you was taken yesterday. She did some digging. I'll let her explain."

Natalya took her cue. "I looked into hospital records in Florida. Four individuals with severe brain trauma and third-degree burns were admitted into Ryder Trauma Center at Miami's Jackson Memorial—no record of their passing away."

"Four? Terry wasn't in that picture," Chris said.

"You were the fourth one. Somehow you were separated from Roland, Tricia, and George at intake." She paused. "It looks like Terry did not make it. Records indicated that a male in his thirties was found deceased on the scene. They weren't able to identify the body, but…"

Her voice trailed off when she saw the look on Chris's face. Alena saw it too. This was a man who rarely showed emotion—a stoic warrior who pushed forward no matter what—but in this moment his eyes betrayed him as he remembered his last conversation with Terry.

"He wanted to get out," Chris said quietly.

"What are you talking about?" Natalya replied.

"Get out. Move on. He was finished with Woodhaven." Chris looked at the screen and the aging spymaster. "Our entire mission was for nothing. There was no viable intel for a whole year. A whole *goddamn* year! We weren't making a difference—if anything, we were just another government agency paid to push papers and pretend like we were serving our country. But you know what happened. We didn't have a choice. Terry didn't have a choice."

He stopped, catching himself. His voice had risen and his body was shaking. Alena touched his arm, not unnoticed by Natalya or Kempe.

"It's okay," she said.

"Sorry—this is a lot for me to take in."

"Completely understand," Kempe said. "I wouldn't expect you to react any other way. This is no longer your fight. You and the Anderson team will all receive new identities. You can finally move on with your lives." He took a puff of his cigar. "But first I need to know everything you learned from Andrew Chew."

Chris nodded. He took a deep breath, calming himself. "It's not good. Nysta's majority shareholder, SMIC, orchestrated the deal with Congress to give Auspex Technology control over Nysta's user data. Auspex is responsible for the software update—so it's impossible to stop—and SMIC is controlled by the Chinese Communist Party, who more than likely put the contract on Alena and her friend Amy. And just to make things more complicated, the FBI is involved. Not sure how far up it goes, but they're using Greenwood Enterprises to do their dirty work—same group responsible for going after my team. I think there's a connection between all this and Woodhaven. I just don't know what."

Kempe's eyes narrowed. "Are you sure Chew was being honest?"

"I am. He was scared, not just for himself, but for his family in China."

Kempe nodded, his eyes darting to Natalya, then back to Chris.

"What exactly do you know about Woodhaven?" he asked.

Chris shrugged. "Gray group funded by the FBI to track and stop NWO activity."

"Woodhaven began under the name *Counterstrike* shortly after 9/11 as a way to combat al-Qaeda—a covert CIA program designed to track terrorist activity both domestically and abroad. The New World Order came later after we discovered that not only were they funding al-Qaeda's operations, but they were the ones responsible for the attack on the World Trade Center and the Pentagon."

"Oh my God," Alena said.

"It was a long-term plan, spanning decades, to weaken the United States from within—create political discourse, economic turmoil, and ultimately, prime the country for the final attack: the big one that will change the course of history forever."

As if rehearsed, Natalya chimed in. "That's when we discovered the New World Order and their connection to the Chinese Communist Party. We didn't know who was calling the shots, but we knew the CIA was compromised. It was time to go dark. But before we could, they wiped out my entire team."

Chris was not surprised. Natalya had always been a woman of secrets—the ultimate spy who never revealed more than necessary.

"It's a lot to take in, Chris," Kempe said. "But you have to understand the stakes. Natalya was deep, *deep* cover, and the CIA had no idea she was involved. That meant we were able to continue Counterstrike through her. My involvement had always been silent. However, I had close ties with former FBI Director Aden Smith, and he agreed to continue the operation, renamed Woodhaven. The FBI funded Woodhaven through secret channels—just like we did at the Agency. Then we discovered the quantum computer and Harry Price's plot to start a war with Russia. You know the rest."

Price was a prominent weapons manufacturer in the U.S. who planned a chemical attack and blamed it on Russia in order to obtain billions in DOD contracts. Chris and the Anderson team had taken him down and were subsequently recruited by Adam Conner to join Woodhaven. They had not been given much of a choice in the matter. It was, *join us or die*.

"I had my suspicions," Kempe continued. "This is not unlike what happened with the CIA. But your intel confirms my worst fear: the New World Order—through its proxy, the Chinese Community Party—has infiltrated the FBI, leaving us, once again, compromised. We need your help, Chris."

Alena's mind was blown. The Nysta story had ballooned into something she could never have imagined, and for the first time in days, she wasn't thinking about her safety; she was thinking about the biggest story of her career—a secret organization pulling the strings of a nation and changing the course of history. Any thought of leaving and going at it alone was now off the table. She was going to see this through, even if it meant putting up with the bitch beside her, the old man on the screen, and the bearded guy she was weirdly attracted to.

Chris shook his head. "I already fought for my country. See

where it got me? I can't speak for Roland, George, or Trish, but I don't anticipate them jumping back in either."

"You don't have to say yes," Kempe said. "We'll drop you and Ms. Moore off in Kentucky, along with everything you need to start a new life. You've already done more than enough. We just ask that you do it one last time."

Chris didn't respond.

"This software update must be stopped," Natalya said. "No matter what their plan is for it, Americans' sensitive financial information cannot end up in the hands of the Chinese. There's no one else to stop them but us. And I can't do it alone. I need the Anderson team. I need Roland, Tricia, and George." She paused. "And I need you…David."

Chris locked eyes with the beautiful spy as he remembered a night in Moscow when he told her that the biblical story of David and Goliath was what motivated him to move forward in the face of adversity. He was scared, unable to decipher the web of lies that surrounded him. But he had been betrayed. Left for dead. Terry had lost his life, days before retiring, and Frank and Susie had been murdered in cold blood. Their deaths needed vengeance. This was his chance.

The former soldier knew what he had to do.

"I need a cigarette," he said.

Natalya smiled and gave him a pack of Marlboro Lights and a Bic lighter from her jacket. He eagerly lit one and took a long drag.

"Okay," he said. "On one condition."

"Anything," said Natalya.

"Keep Alena out of this. I promised to keep her safe, and I intend to keep my word. Her involvement needs to be classified—no new identity, no witness protection."

Alena smiled at him, then stopped smiling when he smiled back.

Stop flirting—this isn't the time.

"I think that can be arranged," Kempe said.

"I need your word."

"You have it."

Chris nodded. "Can't guarantee the rest of the team will go along, but I'll do my best to convince them."

"All we can ask for," Kempe said.

Chris took another drag from the cigarette. "One more thing—I get to put a bullet in the head of the person responsible for this."

CHAPTER 47

Washington, D.C.

"I thought you hated these things, Steven."

The FBI director looked up from his untouched vodka soda to find Congresswoman Robin Valencia leaning against the bar beside him, her eyes locked on his. She didn't wait for him to respond. Instead, she motioned for the bartender.

"I'll have a glass of red wine, please," she said. "Any type of cab will do."

The bartender nodded and went about getting her drink.

Valencia returned her attention to House. "Christmas parties. A waste of time, a waste of money." A glass of wine landed in front of her. She took a sip. "But entirely necessary."

The glittering party was hosted by a prominent D.C. lobbyist and included an open bar and catered menu from one of the top chefs in the city. An extravagant Victorian-era mansion in Georgetown served as the venue, and the guest list brought together the most influential players in U.S. government—men and women who shaped the future of the nation, all dressed in formal attire and drinking and scheming their way through the night.

NEW BEGINNING

"Nature of the job, I suppose." House said, taking a sip of his vodka.

Valencia looked around the room. "Sometimes I wonder how I ended up here."

She was beautiful as much as she was fierce. Her brown hair accentuated her hazel eyes and petite frame. Born and raised in Los Angeles, her mother was a Black school teacher from Louisiana, and her father had immigrated to the United States from Mexico as a boy. Social injustice kept her family from receiving the opportunities they deserved, specifically her father, whose immigration status only changed a year before he died of cancer. This was after a life spent working manual labor jobs. His version of the American dream. Despite a lifelong dedication to educating the children of wealthy families, her mother struggled to earn a livable wage. Valencia blamed a flawed system and the white men who controlled it—businessmen whose sole purpose was to make a dollar, regardless of the human cost.

Valencia had chosen not to have kids until the country progressed into a place where all men and women were equal. She was a bartender through college, and as part of a new generation of politicians, used social media to build a following. Now in her mid-thirties, she was one of youngest, yet most prominent, congresswomen in Washington, D.C., using the very system she sought to change to bring about the world she envisioned.

House did not agree with many of her tactics—like destroying her opponents with social justice warriors on Instagram and X—but he admired her tenacity.

"Everything is going according to plan," he said.

She smiled. "I never doubted it. There's just one thing I wanted to speak with you about." She twirled the red liquid in her glass.

"Andrew Chew."

"A tragedy we are thoroughly investigating. Those responsible will be brought to justice. That I can assure you."

She nodded. "Of course. But I want press on you the importance of timing. This bill is revolutionary in every way, and we only have five days until I take it before Congress. No amount of politicking will alter the outcome if you don't follow through."

"Sometimes I think you forget who you're speaking with, Congresswoman."

"I remember the man whose wife and children love him. A man who will do anything to protect them from knowing things they should not."

She took out her iPhone and navigated to a series of photographs before pointing the screen at House. "I really hate doing this—makes me feel like a bitch—but we're cutting it close here."

He knew what was on the screen before he saw it, but he looked nevertheless. The girl was no more than fifteen years old. Valencia swiped to another picture. Another girl, same bedroom, same lustful look on House's face as he enjoyed her company.

"I remember when I was fifteen," the congresswoman said as she returned the phone to her purse.

House said nothing. He was well aware of the power this young woman wielded over him. Without it, he never would have agreed to facilitate such a harrowing attack on the country. But politics was a dirty game, and weekends on the island with senators, congressmen, and titans of business would not stand in his way. Like the representative from California, he would do whatever it took to survive.

"No mistakes," Valencia said. She finished her glass of wine. "Merry Christmas, Steven."

She left him at the bar, and he watched her walk away, his eyes narrowing. He motioned for the bartender. "Another."

CHAPTER 48

Chinese Communist Party Headquarters
Beijing, China

The lush gardens and lakes of Zhongnanhai bring tourists from all over the world, and its ancient Chinese architecture was nothing short of magnificent. The main entrance was a plethora of red and gold with blue trim and green-accented arches. The Taiye Lake had an island in the middle—General Secretary Zi Jinping's personal residence—and was home to an imperial garden and surrounded by palaces, temples, and shrines. Located directly beside the Forbidden City, the compound referred to by many as the "Gate of New China" was home to the most senior levels of the Chinese Communist Party leadership. Feng Chen had only been there twice before, and each time it engulfed him in awe at what his country had achieved.

Security was intense. Chen was required to go through multiple checkpoints before he was allowed to park his Honda and transfer to the Hongqi N701 government vehicle that would take him to the island. As the car traveled over the bridge, Chen thought about the meeting that was about to take place. This was unlike any other invitation he'd received to Zhongnanhai. He was expected to report to the Politburo Standing Committee, the defacto leaders of the CCP that answered to the Central Committee. Led by Zi Jinping, the committee was made up of seven men—Western-educated politicians whose intellect and ruthless desire to make China the greatest nation in the world was second to none—and met weekly in a marble-floored chamber where they oversaw the entire country. This was the heart and soul of the most powerful communist regime in the world.

Chen both admired and feared them. But on this bright, sunny day, it was mainly fear that pervaded his thoughts. He'd been the one to discover the American spy, he'd taken care of the issues that had plagued the mission, and now it was his job to instill confidence in the committee that the next phase would run smoothly and without incident.

He'd done his job—albeit a few mistakes along the way, all of which could have been avoided if the American government wasn't so incompetent. But no matter, the die had been cast. The Nysta virus would drop, and there was no way to stop it. Today was one of the most important days in Chen's life. His purpose fulfilled. The United States would fall within the week, and China would pick up the pieces and create a new nation in its place.

• • •

Zi Jinping left Chen waiting for over an hour inside a sitting room adjacent to the general secretary's office. Ancient books adorned the walls, and colorful rugs covered the centuries-old hardwood floor. The furnishings were traditional Chinese designs—elaborate woodwork made by the greatest craftsmen the world had ever seen. Chen enjoyed the wait. It was an honor to spend time in a place shrouded in such rich history.

The general secretary entered through a pair of double doors. He was in his seventies and had a thick head of hair parted to the side and a blue suit with a CCP pin on his left lapel. Nearly six feet tall, he towered over Chen—both in grandeur and height.

"*Tóngzhì, xièxiè nǐ jiàn wǒ,*" Jinping said.

In Mandarin it meant: *Comrade, thank you for seeing me.*

"*Zhè shì wǒ de róngxìng, zǒng shūjì.*"

The pleasure is all mine, General Secretary.

"Have a seat," Jinping said, motioning to two couches in the middle of the room.

Once both men were seated opposite each other, the Chinese leader began.

"I've read your report. You have done your country well. The Americans will not see what is coming until it is too late."

"I am pleased you approve, sir."

"President David Douglas is a weak, old man, pandering to a lazy and cowardly people. But he is pliant and will do what we ask of him. Unfortunately, the same cannot be said for all those in American government."

He snapped his fingers. Chen waited in silence as another door opened and a young woman entered carrying an iPad. She gave it to Jinping, took a bow, and exited as quickly as she came. The general secretary swiped up on the screen and handed the tablet to Chen.

"This is why you've been called here today," Jinping said.

Chen stared in disbelief at the grainy photograph of Natalya Palmer exiting a Chinese shipping container at the Port of Los Angeles.

"This can't be," Chen said.

"You underestimated your enemy, comrade. This operation has been the work of many months and will result in the largest cyberattack in history. It will level the United States—bring them to their knees—and as they fall, we will rise as the economic leader of the world."

Panic took hold of the usually calm and collected intelligence officer. "I can make this right."

"It is not only Palmer we are concerned about. Andrew Chew was a liability that should have been taken care of."

"Chew has been terminated."

"But not before he spoke with American agents."

Jinping stood up, prompting Chen to do the same.

"The decision has been made, Agent Chen. It's out of my hands now. You have served your country well. And your family will be dutifully rewarded."

• • •

The Central Committee was waiting inside their marble meeting hall when Jinping entered. And as the general secretary took his seat at the head of the large mahogany table, gunfire sounded in the distance. Outside the ancient building, at the edge of the island—against a stone wall—Feng Chen was executed by firing squad. His last thoughts, before a dozen bullets filled his body, were of his father.

"I did my duty, Father. I did my duty."

CHAPTER 49

Pikeville, Kentucky

EASTERN KENTUCKY WAS a quiet place to live, far from the outside world. The same could be said for the Pikeville/Pike County Regional Airport. It was barely an airport, more like a cluster of sheet-metal hangars and a terminal the size of a one-bedroom apartment in the middle of a cornfield surrounded by rural country. A layer of snow had already accumulated on the frosted ground as more flurries filled the air. A winter storm was brewing—forecasters calling it one of the worst snowstorms to hit the East Coast in decades.

The Gulfstream from California landing at 8:15 p.m. was an unexpected sight for the two people who worked at the airport. Even more surprising was that O'Brien had called ahead and reserved a rental car—which turned out to be a 1995 Ford F-150 that smelled like tobacco and engine oil. Chris, Alena, and Natalya deplaned and were immediately hit with below-freezing temperatures. Even the air smelled cold. Thankfully the chartered jet came supplied with winter coats, hats, and gloves. O'Brien stayed behind. He would refuel the plane and remain onboard until the team was ready to leave.

It was ordinarily a twenty-minute drive to Pikeville, but the two-lane highway was covered in black ice and falling snow, making it difficult to see, so Chris took it slow, doubling their trip to nearly forty minutes. As they neared the town center, the highway widened to four lanes, making way for fast food restaurants and gas stations. The few vehicles on the road seemed to be either full-size trucks or mid-'90s Camaro Z28s. Chris hadn't been to Pikeville in decades. Everything felt foreign yet familiar at the same time. They passed a 24-hour Walmart, and he was immediately taken back to high school—hanging out in the parking lot trying to pick up girls while devouring Mountain Dew and Taco Bell. He swore he'd never return to Pikeville, but here he was, back at Walmart, at night, as if twenty-two years had dissolved into thin air.

Pikeville was part of a lost generation of small towns that had withered with time. These staples of twentieth-century Americana were once flourishing, self-contained communities. Until the mid-1990s, there would have been a drug store, a barbershop, lots of restaurants and bars. Even a local newspaper. These days, the town relied heavily on the University of Pikeville and the manufacturing facility, SilverLiner, to provide jobs. That moved the population from the town center to the suburbs, with its strip malls and chain restaurants. Downtown, though well-maintained, was but a shadow of its former glory.

Chris found himself lost in nostalgia as he watched a nine-year-old version of himself peddle his way down the sidewalk on a red bicycle, dodging pedestrians on the way to Fitch's IGA, the local grocery store that was somehow still in business after sixty-five years. He'd have fifty cents in his pocket—enough to buy himself an RC Cola and a candy bar. They passed the old gas station, which had changed names and faces over the years, but to Chris would always be "Pa's," the single-pump station that doubled as a mini-diner serving up fried chicken and milkshakes. The eleven-year-old version of himself had gone on his first date there. Calling it a date was generous. In reality, he and a girl on his swim team had walked there after practice for Cokes. He wondered what ever happened to that little girl—the skinny kid with brown hair that matched her eyes.

Back to reality. They arrived at the only hotel in town, a surprisingly modern and luxurious Hampton Inn. Natalya had reserved three rooms, and they checked in with the high school kid working the night shift. They paid with a prepaid debit card supplied by Kempe, then walked two blocks to the town's only late-night eatery, a 24-hour diner with Christmas lights dangling from its mid-century neon sign. Inside, there were a couple of old men in trucker hats sipping coffee at the counter while an overweight cook with three teeth worked the griddle—frying up burgers, chicken, and fries.

Chris, Alena, and Natalya took a booth in front of the window looking out at the street. It was a slow night and the waitress appeared instantly. She was pretty, in her early twenties, and was sporting a University of Kentucky sweatshirt—probably a college graduate who ended up back in her hometown. Everyone ordered coffee. Cream and sugar for the ladies and black for Chris. Natalya took a KryptAll phone and a MacBook Pro from her bag and set them on the table.

"We need to make contact as quickly as possible," she said to Chris. "I don't plan on being here any longer than I have to."

He nodded. The only place the Anderson team could remain ghosts would be at George's compound. As a survivalist who didn't trust the government, George had spent his entire adult life in a house in the middle of the woods. Nearly impossible to find, and completely off-grid, George's home was filled with weapons, computers, and every type of high-tech surveillance gear imaginable. He could have been a programmer at Facebook, or even Nysta. Instead, he was a professional hacker who had spent his days alone until he joined the Anderson team.

But Chris wasn't entirely sure they would be there. George's phone number no longer worked. Chris had tried the secure line multiple times in the weeks and months following the explosion—hoping and praying for some kind of response—and just like then, when he dialed the number on the KryptAll phone Natalya had given him, there was no answer. The best way to contact them would be through the dark web. That was how George maintained access to the outside world without compromising his location.

Chris used the MacBook to send a coded message on a dark web chat room filled with patriotic survivalists, libertarians, and anarchists.

> **To the Harvard Man: meet me on the bridge. Confirm time.**

Roland was the "Harvard Man" and the location was a place only George would recognize. Chris logged out of the chat room. It was now a waiting game.

The food arrived, all greasy and hot—southern cooking at its finest—and everyone devoured their dinner in silence, the air as thick as the butter on the hamburgers in front of them. Natalya was silent to a fault, staring out the frosted window as she ate. Alena didn't trust her. Not one bit. And she was scared for her life, while at the same time struggling with her growing affection for the bearded man beside her. Chris ate his food and downed three cups of coffee. He felt the tension the most—two women who disliked each other, an impossible mission, questions that needed answers, and the hope that his friends were still alive.

Alena broke the silence. "How did you two meet?"

There was an awkward pause as Chris made eye contact with Natalya. She shrugged, giving him the opening to answer the question.

"Natalya was our CIA point person in Russia. Of course she turned out to be a double agent. Roland and I almost died in a helicopter crash because of her."

"That's not entirely accurate," the blond spy retorted.

"We thought she betrayed us," Chris explained.

"I made up for that in Irvine."

"Yes, she did." Chris smiled. "We learned that she had been working for Kempe as a covert FBI operative all along."

"I see," Alena said, picking at her food. "And you two never—"

"*Absolutely not*," Natalya said sharply. "Our relationship was strictly professional."

"It was," Chris said.

Alena eyed them both, then nodded, unsatisfied with the answer but not willing to push it either. Chris sipped his coffee. Sure, he'd been attracted to Natalya. But she betrayed his trust. There was no coming back from that, regardless of the circumstances, regardless of the sexual tension that was still obviously there. He would never let himself be drawn into her web of lies again. But he also couldn't deny the connection he felt with Alena, a woman whose past and present were the polar opposite of his. A woman he'd promised to protect. He was ready for this dinner to be over.

The bell above the front door jingled as four men entered the diner. Chris clocked them immediately. His eyes were always on high alert, assessing potential risk. The men were in their late twenties, locals with tan work boots, Wrangler jeans, and camo-colored winter coats. They were loud, obviously drunk, as they plowed through the restaurant and clambered into the booth behind Chris, Alena, and Natalya.

It didn't take long for them to notice the two pretty women seated behind them. They ignored the bearded man, and one of them—a heavy-set fellow with pale skin and scraggly brown hair tucked beneath a tattered Bass Pro ball cap—turned around.

"Hey," he said, eyeing both women.

They ignored him.

"Boys, look at that," he continued. "We got us two pretty ladies. They don't look like they're from here. Where you from?"

Still, nothing.

A skinny guy with five teeth said, "Y'all wanna party?"

No response.

"Come on, don't be shy," said Five Teeth. "We're good guys, aren't we fellas?"

Alena wasn't in the mood.

"Fuck off," she said.

"Whoa, you got a mouth on you." For the first time, he acknowledged the bearded man eating his dinner quietly. "You let your woman talk like that?"

Chris ignored him.

"I'm talking to you, son," Five Teeth pushed.

Chris was exhausted and not in the mood to fight a bunch of drunks who were probably decent guys when the sauce ran dry.

"We don't want any trouble," he said.

This somehow enraged them because they immediately jumped out of their seats and stood in front of the booth, glaring down at the three strangers attempting to eat their dinner.

"But we do," the fat guy in the Bass Pro ball cap said.

Natalya made eye contact with all four of them. "Trust me, you don't."

"Ain't talking to you, honey," said Five Teeth.

By now the commotion had gotten the attention of the old men sitting at the counter, the cook working the griddle, and the waitress who was on her way to get the four rednecks' orders. All of them froze, hoping a fight wasn't about to break out.

Chris was seated closest to the rednecks and had yet to make eye contact with any of them. He kept his hands firmly around the coffee mug in a futile attempt to calm his nerves.

Five Teeth was losing his patience. "Y'all are some stuck-up city folk. 'Round here, we make eye contact when a man speaks to us."

"I couldn't agree more," Chris said, still cradling the mug. "But you're not a man. And you'll leave us alone if you know what's best for you."

"Oh, this boy wants to fight."

The fat guy said, "Why don't we take this outside?"

Alena regretted having engaged them. Her eyes darted between Chris and Natalya before settling on the rednecks. "I'm sorry, guys. We've had a long night. Maybe we can party some other time."

The leader of the group—which turned out to be Five Teeth—considered what she said. But they were all full of bourbon, and fighting was the next best thing to a date. Besides, the bearded man was an asshole. "You ladies enjoy your dinner. We've got some business with your friend. Then we'll join you for that little party." He glared at Chris. "Let's go outside."

"Not gonna happen," Chris said, still not making eye contact.

"Seriously, we're about to leave," Alena said.

Natalya was silent, but her eyes were locked on the four men, scrutinizing their every move. They were drunk. They were out of shape. They were not a threat.

"I'll tell you what," Alena suggested. "I'll give you my number. Just let him go this time. He's a moron. But he's my friend, and I'd hate to see him get hurt."

Five Teeth laughed and smiled. "What about you, blondie? Wanna give us your number?"

There was a long pause, and Chris thought for a moment that she was going to pounce. He hoped she wouldn't. Alena kicked Natalya under the table as if to say, *help me out here.*

"I would love to," Natalya finally said, forcing a smile.

"These gals just saved your life," Five Teeth said to Chris as he handed Alena his phone.

Alena plugged in her number—a fake one, of course—and then handed the phone to Natalya, who did the same. Satisfied, the four men left the restaurant—off to a liquor store, most likely—and everyone inside the diner let out a silent sigh of relief.

Chris raised his hand and motioned for the waitress.

"Check, please."

• • •

Chris, Alena, and Natalya left the diner and walked down the sidewalk toward their hotel. Christmas lights and wreaths hung from every light post. A few cars drove by, but the sound was dampened by a blanket of fresh snow on the pavement. Downtown Pikeville reminded Chris of Bedford Falls from the movie *It's A Wonderful Life*. They were two blocks from the Hampton Inn when four dark figures emerged from an alley and blocked their path. Chris had expected as much. Angry drunks are not easily persuaded. The four camo-laden locals spread out until they surrounded the trio.

"Hey, guys. Thought you were going to call us first," Alena said with a smile, trying to defuse the situation.

Five Teeth pulled out his phone. "Didn't think we would notice a fake number?"

"What are you talking about?"

"We tried calling you," said the fat guy.

Alena blushed. "I must have made a mistake."

"Oh, I don't think you did," said Five Teeth.

"You think we're stupid," said the third guy, the youngest of the group. He had a buzzed head and tattoos on his neck.

"You *are* stupid," said Chris. "Walk away before you get yourselves hurt."

"It's four against one," Buzzed Head replied.

"Four against two," said Natalya.

"Three," Alena added.

The rednecks laughed as they moved in closer. Five Teeth pounced first, sending a clumsy punch in Chris's direction. Chris blocked it and followed up with a side hook to the temple that knocked him to the ground—out cold. The other guys rushed in a frenzy. Natalya blocked the fat guy and Buzzed Head with a wide kick, pushing them both away. The fourth redneck—he had long hair and acne scars all over his face—landed a hit on Chris. A solid punch but not enough to do damage. Chris spun around and kicked him in the shin, breaking the bone. He screamed in pain as he dropped to the sidewalk. Chris grabbed him by the hair and pummeled him in the face. At the same time, he elbowed the fat guy coming at him from the right, causing him to stagger backward.

As Chris continued battering the long-haired man—breaking his nose and jaw in the process—Alena punched the fat guy in the face. It was her first punch, ever, and she reeled back in pain. The fat guy snarled and lunged toward her. Chris dropped the long-haired man like a sack of dead fish and blocked the fat guy before he was able to grab Alena. Chris twisted his forearm, breaking the limb at the joint, then punched him in the gut. The fat guy was tough and still managed to stay upright, even with a broken arm, but Chris hit him two more times in the stomach before landing a kill shot to the jaw. The only teeth he had spewed out of his mouth as he regurgitated cheeseburgers, fried chicken, and bourbon. He hit the concrete with a thud.

Meanwhile, Natalya seized Buzzed Head by the wrist, spun him around, and broke his arm. He shrieked. But she wasn't finished. She grabbed his head with both hands and simultaneously lifted her knee into the air. Buzzed Head's face made contact with her kneecap. The impact shattered his nose. She repeated the hit until he passed out and dropped to the ground with a face covered in blood, mucus, and flaccid cartilage.

Chris, Alena, and Natalya caught their breaths as they admired their handiwork. All four rednecks were out cold—beaten and bloodied, having sustained multiple broken bones, internal injuries, and loss of the few teeth they had. The entire fight had lasted thirty seconds.

"Well, that was fun," Chris said.

CHAPTER 50

Istanbul, Turkey

Once the city of Constantinople and the last remnant of the Holy Roman Empire, Istanbul was home to more than fifteen million people. Europe and Asia converged at the Bosphorus Strait, which cut through the city, connecting the Black Sea to the Mediterranean by way of the Sea of Marmara, and breathtaking architecture from the Byzantine and Ottoman empires populated the skyline. The churches, the castles, the mosques—some of the oldest in the world—filled the urban sprawl. Vendors sold their goods on the winding cobblestone streets, laundry hung from the buildings above, and the sound of daily prayers and street music echoed through the corridors of the ancient city.

It was here where Bashir Mahmoud called home, for now. He'd been at the Ciragan Palace Kempinski for the past month, his suite filled with every extravagance this world can offer. The hotel was once an Ottoman imperial palace. Ornate architecture, manicured gardens, and panoramic views of the Bosphorus provided guests with one of the most luxurious experiences in Europe. But to Mahmoud, it was a place to wait.

NEW BEGINNING

He woke up early. The sun was barely peaking out over the strait, and it cast a blue and yellow glow across the horizon. The woman from the night before was still in his bed. Having enjoyed her company more than the rest, he had decided to let her stay until morning. He lit a cigarette and stared out the window, stark naked except for a gold necklace around his neck. The jewelry was a reminder of his past life—growing up in poverty in Iran, joining the Islamic State, fighting the evil Westerners, and learning the art of warfare. His time in the Islamic Republic of Iran Army had been useful, but it was the years working directly with al-Qaeda, Hezbollah, Hamas, and the Taliban that taught him his trade. That was where he met his partner, Adham Mostafa. And it was during those formative years in the Iraqi deserts and caves that they decided to go out on their own.

To Mahmoud, Islam was nothing more than an idea, no different from any other religion in the world. He craved what he could not have: women, wine, and food—a life fit for a king. And so, they became terrorists-for-hire, mercenaries, and contract killers—anyone who could pay was a potential client—and, in doing so, they had positioned themselves as two of the wealthiest and most feared men in the world.

They'd built their own network of thieves and assassins—in a way, their own army—but riches could only buy so much, and the warmth of a woman's body could only satisfy for so long. The time had come to stand for something bigger than themselves. Now in their mid-forties, they were ready for the most substantial job of their careers. Recruitment had begun more than a year prior. They were tested, providing random acts of violence and mayhem across the globe. And finally, after working their way through multiple layers, they'd been officially contacted by the most secretive and powerful organization the world had ever seen: the New World Order.

There was a vibration on the nightstand as a cell phone received an alert. The woman moaned as the noise woke her. She rolled over, the sheet sliding down and exposing the entire backside of her slender body. Mahmoud admired the curves of her lower back for a moment before grabbing the phone and checking the message. It was from his employer through an encrypted messaging system developed by NASA but used by terrorist cells and criminal organizations worldwide. As he studied the message, written in Farsi, a smile broke across his bearded face. Finally, something worthwhile to fill the void six months of idle waiting had created. He found himself excited, a feeling he'd long forgotten. He read the words again.

> **Phase 2 in motion. Pickup at La Biga Ristoracaffé. Rome, Italy. Await further instructions. Confirm upon receipt.**

As Mahmoud replied with a confirmation, another text message popped up on his screen. It was from his partner, Mostafa, confirming that they had both received the same instructions. He decided to respond with a phone call instead. They hadn't spoken in weeks. Their practice had always been separation to prevent them from being discovered by the many governments who wanted them dead. He had no idea where Mostafa was.

The phone rang four times. Then, "*Salam-aleykom. Chetori, baradare?*" said his partner in Farsi.

Peace be upon you. How are you, my brother?

"The time has come."

"Indeed." Mostafa was a man of few words. He was serious to

a fault.

Mahmoud returned to the window and stared out at the Bosphorus. Morning boats filled the water, and the hustle of the hotel could be heard from the grounds below. He breathed in the cool, salty air. "I feel a change coming on. Unlike anything I've felt before."

"Many things can go wrong, brother. Save your excitement for a time when the job is complete." Realizing the importance of their next step, he added, "There can be no rest until the Americans are defeated and a new world is upon us."

CHAPTER 51

Hampton Inn
Pikeville, Kentucky

Alone in his room at last, Chris took a hot shower—his first in two days. There was still no word from the Anderson team, and he was beginning to worry that the intel of their survival was false. He was lying on his bed smoking a cigarette and drinking a Coors Light—the only beer in the minibar—and trying to make sense of the situation, when he heard a soft knock on the door. He opened it to find Alena standing outside.

"Can I come in?" She seemed concerned.

He stepped aside and motioned for her to enter. He closed the door behind her and dropped his still-lit cigarette into a paper cup filled with water.

"I have a bad feeling," Alena said.

"About those guys?"

"No, they were idiots. Got what was coming to them."

"You carried yourself well."

"The whole thing was my fault. I should have kept my mouth shut."

Chris shrugged. "I thought it was fun."

"You have issues."

"Probably true. What's on your mind?"

She hesitated as if trying to find the right words. Then, "It's about your friends."

"Not my friends—"

"*She* was your friend."

"Are you jealous?"

"This isn't about that."

He stared at her blankly, waiting for an explanation.

She said, "Natalya and this Kempe guy—there's something off about them, about this whole mission. I don't trust them."

"Okay…"

"Why do they need you involved?"

"I'm really good at what I do."

"No, seriously, why you?"

"I don't know."

"And who's paying for all this? It's not the CIA. It's *definitely* not the FBI."

"Kempe, I suppose."

"Well, how's he paying for it?"

"I don't know."

"Exactly," said Alena. "When I'm investigating a story and I get stuck, I follow the money. It never lies."

"So you're saying there's a financial motivation for Kempe?"

"I'm saying it's plausible. The guy is retired military, yet he owns a private jet company and has enough cash hanging around to fund this entire operation. Where did all that money come from? Not his time as a civil servant, that's for sure. Don't remember him writing a bestselling memoir, either. Plus, seems like to me, he's had a hand in every bad thing that's happened to you. And don't get me started on Natalya. Nothing about her is honest. She's betrayed you before. You said so yourself."

"She made up for it later, though."

"The point is, you wouldn't be in this situation if it wasn't for Natalya Palmer and Al Kempe. Neither would your friends."

Chris considered her argument. She wasn't wrong. "Okay, let's say there's an ulterior motive. What's their end game?"

"I don't know." She put her head down.

He could sense her frustration but also her concern. He stepped closer, touching her shoulder. She looked up.

Chris said, "Everything you're thinking right now could be true. The past few days have been a shit show. And you're wise not to trust them. Because you can't trust anyone. But right now they're our only hope of getting out of this mess alive. Even if it's all a lie, we need to run with it. See how it plays out."

She nodded.

"And if I'm being honest," he continued, "I'm excited to see if my friends are still alive."

She smiled. "They're your family. I get it."

"Not my *real* family."

"No, that's exactly who they are."

Chris realized his hand was still on her shoulder. Their eyes met. It was an odd feeling, looking into her eyes. He'd considered her an annoyance the instant he met her, but somewhere along the way—and he would never be able to pinpoint when that moment was because it had come on slowly—he began to feel something when she was near. A kind of tingling sensation. He'd felt it when she entered the room just now.

It wasn't planned, he wasn't thinking—that old mind was a

hell of a long ways away—when he reached out and touched her cheek. She didn't flinch, didn't flick it away. Instead, she stared at him with those almond-shaped brown pools.

Then their lips met.

He felt a rush of dopamine as her mouth opened and her slender arms wrapped around his back, pulling him closer.

He pulled away, realizing what he'd just done.

He started to say something, but she put her finger to his lip.

"Shut up," she said.

Finger went away and their lips met again. As the kiss intensified, their bodies stumbled backward onto the bed. The window was behind them—snow hammering the windowpane and Christmas lights from the street shining through, encapsulating them both in a blue-green haze. Alena wrapped her legs around Chris's torso, and he instinctually grabbed her hips and flipped her around so that she was on top of him. Her brown hair fell in his face as she pressed her body and lips onto his.

And as they continued to explore one another's body—lost in the passion of the moment, tossing clothing to the floor—a dark figure stood outside the hotel. He was dressed in a trench coat, a Fedora hiding his face, and he was staring right up at their room, watching their shadowed bodies moving ferociously against one another. The dark figure removed a phone from his coat pocket and sent a text message. He waited for a reply and once it came through, turned and crossed the street, disappearing into the night.

CHAPTER 52

McLean, Virginia

AL KEMPE LIT a cigar with a match and took three quick puffs, releasing a cloud of smoke into the air. He lived in a colonel house in the upscale Washington, D.C. suburb of McLean. His study was cozy. There was a fireplace, two brown leather couches, a mahogany coffee table, and a minibar—stocked with top-shelf bourbon, vodka, and gin in glass decanters—beside a wall of military biographies and American history books.

Kempe removed two crystal rocks glasses from the bar and filled one halfway with Four Roses Single Barrel bourbon, then turned to the man sitting on the couch behind him.

"Bourbon?"

"Vodka, actually," Steven House replied.

The general sighed with disapproval as he poured the requested drink. No ice, he'd drink this like a man. He handed it to the FBI director and sat down across from him.

"Six hours ago I was in Florida staring at beautiful women, and now I'm here freezing my balls off. Why do you think that is?"

"Duty."

"That's an interesting word. The dictionary calls it a 'moral or legal obligation' and that's where things get complicated. What's moral? What's legal?" He pointed to the books behind him. "In those you'll find a million different definitions of both." A puff on his cigar. Then, "I spent my entire life serving this county. You have too. And in the end, when they no longer find us necessary, they discard us like trash." He dropped cigar ash in a glass ashtray on the table. "But this is our chance to take it all back. It's our *duty* to take it all back."

"I feel betrayed," House said. "You swooping in like that. My man would have finished the job otherwise."

Kempe sipped his drink. "No loose ends. That's what I told you when this all began."

"And I appreciate your candor. You could have eliminated me just like you did Feng Chen."

"I still could."

"We both know that would be unwise."

"You're still valuable, yes. But you need to focus. Stop worrying about Congresswoman Valencia and do the job. This operation is in danger because of your incompetence."

House frowned. "Finding good help isn't as easy as it was in your day."

"In my day we didn't hire foreigners. But times change. We have to change with them. It's called progress." Kempe downed his drink and returned to the bar. As he poured another heaping glass of bourbon he said, "You shouldn't have left Greenwood in the dark."

"He's a paid assassin. It was above—"

"The more he knows, the more dangerous he becomes—yes, that is true, but knowledge breeds confidence." He returned to his seat. "Trust me—Harding, Moore, and the remaining Woodhaven agents will be dead tonight. That I can assure you. Greenwood will be taken care of when that job is completed. Until then, we allow him to do what we paid him to do."

House nodded. He said, "One thing that's been on my mind since the beginning. You helped create Woodhaven. Now you're disarming it. Why?"

Kempe considered the question. Then, "Woodhaven was an idea. But like all ideas, they wither with time. Harding, Anderson, the hillbilly and his wife—these are idealists. They follow orders. That is all. They still believe in democracy and don't possess the wherewithal to consider the bigger picture. When you live as long as I do, you come to realize that there is nothing in this life but money and power…then death. The NWO promises both fortune and power. For me, this was never about socialism, communism—a utopian one-world government. It's about enjoying the few years I have left on this earth."

House smiled and took his first sip of the vodka.

CHAPTER 53

*Pikeville/Pike County Regional Airport
Kentucky*

The Gulfstream G650 landed on the airfield, further confusing the traffic controller on duty. Two private jets in one night, just before a winter storm. What the hell was going on? Steam permeated the air as the Rolls-Royce engines made contact with the freezing temperatures outside. Greenwood stared out the window into the darkness. Somewhere out there in this small town was his ticket to freedom. The largest payday of his career. If properly executed, the last job of his career. After tonight he would retire a millionaire and kiss his treacherous profession goodbye forever.

He zipped his Down jacket to the top and attached a suppressor to his Glock. Then he exited the aircraft. The glowing light from the traffic control tower guided his way. He was joined by another figure out of the darkness. An older man carrying a CIA-issued SIG P226. Jack O'Brien nodded at Greenwood as both men walked side-by-side across the frozen airstrip.

The traffic controller was a young man in his twenties who barely graduated high school and only got the job because his father owned the airport. He worked the night shift and rarely did anything more than drink coffee, smoke cigarettes, and watch YouTube videos on his phone. But tonight had been different. Two G650s had arrived carrying suspicious-looking people. And he didn't recognize any of them. After the first arrival, he thought it was odd. But when the second plane landed, he knew something was off. Should he call someone? He checked the time. It was too late for management. Maybe he should contact the police. Yes, that was the right move.

He picked up the landline phone on the control panel and started to dial 911. That's when he heard the door open behind him. He stopped dialing and turned, but by the time it registered that both men standing in the doorway were armed, a bullet landed in his forehead, ending his short life and splattering blood and brain matter over the control panel behind him. Greenwood lowered the Glock and turned to his companion. It was time to go to work.

• • •

Chris lit a cigarette and exhaled the smoke slowly. He felt more relaxed than he had in years. Sex will do that, but it wasn't the copulation that was on his mind. It was the woman sitting in the bed beside him. They were both still naked, the sheets pulled up over them and providing a resting place for Chris's ashtray.

"She still has a thing for you, you know," Alena said.

"Who?"

She frowned. "You know exactly who."

"Natalya is just trying to get what she wants."

"And I think what she wants is you."

Before he could respond, the KryptAll phone vibrated on the

nightstand. He leaned over and checked the message.

Meet at location in 30 minutes. Please confirm.

"Is it them?" Alena asked.

Chris handed her the phone. "I hope so."

She read the message then gave the phone back. Chris extinguished his cigarette, put the ashtray on the nightstand, and climbed out of bed. Alena had enjoyed the sex and equally enjoyed watching him walk through the room and grab the boxer shorts that had been tossed during their time together—landing on a chair beside the wall-mounted heater.

"What happens after the meeting?" she said.

"Depends. Hopefully it's Roland or George or Trish." He put on the boxers.

"Who else would it be?"

"I don't know." He pulled up his jeans and grabbed his T-shirt from the floor. "But if they *are* alive, I think George's compound would be a safe place for you to lay low."

"I thought Natalya and Kempe were taking care of that."

"Like you said, their motivations can't be trusted. You'll be safer at George's."

"How long?"

"Don't know."

He finished dressing, returned to the bed, and leaned over and kissed her. As he did, the sheet dropped, exposing her breasts. He cupped one as he kissed her again, but she playfully slapped his hand away.

"That's sexual harassment, sir!"

"Shit, don't tell HR."

"I won't. But you have things to do—away with you."

He grinned. "Just a squeeze for the road?"

"Fine."

She guided his hand to her breast. "Enjoy them because I'm not doing this again. One time experience for you."

"What?"

She laughed at his expression of shock and dismay. Leaning forward, she replied, "I'm kidding." With that, she kissed him deeply.

He didn't want to leave. It was warm. She was warm. And he was scared. What if it was a trap? Pushing the thought from his mind, he checked the magazine in his P226 and confirmed it was full. He stuffed the gun in the back of his jeans, grabbed his coat and phone, and headed for the door. He stopped and looked back at her. *Goddamn*, she was beautiful.

• • •

Snow was falling as Chris exited the hotel and crossed the deserted parking lot to the truck. Without bothering to warm up the engine, he pressed the gas and turned onto the street. Inside a parked black SUV, a block away, Greenwood and O'Brien watched the F-150—and the bearded man inside—leave the hotel. It drove right past them.

"That's him," O'Brien said.

Greenwood nodded and checked his iPhone. The GPS tracker he'd installed underneath Chris's truck was activated, and he watched as a flashing blue dot moved across the map. He switched to his encrypted messaging app and sent a quick text to his team leader.

NEW BEGINNING

ETA?

A moment later the response came through.

5 mikes out of Pikeville.

Greenwood put his phone away and smiled. An elite black ops team was on their way from Virginia—former Navy SEALS, Green Berets, and Army Rangers turned PMCs—that would help him take down the remaining Woodhaven agents once and for all.

CHAPTER 54

It was a foggy night, and Chris could see his breath—intertwined with the smoke from his freshly lit cigarette—as he stood alone at the middle of Pauley Bridge, a wire suspension bridge built for pedestrians in the 1930s that stretched nearly four hundred feet across the Big Sandy River. Tree-covered hills surrounded it, and the river was frozen solid beneath it. Chris heard the creaking of the wooden planks and turned. His hand went for the SIG, just in case. He was tense. Ready for anything. A figure was walking toward him, shrouded in a trench coat and a Humphrey Bogart-style hat. The figure came closer, and through the fog, Chris made out who it was: Roland Anderson.

Both men were genuinely glad to see each other. A hug came to mind, but neither would stoop that low. Instead, they stood silently waiting for the other to explain what the hell was going on.

"Why are you dressed like a cartoon character?" Chris asked, breaking the silence.

"Says young Santa Claus. That beard, man."

"You're just jealous because you can't grow one."

"It doesn't make you look tough."

"Says Dick Tracy."

Silence. Then, "It's good to see you, Chris."

"You too—I'm glad you're not dead."

"So am I."

There was another pause. Too much brains and brawn and not enough heart.

"I'm serious," Chris finally stammered. "I thought this might be bad intel, and you all were still dead…like I've thought for six months."

"I was skeptical too when I got your message. But George said only you would pick this place, and obviously no one else calls me the Harvard man. How *did* you find us?"

Chris explained what had happened to him over the past couple of days, including how Natalya was alive and working with Kempe.

"Can't say I'm surprised," said Roland. "Natalya seems to turn up everywhere."

Chris laughed. "*Goddamn*, I've missed you, Roland."

"I'm glad to see you're doing well with the ladies."

"What are you talking about?"

"I did some recon before returning your message. The only hotel in town and sure enough there were three rooms booked last minute. We traced your message—don't ask me how—and I uh, I saw something in the window."

"It's not what it looks like."

"I know what I saw."

"Why were you watching?"

"I wasn't watching; I was confirming."

Chris rolled his eyes. "It's the same thing, dude." Then, changing the subject, "How's everyone doing?"

"Trish and George are good." Roland paused, staring out at the frozen water below. "Terry didn't make it. I saw his body burned to—" He couldn't finish the thought. "He saved our lives, though. He was out of the building, but he came back in."

Chris tossed his cigarette and lit another. "I was out cold."

"Same. Head still hurts like hell."

"Yeah, you've had that Harvard brain knocked around a few times."

He was referring to Roland surviving a helicopter crash and a plane crash in the same day followed by a near-death explosion two days later.

"We spent months searching for you," Roland said. "Looked everywhere. To be honest, Trish and I gave up all hope, but George—he never believed you were gone."

"You guys have been in Kentucky all this time?"

"Pretty much. Somehow we all ended up in the same wing of the hospital. Trish was injured the least and didn't suffer any memory loss. She kept things together. George had it bad, though. It was touch and go for a while."

"He's strong as a bull."

"It was Trish. She nursed him back to health. Wouldn't leave his side. They got married in the hospital."

"You're kidding."

"Hand to God. Honestly, I think it's what saved him. After the hospital, the compound seamed like the best place to go. No clue if anyone was alive. Who we could trust."

"Nothing from D.C., the FBI?"

"Nothing. I was actually relieved. Stepping away from all that—it's been nice. You're going to laugh, but I got a girlfriend."

"Is she blind?"

"Yeah, and she thinks I'm Brad Pitt. No, you asshole, she's

not blind and she's in love with me. She's a waitress at the diner in town."

"I think I met her. The fat one, right?"

Roland glared at him.

"I'm kidding." Chris took a drag from his cigarette. "They want us all back, you know."

"I figured."

"And?"

"No."

"What do you mean, no?"

"I mean, I'm not doing it. Can't speak for George and Trish, but I'm finished. A guy can only get screwed over so many times before he's done. Let Kempe and Natalya handle this one. They don't need us."

"That's what Alena said."

"Maybe you should listen to her."

"I'm surprised they got footage of you guys," Chris replied.

"Traffic cameras."

"I know, but why were they looking?"

Roland shrugged. "We go into town every week. Have for six months. Never once felt like we were being watched."

"You wouldn't see them."

"I know that, Chris." Roland thought for a moment, then said, "The timing is suspicious, I'll give you that."

"So you didn't know I was alive? Didn't see the APB?"

"We would have eventually, but no. When did you say the picture was taken?"

Chris pulled out his phone and showed Roland the grainy photo Natalya had given him. "She said yesterday, no timestamp though."

Roland took the phone and zoomed in on the image.

"That could have been yesterday," he said, handing the phone back.

Chris returned it to his pocket and focused on the water below—darkness, just like how he felt inside. So many people had died or were in danger because of him. He pushed the guilt away and said, "I'll let them know it's a no. But this hideout won't last long. People may come looking."

"George's compound is impossible to find. You wouldn't recognize it. He converted it into the ultimate bunker. I'm talking state-of-the-art AI-controlled weapons throughout the property, high-powered rifles, grenades. And the house is completely bulletproof."

Chris smiled. "I'm not surprised. I'm hoping Alena can hunker down there for a while."

"What about you?"

"I've got some things I gotta take care of."

"That sounds ominous."

"It is."

• • •

O'Brien stood at the edge of the tree line, just beyond where Pauley Bridge reached the shore, and watched Chris and Roland through the night vision scope on his M4. It had been a few years since he attempted a long-range shot like this, but his job was to distract them; if he managed to kill Harding, all the better. Regardless, by night's end, the Woodhaven team would be gone, and he would walk away with more money than he ever made during his entire thirty-year CIA career.

He leaned into his radio and said, "I have the target in my

sights."

"Copy that," Greenwood replied from the passenger seat of a gray Hummer.

Beside him was the team leader, a young man in his early thirties with scraggly blond hair and arms the size of tree trunks. The four men in the backseat were of a similar age and size, and were all dressed in black tactical gear and armed with HK416s and M4s. The Hummer was in stealth mode, engine and lights off, and hidden by trees in a gravel parking area a few yards up the street from where two trucks were parked. Both were F-150s. One was a classic 1970s model, and the other was built in the '90s. A GPS tracking device had been hidden beneath the older truck, just like the one that was already on the newer model—the device that led them to this remote location.

• • •

Natalya was lying on the bed smoking a cigarette and blankly staring at the TV when her phone vibrated on the nightstand. Anticipating the call, she answered quickly.

"Yeah?" she said.

"Everything is going according to plan," replied Greenwood from the parked Hummer. "Be ready with the reporter."

"Roger that."

She disconnected the call and looked out the window. Taking a final drag from her cigarette, she extinguished it in the nearly full ashtray beside the bed and removed her SIG P226 from the drawer. She pulled back the slide and made sure a live round was in the chamber. Then, stuffing the gun in the back of her jeans, she headed for the door.

• • •

O'Brien focused on the two men talking on the bridge. He had a perfect shot. Even though he was out of practice, he knew he could make it. Could probably get Anderson too, but this wasn't the time for that. Killing him would jeopardize the mission. They needed him alive, for now. Greenwood's voice came through O'Brien's earpiece.

"It's a go," he said.

The former CIA agent concentrated his sights on the target. And pulled the trigger.

CHAPTER 55

Had the cigarette in Chris's hand not extinguished from the cold, requiring him to lean forward and relight it with his Bic, the bullet would have blown a hole in the side of his head and ended his life before he knew what hit him. The familiar cracking of the suppressed M4 caused him to immediately drop to the ground.

"Get down!" he yelled.

Roland hesitated, taking a second to register what just happened, before joining Chris on the snow- and ice-covered bridge floor.

O'Brien searched the darkness for his target: nothing.

"Tangos are on the move," he said into the radio. "I'll follow up the rear."

"Roger that, old man," replied Greenwood. He turned to his men. "Time to play, boys."

• • •

Everything was calm. Quiet. Except for a slight breeze that whistled through the frozen trees. Chris removed the P226 from the back of his jeans.

"Are you armed?" he asked the Harvard man.

Roland nodded as he took out his own gun, a Smith & Wesson M19 Classic revolver.

"You would have a revolver," Chris said.

"Tried and true. What happened to your Beretta?"

"Long story. We need to find out where that shot came from."

"And who's shooting at us. Who all knew you were coming here?"

"Alena and Natalya, but I didn't give them the location."

"Maybe they followed you."

"Why?"

"To kill you."

Chris frowned. "You're an idiot." He started to say something else but stopped, put his finger to his lips, and whispered, "Someone's coming."

And there it was. The sound of footsteps crunching through snow.

Chris counted each step. Multiple people, probably four or five, coming from their right, the eastern side of the bridge where he'd parked the truck. He motioned for Roland to follow his lead as he slowly turned his body in the snow and faced the incoming footsteps. Roland did the same, and soon they were both facing the threat head-on with their pistols aimed at the darkness.

The footsteps grew closer, faster, confident in their rhythm.

Operators, thought Chris. He tightened his grip on the SIG, his finger touching the trigger. He was ready, focused. Roland was surprisingly calm, but his hands were shaking. It had been a long time since he'd fired a gun at another person, and the natural reflexes from his CIA training had worn down, like muscles unused and weakened with time.

The footsteps stopped. Their attackers were being cautious.

They know who we are, Chris realized.

Did they have night vision?

No, we'd already be dead.

Find advantage in the situation.

These assholes were just as much in the dark as they were, only they were walking, making themselves easier targets. That was it. Chris fired three shots in quick succession. The unsuppressed fire echoed through the trees.

Footsteps running.

He'd missed. But whoever it was, they were on the move. Chris jumped to his feet and charged, gun leading the way.

Roland wanted to stay on the ground, but as soon as the crazy, bearded soldier darted into the night, he knew he had to follow, so to his feet he went, grasping the revolver with both hands.

He felt the rush of a bullet whizzing past his head.

"Shit, shit, shit!"

Another suppressed gunshot, then another, each one barely missing him. The shots were coming from behind which meant there was another shooter. They were surrounded.

• • •

After a long, hot shower, Alena dried herself with a towel and stared into the steam-frosted mirror. Her life had changed drastically over the past couple of days, and it felt odd seeing herself, the same person she'd always been, now in a strange town with strange "spy" people—on the run from the police, the FBI, and the CIA. She had given little thought to completing her story. Staying alive had taken over. For the first time in years, her mind was not dedicated to her career. And then there was Chris. Why couldn't she stop thinking about him? He was an asshole who killed for a living. Talk about red flags. But he had kept her safe, and from what she could see, was trustworthy. Not as much could be said for Natalya, or this Kempe guy, or the Irish pilot who hadn't said a word to her since she boarded the Gulfstream, her first experience on a non-commercial flight. The journalist in her was weighing everything in her mind—exploring every angle.

Why did they want Chris on this mission? Why was Kempe and Natalya alive when the others had been targeted? Natalya had barely explained her "escape," and Kempe hadn't even acknowledged his involvement since the Woodhaven hit. And he should have. Or was all this a coincidence? Chris seemed to trust them enough to go along with it. Or was he blinded by the thought of his friends being alive?

The knock on the door startled her. She hadn't heard from Chris yet, and it had only been thirty minutes since he left. She went to the door and timidly looked through the peephole.

Oh.

• • •

Chris charged into the night, following the sound of footsteps in the snow, and emptied his magazine, the cracking of gunfire pounding through the forest. He replaced the empty mag with a fresh one and continued toward his targets. The shooter who initiated the attack had disappeared somewhere behind them in the darkness. Chris figured he had lost his sights and was working toward a new position.

As they neared the end of the bridge, Roland joined Chris's side, aimlessly spraying bullets into the air. They were doing their best to survive, pushing forward in the face of danger. In the face of certain death. Chris hit the edge of the bridge first. The road was

NEW BEGINNING

empty. Their attackers had vanished. Then he heard the crunching of feet on snow and saw a lone figure dart into the trees. He motioned for Roland to follow and made his way past the spot where the figure had disappeared. Not an ideal situation since whoever was out there now had the higher ground. Chris saw his truck. It was only a few yards away. If they could just make it there.

"Cover me," he said.

Roland fired into the woods, but after one round his gun clicked. He was out of bullets. No time to reload the revolver. Without hesitation, Chris picked up the slack and discharged a series of shots into the trees as they ran past. They made it to the truck and crouched behind the driver's side, away from the tree line. No one had shot back. Was this an ambush?

Focus.

"You have more ammo?" Chris asked.

"No."

"Shit."

"Didn't expect a gunfight."

"Always be prepared, Roland."

"You brought this to me. I was minding my own business." The gravity of the situation sank in. "I finally get a girlfriend, and then I get killed."

"You're not dying."

"We're outnumbered."

"It ain't over till the fat lady sings."

Before Roland could reply—

"Don't fucking move."

O'Brien was standing behind them with his M4 aimed at their heads.

Chris hesitated, considering his options. There was a rustle in the trees, and he looked up to see dark figures emerging from the darkness. Dan Greenwood led the way, followed by five men in black tactical gear. Three were armed with M4 carbines. The other two, including Greenwood, had HK416s. Chris dropped his pistol. Seven fully automatic rifles against one semiautomatic handgun. The odds weren't good.

"I think the fat lady just sang," said Roland as he dropped his empty revolver and raised his hands in the air.

Greenwood lowered his weapon and approached.

"Chris Harding," he said.

"Dan-fucking-Greenwood," Chris replied. "You're dumber looking in person. All those steroids must be taking their toll."

The insult didn't phase the PMC. "I've read your file. Impressive resume. You killed two of my best men."

"Obviously they weren't your best."

"Perhaps not, but either way, you will die tonight. So will your friends. That is a certainty. What is not certain is the fate of Alena Moore."

Chris's eyes narrowed.

Greenwood smiled. "That got your attention. Now listen closely. I need to know where the rest of your little band of outlaws are hiding."

"Fuck you."

"I thought you might say that."

He took out his cell phone and clicked the first number in his call history. A second later, someone answered on the other end.

"He needs confirmation," Greenwood said.

He pressed the FaceTime option and turned the screen so that Chris could see. It was Alena in what appeared to be her hotel room at the Hampton Inn. Natalya was beside her, holding a pistol to her forehead.

Chris's heart rate increased, his breath quickened, and his eyes turned red—unable to form words, his teeth clenched in silence.

"I'm sorry," Natalya said in a low voice.

Greenwood disconnected the call and returning the phone to his jacket pocket. "See, Ms. Moore is a guarantee that you will do what is needed."

"You're going to kill her, regardless," said Chris.

"I can see why you'd feel that way. But you have my word. No harm will come to her if I get what I want. And what I want is Woodhaven."

"Then you must want Natalya as well," Roland said. "She's one of us."

"You'd like to think that, wouldn't you," Greenwood said with a hint of laughter in his voice. "Lead us to your safe house, along with your two surviving partners, and the reporter lives. Don't, and Natalya Palmer will put a hole in her pretty little head. Come on, guys, be gentlemen. Let the lady live."

"Who are you working for?" Chris said.

"I think you know."

"But I'd like to hear it from your mouth. I'll be dead soon, so it won't matter. Call it professional courtesy from one operator to another."

Greenwood considered the ask, but he and the bearded man were the same breed and he knew what he was doing. He was stalling.

"Let's get this going," O'Brien grunted. "It's fucking cold out here."

"All right." Greenwood sneered at Chris. "What is it with Americans and trucks? Can't fit more than one passenger in the cab. But it's okay. We really don't need both of you."

Chris glanced at Roland. *Shit.* He clenched his teeth, searching for a window of opportunity, so much so that his body flinched.

O'Brien brought the M4 to Chris's back. "Don't fucking move."

"Kill me, and you'll never find the safe house," Chris said.

"No one is killing you," Greenwood said, "yet."

He raised his rifle and pointed it at Roland's head. The Harvard man glared back. Once upon a time he would have closed his eyes and pissed his pants, but this wasn't the first time he'd stared death in the face. Fuck this guy. He'd die a man.

Greenwood put his finger on the trigger. "Goodbye, Mr. Anderson."

CHAPTER 56

Pink chunks of brain matter splattered on the side of Greenwood's head. But it wasn't Roland's brain that had been dispersed over the ground, adding color to the white snow and ice; it was the blond-haired team leader standing guard beside Greenwood, and it startled the PMC, causing him to lower his weapon and turn, his eyes widening in horror at the sight. An arrow was sticking out the front of the operator's head where his left eye used to be. The man jerked—the neurons in his brain flickering like a dying light bulb—then he went limp. His body hit the ground with a thud.

"What the fuck?" Greenwood said.

His next thought was interrupted by another arrow that whistled as it glided through the air, landing in the back of another man.

Chris smiled, knowing exactly who was responsible. No time to gloat, though. This was his window of opportunity. In one smooth motion, he jumped to his feet, turned, and grabbed the M4 from a stunned O'Brien. It would have been great to keep the old man alive—discover why he'd betrayed them when he was supposed to be on their side—but right now Chris's focus was on neutralizing the situation. Two shots to the head and O'Brien was down. Chris dropped to one leg as he spun around and took aim at the rest of the operators. Three more shots sent another man to the ground. As the bullets entered his body, making wet thumping sounds as they tore through flesh and entered the heart, another arrow whistled through the trees and landed in the man beside him—right in the neck, splitting his trachea and thyroid cartilage in two and causing an avalanche of blood to pour out like an open faucet.

The two remaining operators began shooting aimlessly in every direction, moving around to avoid contact with the incoming deluge of arrows. They glanced at each other, both discerning the same thing: Whoever was out there was on the hunt, and they were his prey.

Those were their last thoughts on this earth.

An arrow landed in the right man's head, much like it had their team leader, only this time it entered the skull from the temple. It made a clean exit—no brain matter and skull fragments—but the force of the wood and metal traveling through the head disconnected the eyeballs, causing them to shoot out of the sockets like baseballs out of a batting cage pitching machine.

Chris stood up, flipped the M4's selector switch to full auto and opened fire on the remaining operator, filling his body with lead. The force of the rounds in quick succession made him dance, jerk, and twerk like a drunk Gen-Z at a rave, before dropping to the ground in a pile of blood and loose organs. Chris lowered his weapon and surveyed the carnage.

There were six dead men scattered over the road, and his rented truck was filled with holes, smoke spewing from the engine. Roland stood up from behind the truck. Everything had happened so fast that he'd barely had a chance to move. He and Chris looked at each other, and both let out a sigh of relief. But then it hit them at the same time.

Where is the man in charge?

"Greenwood," said Roland.

"Shit."

Chris brought the rifle back to his shoulder and scanned the tree line. The PMC was nowhere to be seen. That gym-rat wanna-be tough guy had disappeared the moment the fighting started. Was he out there waiting for the right time to strike? What was his plan B?

There was a rustling in the trees followed by footsteps. Chris aimed his weapon in that direction and inched toward it.

"Don't shoot," came a bellowing voice.

A large man appeared out of the darkness, revealing himself. It was George Hartman, brandishing a military green crossbow with a laser sight mounted on top. He had a Smith & Wesson M&P15-22 strapped to his shoulder and a .45-caliber Colt M1911 in a holster on his hip. He was wearing full winter camo, and his long beard was covered in snow. He looked like a mountain man on a hunting expedition.

"Chris Harding," he exclaimed. "You look like a dump truck took a shit on you."

Chris dropped the rifle to his side. "You're still the ugliest guy in the room. I'm glad you're here."

"Always saving your ass," replied George. He came in for a bear hug. "Mind the guns."

"You finally got to use that crossbow."

The big man laughed. "I figured y'all might need a hand."

"I told him not come," Roland said.

"Glad he didn't listen to you," Chris replied.

"Actually, I did," said George. "It was the message I got in the chat room that made me come."

"What message?"

George pulled out his cell phone and navigated to the dark web chat room. The same one Chris had used to contact them earlier that evening.

"You have a cell phone now?" Chris asked.

"You're an asshole." He pointed to the screen. "Right here. Says, 'The smoker and the Harvard man are under attack.' Signed, *N*."

Chris stared at the screen, confirming what George had read. *N*? Could it be?

"Natalya?" he said.

"No clue," said George. "But I wasn't taking chances."

The sound of tires spinning on the snow startled them. Chris brought his M4 back to attention, and George dropped his crossbow and switched to the M&P15-22. Roland froze. Headlights from an approaching vehicle lit them up, then a gray Hummer roared out of a break in the trees and turned left onto the road.

"That's Greenwood!" Chris said.

Both men opened fire on the utility vehicle as it sped away. But it was in vain, and the Hummer disappeared around the bend. Chris's mind went from *survive the battle* to *win the war.*

Alena.

CHAPTER 57

Uncomfortable was an understatement. Alena sat on the bed in her hotel room with her arms crossed. She was staring at Natalya's pistol, which was conveniently placed beside her on a dresser that doubled as a TV stand. Natalya had betrayed them. And Alena felt a combination of rage, regret, and confusion as she realized she should have listened to her gut and got out while she had the chance.

For her part, Natalya was calm. She smoked her cigarette, and she watched the reporter fume. It wasn't the first time she'd held someone hostage, and it wouldn't be the first time she killed someone when a "ransom" wasn't delivered, but still, she felt a twinge of guilt, having double-crossed Chris and this woman he so obviously had feelings for.

Alena broke the silence. "You're going to kill me either way, aren't you?"

Natalya didn't respond.

"I'll take that as a yes."

The spy took a long drag from her cigarette, letting the nicotine fill her lungs before exhaling the smoke into the room. "You talk too much."

"You're going to murder me, so why not just tell me why?"

"Would it make a difference?"

"Yes."

"How?"

"Maybe I can persuade you to consider other options."

"There it is."

Alena stared out the frosted window. "I don't want to die."

Natalya snuffed the cigarette in an ashtray beside the TV and lit another one. Her upbringing in L.A.'s San Fernando Valley in the 1990s had been far from normal. Her parents were Russian spies who lived and worked among average Americans while at the same time sending U.S. government secrets back to Moscow. Natalya learned early on that no life was more important than the mission. But she cared for Chris. And those "feelings" had caused her to make a few judgments of error in the past. She looked at the woman sitting on the bed. It was easy to see what Chris saw in her.

"I wish it didn't have to be this way." Natalya was surprised the words came out of her mouth, but they did. Might as well run with it. "I'm only doing what has to be done."

Alena looked at her. Long, hard. Then, "Why?"

"For starters, you know too much."

"But what do I *really* know?"

Natalya raised an eyebrow.

"Fine," Alena conceded. "I know too much. But I don't have the flash drive. You do. So even if I wanted to write the article, I couldn't prove anything."

"Doesn't matter. My employer doesn't like loose ends."

"Al Kempe?"

"It's more complicated than that."

"We have time. At least I'll die understanding the 'complications' of it all."

Natalya's cell phone vibrated in her pocket. She ignored Alena's last remark and answered. "Yes?"

Alena tensed, knowing what the call probably meant. She wanted to fight back, thought about every possible outcome, but she had no idea how these people did what they did. She had never held a gun, let alone extracted one from the hands of a trained assassin. No, this was it; she was going to die in a cheap hotel room in a town she'd never heard of in the backwoods of Kentucky. Natalya made eye contact with her as she listened to the voice on the line, nodding as she received the information.

After what felt like an eternity, Natalya said, "See you soon," and disconnected the call.

Phone back in the pocket.

Cigarette crushed in the ashtray.

Alena fought the urge to say something. Should she make a run for it? Her eyes darted between the door and the blond spy.

Natalya hopped off the dresser and grabbed the SIG. She looked Alena in the eyes.

"It's time," she said.

• • •

The 1978 Ford F-150, George's pride and joy, flew down the winding road at a breakneck speed. Its off-road tires did their best to stick to the asphalt, but it was a challenge. Patches of black ice hidden beneath the snow are impossible to see until it's too late. Chris focused on the road. Darkness in every direction, only his headlights to guide the way. George and Roland followed in George's other vehicle, a dark blue '94 Ford Bronco in perfect condition. Although Greenwood had a head start, Chris had a good idea where he was going. There was no telling how many more men were waiting for them, but one thing was certain. *Alena was in danger.*

If she was even still alive.

Chris turned another bend in the road, nearly sliding into the tree line, but regained footing and continued, passing older homes and a newly constructed Methodist Church. Still no sign of Greenwood. He made a right turn onto Main Street, and the collection of brick buildings that made up downtown came into view. He pulled back the slide on his handgun, arming the chamber, and slammed a new magazine into the M4. Thankfully the dead PMCs carried plenty of ammo, and Chris had liberated three spare mags. He had no idea what was about to happen, but that feeling of dread in his gut was pumping like a vein. And it was rarely wrong.

• • •

Downtown was deserted, and there was no sign of Greenwood or the Hummer. Chris parked the truck on the street directly in front of the Hampton Inn. He didn't wait for Roland or George and entered the hotel with his rifle guiding the way. There was one thing on his mind and that was rescuing Alena.

He passed through the lobby.

Empty.

He entered elevator, hit the button, and went up. The aging lift hummed as it moved and dinged when it reached the fourth floor. He exited and scanned the hallway.

All clear.

Two doors down from the elevator and he was standing in front of Alena's room. He tightened his grip on the M4 and used his right foot to kick in the door. The lock broke through the wooden frame and he stormed inside—finger on the trigger, ready to take out anyone in his path. The barrel of his rifle scanned the room with speed and efficiency. With his back to the wall, he checked the bathroom on the right.

Clear.

Then the rest of the room—

Empty.

Bed was made, bag was gone; it was like she'd never been there. He lowered the gun and crossed to the window. The hotel was the tallest building in town and gave him a panoramic view of the entire "urban" sprawl below—all six blocks of it. The streets were empty. It was a ghost town. And then he saw it. A vehicle's headlights heading out of town.

• • •

Chris came out of the hotel in a fury, nearly colliding with George and Roland as they exited the Bronco.

"What happened?" said Roland. He was holding one of the dead operator's HK416s. It looked funny in his flabby arms.

"They're headed for the airport. They have Alena."

"Shit," George said.

"Any sign of Greenwood?" Roland asked.

But Chris was already in the truck.

"Let's go," George said, spinning around and diving back into the Ford.

The stick shift was a long bar that came up from the floor with a plastic ball on top indicating five gears and reverse. Chris slammed the shift into first, released the clutch, and floored the pedal. Back tires spinning in the snow, the F-150 fired off down the road.

Chris navigated Pikeville the same way he once did as a seventeen-year-old kid in a '97 Camaro Z28, moving up from each gear to the next and punching the pedal with his foot, making the engine roar. Two more turns and he was out of downtown, passing gas stations and fast food restaurants. The road became four lanes. That made it easier to speed without losing control.

Faster and faster.

Gasoline and air exploding as the RPMs hit red.

Snow hitting the windshield faster than the wipers could clean it off.

Then, out of the darkness, the red glow of taillights appeared. Chris tightened his grip on the steering wheel and clenched his teeth as he got closer to the other vehicle. It was a black Dodge Durango Hellcat. The same SUV he had noticed when he left the hotel earlier that night. And he could see two people inside.

Alena.

The Dodge sped up. The driver had spotted him. He tried to pass, but the Hellcat was more powerful and prevailed.

"Goddamnit!"

He dropped down to third gear—causing the RPMs to redline once more—then as he released the clutch, slammed it into fourth. The engine found power it didn't know it had, and Chris pulled up alongside the newer vehicle. Natalya was behind the wheel, Alena in the passenger seat. Their eyes locked. She was terrified.

He looked back at the road. Tree.

Shit, Fuck.

He swerved just in time to avoid a collision with the goddam log in the air and returned to the highway that had abruptly become a two-lane nightmare. But the quick turn caused the truck to hydroplane over the ice- and snow-covered asphalt. Chris slammed the steering wheel the opposite way and pumped the brakes. This stopped the spinning, but he lost speed. The Hellcat continued on, its lights disappearing into the night—leaving nothing but darkness and a furry of snow. Chris took a deep breath. Took in his surroundings. He knew these roads like the back of his hand. And there was only one place the Hellcat was headed. He released the clutch and fired off into the night.

• • •

The Hellcat entered the Pikeville airport parking lot and continued through the open gate onto the tarmac, passing a gray Hummer that was parked as if the driver had been in a hurry. Natalya made note of the vehicle and mentally prepared for what was about to happen. Timing was key. Every little detail had to be accounted for. She kept her P226 on Alena as they passed the SUV and headed toward the runway.

Alena was frozen in place—scared, yet hopeful. Natalya had a plan, but did that plan include Chris? His crazed eyes when he pulled up beside them told her he was oblivious. Would he jeopardize everything? Would he be able to help her? Or was this mission doomed from the start? No, he was going to rescue her. She had faith in that. More than she did in the blond spy holding a gun to her head. But if it came down to it, did he have what it took to kill the woman he'd once loved? She brushed the thought from her mind as the SUV came to a stop.

There were two Gulfstream G650s on the runway. Alena recognized one of them as the plane they arrived in earlier that night. The lights were off, and it appeared to be empty. Where was O'Brien? Was he dead? Was he part of this whole thing? The second Gulfstream had steam coming from its two engines, and the lights were on. A man was standing in front of it. Alena immediately recognized him from his website: Dan Greenwood, CEO of Greenwood Enterprises and, according to Chris, the leader of an elite team of assassins. He had on black tactical gear with a handgun holstered to his side and looked like a real-life GI Joe, down to his oversized arms and shoulders—lots of time spent in the gym, no doubt. His eyes were cold, dark, and calculating—and he looked upset, almost like a child whose toy had been taken from him.

"Stay in the car," Natalya instructed.

Alena nodded. What choice did she have?

Natalya climbed out of the Hellcat. She locked the doors behind her and approached Greenwood.

"Do you have it?" he asked.

She removed the flash drive from her coat pocket and dropped it in his hand.

"Kempe will want an update on Woodhaven," she said.

"Tonight was a setback, but we'll get them."

"And the reporter?"

"No longer necessary," Greenwood replied.

"Roger that."

"Glad we're on the same page."

Headlights from an approaching vehicle illuminated them both, creating silhouettes out of their frames as an F-150 charged onto the airstrip.

Chris, Natalya thought, a smile breaking across her face.

The Glock G21 came out of its holster like a gunslinger in a western. It threw Natalya off guard, a split-second delay. She saw the weapon. Went for hers. But the moment her hand touched the grip of her SIG, Greenwood's own gun was already aimed at her head.

Chris jumped out of the truck with his M4 on his shoulder.

He saw Greenwood.

He saw Natalya.

He saw the Glock.

The gunshot echoed across the airstrip.

Shards of Natalya's skull escaped the back of her head along with spews of bright red blood and gooey pink brain matter. The force of the bullet knocked her head back and sent her body to the ground. Greenwood immediately followed up with two more shots to the chest—the bullets bouncing her body with each impact.

Alena witnessed everything from the passenger seat of the Hellcat. She let out an audible gasp as her eyes widened in horror. Never in her life had she seen a sight so brutal as a woman's head exploding like a watermelon.

The violence was abrupt and would have stunned most people, but Chris reacted on instinct. Muscle memory from years of training. He opened fire and sent an avalanche of lead in Greenwood's direction. The PMC ducked and ran for the stairs leading to the open door of the Gulfstream. Chris's marksmanship was rusty. He was finding it difficult to hit his mark, so he stopped. Took a deep breath, aimed, and pulled the trigger. He missed. He fired again. This one landed, sort of. The bullet skimmed the top of Greenwood's right thigh just as he was about to enter the plane. Not enough to stop him, though. Chris emptied the rest of his magazine as he charged forward. But Greenwood escaped inside.

"Fuck." Chris slammed in a new mag and headed for the stairs.

He ignored Natalya's body on the ground.

Later. Focus on the target. Kill this son of a bitch.

The barrel of a Mk 48 MOD 1 belt-fed machine gun appeared in the doorway.

Shit.

Chris dropped to the ground as hundreds of bullets lit up the night like firecrackers.

Alena ducked below the dashboard of the Hellcat and screamed. The windshield was obliterated and plastic, metal, and glass covered the inside of the car.

The Ford Bronco turned into the airport parking lot. George and Roland could hear the gunfire. And they could see the muzzle flashes. They continued toward the airstrip, weapons ready to go. A bullet shot through the windshield. Another took out the left mirror.

"Fucking A," yelled George.

He steered the SUV to the right, taking refuge behind the terminal building.

Back on the airstrip, Chris kept his head down. An inch higher and he'd be blown to bits.

Just wait; you'll get your chance. Don't let that piece of shit get away.

Suddenly, the jet's twin engines made a high-pitched screeching sound and the aircraft started to move. The machine gun fire continued as the plane headed toward the runway. Then the doors closed, and the gun disappeared inside.

Now.

Chris jumped to his feet, flipped the M4s selector switch to full auto, and pressed the trigger, emptying the entire magazine. But the plane was traveling too fast, was too far away. Chris stopped running. He dropped the rifle to his side and watched as the Gulfstream gained momentum and speed then took off into the dark sky, disappearing into the incoming snow.

CHAPTER 58

Alena nearly fell into Chris's arms as he opened the passenger door of the Dodge Hellcat.

"Are you okay?" he asked.

She was shaking. From fear. From shock. Didn't bother responding. Instead, she wrapped her arms around his neck and squeezed him with all she had. After a long moment, she pulled away and searched his face for answers. In his eyes she saw a new man—not the one she said goodbye to a few hours ago, but a battle-hardened killing machine with nothing but death and destruction in his sights.

The airstrip was calm. Fresh snow was falling. Alena tore her eyes away from Chris's. She stared at Natalya's body behind them, only to immediately turn away and refocus her gaze on the bearded man in front of her. She wanted to say something. But the words didn't come.

"I know," he said.

Before she could respond, they were lit up by headlights. The Ford Bronco drove onto the airstrip and came to a screeching halt a few yards in front of them.

"You good?" George said as he climbed out of the driver's side.

"Never been better," Chris replied sarcastically.

Police sirens echoed in the distance.

"We gotta get out of here," George said. "Pikeville might only have two cops, but they've sure as hell called state police by now."

Chris grabbed Alena's hand to go, but she hesitated, glancing back at Natalya.

"We can't just leave her there," she said.

"She made her choice."

"She saved my life."

Alena removed a black flash drive case from her coat pocket and pressed it to his chest.

He said, "Is that the?"

"—Yes, *'nothing is what it seems, David.'* That's what she told me to tell you if she…" There was no need to finish the thought.

Chris took the case and stuffed it in his pocket. This was going to have an effect on him. He knew it. But reflection would have to wait. Right now he needed to get Alena to safety.

Blue and red lights illuminated the sky, and the sirens grew louder.

"We have to go. *Now!*" Chris said.

Alena followed him to the Bronco, and they both jumped in the backseat as George slammed the gear into reverse.

• • •

Greenwood leaned against the leather seat and closed his eyes. He was exhausted. The weather had not been ideal for takeoff and turbulence had nearly caused the cabin to lose pressure. But the pilot was a pro. He guided the Gulfstream until it reached a cruising altitude of thirty-five thousand feet.

Hydration, electrolytes—replenish and focus.

NEW BEGINNING

Greenwood downed a sports drink and opened a Cliff bar, killing it in two bites. He was frustrated. Tonight had been a shit show; had he been allowed to work alone, none of this would have happened. Good men had died, and now he would have to expend more resources on a counterattack. First things first—he used his iPhone to check the coordinates for the GPS he installed on Mr. Anderson's vehicle, hoping it was already en route to the safe house. No such luck; the goddam truck was at the airport. Not ideal. Not the end of the world either. If local authorities got their hands on it, they were back to square one.

He flipped open his laptop and inserted the flash drive Natalya had given him. Thankfully there wasn't a password. The drive contained a single folder named *Nysta Update*.

So far so good—

It was empty.

What the fuck?

He clenched his fists trying to control his anger. Natalya, that bitch, had double-crossed him. She worked for Al Kempe. Was he in on this? Greenwood needed answers.

He called House's secure line.

CHAPTER 59

THERE ARE THOUSANDS of acres of undeveloped land in Eastern Kentucky. Forests that spread out for miles and winding roads that seem to lead nowhere. The incoming snowstorm would soon render those roads nearly impassable, but George Hartman knew them like the back of his hand, and the 4x4 Bronco was fully equipped to handle the snow and ice. After a thirty-minute drive, they arrived safely at George's property.

The last time Chris had been there was when he returned from Russia—right before going to Los Angeles to take out a quantum computer-controlled nuclear bomb. The deed to the property was in the name of a trust owned by a moonshiner who died in the early 1970s. Chris had asked George many times what the connection with the old man had been, but George would simply grin and change the subject. Regardless, this was a patch of land—about twenty acres worth—the U.S. government could never trace back to Mr. George Hartman.

There was a gravel driveway that stopped a few feet into a wall of trees. Then a metal gate—towering thirty feet in the air—with barbed wire on top and a security camera staring down at them. George pressed a button on his phone. There was a loud beep and the gate opened, allowing them to pass through. The gravel driveway through the woods had only whispers of snow. But the ice was there. So were the security cameras. They hung from trees, hidden but watching. This was home for George and Roland—an old familiar place for Chris—but to Alena, it felt like she was traveling into a James Bond villain's hideout.

She squeezed Chris's hand.

He smiled and whispered, "We're almost there."

It took them five minutes to get to the house, which was in the middle of a clearing with a yard—though calling it that was a stretch as it was mainly dirt, gravel, and weeds—filled with old vehicles covered in snow. The house itself was built in the early 1900s and had a large wrap-around porch, complete with four rocking chairs. George parked the Bronco in front, beside several other "old" vehicles. Chris recognized all of them but one: a late model GMC Hummer painted military green.

"Where'd that come from?" he asked.

"Won it playing cards with a guy in town," said George.

"Really?"

"Yeah—Trish hates it. Don't bring it up." He turned off the engine and made eye contact with Alena through the rearview mirror. "Welcome to my humble abode, Ms. Moore."

She smiled meekly. "Thank you. And it's Alena."

"Alena—that's a purty name." Then, "Inside we go."

A roaring fireplace, hardwood floors, and walls adorned with stuffed animal heads greeted them as they entered. Tricia was waiting in the living room. She nearly jumped across the room to give Chris a hug, and a few tears followed as the old team reunited for the first time in six months.

CHAPTER 60

Washington, D.C.

STEVEN HOUSE STARED out the window of his office with a hot cup of coffee in his hand. He'd been burning the midnight oil lately, and a steady flow of caffeine was about the only thing keeping him going. Greenwood had informed him of the failure in Kentucky. That was concerning. But more than that, he felt betrayed by Kempe. Did the general plan for Palmer to keep Amy Dotson's flash drive? Was the old man toying with him? Valencia had him by the balls and now Kempe—someone who could order his death at any moment—had proven untrustworthy. But if House had learned one thing in his long career, it was the importance of controlling the narrative. He was the only one with the contacts to carry out the final phase of the mission, a responsibility bestowed upon him by none other than Kempe himself. His ability to retain information across every government agency made him the perfect candidate to ensure each player did their part. It was time to capitalize on that fact.

He used a unique passcode to open a safe hidden in the wall behind his desk. After punching the code into the digital pad, he was prompted to approve a two-part authentication on his phone. He did so, and the safe door popped open. Inside was an array of hard drives containing years of confidential information—the nation's secrets going back to the days when J. Edgar Hoover still roamed the halls—as well as Glock 17 and House's birth certificate. But his focus was on something else inside the metal box: a KryptAll secure mobile phone. He placed the encrypted phone on his desk, took a seat—and another sip of coffee—before dialing one of four contacts saved on the device.

The unlisted European cell phone number rang several times before a man answered in a deep voice and an accent that was distinctively Texan.

"You're not supposed to be calling me, Steven," said Auspex CEO Jean Mackler. "What time is it there anyway?"

"Late."

"Obviously something is wrong. Is this about Andrew Chew? I read what happened. Murdered in his own home by an illegal immigrant. Only in California."

"Terrible, but listen, this isn't about that. How quickly can you launch the Nysta update?"

CHAPTER 61

George's Compound
Pikeville, Kentucky

The Miller Lite was far from being an IPA, but at least it came in a good pint glass. It was a known fact that George had terrible taste in beer. That couldn't be said for his taste in glassware. He had a small collection of handmade beer glasses manufactured in Wisconsin by a family business called BenShot. Each one was unique. The one Chris had grabbed from the cabinet was called the "Bulletproof" glass. It was hand-embedded with a .50 BMG bullet and had an American flag laser etched on the side. One hell of a glass. Chris planned to steal it and save it for the next time he got his hands on a 21st Amendment West Coast IPA. He took a healthy pull of Miller Lite, followed by a drag from his cigarette as he melted into the couch, his body warmed from the fire inside the brick fireplace. George's living room was a man cave with a woman's touch. There were shotguns and dead animals on the walls, but there were also throw pillows covering the leather couches and scented candles on the pinewood coffee table.

With everyone seated, drinks in hand, Chris gave an update

on the situation. It was a lot, and when he finished, he paused. Then he said, "I'm sorry I got you guys involved."

"Shut the hell up," said George. "This was always our problem."

"I didn't see it coming with Natalya. That O'Brien guy, something was off about him, but I thought she was—"

"Dude, she's betrayed us before. And just because she saved our lives once doesn't mean she can be trusted. She's a spy."

"Aren't all of you spies?" Alena said.

George shrugged.

"Let's not jump to conclusions," Roland said. He smiled at Alena. "What did she tell you?"

Alena was beside Chris, a pint of beer doing its best to numb the pain of the day. She said, "All I know is that Natalya didn't kill me when she was supposed to. And she gave Greenwood a fake flash drive. Chris?"

"Right." He removed the flash drive she had given him from his pocket and placed it on the coffee table. "Here's the real one—Amy Dotson's copy of the Nysta update."

"The virus," Roland said.

Chris nodded.

"I think there's more," said Alena. "Natalya told me there was information you all needed to know—something about her mission, about Kempe."

"That's it?" Roland asked.

"We didn't have a lot of time together. And I don't think she expected to die."

"One never does," Chris said.

"Greenwood caught her off guard," Alena replied. "I'm pretty good at reading people, and I'm telling you, she had no idea he was going to kill her."

Roland leaned back in his seat and removed a walnut pipe from his shirt pocket and a pouch of tobacco from a box below the coffee table. As he packed the pipe with the toasted leaves, he said, "We need to see what's on that flash drive."

Chris was shocked. "You smoke a pipe?"

"Yes."

"It fits you."

• • •

Everyone crowded around the MacBook Pro, open on the coffee table. George inserted Amy Dotson's flash drive into the computer and clicked on the icon that appeared on the screen. There were two folders inside. Chris and Alena recognized the first one as the update code they'd seen while in California. But the second one was new.

"Let's see that one," Chris said, pointing to the folder labeled *N*.

George did as he was told. The folder contained a single MOV file, which he double-tapped. A cell phone video filled the screen: Natalya sitting on the bed in a hotel room.

"That's the Hampton Inn," Chris said.

"Shhh," Roland said.

Natalya took a drag from a cigarette and looked into the camera. She seemed tired, stressed—an unusual trait for the beautiful spy. She said, "If you're seeing this, I'm dead. Happens to us all, I suppose. You've all been betrayed, and if you're still alive after tonight, it's important you know who's responsible." She paused as if torn whether or not to proceed. Then, "General Al Kempe and I have betrayed you."

"No shit," said George.

"Quiet," Tricia hissed.

Natalya said, "We have both been working directly for the New World Order."

There was a gasp from everyone but Chris. He was no longer watching the screen. Instead, he was puffing on his cigarette, his eyes dark and brooding.

Natalya continued.

"I was a sleeper agent from the time I was born until I was activated by Russian Foreign Intelligence, known throughout the world as the SVR. Kempe was my handler. He was recruited sometime in the mid-2000s—probably around 2006, I would guess—after decades of public service to the country he loved. His compensation was pathetic—pension would be worse—and I think he realized his ideas would never be appreciated. He became jaded. Russia works that way. They placate to our deepest desires, and in Kempe's case, it was recognition."

She hesitated, contemplating how far she was willing do go with her confession. Finally, "When I made it out of Beijing, I knew I'd been betrayed. So I returned to Moscow. I went dark for months and used Russia's Internet Research Agency to dig deeper into Woodhaven, the SVR, China's Ministry of State Security, and the NWO. What I found was shocking."

She paused again, searching for the words that followed.

"Kempe started Woodhaven because he wanted to form an alliance between Russian and U.S. intelligence to fight the NWO, which he believed originated in China. But geopolitical landscapes change, and six months ago the Russians joined forces with the NWO—and the Chinese. Woodhaven was no longer necessary. In fact, it was a liability. So Kempe ordered the termination of all Woodhaven operatives, including me. FBI Director Steven House was his proxy, and he used Greenwood Enterprises to do the dirty work."

George paused the video.

"I'm confused," he said.

"Why are you confused?" Tricia asked.

"Was Natalya working for the Russians? Or was she working for Kempe?"

"Both," said Chris.

George stared back blankly.

"Kempe and Natalya were both Russian spies," Tricia explained. "Woodhaven was formed to fight what they considered a bigger threat."

"The NWO," said George.

Tricia nodded. "Yes, honey, and when the NWO joined forces with Russia, Kempe decided to terminate Woodhaven. That meant Natalya too."

"Basically, Kempe's a traitorous piece of shit who betrayed all of us," Chris said.

"I get it," George said. He pressed play on video.

Natalya took another drag from her cigarette. "There was a congressman from Kentucky who died in a car accident earlier this year. His name was Seth Wilson. The media speculated that it was no accident, that he was killed by the Deep State for not voting "yes" on the Nysta deal with Auspex. That is partially true. But the real reason he was killed was because he knew too much. Information can either save you or kill you. I wanted to avoid the latter. So I took matters into my own hands and contacted Kempe myself—convinced him *and* Moscow that I was still valuable."

She almost shed a tear but stopped herself. Instead, she took a very long drag, shrouding her face in a cloud of tobacco smoke. "And I proved my value by betraying all of you—by discovering evidence that you were still alive. The plan was for me to assist Greenwood in taking you out. All we needed was the flash drive and the location of George's compound."

George hit pause. "Goddamnit, she was using us to save her own skin."

"Yes, dear," said Tricia as she leaned over and restarted the video.

Alena took a final hit from her cigarette and crushed it in a plastic ashtray beside the bed. "My loyalties have always been and always will be with Russia. And I believe in a communist society, but," she took a deep breath, "I couldn't go through with this plan. So I sent George the alert that something was wrong."

George stopped the video.

"That's what the N stood for," he said. "She texted me, and that's why I showed up at the bridge. If she hadn't," he looked at Chris, "you and Roland would be dead. She double-crossed Kempe when she was supposed to be double-crossing us. But why the change of heart?"

"If you would stop pausing it, maybe we could find out," Tricia said, restarting the video once again.

Natalya said, "I will not shoot Alena, even if Greenwood orders me to. And I plan to give him a fake flash drive, leaving the real one with you. I'm doing all of this—risking my life, betraying my country—because I broke a cardinal rule." She could no longer hold back the tears. "I love you, Chris. I've loved you since the moment I met you in that farmhouse in the middle of nowhere. And I couldn't bear to see you die…or those you love."

The video ended.

No one said a word.

Finally, Chris stood up. "She knew she was going to die."

With that, he took his beer and disappeared out the front door.

CHAPTER 62

CHRIS STOOD IN stoic silence on the front porch. The snow was coming down hard, but he couldn't feel it. The cigarette in his hand stayed between his fingers, slowly burning—he was too lost in thought to smoke it. Even the nicotine couldn't numb the pain. An IPA would be nice, but he wanted his mind clear—his thoughts pure of outside elements. He kept replaying Natalya's words and the moments leading up to her death. She had "died" before, but it had always been a ruse—spy tricks. Today her life actually ended. Was he in love with her still? It didn't matter. She was gone. And she was gone because she loved him.

The front door opened, and he felt the presence of someone else. Alena took the cigarette from his limp fingers and tossed it into the air where it landed on the snow-covered gravel driveway. She touched his shoulder.

"Are you okay?"

He didn't respond.

She pulled her hand away. "I'm leaving in the morning. Your friends want nothing to do with this. And I can see you don't either. I just wanted to say that I…"

There was no point. She turned to leave.

But he grabbed her hand.

"I'm sorry you got dragged into all this," he said. His voice nearly cracked.

She returned to his side, still grasping his hand—a hand that was shaking. "I'm the one who should be apologizing to you. If it wasn't for me, you'd still be living your life."

"I wasn't living, not really." His eyes darkened. "I was hiding."

"Maybe, maybe not, but you've saved my life more than once. Whatever you decide to do, I'm here for you. Even if that's standing outside in the cold." She laughed. "When there's a roaring fireplace a few feet away."

He attempted a smile, almost a laugh. He thought about responding—saying something, perhaps expressing his feelings—but he couldn't. Instead, he removed the pack of Camels from his coat pocket and lit another cigarette.

• • •

George and Roland were already in bed when Chris and Alena returned from the front porch. Tricia was waiting for them, sipping a hot cup of tea like a mother waiting up for her children. She smiled when they entered, then showed them to the guest bedroom—neat and clean with new furniture and pictures of mountains and lakes on the walls.

"One of the few rooms without animals," she said. "There are fresh towels in the closet and extra toiletries in the bathroom. Alena, I put some of my own stuff in there for you. I hope it's to your liking."

"It'll be fine," Alena said. "Thank you, Tricia."

"Call me Trish." She turned to Chris, her eyes tearing up. "I'm glad you're alive."

"You too, Trish. More than you know." He meant it.

She smiled. "Get some sleep. Both of you."

• • •

A meteor the size of a basketball that looked like a ball of fire shot through the sky, lighting up the night as it traveled over the hills of Eastern Kentucky. It began to fall, descending on an open clearing in the middle of a hundred acres of woods—George's house.

Fire flooded through the building, its flames disintegrating everything in its path. Tricia and George were instantly killed in their sleep, while Roland—reading a book in bed—looked up long enough to realize he was about to be consumed by fire. Chris awoke as smoke powered into his room, first from underneath the door, then through the cracks in the ceiling, in the walls.

Clouds of black and gray.

He struggled to breathe.

He choked.

Then came the heat as flames seeped into the room, surrounding him in a fiery haze. He scanned the room. If he could make it to the window, he could escape. He attempted to climb out of bed, but his legs didn't seem to work. His entire body was paralyzed, rendering him unable to move. He heard the screams echoing through the house. His friends were burning alive.

I have to save them.

Another attempt to climb out of bed. Only this time he felt the blankets growing heavier on top of him like a five-hundred-pound block was pressing him down, deeper into the bed.

"Chris! Help me!"

It was coming from outside the window.

Alena was on the roof of the porch engulfed in flames up to

her neck, and Natalya was standing beside her holding a knife.

"I'm coming," Chris said.

But the blankets were still holding him down. He looked in horror as the flames consumed Alena. Her screams were deafening. Chris struggled to move.

Goddammit, what is wrong with this fucking blanket? I'm coming, Alena, I'm coming!

"No, you're not," said Natalya.

She pressed the twelve-inch blade to her own neck and sliced through the skin from end to end, severing the esophagus and trachea. An avalanche of blood shot out of the gaping wound, bathing her entire body in red.

"You can't fucking save her," said a gravely voice. "You can't save any of them."

Chris's eyes darted to the other side of the room. Standing in front of the closet was Terry Harper. But it wasn't the Terry he knew. This creature was a corpse who'd spent the last six months rotting. It was purple and gray, and its eyes were black. Void of a soul.

Chris said, "I did the best I could."

"The best," scoffed Terry's corpse. "You think you're good? The villain never realizes he's the villain. Never knows what a piece of shit he really is."

Frank and Susie Boone appeared beside him with fresh bullet holes in both of their heads.

"You betrayed us," said Frank.

"We brought you into our home, and this is how you repay us?" said Susie.

The creature that was Terry laughed. "Chris, you're God's only regret." Then, in a sinister voice, "Chris, Chris! CHRIS!"

NEW BEGINNING

The last one sounded different.

Everything went blurry. Then, "*Chris!*"

I know that voice. Can't get that voice out of my head.

His vision began to clear, like putting on glasses, and he looked up to see Alena standing over him. She wasn't burning. He blinked. Trying to focus. The fire and smoke were gone—so were the ghosts of Natalya, Terry, Frank, and Susie.

"Are you okay?" she asked, touching his shoulder. "You're soaking wet."

He rubbed his eyes. Thank goodness he could move again.

"A nightmare," he said.

Their eyes met. She smiled and leaned down and kissed him. He kissed her back, savoring her lips on his. She was alive. He was alive. For a moment, nothing else mattered.

"You had a rough night," she said. "You should get more sleep. It's still early."

He sat up and looked around the room for his cigarettes. The nearly empty pack of Camels was on the nightstand beside his lighter. He pulled a smoke from the box and lit one.

"Unbelievable," Alena said, throwing her arms in the air and standing up. "You're obviously fine."

Chris felt the nicotine fill his lungs and invigorate his spirit. He looked up at the angry woman staring at him with crossed arms.

"We've got work to do," he said.

CHAPTER 63

Taormina, Italy

SICILY IS AN island just south of the Italian peninsula, and the ancient town of Taormina looks out on the Ionian Sea. Medieval buildings cover the mountainous coastline, perched on the rocky cliffs like homes in the Hollywood Hills. Even in winter the waters are blue, the weather warm, and the palm trees sway in the evening breeze, making it paradise on earth for those who can afford it.

Above the city, on a balcony in one of the most expensive villas in Italy, stood Auspex Technology's CEO and founder, Jean Mackler. A large man in his early sixties, Mackler was still athletic with a thick mane of salt and pepper hair that matched his immaculately trimmed goatee. He was dressed for dinner—white suit, leather boots, and a black button-down that revealed an abundance of chest hair. No jewelry except for a gold class ring with the University of Texas at Austin crest on top and "Class of 1982" engraved on the side. No matter how far he came, he would always be the kid who *almost* went pro. A jock from the start, Mackler had worked his way up from a blue-collar family in south Texas to a full-ride scholarship at UT Austin. As a linebacker with nearly four hundred tackles—number two on the team for forced fumbles—he took the Longhorns to the National Championship his junior year and was subsequently recruited by the Dallas Cowboys.

Then came the knee injury. His football career was over, but it sparked in him a drive to become invincible in this cruel world. Never again would he suffer the agony of seeing his dreams ripped from his hands. He learned to code and jumped on the '80s computer software bandwagon, following in the footsteps of Bill Gates and Steve Jobs. Mackler became a millionaire in 1986 when he sold his software company to Microsoft, a business he'd started in his studio apartment and built while moonlighting as a bartender at a local dive bar in Austin.

From there it was off to the races. He launched Auspex Technology in 1991 with one of the leading data scientists in the country and earned his first government contract five years later. In 2000 he beat the Y2K scare, and when the internet bubble burst the following year, he bought out his partners, making him the sole owner of Auspex and one of the richest men in the world. But Mackler was not satisfied. He wanted more. Robin Valencia's offer was too good to ignore, and though he doubted its validity at the start, when he learned of her intrepid plan to introduce legislation that would give him oversight over every corporation in the United States, he was on board. Damn the legality of it all; he had been given the keys to the kingdom.

It had been exactly twelve hours since Mackler's impromptu call with Steven House. The FBI director had become Valencia's proxy, a secret intermediary between him and the treason he was committing. Andrew Chew's fate was concerning, but it changed nothing—that spoilt little shit was nothing more than a frontman. As the sun set over the Ionian Sea and the lights from Taormina spilled out onto the water, he realized the wheels were finally in motion. It took him the entire day, but he'd managed to move the timeline up by more than twenty-four hours, the complexity of which made this no small feat. No matter what "emergency" had befallen House, the mission would be consummated. The United States would be forever altered, and he would be in the final stages of becoming one of the most powerful men in history.

The AI tablet had been a collaboration. Powered by state-of-the-art AI chips manufactured in China, the original prototype had been developed by a third-party tech consultancy in Oakland, California. From there it was delivered to Auspex headquarters in Dallas, Texas for assembly. The result was machine learning technology like never seen before—an AI-powered computer named Octavia, designed to control information without oversight; meaning it was impossible to hack. In a fraction of a second, it could steal billions—even trillions—of dollars and hide the assets with artificial paper trails.

Mackler had overseen the entire development process, ensuring that he had the necessary tools to complete the task required of him by the congresswoman, but also the ability to automate his new role as Chairman of the soon-to-be-inaugurated United States Corporation Oversight Committee. The next step had been production of a tablet-sized remote control for the computer, again provided by third-party vendors—this time in Italy. Parts were separately manufactured by four independent factories and assembled by a single craftsman out of a small shop on an unassuming street in Rome where the tablet was currently being stored.

The final stage was the Nysta update. As soon as the update dropped, bank accounts, pensions, and investment portfolios from millions of Americans would instantly transfer to the AI tablet. From there, the money would be deposited into thousands of offshore bank accounts belonging to shell corporations, all controlled by Auspex Technology's AI computer in Dallas: Octavia. Mackler's job would be complete.

His cell phone buzzed in his pocket. "Barry Allen" appeared on the caller ID.

It was time.

Mackler lit a cigarette with his gold lighter and inhaled the smoke, taking the nicotine deep into his lungs. Exhaling slowly, savoring the moment, he answered the phone.

The Nysta COO was a company man through and through, which made him loyal as a goddam Labrador; there wasn't an ounce of independent thought in his entire body. The corporate stooge was in his office at Nysta headquarters, working through his third Coke of the day. And it was only ten o'clock in the morning in California.

No pleasantries, Mackler got straight to the point. "Are we good?"

"We are," said Allen. "Just not as fast as we'd hoped. The update should be available for download in six hours."

"What part of 'immediately' do you not understand?"

"We're doing the best we can, Jean. This was last minute, and we've had a lot on our plate after what happened to Andrew."

"You assured me you had things under control. Can I count on you?"

"Yes, yes, you can," Allen quivered.

He'd surely wet his pants.

"Good," Mackler said. "Then you'll have the update live in two hours."

There was a pause. Then, "Yes, sir."

Mackler disconnected the call and grabbed his keys. It was time for dinner.

CHAPTER 64

Bert T. Combs Mountain Parkway
Kentucky

CHRIS KEPT THE Ford Bronco at a steady speed. Fast enough to make good time but slow enough to avoid a state trooper trying to achieve his monthly ticket quota. The Bert T. Combs Mountain Parkway traversed Eastern Kentucky to the central part of the state. Unlike the snow-capped mountains of Colorado, the only things visible from the freeway were dead trees and open fields covered in snow. There weren't a whole lot of vehicles on the road either. But that would change when they merged onto I-64 and made their way into Fayette County.

The large McDonald's coffees in the Bronco's cupholders were Chris's and Alena's third that day. It had been a busy morning. Roland, George, and Tricia were up early—discussing the previous day's events over coffee and a homemade breakfast of eggs, bacon, and toast when Chris and Alena emerged from the guest bedroom.

Chris's nightmare had sparked a fire that could only be tamed by one thing: death to the perpetrators of their betrayal. He was tired of running. It was time to turn things around. Go after the devil himself—head-on. And he wasn't the only one who felt this way.

One of George's friends, a crusty old Pikeville police officer, had been on the scene with state police at the airport. He recognized George's truck—riddled with bullets, the windshield shattered, the classic V8 engine destroyed—and he found something hidden underneath.

"A goddam GPS tracker," George had said. "It's time to hunt these assholes down. Like animals. No mercy. If we don't, they're gonna keep coming until we're all dead."

"I agree," Tricia had said as she filled everyone's plates with second helpings of her home-cooked southern breakfast. "We're no longer safe here. And I'm sick and tired of the federal government. I'm ready to be done with all of them."

She's sounding more and more like George, Chris had thought.

Roland had smoked his pipe and listened to what everyone had to say. Then he'd said, "If we do this, we go all the way. That means evidence."

Alena had agreed. "There is power in the public knowing the truth. But it requires evidence. An FBI director and a former Chairman of the Joint Chiefs of Staff colluding with Russia and China. A private military contractor carrying out targeted assassinations on American citizens. Two of the largest tech companies in the world stealing users' financial information. We can stop this; we just have to prove it."

George and Tricia wanted to protect their home. Roland wanted to start a new life. And Alena wanted to expose the truth. But Chris—he wanted to send the people after them straight to hell.

Regardless of motivations, they were all on board. And they had a plan.

Chris saw a blue sign above the freeway indicating their exit was a mile away. It was followed by another one that said LEXINGTON 18 MILES. He put his blinker on as he moved to the right lane and prepared to merge onto Interstate 64.

CHAPTER 65

The Hay-Adams
Washington, D.C.

OFF THE RECORD is an upscale bar beneath The Hay-Adams hotel with red leather-backed chairs and matching walls adorned with caricatures of the country's political elite. The dimly lit downtown haunt is frequented by politicians and lobbyists looking to hide in plain sight. Within this historic hotel, deals are made, bribes taken, and the gears of the United States government continually oiled. Robin Valencia left her black Tesla Model S with the valet and entered the hotel lobby, her Gucci sunglasses still shielding her eyes. She was active on social media, and that made her a recognizable figure wherever she went—ergo her disdain for taking meetings in crowded restaurants. But today was an exception. The man she was meeting was not someone you said no to.

She took the elevator down to the basement bar and made her way through the busy eatery—passing senators, congressmen, and lobbyists in tailored suits all hunched over their tables, wheeling and dealing over top-shelf whiskey and filet mignon lunches. Al Kempe was comfortable in a red lounge chair in the back, beneath a caricature of President Obama, nursing a Woodford Reserve on the rocks. Valencia took a seat across from him, placing her purse on the small circular table between them but keeping her sunglasses on.

"Take those goddam things off," Kempe said.

"As you wish," she replied, removing the sunglasses and setting them beside her purse.

"Much better. Now I can see those big brown eyes."

"You're a little old for me."

"Not from what I hear."

She ignored the insult and motioned for the waiter, who appeared instantly as if he worked for her personally. She ordered a Manhattan and spring water, no tap, and then shooed him away with a flutter of her French-tipped nails.

"Why did you want to see me?" she said.

Kempe took a healthy taste of his bourbon. Then, "What's your evaluation of FBI Director House?"

She considered the question. Before she could reply, the waiter appeared with her cocktail and water. He stalled a moment to see if they needed anything else, and when his presence was ignored, he disappeared.

"House has been a competent performer," Valencia answered, sipping the whiskey drink. "There's been a few mistakes, specifically with Woodhaven. But he's managed to thwart cybersecurity and espionage investigations into China and Russia. Why do you ask?"

"It's always good to get outside opinions."

"Is there a problem?"

"Depends on how one looks at it."

"So there *is* a problem."

"Not one lacking a remedy. And not one you need to concern yourself with. Your focus should be on legislation. What's your read on the president?"

"He's on board."

"Has he seen the bill?"

She smiled. "Of course he has. And he knows as well as I do that it's in his best interest to do as he's told."

"Good."

"I still don't understand the reason for this meeting." She leaned forward. "How do you know we're not being followed?"

Kempe laughed. "By who? House? He's got too much on his plate right now to worry about you."

"I wasn't talking about me."

The Russian spy shook the glass, swirling the brown liquid around the two ice cubes. He took a sip. Then, "I'm too old for the field. I was supposed to be hands-off, on a beach somewhere. But alas, incompetence runs rampant in this country. It's always been that way in government, though. How do you think I maintained my cover for so long?"

"Blind eyes."

"That too." He smiled. "Money is the great equalizer. And it's why I'm sitting across the table from you. Just a few blocks from where I spent thirty years serving this country."

Valencia didn't respond. She'd long known Kempe was a Russian spy with ties to America's deep state. Ever since he approached her with the opportunity of a lifetime. Money cured all sins, and her dream of creating an equitable society for unrepresented groups would finally come to fruition thanks to him and those he worked for—a blind eye was the least she could offer in return.

"It is important that you continue what we started," Kempe

said. "The final phase is upon us. The Nysta update will go live today. Another twenty-four hours and users will have updated their applications and the AI computer will be activated." He leaned forward, his expression stern. "There can be no turning back."

"I am fully committed."

"I'm glad to hear it."

He downed his drink and placed both hands on the table. Sensing the meeting was over, Valencia couldn't resist another question.

"The update was scheduled for three days from now. Why the change?"

Kempe's eyes narrowed. They were ice cold. The Russian spy emerging from his shell. She nearly shuddered inside. Almost took back the question. After all, he had said the issue was none of her concern.

Then, his eyes softened. "I made a judgment of error, so I will tell you. Woodhaven is still at large. As a precaution, House wisely decided to move the timeline up for launch. Auspex has been notified, so has Nysta, and my team in Italy is ready to go."

"How did this happen?"

"One of my operatives betrayed me. I should have seen it coming."

"There's been a trail of blood from California to Kentucky."

Kempe nodded. "No one will know the truth, but nevertheless, the surviving members of Woodhaven—and the journalist—have enough information to be a problem."

"How much do they know?"

"Not a lot, but enough—don't worry, they are not aware of your involvement. That knowledge died in Kentucky six months ago. Nor do they fully comprehend what is really happening. Or the gravity of the information they possess." His eyes grew heavy.

"But I've become too visible, and I fear they may come after me. It's no longer safe for me to be in the country. Which is why I wanted to see you today."

"You're leaving."

He nodded. "You and I will never speak again, but you must do your part. There can be no failure. We both know how that ends."

She swallowed as she nodded, knowing damn well what he was implying.

CHAPTER 66

Lexington, Kentucky

"This place has changed," said Chris.

He was staring out the window as they drove down Main Street. Much of downtown was historic, though a recent surge in development had added a plethora of modern buildings to the mix. There were bars and restaurants—none of which Chris recognized—as well as a few retail shops, the courthouse, a brand new civic center. The University of Kentucky was nearby. So was Keeneland race track. Lexington was a small city, a big town. And it brought back memories.

"When was the last time you were here?" Alena asked.

Chris turned right onto Tates Creek Road, entering Chevy Chase—a village-like neighborhood filled with bungalows and cottages from the 1920s and '30s.

"A lifetime ago," he said. "George and I drove up senior year. Spent the weekend partying with college girls. That was fun."

Alena rolled her eyes. "I'm sure it was."

"Place seemed different then."

"Perhaps you were different."

"Yeah, a lot of water under the bridge." He changed the subject. "You think this Laura Wilson will talk to us?"

"She agreed to see us when I called her. I don't know how much she'll talk, though. I reached out when her husband died six months ago. That was during the Nysta hearings—when I first had the idea for the article. She refused to speak with me then. Refused to speak with anyone in the press, for that matter."

"I don't blame her."

"I don't either. What happened was—it was awful. His body was cut in half."

"Jeez."

"She's a nurse, was a nurse. They have a little girl. Last I heard she was living with her parents and taking care of her daughter full-time."

"How do you know all this?"

"Facebook, Instagram," Alena said.

"You're a stalker."

"I'm a journalist. And it's a good thing, too. If Seth Wilson had information on the Nysta update, she's our only lead."

Chris nodded. He would have much rather been headed to D.C. with a truckload of weapons. Never mind the potential cyberattack, or the government collusion with Russia, with China; all he cared about was putting those responsible for his friend's deaths in the grave. But first they needed information. They needed to understand what was going on, who the players were. Revenge would have to wait.

Tates Creek Road became four lanes, separated by a grass median and surrounded by expensive homes and gigantic churches. They had entered Lansdowne, an upper-middle-class neighborhood developed in the '50s and '60s. Chris's KryptAll phone vibrated. A text message from Roland confirming his arrival at the safe house. George's compound was no longer a secure location, so while Chris and Alena met with Wilson's widow, Roland, George, and Tricia were tasked with establishing a temporary base of operations in Lexington. In order to maintain secure comms, George had outfitted the entire team with new KryptAll phones.

Laura Wilson's parents lived in the smallest house in Lansdowne. Incidentally, it was also the largest lot in Lansdowne. Her father was a barber, and her mother was a retired kindergarten teacher. Laura had moved in with them less than a month after her husband's death. Attention from the media outside her home had been unrelenting. And anyway, it was no longer a home; it was a house without a future. Only memories of a life she would never get back.

"All this from Facebook?" Chris said as he parked the Bronco in front of the mid-century ranch and turned off the engine.

"Not just hers—her friends', her family's," said Alena. "You can piece together a person's entire life from social media."

• • •

Laura Wilson set two coffee mugs on the glass coffee table and took a seat opposite Chris and Alena. She was beautiful, couldn't be more than thirty-five or thirty-six, with blond hair that cascaded over her black turtleneck sweater. There was a warmth in her blue eyes but also a sadness that made her appear older than she was.

"Thank you for seeing us," Alena said, taking one of the mugs and sipping the hot beverage. "Oh, this is good."

"It's my sister's coffee," Laura said. "Cherry Seed Coffee Roastery is her brand. She used to have a store over on Southland.

COVID lockdowns put her out of business, and now she roasts out of her garage for family and friends."

Chris tried the coffee. He smiled. "It's excellent."

"Lizzy will be up from her nap in fifteen minutes, and my mom won't be back from her pickleball game for another hour. So let's make this quick. What did you want to see me about?"

Alena removed a manila envelope from her jacket and placed it on the table. She had printed screenshots of the Nysta update code while back at George's to make things easier.

"Do you know what this is?" she asked.

Laura looked at them, then shook her head. "Looks like computer coding or something. I don't know."

"It's a software update for the Nysta app."

Laura looked down. "I don't use that."

"And you shouldn't. We believe this update will be used to steal sensitive financial information from its users."

"I know."

Alena looked at Chris, then back at Laura.

"What do you mean?"

Laura hesitated. "I'm really not comfortable talking about this."

Alena hid her frustration. "I understand."

"I know I agreed to see you, and I knew you would bring this up, but I just—it's still fresh. The past six months have been really hard. Seth was my whole world." She fought back tears. "I'd known him since we were kids. I don't know what life is like without him."

Chris thought of Jessica and Claire and how much his life had changed since losing them. They were still alive, though, and the loss had been his doing. He couldn't even imagine what Laura was going through.

"I'm sorry," Alena said. "We shouldn't have come."

Laura grabbed a tissue from a box beside the couch and wiped her eyes. "It's fine. I'm just—Seth dedicated his life to two things: his family and his country." She pointed to the pages on the table. "In the months before he died, this was all he thought about."

"He was going to vote against Nysta at the hearings," Alena said.

"Yes, he was. But it was more than that. He knew about this, this update. He was obsessed with it, actually. Said it was the biggest threat to our country since World War Two."

"He knew there was going to be a cyberattack?"

"He didn't call it that."

"What did he call it?"

"You think he was killed because of this, don't you?"

Alena didn't respond.

"It doesn't matter how my husband died, or why. None of that will bring him back. What matters, Ms. Moore, is that he stood up to evil. He was David fighting Goliath. And he died protecting me and Lizzy from that evil."

Chris felt a knot forming in his gut. Was it guilt? His conscience? If Seth Wilson was a patriot, what did that make him? A mercenary? Would Jessica or Claire speak of him the same way Laura did of her husband? He felt a resolve.

"We're trying to stop that same evil, Mrs. Wilson," he said. "The people responsible for your husband's death are still out there. The threat is still real. Help us finish what he started."

Laura looked at the bearded warrior and the journalist in front of her. Her eyes darted between them as if she was trying to decide whether or not she could trust them.

Finally, she said, "Seth was always concerned about cybersecurity. He was one of those guys who put tape on his laptop's camera. Changed his iPhone password daily. I used to make fun of him, but he would always respond with, 'Laura, technology will be our downfall,' and I'd just shake my head and go back to shopping on Amazon." She laughed. "We were polar opposites, which is why I thought he was crazy when he began saving hard copies of his investigation into Nysta. But it wasn't just Nysta; it was the people he worked with in Washington. You could call him a conspiracy theorist, but he wasn't the type. Everything was black and white to him—nothing was gray. He would never have pursued this if he didn't believe it was true."

She took a deep breath. "As you know, there was a lot of news coverage when he passed away. There was also a police investigation due to the nature of his death." She nearly teared up again but powered through. "I received a visit from two FBI agents the day after the accident."

"That's fairly routine considering your husband's occupation," said Chris.

"Yes, but their questions were not," Laura replied. "They wanted to know what his involvement was in the Nysta hearings. Of course, I knew very little. Seth never told me much. Always preferred to leave his work at the office." She looked down. "Now I know it was to protect me."

"What did the agents say when you told them?" Alena asked.

"They weren't kind. They pushed. Found it hard to believe I

didn't know what my husband was involved in. Said they would return with a federal warrant."

"Did they?" Chris asked.

She nodded. "They came back the next day. Went through everything, even our safety deposit box at the bank. I felt violated. It was awful. They found nothing, of course. After that, I started staying here with my parents. I just couldn't take it any longer."

"So where did your husband keep his Nysta files?" Alena asked.

"For that you'll need to speak with my father."

CHAPTER 67

The Lansdowne Barber Shop was only a mile from Laura's parents' house at the Lansdowne Shoppes. Chris passed Malone's and Drake's—local eateries serving up prime steaks and upscale bar fare—and parked the Bronco in front of the Old Kentucky Chocolates store. A white sign with red lettering indicated that the barbershop was located down an alley between another steakhouse and a Baskin-Robbin's. Laura had given them the address and told them to speak with the barbershop's owner, Billy. Her father. That was the end of their conversation.

A red-and-white barber pole turned above a green front door. Chris opened it for Alena, and they entered what felt like a time machine—cast-iron barber chairs, backbars laden with shears and jars of Barbicide. And a smell. One so familiar it brought Chris back to his childhood and the monthly visits to the barber with his dad. The shop had always smelled of cigarette smoke, mint gum, and hairspray. But also "cut hair"—an indescribable scent, really, only known to those who've been to barbershops. No gum or tobacco smell at the Lansdowne Barber Shop, but the "cut hair" scent and hairspray were the same. There were four men in their sixties and seventies working behind antique barber chairs and customers waiting their turn in a small seating area at the front. Piles of hair on the tiled floor, the steady hum of electric clippers, framed black-and-white photographs of 1930s baseball players on the walls. Chris immediately felt at home.

A trim man in his sixties wearing Dri-FIT khakis and a forest green button-down smiled at them as they came in.

"Welcome," he said. "Do you have an appointment?"

"We do not," Chris replied.

"No problem. Jeff over there will take care of you as soon as he's finished."

Chris noticed the five other men seated in the waiting area.

"They're all waiting for me," the barber explained.

"I'm here to see Billy. Laura Wilson sent me."

"I'm Billy, but I'm full the rest of the day." He paused for a moment. Then, "Come back at six, and I'll get you in."

"Perfect. Any good spots nearby to grab a bite to eat?"

• • •

Billy recommended Drake's.

Chris and Alena grabbed a table near the bar and both ordered Juicy Lucy cheeseburger sliders with fries and a West Sixth IPA from a local brewery. Food was excellent. So was the beer. They had two hours to kill, and they spent it discussing the day's odd turn of events. How was a local barber in Lexington connected to Congressman Wilson's investigation into Nysta? It was strange that Laura had trusted them, two people she hardly knew, with the whereabouts of her husband's files. Files the FBI had unsuccessfully tried to ascertain. Chris wondered if it was the information they'd shown her about the Nysta update. But Alena knew it was Chris himself who had gained Laura's trust. He'd somehow accomplished what she could not: assure Laura that those responsible for her husband's death would be brought to justice.

They returned to the barbershop at exactly six o'clock. A guy in his fifties wearing jeans and a blue polo shirt with "UK Wildcats" embroidered on the chest was paying Billy for a haircut, and the other three barbers were cleaning their stations. Chris and Alena took a seat and waited, but not for long. Billy finished his conversation with the customer—who promised to be back the following week, then waved as he left. The other barbers grabbed their bags and coats, and each one said goodbye and headed out into the cold. Once the shop was empty, Billy motioned for Chris to have a seat in the mint-green chair in front of his station.

"What are we doing?" he said, wrapping a disposable neck strip around Chris's neck.

"Just a trim."

"You got it." Billy draped a black barber cape over Chris's chest, then turned on an electric clipper. He started with the sides, skillfully working his way up from the base of the hairline to just below the top of Chris's head. "What kind of work are you in, Mr.—"

"Harding," Chris replied. "Chris Harding." He wasn't sure why he used his real name. Perhaps he was tired of hiding. Alena shot him a confused look. He ignored her and said, "Right now, no occupation."

There was no discernible reaction from the barber. He simply nodded and continued with the haircut, switching to sheers and focusing on the unkempt mane in front of him. Once he'd taken off a good inch, he returned to the clippers and began blending the sides.

"What kind of information are you looking for?" he finally said.

NEW BEGINNING

There it was. He knew why they were there.

"How much did Laura tell you?" Alena said, answering the question for Chris.

Billy's eyes didn't leave his work. "I went to high school with Seth's father."

"You grew up here?" Alena asked.

"Sure did."

"It's a beautiful town. Reminds me a bit of home."

"And where's that?"

"Austin, but I've been in New York for a long time."

"The city?"

"Yeah, you've been?"

"Never, but I've had quite a few customers move down from New York. Lexington is a nice place to live—a nice place to raise a family. You two have kids?"

Alena blushed. "No, uh—"

"We're not married," Chris said.

"Hmm," said Billy. "I wouldn't have guessed that." He handed Chris a mirror. "Let me know if I need to take any more off."

Chris was accustomed to thirty-minute, even forty-minute haircuts; this one had taken less than ten. Billy was a pro. A true craftsman.

"Looks great," Chris said, handing back the mirror.

Billy nodded and removed the cape and neck strip. Next came the warm shaving cream to the back of the neck.

This is the point where he kills me, thought Chris as he watched the reflection of Billy dipping a straight razor into the jar of Barbicide from the mirror in front of him.

The barber moved Chris's head forward, keeping the skin taut, and pressed the steel blade to the back of his neck. A series of quick, smooth upward motions followed. The front of the neck was the final step in the process. And the most intimate. The barber was holding a straight razor mere inches from his throat.

"What will you do to the men responsible for my son-in-law's death?" Billy asked.

His tone was no longer the grateful customer service savant of moments before. He had waited until Chris was at a disadvantage before asking the only question that mattered, proving he had known why they were there the entire time. And Chris respected him for it. He would have done the same thing.

"Kill every goddamn one of them," Chris replied.

"Good," said Billy. He wiped away the residual shaving cream with a towel and then splashed on a dab of aftershave. "All done."

Chris stood up and faced the barber. They were of similar height, though Chris was easily fifty pounds heavier, but Billy was athletic—spry would be the right word—and Chris sensed this wasn't a man to tangle with.

"What do I owe you?" Chris asked, taking out his wallet. For once he was in a place that welcomed the only form of payment he had—cash.

"I don't want your money," Billy said. "Laura told me what's going on. I just wanted to meet you first. Not sure if I can trust you, so I'll tell you this: What you're about to see did not come from me. In fact, we never met. Understand?"

"Yes."

"And one more thing—you hurt Laura, or anyone else in my family, I'll make sure it's the last thing you ever do."

Chris didn't doubt it. "I'd expect nothing less."

"Now with that out of the way, there's something you should see."

NEW BEGINNING

The barber went to the front of the shop and closed the blinds and locked the door. He then returned to his station. The barber chair consisted of three distinct parts. The base was made of steel, the mint-green frame was ceramic, and the seat cushions were wrapped in thick, brown leather upholstery. There was a lever on the side—also made of steel—and the barber pulled it, releasing pressure on the hydraulic pump beneath the seat and causing it to drop downward. Typically one would let go, and the chair would be ready for the next customer, but Billy continued to press the lever until a loud clicking sound alerted him to stop. He then used both hands to turn the seat cushion clockwise and, in one swift motion, lifted the cushion out of the chair, leaving a rectangular compartment in its place. Inside the compartment was a small safe with an analog locking system.

Billy said, "I began my career in 1976. And since then I've had customers from all walks of life. Being a barber means information is exchanged as often as cash." He spun the dial on the safe, pinpointing a series of numbers. The door clicked open. "From time to time that information must be stored. I don't just do it for the money, I do it to help preserve the freedoms we enjoy in this country. In a world of technology, no one is truly safe—truly free."

"So you're a broker," Chris said.

"Only when necessary," Billy replied. "I cut Seth Wilson's hair for many years, long before he became a congressman."

"You're selective."

"Very."

Inside the safe was a stack of envelopes and files. Billy thumbed through them, found the one he was looking for, and removed a thick 9x12 padded envelope. It was sealed shut with a large sticker on top. "Seth told me about his investigation into Nysta. Said he discovered something that, if true, could alter the course of our country forever. He never got into specifics, didn't want to put anyone in danger—myself included—but he was very clear on one thing. What he discovered could not fall into the wrong hands. The day before he left for D.C., to cast his vote on the Nysta hearings, he came in for a haircut. Asked me to keep this envelope safe for him." A sadness fell across Billy's eyes. "It's like he knew something was going to happen. It was the last time I ever saw him."

Chris looked at Alena, then back at the barber. "He knew someone would come looking for this."

"And they did."

"FBI?" Alena asked.

"FBI, CIA, Secret Service—you name it." Billy pressed the envelope with both hands. "Whatever is in here was enough to get Seth killed. But this isn't my first rodeo. I told those bastards exactly where they could shove their warrants."

"Why are you showing it to us?" Chris asked.

Billy handed him the envelope. "Because it was intended for your eyes only."

Chris stared at the sticker on top and the name printed on it: CHRIS HARDING.

CHAPTER 68

La Biga Ristoracaffé
Rome, Italy

Bashir Mahmoud and Adham Mostafa met face-to-face for the first time in six months. The small restaurant was a popular tourist destination in the heart of the ancient city. It had a patio with views of the Colosseum directly across the street and served traditional Italian cuisine along with a large selection of pastries and coffee. Though it was December, the rainy season in Rome, the sun was shining and the temperature was a comfortable fifty-eight degrees. The two men ordered caramel lattes and found a table on the patio. Both were dressed in designer clothes—fitted jeans, tailored shirts, and sports coats paired with Italian dress shoes—looking every bit the part of wealthy Iranian tourists. A believable ruse considering Italy's longstanding economic ties with Tehran.

Earlier that day, Mahmoud and Mostafa had received instructions from their employer to meet at this address for the hand-off. An exact time was not specified so they spent the better part of an hour guzzling lattes and discussing their recent escapades with women. Mahmoud was the ladies' man, and his appetite for big-breasted prostitutes was rarely satisfied. Mostafa, on the other hand, was more subdued, serious even. He rarely spent time with the opposite sex but enjoyed Mahmoud's stories. It had been six months, and there were many.

Finally, their contact arrived. She was an Italian woman in her mid-twenties—beautiful by anyone's standards—with jet-black hair, large almond-shaped brown eyes, and a tight body that matched her enhanced chest. She carried a black leather briefcase in her right hand. She recognized Mahmoud and Mostafa based on a picture her handler had sent her a few hours before and made a beeline for their table.

She removed her sunglasses and set the case on the ground beside Mahmoud's feet.

"Wait here until you receive further instructions," she said in perfect Farsi.

The men nodded. Mahmoud was about to comment on her beauty, but she turned and walked away before he had the chance. He shrugged. There would be time for pleasure once the mission was completed.

The woman had barely made it to the sidewalk when their phones vibrated inside their pockets. Both encrypted messages were the same, and like the ones they received before, they would disappear once read. Mahmoud memorized the numbers in the text then placed the briefcase on the table, careful not to spill the drinks. He plugged the six-digit password into a small digital screen, and the case clicked open.

Inside was a metallic-gray thirteen-inch tablet similar in design to an iPad Pro. Mahmoud powered up the tablet and used

NEW BEGINNING

another password followed by facial recognition to complete the two-part authentication process required to unlock the device. There was only one preloaded application on the home screen. And it was named Octavia.

CHAPTER 69

Lexington, Kentucky

It was dark when Chris turned the Bronco onto the two-lane highway just outside of town. Their destination was a house on a ten-acre lot that backed up to one of the largest horse farms in Kentucky. George's uncle owned the property. But it was winter. That meant he and his wife were enjoying the beaches of Fort Myers. They wouldn't return until late March, which made it the perfect place for a group of wanted criminals to crash. George, Tricia, and Roland were waiting for Chris and Alena in the living room in front of a roaring fireplace. Much larger than George's home, it resembled a log cabin, like something in Vail or on a ranch in Montana. The ceiling was two stories high, with the second-floor hallways surrounding the living area below, and everything seemed to be mahogany or red and smelled of leather and wood.

Chris and Alena had already read the contents of Seth Wilson's file. They had done so while at the Lansdowne Barber Shop and then spent the drive processing what they'd learned. As much as Chris wanted an IPA, he knew it would have to wait. Everyone crowded around the two leather couches that faced the stone fireplace, and Chris opened the envelope on the oak coffee table and began.

The envelope was easily an inch thick, filled with at least a hundred pages of documents as well as several glossy 8x10 photographs, newspaper clippings, and website printouts. It was a case file for what appeared to be a months-long investigation, and Wilson had left no stone unturned. He had discovered a conspiracy to push through a legislative proposal as early as 2022, a congressional bill titled the United States Corporation Oversight Act and authored by California Congresswoman Robin Valencia. The fifty-page proposal asserted that capitalism in the United States had become "too big to fail" and that the American people, specifically minorities, were no longer able to live a quality life. This concept that the middle class was gone, that the rich were getting richer, wasn't a new idea. For decades, large corporations had monopolized every aspect of commerce. But now private equity firms were buying up every house in the country, ballooning values and pricing average Americans out of the real estate market. And they hadn't stopped there. Hundreds of thousands of small businesses across the country had been acquired in droves by the same private equity firms who now owned eighty percent of the country's single-family homes.

COVID-19 had only exasperated things. An entire country shut down. Political unrest, racial tension—the country had never been more volatile than it was now. They were primed. Ready for a change. And Robin Valencia had a plan. The United States Corporation Oversight Act would grant the federal government complete control over the private sector. Valencia argued that the only way to truly build an inclusive and equitable society was federal oversight over all commerce in America. Her groundbreaking bill had received some traction from the far left, but most—including many Democrats—felt it was too much. As one Democrat congressman from Tennessee said: "This is pure, unadulterated communism."

And it was. State-controlled means of production is one of the pillars of communism. Valencia knew that, of course, which was where Nysta came in. The social media app had taken the country by storm. With over a hundred million users, it was by far the most used application on the market. But it had a problem. It was Chinese-owned. Congress had been cracking down on cybersecurity involving foreign corporations for some time, and Nysta was first on their list. This created the perfect storm. The perfect tool.

The New World Order wasn't necessarily a communist organization, though that was part of it. Their goal was to create a one-world government controlled by them and them alone. Accomplishing this meant seizing every opportunity that presented itself, and Nysta and Valencia were too good to be true. They decided to weaponize the popular app and use Valencia to push the United States closer to Marxism than one could have ever imagined possible.

To achieve this plan, the NWO needed an economic disaster. So they partnered with the Russians and the Chinese to develop a virus, stealthily hidden within one of Nysta's routine software updates, that would give the app complete access to users' sensitive financial information. Simultaneously, they built an AI-powered computer—appropriately named Octavia, which in Latin symbolized "new beginnings"—that could take that sensitive financial data and wipe out a third of the United States' wealth in a fraction of a second. Octavia would then hide the stolen funds within thousands of offshore accounts. The money would never be found. The NWO used a new cryptocurrency called HX5 to purchase the AI

NEW BEGINNING

chips needed to power the AI computer from a Chinese semiconductor chip manufacturer called SMIC—a transaction brokered in Geneva by a Swiss banker named Mikael Gerber and facilitated by two Iranian terrorists, Bashir Mahmoud and Adham Mostafa.

SMIC held a majority stake in Nysta and was more than happy to see the company take the fall if it furthered China's ultimate goal of dominating the world economy. The American people already suspected the Chinese, and Nysta for that matter, of engaging in cyber espionage and wouldn't blink an eye when they were discovered to be responsible for stealing billions of American dollars and plummeting the country into a depression not seen since the stock market crash of 1929. Auspex Technology, already installed by Congress to protect Nysta's user data, would swoop in and save the day by "stopping" the virus from completely wreaking havoc on the country. But the damage would be done, and the American people—through their representatives—would welcome more oversight if it meant foiling future attacks. As an added precaution, a list of congressmen likely to be "on the fence" were to be provided substantial payments—bribes—all derived from the money that would be stolen from the American people.

The promise of power was used to engage Auspex CEO Jean Mackler. He met with Valencia on more than one occasion and was subsequently given the contract to manage Nysta's data. He was a perfect partner, having already established himself as the largest network security professional in the world. As a multi-billionaire, money would not have been enough to entice him. What he wanted was power. So as payment for building Octavia, he was promised the role of a lifetime: Chairman of the United States Corporation Oversight Committee.

Conversely, Nysta CEO Andrew Chew and FBI Director Steven House had not been given a choice; their payment was their lives. Chew was already beholden to the Chinese Communist Party, due to their ownership stake in Nysta through SMIC, and was forced to build the software update. House was blackmailed by Valencia, as one of the glossy 8x10s indicated in a career-ending scene: the FBI director exiting a helicopter in front of a certain mansion on a certain private tropical island owned by a recently deceased millionaire. Another picture showed House enjoying the company of a fifteen-year-old girl in a bedroom of that house. The FBI director's job was to shut down any investigation into cyber espionage. That included Woodhaven. The contract to terminate was given to Dan Greenwood. Everyone, even FBI Special Agent Adam Conner, was on that list. Seth Wilson had Woodhaven's entire file, including their true identities. And the man responsible for overseeing this entire operation was an aging Russian spy hidden deep within the United States government named Al Kempe.

The most damning piece of evidence was Woodhaven's source of funding. It had never crossed Roland's mind, or George's, Tricia's, Terry's, or Chris's, to look into how they were getting paid. Woodhaven was a gray group funded by the FBI. Only it wasn't. Wilson had tracked the bank accounts responsible for payroll to a holding company in Saint Petersburg, Russia. Further investigation led to Yevgeny Prigozhin, the recently deceased co-founder of the Wagner Group. A proxy of the Russian government, the Wagner Group was the most corrupt private military company in the world, and Prigozhin had been their leader—though he would never admit it—until he died in an "accidental" plane crash on August 23, 2023. As the second most powerful man in Russia, it was believed President Putin had ordered Prigozhin's death to cover up the Wagner Group's involvement in the Russian invasion of

Finland in 2022. Woodhaven had been a Russian-funded organization—ramifications of which inadvertently made Chris, Roland, George, and Tricia agents of the Russian government.

When Chris finished explaining the contents of the file, the steady crackling of the fire was the only sound in the room. It was a lot to take in. Seth Wilson knew of the NWO's existence. He knew about their planned cyberattack using Nysta as the catalyst. And he knew about Woodhaven. The congressman had obtained enough information to expose some of the most powerful people in the country. No wonder they killed him.

Alena broke the silence.

"We have enough here to blow this whole thing out of the water," she said. "The Nysta update is scheduled to drop in three days. The country will spiral into chaos. And Robin Valencia will introduce her bill to Congress. But we can stop the attack simply by exposing Valencia, exposing House, Mackler, Greenwood, Kempe—all of them will go to prison. The public will be able to protect themselves from the cyberattack, and Valencia's bill will disappear into oblivion."

"She's not wrong," Roland said. "But remember, our involvement in Woodhaven makes us culpable for this whole thing too."

"Unwittingly," Alena replied.

"I don't think that would hold up in court."

"Sure, it's a risk—we have to hope the attorney general sees this in context—but that's where I come in. My story will give that context." She looked around the room. "Honestly, from what I've seen, this is the *least* dangerous thing any of you have done."

She had a point.

"Words are a powerful weapon," Roland said. "But how can we trust this intel?"

"It's all in there," said Chris. "Photographs, transcripts—Wilson uncovered everything."

"But how?" Roland pressed. "He must have had a source. Someone on the inside."

"He did," said Alena.

"Who?"

"We have no idea," Chris replied. "And it doesn't matter."

Roland frowned. "It does matter."

"Everything in here is well documented. This isn't a history on how he got it."

Their argument was cut short when Alena gasped, "Oh my God."

All eyes turned to her.

She was staring at her phone with a concerned look on her face. "The Nysta update just dropped." She looked up from the screen. "Three days early."

CHAPTER 70

Roland struck a match and lit the tobacco that was firmly pressed inside his pipe. Then, settling into the back of the leather couch, he said, "According to the model described in Wilson's report, the Nysta update alone will not instigate the attack. The AI computer will need to be activated first."

"Correct," said Alena. She was on the couch across from him nursing an IPA and writing notes for her article on his MacBook Pro.

Tricia stood by the fireplace warming her hands. "What happens if someone doesn't download the update? Are they safe?"

George cracked open a Miller Lite as he entered the living room. "Nope, they're all screwed. If you have the Nysta app on your phone, it will automatically update as soon as you connect to the internet, which these days is pretty much all the time."

"Excellent," Roland replied sarcastically.

Chris joined them in the living room with his own IPA. In the BenShot "Bulletproof" pint glass he had stolen from George's house. He lit a cigarette as he sat down. George looked at the glass suspiciously—didn't make the connection—then longingly turned his attention to the cigarette.

"The woman made me quit," he said.

"The *woman* did no such thing," Tricia replied. "That was all you."

Chris laughed. "I need to quit too." He took a drag. "Just not today."

Alena looked up from the computer screen. "I can have this story finished and sent to my editor within the hour."

"That won't stop the attack," Chris said.

"No, it won't, but those responsible will still be brought to justice."

Chris shook his head. "We have to get to that AI computer before it's activated. Neutralize the threat. Then we go after the sons of bitches responsible."

The Harvard man relit his pipe with another match. "I think we can accomplish both at the same time."

• • •

Always follow the money. The root cause of any crime is financial gain, and Roland used that philosophy to construct his plan. It came to him quickly, as if like magic. Like that little voice within an artist's mind that controls what he creates—the story inside a novelist, the character inside an actor, the melody inside a musician. The god of ideas that lives within us all.

This ragtag group had come together because of the Harvard man. He would always be their leader. He wasn't the strongest man alive—fighting was his worst enemy—but he was smart, despite his flabby arms and soft midsection. And goddamn, he could bark orders.

"George, get your computer," he said. "Tricia, I need Robin Valencia's itinerary for the next seven days. And Alena—write that story."

Everyone nodded except Chris.

"What about me?" he said as he crushed his cigarette in a glass ashtray on the coffee table and lit another one.

"We're the brains; you're the brawn," replied Roland. "Just relax and don't drink too much."

"Fuck you. And roger that," Chris said with a grin.

Fifteen minutes later he had downed two West Sixth IPAs from the house's well-stocked beer fridge—the local brewery was quickly becoming his new favorite—Alena had completed a first draft of her article, and Tricia and George had news to report.

George turned his laptop around so that everyone could see the screen. Instead of a typical MacOS or Windows operating system, George operated within the dark web, a digital realm populated by the world's criminal elite.

"Artificial intelligence works by connecting to every part of the internet," George explained. "It collects data and stores it away, using it to increase its 'intelligence' and ability to perform."

"Just like humans," Alena said.

George nodded. "That's what makes it so dangerous. Octavia was built to steal currency and make it disappear into thousands of different accounts. Using a typical web browser, it would be impossible to track. However, the only way for the AI to transfer money in such a complex way would be to transmit it through the dark web. And that's how we catch it." He pointed to the screen. "This code represents instances when Octavia has accessed the dark web. As you can see, there is only one entry."

"In layman's terms," Chris said.

"Each time Octavia is turned on, it travels through the internet where it accesses everything in the world—all at once. But it does it from a single point of entry."

"The location of the computer," said Roland.

"Exactly," said George. "Octavia has only been turned on once, and there wasn't any financial activity, so it was probably just a test to see if the device worked. Anyway, I tracked the code from this entry point to this address." He clicked on his TOR network browser, navigated to a map, then plugged in a series of numbers. "The coordinates from the last time, and only time, Octavia has been powered on leads here: La Biga Ristoracaffé in Rome, Italy."

A quick Google search on Alena's phone revealed that it was a small restaurant across the street from the Colosseum. The Roman Empire's mark on the world had only been surpassed by the United States, and the irony was not lost on Chris that the heart of the old empire had become part of its greatest rival's potential downfall.

"When was this?" Roland said.

"Forty-five minutes ago," George replied. "But it's at a restaurant, and that means Octavia is mobile."

"Someone is accessing it with a tablet or a laptop."

"They sure are."

"But why Italy?" Chris asked. "Auspex is headquartered in Dallas. If they built this thing, wouldn't it be there?"

"Not if they wanted to use it in Italy," Tricia said. "They have something else planned, and I don't think Italy is a coincidence."

It was now her turn for a show-and-tell. She aimed her laptop at the group and said, "Robin Valencia is scheduled for back-to-back meetings with members of Congress all week. So she's not leaving D.C."

"She's building support for her bill," Roland said.

"That's exactly what she's doing. But here's what's concerning: The president will be in Rome the day after tomorrow for the G20

NEW BEGINNING

Summit."

Founded in 1999, the G20, or Group of 20, is an international correlation of governments—nineteen sovereign nations, the EU, and most recently, the African Union—that meet annually to address global economic issues. As a leader of State, the president attended every year, and this would be David Douglas's third summit since taking office in 2021. This year it was to be held at the Roma Eventi conference center in Rome.

On the surface, nothing out of the ordinary, but the timing was suspicious. A coincidence, maybe, but Chris didn't believe in coincidences.

"Is there a way for us to know when Octavia is powered up again?" he asked.

"GPS," said Tricia.

Everyone turned to look at her, waiting for her to explain. She blushed. "George, could you program a malware GPS so we'll be alerted the next time Octavia is turned on?"

"Obviously," he said with a grin. "Who the hell do you think I am? There is no way I'm letting our daughter down."

Chris nearly choked. "Wait—what?"

Tricia let out an audible sigh. "Damnit, George."

"What is he talking about?" Roland said.

She paused. Then, "We planned to tell everyone, but—"

"Trish is pregnant as shit," George blurted out. He was beaming.

"Oh my God, congratulations!" Alena exclaimed.

"Why is this the first time I'm hearing this?" Roland asked.

"Yes, I'm pregnant," said Tricia. "Eight weeks—we don't know if it's a boy or a girl yet."

"We're not doing a goddam gender reveal," said George. "Just gonna wear pink shirts when we find out it's a girl. Because it will be a girl. I drank White Claw for a year to make sure I'd have feminine sperm genes."

"That's a gender reveal, George," Chris said. "And I don't think it works like that."

"We were going to tell you, Roland, but then all this happened," Tricia said.

Roland was visually hurt, but he brushed it off. "I understand. Well, in this case, maybe you should stay here, Trish."

"The hell I am."

"You're pregnant."

Tricia raised one eye and narrowed the other. "There are laws about that, Roland."

"She's right," Alena said.

Roland threw his hands in the air. "Fine! But we have to protect you."

George slammed his 44 Magnum Smith & Wesson Model 29 revolver on the coffee table.

"Protected," he said.

Chris laughed. "You're outnumbered, old boy."

Roland went for his pipe and refilled it with fresh tobacco from his tin jar. Lighting the leaves with a match, he said, "Let's get to work, then."

"There's just one tiny little problem, guys," Alena said.

All eyes on her.

"How are we getting to Italy?"

CHAPTER 71

*The White House
Washington, D.C.*

President David Douglas stared out the window of the Oval Office at the Rose Garden, all covered in snow. It reminded him of growing up in Connecticut in the '40s and '50s and celebrating Christmas with his family. Now in his eighties, he was the oldest president in U.S. history to hold the office. Though he was growing frailer by the year, one could look at him and remember the dashing young politician he'd been in his youth—the young Turk who was going to change the world.

But times changed. The country changed. The year before, he had fraternized with Russia, negotiated with Putin, and turned a blind eye when the bald-headed demigod threatened to launch a nuclear attack on the country. Publicly, Douglas had been regarded as weak, and turning that perception around was no easy task. He'd thought he could do it on his own; one more term would do the trick. But the American people were lost. And their incredulousness had left him with no choice.

His thoughts were interrupted by the door opening. His last

meeting of the day. Congresswoman Robin Valencia shut the door behind her and extended her hand to the president.

"Mr. President," she said.

"Hi, Robin, thanks for seeing me."

"Pleasure is all mine."

He firmly shook her hand and motioned toward two couches in front of the fireplace that faced a mahogany coffee table. They both took a seat opposite each other.

"Can I get you anything? Coffee? Tea?" Douglas asked.

"I'm good, thank you."

The president crossed his legs and leaned back in his seat. What he was about to say had to be worded perfectly. "First, I want to thank you for your support. Recent developments in U.S.-China relations would never have been possible without you."

"California is on your side."

"I'm glad to hear that."

He shifted in his seat, then decided it was best to lean forward. It had been a long day. His mind would soon grow cloudy and he needed to stay sharp, at least until this meeting was over.

"I've read your bill, and I have some concerns," he said.

Valencia had been expecting some pushback from the president but maintained an expression of concern and reverence. "It is indeed a bold piece of legislation, Mr. President. But I'm confident the bill is in the country's best interest and that Congress will vote in favor of it."

"Both Democrats and Republicans have stated publicly that they will not support a bill of this magnitude—that it is quote 'Un-American' in nature. This must be bipartisan, Robin. Our country is divided, more so than ever before. We need to bring the people together, not force them into civil unrest."

"Are you saying you'll veto the bill?"

"I'm saying, get two-thirds from the House *and* the Senate. Show the American people that their elected leaders have their best interests at heart. I understand the magnitude of the attack that is coming and am well aware that my support has been required. But don't for one moment think I will put the interests of the establishment ahead of the American people. I've been silent for far too long. That ends today."

"You'll make enemies, sir. The economy may not recover, and the American people will resent you for that. This bill is the only way forward."

The president stood up and walked to the fireplace. He rested his hand on the mantel. He was tired but refused to succumb to it.

Looking back at Valencia, he said, "We both know who elected me—and why. I agreed because I wanted my shot. It was selfish." Nostalgia took over his expression. "There was a time when I would have crushed the NWO rather than surrender to their wishes." His eyes narrowed. "I hold the most powerful office in the world. It may be too late for me to stop the attack, but I will do everything in my power to bring the country back from the dead. And I will expose everything if you attempt to pass this bill. Do we understand each other, Congresswoman?"

"Perfectly."

• • •

Valencia left the Oval Office and made her way through the blue and beige carpeted halls of the West Wing. Staffers in navy suits scampered by as she passed offices and conference rooms adorned with American flags. Her meeting with the president had not been a surprise, but the resolve in his position had. It gave her a newfound respect for the old man, and for a moment she felt a twinge of guilt for what would soon befall him. But the wheels of progress were in motion. There was nothing she could do to stop it. This contingency had always been on the table and, unfortunately, it was time to exercise it. She brushed any feelings of remorse from her mind as she pulled out her iPhone and dialed the office of the vice president.

She was greeted by the cheery voice of Vice President Kim Walter's secretary, a young man who graduated from Stanford and drove an electric scooter—with a helmet—to the White House every morning in an attempt to help the environment.

"This is Robin Valencia."

"What can I do for you, Congresswoman?"

"I need a meeting with the vice president."

"Let me check her calendar—"

"Tonight."

CHAPTER 72

Lexington, Kentucky

Flying commercial to Italy was out of the question. Everyone but Alena had fake IDs, but those would have already been flagged by the FBI—as would Alena's real one—and they would all be arrested the moment they set foot in the airport. Roland's plan for stopping the cyberattack while also eliminating Greenwood and House could be achieved only by traveling to Rome that very night.

"My best guess—we have less than twenty-four hours before Octavia is activated again," the Harvard man had said.

It was snowing, and the temperature had dropped below freezing. Everyone was huddled around the coffee table in the living room, keeping warm by the fireplace, its flames sparking off the firewood and creating dashes of gold, black, and gray. Frozen pizzas from George's uncle's freezer had been supper, its remnants now scattered over paper plates on the table beside an overflowing ashtray and cans of West Sixth IPA and bottles of Miller Lite.

Time was of the essence, but no one could figure out how to transport five people wanted by the FBI, the CIA, INTERPOL, not to mention every police agency in the country, overseas.

"It's hopeless," Roland said.

"I'm depressed," echoed George.

"You two are pathetic," Tricia replied.

"Are they always this helpless?" Alena asked.

"Always," said Tricia. "I don't know what they would do without me."

Chris finished his fourth beer of the night and stood up. He lit a cigarette as he approached the fireplace, then turned and faced the group.

"I think I have an idea," he said. "George, how long would it take you to find an unlisted cell phone number?"

"Depends. Who you looking for?"

"Someone who just might fly us to Italy."

• • •

Chris went to the kitchen to call the Tennessee cell phone number George had given him. It went straight to voicemail. Either the recipient's phone was off, or he was screening his calls. Chris knew it was more than likely the latter. When the automated voice message came on, Chris waited for the beep and then left a simple message: his name and callback number—his real name. The man he was trying to contact only knew him by that name and would call back if he was able to help. And two minutes later, he did.

The familiar voice on the other end of the line was surprised. But when Chris explained in detail the events of the last year and a half, the man agreed to help them.

"Can you be at Fort Knox by 0100?"

"Sure can."

"See you soon, brother."

When Chris returned to the living room, Alena was gone.

Tricia noticed his concern and said, "She stepped outside, Chris."

"What's the word?" Roland asked.

"He came though. We leave tonight."

• • •

Alena was on the porch staring out into the darkness, the wonted glow of lights from downtown Lexington shrouded by falling snow. Chris closed the front door behind him and joined her.

"Got us a ride," he said. "We leave within the hour."

She said nothing.

"What's on your mind?" he asked.

"Lots of things." She turned and faced him. "What happens when this is all over?"

"No clue."

"You don't think about it?"

"I just take one day at a time."

"Must be nice."

"When I was deployed, each day was all you got. Anything more was wishful thinking."

"Makes sense." She paused, thinking. Then, "My whole life has been about preparing for what's next—that big break, the life I want to live. I never put much stock in the moment. But these past few days—life is precious. And it's fleeting."

"That it is." He put his head down. "I'm sorry."

"None of this is your fault." She touched his arm. "Thank you for keeping me alive."

Their eyes met.

"We'll get through this, Alena."

"How can you be so sure?"

"I'm not. But there's one thing I've always believed—what keeps me going, I suppose. Good will always triumph over evil. Sounds cliché, but I've found it to be true." He paused. "I think you should stay here. No one will think less of you for not going."

Music to Alena's ears but not what she wanted. "You don't want me with you?"

"Of course I do. But I can't stand the thought of you being in danger again."

She smiled. "You're a sweet man, Chris Harding. But I'm going."

"It's too dangerous."

Her eyes flared. "I'm seeing this through."

Chris stared at her for what seemed like an eternity before he responded. "Okay." He removed his SIG P226 from the back of his jeans. "But you're going to carry one of these."

She shook her head. "No, I don't like guns. Besides, I've never—"

"Don't give me that bullshit. A gun might be the only thing that keeps you alive. You'll carry a weapon, or you don't go."

"I'm not qualified to use one."

"Point and aim." He handed her the pistol. "Now you're qualified."

CHAPTER 73

Greenwood Enterprises
Fairfax, Virginia

It was nearly two o'clock in the morning, and Greenwood had arrived at the compound earlier than usual. He couldn't sleep. For him, waiting was hell, and for the past twenty-four hours all he had done was wait. He did a quick calisthenics workout in his office—a combo of push-ups, sit-ups, and burpees—then made himself a breakfast shake. He stripped off his sweat-soaked T-shirt and stared out the window. The blacktop driveway below was covered in a fresh coat of snow, illuminated by the giant strobe lights that turned the compound into a glowing little city. Beyond the gates of his empire were acres of open land—ten miles to the nearest interstate.

The darkness beyond the compound created a reflection in the window, and Greenwood used it to admire his bulging biceps and six-pack abs, a physique built from a strict diet and years of intense strength training. None of that had helped him achieve his goal, though. The chain-smoking, beer-guzzling, middle-aged former soldier, Chris Harding, and his group of outlaws had outwitted him and outfought him every step of the way. This was no longer about money; this was about revenge.

His iPhone vibrated on the desk behind him. Intelligence analysts at the FBI had been hard at work tracking the rogue Woodhaven operatives. Perhaps they had finally found something. Greenwood opened the Threema app and clicked on the first of two videos embedded in the secure text message. The timecode at the bottom of the screen said 0058. It was a grainy, black-and-white image of a Ford Bronco pulling up to the main entrance of Fort Knox in Hardin County, Kentucky. Greenwood enlarged the video with his fingers, focusing on the faces of the people inside the vehicle. The bearded man driving looked like Chris Harding, and the man in the passenger seat resembled Roland Anderson. Greenwood moved to the second video with a timecode of 0116. It was shot from the roof of an airplane hangar with a wide-angled view of the Godman Army Airfield. Five figures crossed the airstrip. They were met by two men in Army fatigues and escorted to a Gulfstream C-37A twin-jet aircraft with United States Army printed across the side.

Another message popped up on the screen. It was a link to a detailed report from the FBI's facial recognition database indicating that the individuals in the Fort Knox security footage were an eighty-nine percent match for the Woodhaven operatives.

CHAPTER 74

McLean, Virginia

STEVEN HOUSE'S FOUR-BEDROOM Cape Cod house—clad in white shingles with a matching picket fence and a large oak tree in the front yard—screamed upper middle class. It was where he and his wife called home, along with their teenage daughter and a Golden Retriever, and it was the only place he found solace from the dirty business of Washington politics.

His iPhone vibrated on the nightstand beside his bed. Normally, the director would have ignored the call and gone back to sleep. But not today. He fumbled for it, then silenced the ring and checked the caller ID.

"Fuck," he said under his breath.

The past twenty-four hours had been a whirlwind, and he was hoping for an update, just not at two o'clock in the morning. His wife of twenty-three years rolled over in bed. She'd won Miss Georgia in 1997 and still looked as beautiful as the day he married her.

"Who is it, honey?" she whispered.

"It's work. Go back to sleep."

House climbed out of bed and made his way through the darkness to the bathroom. Once inside, he closed the door and pressed the green "Accept" button on the phone's screen.

"Yeah?" he answered.

"Your minions in intelligence found something."

"This couldn't wait until tomorrow?"

"No."

"Our conversations always make me feel dirty."

"It's because you probably are."

House ignored the insult. "What do you have?"

"Facial recognition surveillance tracked them to Fort Knox, Kentucky."

"What the hell are they doing there?"

"Seems they know someone, someone high-up. Got them a military escort to Camp Ederle, a U.S. Army installation in Vicenza, Italy."

"I know where it is. *Shit!*"

"What the hell's going on?"

"I don't understand how they could possibly know about Italy."

"We should assume they know everything."

House stared into the mirror above the sink. His reflection stared back. Pre-mature gray hair and bags beneath his eyes. He was ready for this goddamn job to be over.

"How quickly can you assemble a team?"

"We can be wheels up in less than thirty minutes."

"Make it sixty. I'm coming with you."

"You sure that's a good idea?"

"None of this is a good idea. But I've delegated long enough.

This ends today. They're headed for Rome. We'll be waiting for them."

"Copy that."

"And Dan? No survivors this time."

CHAPTER 75

Vicenza, Italy

The U.S. Army Gulfstream C-37A touched down at Aeroporto di Thiene, a single-runway military airport northwest of Vicenza. Northern Italy in the winter was cold, and the mid-afternoon air was crisp, but there was no snow—not a cloud in sight—and the rolling green hills surrounding the ancient city seemed to go on forever. The all-night flight had been comfortable enough, and everyone took advantage by catching some much needed shut-eye. But not Chris. He never slept the night before an op. Instead, he stared out the window into the darkness, wondering if this would be his last day on earth.

Roland didn't bother sleeping either. Forever a man of data, he kept his eyes on Octavia's location using the GPS tracker George had installed on his phone. Roland's studiousness paid off. Halfway across the Atlantic someone turned on whatever was controlling the AI computer, revealing its new location: the Anantara Palazzo Naiadi Hotel in Rome.

Vicenza is a historical city less than forty miles from Venice that dates back to the second century BC, with much of its architecture either built by or inspired by Andrea Palladio, a fifteenth-century architect widely known for designing the Basilica Palladiana, an ornate structure in Piazza dei Signori within the heart of the city.

The first and last time Chris set foot in Italy was not something he wanted to remember. It was 2016, and he had taken a contract job with the Central Intelligence Agency to apprehend an al-Qaeda leader named Ayman al-Rahman. The covert operation was led by Roland Anderson, an up-and-coming CIA agent at the time. After months of surveillance, al-Rahman had been located at a palace in Casablanca, Morocco. The exfil was to be a quick in-and-out. Vicenza was the starting point, and it was to be the end point less than five hours later. Bad intel, poor communication, Chris and Roland would never know, but that night cost them everything. Their entire team was massacred, and as the only survivors, the shame of having failed their men began the downward spiral that destroyed Chris's marriage, Roland's career, and made them who they were today—fugitives of justice, operators living in the gray, men without a home.

As soon as they deplaned, the team was met on the airstrip by a young uniformed Army Sergeant standing beside a military-green Jeep Wrangler.

"Welcome to Vicenza," he said.

Chris led the way from the plane to the 4x4 utility vehicle. He opened the back door for Alena and Tricia. George and Roland climbed in the other side, and Chris joined the young soldier in the front, dropping his bag between his legs.

"It's a forty-minute drive to the base," the sergeant explained. "Colonel Elgerson is expecting you."

...

Camp Ederle has been an intricate part of United States foreign policy since its constitution in 1955. Today, though under Italian military control, it is headquarters for the Southern European Task Force, Africa (SETAF-AF), which includes the 509th Signal Battalion, the 414th Contracting Command, the 207th Military Intelligence Brigade, and the 173rd Airborne Brigade. The garrison is an expansive compound on the eastern side of the city with all the trappings of a U.S. military installation: offices, commissaries, barracks—even a bar and a Taco Bell.

The Jeep passed through the main gate, its walls covered in barbed wire. Chris felt a twinge of nostalgia as he watched soldiers marching in formation and officers zipping through the mini-city in open-topped military Jeeps. He missed the action, the precision, the uniformity of it all. George wondered what kind of weapons they had onsite. Roland was glued to his phone, waiting for an update on the AI tablet's next location. Tricia wondered how many women lived on the base—turned out quite a few. And Alena was feeling an overwhelming sense of excitement about the environment she'd found herself in.

Post command was located in a three-story structure at the center of the complex. The sergeant parked the Jeep in front of a manicured lawn and a walkway that led to the building's entrance. Everyone climbed out, taking their bags with them. They were met by an athletic man in his forties with a tan and salt-and-pepper hair cut high and tight.

"Chris Harding as I live and breathe," he said.

"Aaron Elgerson," Chris said, shaking his hand. "Or should I say, Colonel."

"That part's new, and you're no longer in the service. You'll call me Aaron." He noticed Roland standing by the curb. "Anderson, didn't think I'd ever see you again."

Roland laughed. "You and me both. Thanks for helping us out."

"When Chris told me what was going on—hell, this is the least I could do. You all must be hungry. I'll walk you over to the commissary. Get some chow in you, then we can talk shop."

"We're on a bit of a time crunch," said Chris. "Let's talk first."

"You got it, brother."

Elgerson led the way through a maze of hallways with offices on either side filled with uniformed officers hard at work. The place was buzzing with activity.

"Believe it or not, we're pretty busy out here," the colonel explained. "We've been on standby ever since Hamas attacked Israel." He motioned to an open door. "I'm in here."

The post commander's office was small, but it was neat. There was a desk, two chairs, and a couch. Maps covered the walls. Chris noticed a framed photograph. A group of soldiers wearing tan fatigues posing in front of a tank.

"You still have it."

"Damn straight, brother. You don't have yours?"

"I'm sure it's somewhere. A lot of things went missing after the divorce."

Elgerson pointed at the photograph. "This was taken when Chris and I were young, crazy, and full of piss and vinegar."

"He's still full of piss and vinegar," Alena said.

"That I believe," Elgerson replied with a laugh.

Everyone took a seat, coffee was served, and a quick round of introductions were made. Chris and Elgerson had met right after boot camp at Fort Bragg—now Fort Liberty—in North Carolina when they both joined the United States Army Special Forces Airborne command. They served together on multiple deployments to Afghanistan and Iraq, saving each other's lives enough times to make them brothers in arms for life. When Chris was honorably discharged following a knee injury that required surgery in 2015, the two men drifted apart. Elgerson continued climbing the ranks, making colonel in 2023, and now with a daughter in college was considering retirement. Maybe sell real estate in his home state of Tennessee. But recent events in the Middle East changed all that. He was needed right where he was, serving out his commission at Camp Ederle. His wife understood. She even left their home in Franklin to be with him on base.

Elgerson was as good a man as they got. For that reason Chris had been hesitant to reach out. It was risky. After all, everyone he came into contact with seemed to either end up dead or on the run. But Elgerson was the only one who could help them stop the largest cyberattack in history. And he was a patriot. So much so that he would have been upset if he discovered Chris *hadn't* called.

Once Elgerson was fully briefed on the plan of action, he said. "Sounds like you've got your work cut out for you."

Roland said, "When Octavia is activated, there'll be no turning back. We need to get our hands on the tablet before that happens."

"It's a ticking time bomb," Chris added. "The operation is risky, Aaron, but I just don't see any other way."

"Because there's not." Elgerson sipped his coffee, considering the situation his old friend was in. "Last time I saw you and Roland was 2016."

"What a shit show," Chris replied.

"Casablanca wasn't your fault," said Elgerson. "It was bad intel. And you know—there's a good chance that son of a bitch is still out there. I guess that's what we get for coordinating with the

NEW BEGINNING

goddamn CIA."

"I still think it was an inside job," Roland said.

"I'd believe it. The Agency is corrupt as shit. So is the FBI. And I'm not surprised by any of what you just told me. Stealing American dollars so some asshole in Washington can pass some goddamn bill. It's treason. And you can bet your ass my daughter has deleted her Nysta app. I want those responsible to have their lights turned off. Chris, you were always pretty good at making that happen."

"I still am."

"I can't believe you're alive. This is some real spy shit."

"It's a long story."

"We'll save that for another time."

"I don't want to jam you up."

"You're not. Of course, it goes without saying that the United States Army cannot be involved in this operation. You're on your own."

"Wouldn't want it any other way."

"You can hitch a ride to Rome with the Airborne. We'll rent you a car there too."

"Thank you for helping us," Roland said.

"Pleasure's all mine," Elgerson replied. "We're tasked with assisting Secret Service, so we're headed there anyway. Pushing out within the hour. We've got Iranian proxies firing at our ships in the Mediterranean, war in Gaza, and President Douglas decides this is a good time to go to the G20 Summit."

"Fucking idiot," George said.

"This could be related to the cyberattack," Alena said.

"I sure as hell hope not," Elgerson said. "Chris, Roland—you two remember how we did things with the Agency. Same goes with this. Don't get caught by local police, don't talk to anyone on base. Sounds like you're dealing with some real bad guys. Of course," he leaned back in his chair, "if a fight comes to our door, we'll blow those sons of bitches right back to hell."

Alena shuddered at the thought. Every problem was solved with violence. And it was strange that she was growing numb to it. She glanced at Tricia. She was calm. Her right hand resting on her belly was the only indication that she was scared. But Alena knew this was a woman who had killed before and would kill again if it meant protecting her family—including the little one growing inside her.

"We could use some weapons," George said.

Elgerson smiled. "That, I can do."

CHAPTER 76

Rome, Italy

A BEAUTIFUL WOMAN climbed out of the Mercedes S-Class sedan that had delivered her from her apartment to the Anantara Palazzo Naiadi Hotel. The nineteenth-century white-marble building was located in the heart of Rome—known as "The Eternal City"—on a stone roundabout with an elaborate fountain in the middle called the Piazza della Repubblica. The woman's red dress and black heels did little to give away what she truly was, but the luxurious surroundings helped her stomach the reality.

She passed through the opulent lobby, up the elevator to the top floor. She knew the room number, having confirmed it when she received the job. She knocked only once and waited. Seconds later, the door opened and she was ushered inside.

The 2,000-square-foot suite had a private terrace with panoramic views of Vatican City, the Trevi Fountain, and the Colosseum. Bashir Mahmoud greeted her with a glass of champagne and immediately led her to the bedroom. After receiving the AI tablet, he and Mostafa had returned to the hotel to finalize the last stage of the operation. The heavy lifting was over, and it was now a waiting game until the following morning. That gave Mahmoud time to indulge in his favorite pastime. He leaned over and kissed the woman's neck, working his way up her jaw to her lips. Her perfume was sweet, her skin soft. Unable to delay gratification any longer, he took the champagne from her hand, placed it on the table beside the bed, and unzipped the back of her dress.

• • •

Adham Mostafa listened to the carnal sounds coming from the suite beside his. Part of him wished he hadn't reserved an adjoining room with Mahmoud, but the other part relished in what he was unable to do. He poured himself a cup of hot water from a small kettle, added Persian tea leaves, then finished with a dollop of honey, a habit he'd developed during his time in Morocco. He sipped his tea and stared at the AI tablet on the coffee table in front of him. It had been nearly twenty-four hours since the Nysta update had dropped. By now, it would have been installed on millions of American's smartphones. Once the sun came up in a few hours, he would activate the tablet, and Octavia would do its job of stealing billions of dollars and dispersing them into thousands of hidden bank accounts throughout the world.

But he and Mahmoud had another responsibility. Everything was in place. The team consisted of a select group of Palestinian and Lebanese militants willing to martyr themselves in the name of Allah. Armed with suicide vests and Italian passports, they would stealthily move through the crowds of Rome, undetected by law enforcement. Everything had been planned weeks in advance, and the soldiers of Allah had worked in tandem with the vice president of the United States to carry out the attack.

The money Mostafa and his partner would receive as payment

for facilitating two concurrent strikes against the United States would be enough to disappear forever, spending the rest of their lives enjoying the fruits this world had to offer. But they would have also accomplished something else. Something everlasting that would make their families proud. In less than twelve hours, they would help take down Islam's greatest enemy.

CHAPTER 77

Chris stood in front of a fourth-century Roman bathhouse—now an archaeological museum—and lit a cigarette. Across the street was the Anantara Palazzo Naiadi Hotel. Traffic was heavy, and cars and scooters filled the Piazza della Repubblica, honking their horns as they passed the Fountain of the Naiads—another night in Rome. Chris smoked his cigarette and mentally prepared for what he was about to do.

Elgerson had supplied them each with a SIG Sauer P365-AXG LEGION outfitted with a Dead Air Odessa-9 suppressor and two extra 17-round magazines.

"Concealed carry only," he had said. "These are clean, so they won't come back to me."

Along with the 173rd Airborne Brigade, they flew into Fiumicino Airport, arriving just after one o'clock in the morning. True to his word, Elgerson had a vehicle ready and waiting for them. A rental through a corporate account—incidentally, the same one used for many of the CIA's covert activities in southern Italy. Chris, Alena, Roland, George, and Tricia piled into the yellow Fiat 500X Trekking SUV—it was an atrocious automobile, but it would get the job done—and Roland monitored the AI tablet's location during the thirty-minute commute along the A91 highway to the city center.

They parked across the street from the hotel and went through the operation one last time. Whatever was controlling Octavia had not moved in several hours. A schematic of the hotel confirmed its location to be on the sixth floor—suite 606. There were virtually no comms to speak of, only their KryptAll phones, and there was no telling how many hostiles were inside, so they opted for a three-man team. Two would go up while the third stayed in the lobby. Chris and George had the most tactical experience. They would retrieve the asset. Alena would be on point in the lobby. From the Fiat, Roland would monitor the tablet's location, alerting the team if anything changed. With George's help, Tricia had hacked the emergency response line so she could provide updates on any police activity nearby.

There was no room for error. In and out. Just like the last time Chris was in the Mediterranean. He could feel the history seeping out of the ancient buildings. Millions of lives over centuries filled his senses, and then a memory from eleven years ago. Back when he was married. Back when he was still in the Army. And back when he had a future. His ex-wife, Jessica, had bought a vacation package to Rome. It was to have been a week of museums for him and restaurants for her. But when the pregnancy test came back positive, they'd decided to wait on the trip—better to spend the money on baby food and diapers. One day they would make up the trip. Of course, they never did.

"You good?" Alena asked, joining Chris on the curb beside the Fiat.

"Yeah," he said, pushing the bittersweet memory from his mind. "I'm good."

George climbed out of the SUV and adjusted his holster.

"This gun is way too small," he said. "I need my Smith and Wesson."

"That one stays in the car," Chris said.

"Yeah, figures," George grumbled. "Everything in this city is small."

Chris checked his own firearm. Good to go.

Alena felt odd with the SIG P365 concealed beneath her leather jacket. It went against every grain in her body to carry a weapon. Would she even have the nerve to pull the trigger? Hopefully it wouldn't come to that. She looked at the two bearded men beside her: Levi's jeans, Wrangler jackets, boots, ball caps—American as apple pie. Both had killed. Both would do it again. That calmed her nerves; they would keep her safe.

"Let's do this," Chris said.

He crushed his cigarette and led the way across the street toward the hotel.

CHAPTER 78

MOSTAFA POURED HIMSELF another cup of tea. It helped to calm his nerves. The noises from next door had subsided, only to return an hour later—this time in force. He knew Mahmoud was anxious as well. And that was okay. In a few hours they would achieve what no other *mujāhidīn* had been able to achieve before. It was okay to be nervous. In fact, it was wise.

His cell phone vibrated on the couch cushion beside him. An incoming text. He read the encrypted message from his contact in Washington, D.C.

You've been compromised. Get out now.

Mostafa went to the window. Nothing out of the ordinary. No helicopters, police, or Secret Service outside. He opened the door to his suite. The hallway was empty. Closing the door, he went to the bedroom and removed a leather chest holster containing a Glock 17 from the top drawer of the dresser. He strapped on the holster, confirmed the magazine in the pistol was full, and then grabbed his suit jacket from a hanger in the closet. The sounds from Mahmoud's room had grown louder. That sex addict had clearly not bothered to check his messages.

Mostafa's phone lit up again. Another text from the same number. This one was longer and included detailed instructions on what was to happen next.

• • •

Alena ordered a gin martini at the hotel bar. Even though it was two o'clock in the morning, the place was full. The bartender, a tall man in his twenties with a chiseled jawline and slicked-back hair, stared her up and down as he poured the drink.

"*Sei troppo sexy per bevere da sola*," he said, dropping an olive into the glass and pressing his lips together.

You're too sexy to drink alone.

"*Ovviamente, idiota*," she replied. One of the few phrases she knew in Italian.

Obviously, idiot.

Chris and George watched the interaction from across the bar in the lobby.

"Should we help her?" George asked.

"I think he's the one we should be worried about," Chris said.

They moved through the lobby to the elevator bays. Chris's phone vibrated in his back pocket. It was Roland checking in. Chris ignored the message and returned the phone to his pocket as he and George entered the elevator and pressed the button for the sixth floor.

• • •

"Chris didn't respond," Roland whined.

He was in the passenger seat of the Fiat beside Tricia, eyes glued to his phone.

"Of course he didn't," she said.

"What if it was important?"

"But it wasn't."

Roland grunted and switched over to the GPS tracker. The AI tablet was still in the room.

There were no hiccups, yet.

• • •

Chris and George exited the elevator, their P365s leading the way. Chris checked the right, George the left. All clear. They moved down the hallway. No bad guys guarding the doors. No tourists coming back from a night on the town. All was calm. All was quiet.

Until they reached suite 606.

Muffled sounds of moaning. It was a woman. Sounded Italian. Chris signaled for George to take the left side of the door. The AI tablet was in that room. Everyone inside was going to die. No telling how many there were, how many were watching whoever was in the throes of passion. It didn't matter; they were all going to hell tonight. Chris did a countdown with his fingers.

Three, two, one—

• • •

Mahmoud could tell the woman was enjoying herself. Not that it mattered. He grasped her hips with both hands as her naked body writhed against his. She moaned louder. He pushed harder. She was about to climax. So was he.

The door slammed opened.

What the fuck?

Two armed men with beards and baseball caps entered the living room. Mahmoud's eyes met theirs. They were American. He recognized one of them. He'd seen him before. But where? His gun was across the bedroom. He would never reach it in time.

The Italian woman noticed the intruders and screamed. The bearded American Mahmoud recognized entered the bedroom. His eyes met the woman's.

"Get out of here," Chris said to her.

Before she could move, Mahmoud grabbed her by the hair and yanked her up so that her body was in front of his. A human shield. He stared into the eyes of the gunman.

Geneva, that's where I know him from. He was the American operator who—

Darkness.

The 9mm bullet from the suppressed P365 entered Mahmoud's forehead, blasting through both sides of the skull and splattering brain matter, bone, and blood over the bed and the woman. She screamed as his lifeless body dropped to the carpet, releasing her from his grasp.

The bearded man turned his sights on her. "Go," he said. "Now!"

Tears in her eyes, she did as she was told—grabbing her clothing and heels from the floor and running out of the room, past the other bearded man, and out of the suite.

• • •

Mostafa heard the suppressed gunfire from the adjoining room. He was out of time. His partner was surely dead, and he would be next if he didn't leave immediately. He returned to the living room and snapped the briefcase containing the AI tablet closed.

• • •

NEW BEGINNING

Chris stared at Mahmoud's body—naked, sweaty, and soaking the carpet beneath it with blood. He'd recognized him the moment he entered the room. The man from Geneva who had killed the Swiss banker. The man who was after the crypto ledger that tied the NWO to the Chinese AI chip purchase.

"The tablet isn't here," said George, entering the bedroom.

"Shit."

George eyed the body on the floor. "Who is this guy?"

"Bashir Mahmoud."

"The terrorist from Geneva?"

"Yup."

"Pathetic."

"If the AI tablet isn't here, then where is it? Adham Mostafa—that's who this piece of shit works with. He's gotta be nearby."

George pointed to a door beside the bed. "Connecting rooms?"

Chris nodded. "It's a dual suite."

The door was locked.

"Your time to shine, big fella," said Chris.

"I got a bad back."

"You're kidding me."

Chris fired twice into the lock. The door swung open and both men charged through, guns leading the way. What they found was a suite identical to the one they'd just been in. The room smelled of cologne. There was a cup of tea beside a kettle on the coffee table—still hot, still steaming. Someone had just been there. Chris and George cleared every room, finding nothing—no terrorist, no tablet.

"Shit," Chris said, dropping the gun to his side.

He pulled out his phone and was about to call Roland when the screen lit up. The Harvard man had beat him to the punch.

Chris answered, putting it on speaker.

"Tablet is gone," he said.

"That's because it's on the move," Roland replied.

• • •

Alena had spent the past five minutes fielding pickup lines from different men at the bar. It was unnerving how forward Italians could be. She finished her martini and was about to order another one when her phone lit up on the bar. It was a text from Chris.

> **Middle Eastern man headed your way. He has the tablet. I'm coming.**

Forget the second martini.
What the hell happened upstairs?

She scanned the room: four young men on barstools who had already hit on her, a man and a woman sharing drinks at a little table by the bar, and an older man in the corner eyeing her with unscrupulous intentions. No one who hadn't been there the entire time she had. She got up from her seat and casually walked toward the lobby. It wasn't busy, just a couple of clerks behind the desk and a man standing near the front door on his cell phone. Her eyes went to the elevator. She waited. Five seconds. Ten seconds.

The elevator opened and a well-dressed Middle Eastern man in his forties came through the doors. He was holding a black leather briefcase. As a writer, Alena studied human nature and was able to recognize when someone was nervous, when they were excited, when they were scared. She saw all three in this man.

And then he saw her. His brown eyes darkened, and he quickened his pace.

Alena had a gun. She could stop him. But that would be murder. And she was in the middle of a public space, one of the most luxurious hotels in Rome.

Where are you, Chris?

The Middle Eastern man made the decision for her. As he came closer, his left hand went inside his suit jacket. It happened as if in slow motion. She saw the hand. She saw the gun—a small pistol similar to the one she had hidden beneath her own jacket.

She froze.

The man aimed the gun at her. There were probably screams from hotel guests, but she didn't hear them. She was about to die. This was it.

Two sharp *cracks*.

The man dropped the gun. A bullet had grazed his right arm, just below his shoulder. Another had shattered a large ceramic vase to his right. Standing behind him was Chris, holding his SIG P365 with two hands, smoke still spewing from the muzzle. An almost perfect shot. He'd aimed for the man's back.

Mostafa felt the pain shooting through his bicep. He felt the blood dripping down to his forearm. But it was nothing he hadn't felt before. This was a flesh wound. As long as he kept his focus, he would survive. He made a run for it, dashing through the now crowded lobby—hotel and bar guests screaming in fear as he ran past them and out the front door.

Chris was unable to get another clean shot. Too many innocent people in the way.

Fucking terrorists and their human shields.

He ran, full speed, after the son of a bitch, flying through the front door to the plaza outside. Luxury vehicles filled the roundabout in front of the fountain. It was the middle of the night, but hotel guests in suits and cocktail dresses were still coming and going, and there was a steady flow of traffic on the adjoining street. Chris could hear police sirens in the distance.

He spotted Mostafa.

The terrorist opened the door of a black Audi A8 sedan and forced the driver out of the vehicle at gunpoint. Chris aimed his SIG. Still too many innocent people for a clean shot. Mostafa jumped inside the car and hit the gas, the tires squealing as he peeled out of the roundabout. Chris lowered his weapon. George and Alena joined him on the steps as the Audi disappeared into a sea of red taillights.

CHAPTER 79

"You tracking this guy?" Chris said to Roland as he climbed into the backseat of the Fiat.

George and Alena piled in behind him.

"Already on it," the Harvard man replied.

He'd been monitoring the GPS and was now staring at a pulsating dot traveling through Rome's congested grid. Tricia, who was already behind the wheel, hit the gas and skillfully merged into the heavy traffic that surrounded them.

"Bashir Mahmoud and Adham Mostafa have the tablet," Chris said. He glanced at Alena. "Mahmoud won't be a problem anymore."

Tricia looked at him in the rearview mirror. "Should I ask?"

"No."

"He's dead," George said.

They followed the pulsating dot through the center of the ancient city, passing the Colosseum, the Pantheon, and the Roman Forum—all lit up in blue, green, and red for Christmas. A little over an hour later, they were on a two-lane highway in the middle of the Italian countryside. A long, straight road and almost complete darkness. Then taillights up ahead. Roland confirmed it was their target, and Tricia slowed down to avoid exposing their position.

Roughly five kilometers later the Audi turned off the highway. Tricia pulled over to the shoulder, turned off the lights, and put the engine in park. Then they waited, watching the Audi's headlights bounce through the darkness, until they disappeared completely.

"I think we're good," Roland said.

Tricia nodded and pulled back onto the highway, then turned off where the Audi had. It was a gravel road lined with hundred-foot Mediterranean cypress trees. The sun was beginning to creep over the horizon, creating a dark blue haze in the sky, and it revealed a towering structure in the distance made of stone—elaborately constructed pillars standing thirty-forty feet in the air.

"What is this place?" Alena asked.

"Ancient ruins from the Roman Empire," Chris replied. "This has to be an old estate, probably dating back to the first century BC."

"How do you know that?"

"He's a nerd," George said.

"Student of history," Chris replied.

"You never cease to amaze, Mr. Harding," Alena said with a smile.

There was a sharp bend in the road, and Tricia nearly drove straight into the wall of cypress trees but corrected herself just in time. That's when they all saw it. A mansion at the top of a hill, or since they were in Italy, a villa, that was at least two hundred years old. It had three stories with vines decorating the sandstone walls and a paved circular driveway at the front. The Audi was parked in the driveway. The only light was coming from the right side of the building.

"Feels like a trap," Chris said.

"I was thinking the same thing," said Roland.

"I'll run some recon."

"I'm coming with you," George said.

Roland shook his head. "You should stay here. Someone else could be arriving later."

"He's right," Chris said. "Stay with the girls."

"Damn, I always miss the action," George grumbled.

"You're staying here," Tricia ordered.

"I'm staying here," he confirmed.

"I'd like to go with you," Alena said.

"Not an option," Chris replied.

"You think I'll slow you down because I'm a girl?"

"Yes."

"You're an asshole."

"I know."

Chris removed the magazine from his SIG and counted the rounds he had left. Thirteen plus one in the chamber, and he had two extra mags in his back pocket. Not a lot of ammo, but it would have to do. Roland checked his weapon as well. Nothing had changed since it was given to him by the armorer back at Camp Ederle. Both men took deep breaths and exited the Fiat.

• • •

Chris and Roland passed the cypress trees as they jogged up the hill toward the right side of the villa, where the light was coming from. They kept their weapons in front of them, held steady with two-handed grips. There was no sign of life, not a guard, nothing. It was almost *too* quiet. They reached the top of the ridge and pressed against the side of the building. Inching their way around the corner, they continued along the stone walls until the single light grew brighter. It was coming from a window on the ground floor. Keeping their bodies firmly against the wall, they made it to the window and peered inside.

It was a large room with a medieval fireplace and two leather couches facing an oak coffee table. The floor was a dark-stained hardwood with a Persian rug covering most of it. A dining room table big enough to seat a dozen people completed the space. And sitting at the end of that table, like a king in his castle, was Adham Mostafa. The black leather briefcase was open on the table in front of him with what appeared to be some sort of iPad or tablet inside.

"That's what controls Octavia," Roland whispered, pointing to the device inside the briefcase.

"The AI tablet," Chris said.

Roland nodded. "What do we do now?"

"I don't know. I need to think."

But before he could, Roland was shot in the back.

• • •

Chris hit the ground.

Find the shooter.

But it was too dark.

Check on Roland.

The Harvard man wasn't moving, but he was breathing. Chris assessed the damage, feeling every part of his body in an attempt to find the bullet entry point. He found it. In the left side of Roland's lower back, just above his hip. The spine didn't appear to be hit, which was good, but if the bullet had impacted an organ, the outlook wouldn't be so positive—fatal if they didn't get him to a hospital.

Chris slapped him across the face and said, "Roland."

No respone.

"*Shit!*"

He pulled out his cell and dialed Tricia's number. She didn't answer. It just kept ringing.

"*Fuck!*"

He tried Alena. He tried George. Same thing.

Something was wrong. Chris checked his surroundings again for any sign of movement. Still, nothing. Just a soft breeze rustling through the cypress trees. They were compromised and needed to get the hell out of there. But first, where was that goddam shooter?

He carefully stood up, keeping his back to the wall as he inched his way to the corner of the building and peered around. All clear. He could see the Fiat at the bottom of the hill. It was too dark to see who was inside. Everything seemed fine.

Why aren't they answering their phones?

Time to move Roland. Worry about comms later.

He turned around and found himself face-to-face with the butt of an AK-47.

Then everything went dark.

CHAPTER 80

Chris opened his eyes. His head was pounding, like he was in a fog—another concussion no doubt. His nose was broken, and he could feel the crisp blood that had dried around it. He was seated at the dining room table in the room with the fireplace with his wrists and ankles bound by plastic zip-ties. The sun had come up, sending beams of light into the room. From the very window he and Roland had looked into. Had that been minutes ago? Hours ago? He couldn't tell. The black briefcase was still open on the table in front of him, the tablet still inside, and sitting directly across from him with a Glock 17 pointed at his heart was Adham Mostafa.

"Glad you're finally awake," Mostafa said in accented English as he checked the time on his Rolex watch. "It would have been a shame for you to miss all the action."

"Fuck you."

Mostafa smiled. "I know all about you, Mr. Harding. Former Special Forces, CIA contractor. And most recently, Woodhaven operative. Divorced with one child, a girl. They live with your wife's new husband in Arizona."

Chris's eyes narrowed.

"This isn't about them," Mostafa said. "It's about you."

"Where's Roland?"

"Sadly, he did not make it."

Chris struggled with the zip-ties.

"Don't bother. They're American made. You won't break them."

"Then cut me loose," Chris snapped. "Fight me. Man-to-man."

Mostafa laughed. "And why would I do that? I saw what you did to my colleague. You are more than capable of killing me, that I am sure." He took a moment to choose his next words. Then, "You have more reason to kill me than you might think. Rather, we have more in common than you might think."

"I have nothing in common with you."

"Defiance is a common trait with you Americans. So is pride. And it's that pride that has allowed your enemies the upper hand. Allowed them to penetrate your very government and, in the end, destroy everything you hold dear."

Chris said nothing. The terrorist wasn't wrong.

"You don't remember me do you?" Mostafa said. "This is not the first time we've met. It was a long time ago. I wouldn't expect you to remember me. But I know you remember what I did." His eyes locked on the former soldier's, reading him, searching for his greatest weakness. Then he said, "The very same people who hired Mahmoud and I for this job hired us in 2016 to terminate your team in Casablanca. We may have failed to kill you and Mr. Anderson before. We won't make that mistake again."

Visions of Navy SEALs and Special Forces operatives dying in an explosion of gunfire as they entered a Moroccan mansion in the middle of the night filled Chris's mind. They'd been tipped off from the start, resulting in a hundred percent casualty within minutes of entering the building. Hand grenades and bullets blew heads and limbs from their bodies as debris and smoke suffused every hallway and room in the house. Chris was knocked to the floor and found himself looking into the lifeless eyes of a man who had, moments before, expressed his fear of dying.

Back to the present. Back to the man watching him from across the table. Mostafa was enjoying the pain and misery permeating from Chris's eyes. And the former soldier could do nothing. He pulled at the zip-ties but was unable to break free.

"Before this is over, I'm going to kill you," Chris growled.

His tone sent shivers down Mostafa's spine. Had he made a mistake telling him?

No, there's nothing he can do about it but suffer.

Mostafa reached for the briefcase, pulling it toward him and admiring its contents.

"Do you know what this is?" he asked.

Chris didn't respond.

"Of course you do. Why else would you be here? But what you may not know, is that this is not the only attack on your country taking place today. In exactly two hours, *mujāhidīn* from Lebanon and Palestine, armed with suicide vests—"

"Terrorists," said Chris.

"Freedom fighters, Mr. Harding. They will intercept the American presidential motorcade on its way from the airport to the G20 Summit at the Roma Eventi conference center. By the time your military and Secret Service are aware of their presence it will be too late. Hezbollah and Hamas will take credit for the assassination of the president as retaliation for his support of Israel in the War on Gaza. The United States will be forced to send troops back into the Middle East while at the same time reeling from the most significant economic free-fall since the stock market crash of

1929."

Mostafa wished he'd thought of this himself. But saying it out loud made it seem more real and his important contribution all the more satisfying. "A new bill will be passed by Congress almost immediately."

"The United States Corporation Oversight Act," Chris said.

"Not as uninformed as I thought. Once American production is controlled by the federal government, it's only a matter of time before the rest of the world follows."

"What does that have to do with you?"

"It has everything to do with me. My entire life has been dedicated to destroying the West. The New World Order has given me the opportunity to fulfill my destiny."

"I'm sure what they're paying you didn't hurt."

"Where do you think all that stolen money is going? So many people in your government are more than willing to betray their country for the right price."

"Congress," Chris said, finally grasping the entire plan.

"How astute of you," Mostafa said, "but don't limit yourself to congressmen and senators. Even your vice president will enjoy a piece of the pie."

"She gave you the president's motorcade route."

"And she'll be more than rewarded."

"Why are you telling me all this? You know I'll never let you get away with it."

Mostafa laughed. "Who's going to believe you? You're a murderer, a domestic terrorist. You are going to die, and your daughter will spend her entire life trying to distance herself from the shame of being your daughter." He stood up. "And you'll die knowing that you couldn't even save your closest friends. Or the woman you love."

Chris tensed. His eyes narrowed. Darkness was taking over his soul—a thirst for the kill, to destroy everyone and everything in his path, starting with the terrorist standing before him.

Mostafa removed an iPhone from his suit jacket, pressed a button, and turned the phone's screen so Chris could see. It was a FaceTime call revealing Alena, George, and Tricia bound and gagged in the backseat of an SUV. And each one of them was wearing a suicide vest filled with explosives.

Mostafa disconnected the call. "We had a few extra vests lying around. Thought your friends might like to join in on the fun."

He scrolled to a different application on the phone and then turned the screen toward Chris. It was an app used to detonate bombs remotely. And it was connected to the suicide vests worn by the terrorists—the same ones that were strapped to Alena, George, and Tricia.

CHAPTER 81

Chris was furious. He wanted to take a knife and slit Mostafa's throat, but the goddam zip-ties were American-made—not Chinese—and the more he struggled, the more they tore into his skin, restricting the blood flow to his wrists. He needed a weapon.

Keep this piece of shit talking while you formulate a plan.

"Who do you work for?"

"I think you already know," Mostafa replied as he returned the phone to his jacket pocket.

"Who's your handler?"

"That is the least of your concern right now."

"Yeah, but I'm curious. Unless you *don't* know. Maybe you're just a low-level cocksucker who's not important enough to know who pays him."

"I know what you're attempting to do," Mostafa said. "And it won't work."

"What won't work?"

"You're stalling. It's pathetic, really—a man with your background. You have been defeated. Your friends have been defeated. Your country has been defeated. Show some dignity in your resignation."

"Go fuck yourself."

"Have it your way," the terrorist said with a sigh. "You should know that your American FBI is on their way. You'll be arrested. The report will show that you attempted escape. Killed onsite. But myself and those I work for will be here long after you've left this world."

Mostafa returned the Glock to his leather chest holster, buttoned his jacket, and closed the briefcase containing the AI tablet.

This was Chris's last chance. It was now or never. As the terrorist taunted his prisoner, Chris had been analyzing every aspect of his surroundings. The roaring fire in the fireplace. The leather couches. The hardwood floor. The coffee table with its sharp corners approximately five and a half feet behind Mostafa. The dining room table in front of him made of heavy oak. The chair he was strapped to, four feet from his captor.

"Goodbye, Mr. Harding."

Mostafa turned to leave.

Chris's movement was quick, almost instant. He tipped the chair back and, as he went down, used what little movement he had in his feet to push the top of the table in front of him, causing it to tip forward. Mostafa was caught off guard. The oak table knocked him backward. He lost his balance. Being exactly five-foot-eight was what killed him. The side of his head landed on the corner of the coffee table. It was just the right spot—the weakest part—and his skull cracked wide open. He dropped to the hardwood floor like a sack of shit, a pool of blood spreading across the Persian rug.

There wasn't time to dwell on the death of Mostafa. Chris used the heels of his boots to push himself toward the fire, feeling the heat as he inched closer. When he was less than a foot from the hearth, he spun himself around, closed his eyes, and reached out his zip-tied wrists. The pain was excruciating, the smell of burning flesh and plastic overwhelming, but it took only five seconds to melt the zip-ties enough for him to snap them off. Hands free, he searched his pockets for his Buck 119. The knife was gone. So he turned himself back around so that he was facing the fire, and pressed his bound feet against the flames and clenched his teeth, trying to ignore the pain. After ten seconds of hell, he attempted to pull his ankles apart. They wouldn't budge. Back to the fire. Another ten seconds. This time it worked. He was free.

Now he needed a weapon. Mostafa was lying on his back—eyes open with a look of surprise like he hadn't expected to meet his maker so suddenly. Chris removed the Glock from the holster strapped to Mostafa's chest and did a quick press check. The 17-round magazine was full. He stuffed the gun in the back of his jeans, then opened Mostafa's jacket, removed his iPhone, and used the dead terrorist's eyes to unlock the screen. He opened the detonation app and searched for a "deactivation" button. There was none.

Shit.

Voices in the distance. He pulled out the Glock and went to the door. The voices were coming from just outside the room—sounded like Arabic.

Terrorists.

Chris grabbed the briefcase from the floor and prepared himself. No telling how many men were out there. He only had seventeen bullets. No backup, no air support, no Trish on comms giving him instructions; he was on his own. But he had a mission. Find Roland, then rescue Alena, George, and Tricia—and stop the president from being assassinated by Islamic terrorists.

• • •

Chris opened the door, Glock leading the way. There were two terrorists with AK-47s standing guard, and they were expecting Mostafa, not the American, to come out of the room. Their delayed reaction was enough to seal their fate. Chris sent two 9mm rounds into each of them—one in the head, one in the chest. He returned the Glock to the back of his jeans and picked up an AK and two extra mags from one of the dead terrorists, then stepped over their bodies into a wide corridor with oil paintings and ornately designed light fixtures hanging from the walls. The gunfire brought three more Middle Eastern men from around the corner, all young and skinny with tangled beards and tattered clothes. Chris sent them to the afterlife and continued through the house, checking each room one by one—killed two more men in the process. The years away from the fight had taken a toll on his concentration, but right now, he was dialed in; his mind and body were one.

He climbed the stairs to the second floor. A terrorist came running toward him. Chris shot him twice in the face, leaving behind a gaping red hole where his eyes and nose once were. The second floor was a long hallway with closed doors on either side. Chris methodically worked his way through each one. Killed two more men. Still no sign of Roland. He cleared the third and final floor and then returned to the first level. As he entered the kitchen, he was met by four angry terrorists and an onslaught of automatic gunfire. A bullet nicked his shoulder, but he ignored the sting and the blood spurting down his arm and dived for cover. A hail of bullets followed, passing over his head—destroying cabinets and glassware and sending chunks of Venetian plaster into the air.

"Shit," he said, crouching behind a marble-topped island in the middle of the room.

He aimed his rifle around the corner and let off two blind shots. He heard a scream, then the shooting stopped. That was his opening. He jumped to his feet and opened fire. The Soviet-made Avtomat Kalashnikova, known throughout the world as the AK-47, is a powerful and precise weapon and for that reason has survived eight decades of combat. Chris used the efficiently designed tool to kill three of the terrorists that surrounded him.

The fourth man was too close to shoot. Chris met his body head-on. The terrorist swung his rifle like a bayonet, but Chris blocked the hit with his own weapon. He then dropped the AK and followed up with a punch to the man's ribcage that sent him several steps backward. The terrorist cowered in pain but returned with a large knife and eyes red with vengeance. He charged toward Chris with the outstretched blade. Chris swiftly removed the Glock from his jeans and shot him three times in the head. The force of the bullets exploding through his skull sent the terrorist's lifeless body to the floor.

Chris let out a sigh of relief as his adrenaline subsided. But before he could fully recalibrate, he heard footsteps behind him. He spun around with his pistol and pulled the trigger.

The Glock jammed.

"Fuck!"

He found himself face-to-face with a fat terrorist and a Kalashnikov pointed at his heart. The man smiled, revealing a mouthful of gold teeth, and pulled the trigger.

CHAPTER 82

The wet thump of lead making contact with flesh came first and was followed by a splash of blood and brain matter exploding from the fat man's head. It happened a second before Chris heard the cracking sound of an automatic rifle. The terrorist fell to the ground. Standing behind him with a smoking AK-47 pressed against his shoulder was Roland Anderson. He was limping. And a makeshift bandage made from part of his shirt was wound tightly around his waist. He was obviously in pain, and he was struggling to stand. But he'd managed to hold onto the gas-operated assault rifle. And he'd managed to make the shot.

"How the hell are you still alive?" Chris said.

"No idea, but you're welcome—for saving your life." Roland's face was white.

"You don't look good."

The Harvard man struggled to speak, having exhausted what energy he had. "They put me in a room." More panting. Then, "I woke up and thought I was dead. I think it's just a flesh wound, though. Missed everything important. But I'm losing…" He dropped to the floor.

"Shit."

NEW BEGINNING

Chris knelt beside him, removed his bandages, and inspected the wound. The projectile had gone straight through. It had missed vital organs, and the blood had begun to coagulate, which was good, but it was still inside and an infection was setting in.

"I'll be right back," Chris said.

"Take your time."

Chris finished clearing the rest of the house—thankfully, everyone was dead—and then returned to the kitchen and searched the cabinets for a first aid kit. Miraculously, he found one. A plastic container with the Red Cross emblem on top. He also found a half-empty bottle of vodka.

"This is going to hurt," he said, tearing open two packets of disinfectant wipes.

Roland nodded. He'd seen Chris play doctor before—on Terry, twice. Not a pretty sight, but it had saved Terry's life.

Chris applied the wipes to the wound. It bubbled and oozed and fizzed. He removed his leather belt and handed it to Roland.

"Bite down on this," he said.

Roland did as he was told while Chris picked up the dead terrorist's knife from the floor and doused it with vodka.

"Ready?"

"Yeah," Roland whispered.

Chris dug into the wound with the knife, tearing through the dried blood exterior to the pink flesh inside.

"Fuck!" Roland screamed.

"Almost done." Chris got the bullet out, then used the kitchen's gas stovetop to heat the knife's blade. "Ready?"

Roland nodded.

Chris pressed the hot steel against the open wound and moved it across like a baker kneading dough. Roland screamed in agony, but thirty seconds later the hole was soldered shut, leaving behind a tangled mess of burnt skin cells all black and orange. Chris repeated the process on the exit wound, then applied fresh gauze before wrapping the old bandage tightly around Roland's waist.

"How you feeling?"

"Better," Roland said. He tried to stand. "I could use some water."

Chris got him a glass from the sink. Roland finished it in one gulp.

"Where is everyone?" he asked, knowing damn well what the answer would be.

Chris's response wasn't what he expected, but it wasn't much better.

• • •

Sunshine and blue skies welcomed Chris and Roland as they came out the front door. The cypress trees scattered across endless rolling hills, the pines, the ancient Roman ruins; it was beautiful. But they didn't care. Chris had brought Roland up to speed on the situation. He had the tablet that controlled Octavia, so the Nysta cyberattack was no longer a threat. And Mostafa was dead. However, in less than an hour, the president of the United States was scheduled to be assassinated by terrorists in suicide vests controlled by a detonator on Mostafa's iPhone. Worst of all, George, Tricia, and Alena had been captured and given suicide vests of their own.

"Is there a way to disarm the vests?" Chris asked.

The Harvard man examined the detonator app for a moment, then said, "No, this app only allows you to detonate the bomb. Once it's armed, and it is, there's nothing we can do."

"Shit."

NEW BEGINNING

Roland navigated to the settings and studied the screen. His eyes lit up when he found what he was looking for.

"I can track their location with the detonator app's GPS," he said, pointing to the blue dot moving across the map.

"We can work with that."

"Even if we had a car, there's no way we'd catch up to them in time."

"Unless…" Chris grinned. "Follow me."

They took the driveway around to the back of the house, where it opened up to a large blacktop parking area with a six-car garage. Three spaces were empty, but the others were filled with exotic cars: a Rolls-Royce Phantom, a Bentley Continental GT, and an immaculately restored ruby-red 1963 Corvette Sting Ray convertible.

"Not fast enough," Roland said, eying the red sports car.

But then he saw what Chris was staring at, and it wasn't a car; it was a much larger vehicle parked in front of the garages.

Roland's eyes nearly came out of his head. "No, no! Absolutely not!"

CHAPTER 83

THREE IDENTICAL BLACK Land Rover Defenders traveled one in front of the other down the A1 motorway toward Rome. Traffic was light but would increase as they got closer to the city center. Their destination was an intersection a mile from the Roma Eventi conference center, the only spot along the United States presidential motorcade route where a civilian could be within yards-length of the president's armored SUV. The black Defenders were chosen for two reasons. First, they were capable of seating five people. Second, and most importantly, they were identical to the vehicles used by Italian military and intelligence agencies. By the time the American Secret Service realized the license plates were not cleared, and before their snipers—perched on rooftops at every corner of the motorcade's route—had time to fire a single shot, the damage would be done. There were five people in each Defender, each one wearing a suicide vest filled with dynamite. Combined, it was enough explosive power to take out an entire city block. The president wouldn't even know what hit him.

Alena, George, and Tricia sat silently—they didn't have much choice with the gags in their mouths—in the backseat of the third Defender in the caravan. There were two skinny young men in the front seat—boys, really, barely eighteen years old—dressed in street clothes and suicide vests and armed with AK-47s. They were silent as well, staring stoically at the SUVs in front of them, well aware they were moments away from meeting Allah. Their sacrifice would bring great honor to their families, and it would solidify their place in heaven. But human nature longs for survival, and fear transcended the excitement that filled their souls.

George kept his eyes on the front seat, searching for a way out. They'd been ambushed by a dozen armed terrorists moments after Chris and Roland left the Fiat. Fighting back would have been suicide. But when the vests came out, they all knew what was about to happen. George was terrified, and he was angry. His wife and unborn daughter were about to die, and there was not a goddamn thing he could do about it.

The women were calm. Perhaps it was intuition. Perhaps it was how they handled their own fears. Even though Alena had nearly died many times over the last few days, it still felt surreal to know her time on earth was about to end. She wondered if Chris was still alive. And if he was, would he try and rescue them? But how could he possibly do that?

It was Tricia who seemed to know something. While George focused on an impossible escape plan, she looked Alena straight in the eyes and attempted communication—Morse code with the blinks of her eyelids. At first Alena was confused. But then she got it. After a couple minutes of trial and error, she understood what Tricia was trying to say: *Chris never gives up.*

• • •

The Airbus twin-engine H145 helicopter was painted blue and white and stood alone in the middle of the blacktop parking area.

"I'm not doing it," Roland said.

"Stop whining."

"Who needs a private helicopter, anyway?"

Chris shrugged. "I dunno, rich people?" He opened the helicopter door.

"We're taking the Corvette. It's fast. We'll catch up."

Chris reached inside the aircraft. Out came the key. He smiled. "It's a sign."

"That we're going to die."

"Didn't die last time."

Chris was referring to the helicopter crash he, Roland, and Terry had survived a year before in the Russian wilderness.

"That was luck," said Roland.

"Luck of the Irish."

"I'm not Irish."

"But you're a lucky guy. You always get hurt, and yet you survive. You're a survivor."

"Your logic is illogical. You can't even fly this thing."

"I flew a plane."

"And you crashed it."

"I was being shot at."

"You don't think they're going to shoot at us? No, this is a bad idea."

"Of course it is. But it's the best bad idea we got."

• • •

And it was a bad idea—a terrible idea, actually. Before takeoff, Chris and Roland stocked up on extra Kalashnikov rifles from the dead terrorists and a box of fully loaded magazines from a storage closet in the villa. Headphones on, Chris powered up the Airbus, and the propellers began to spin. But the challenge was getting the damn thing in the air without losing control. Roland's eyes were closed the entire time, but somehow Chris managed to pull it off. Steady all the way. The thumping of the propellors, the humming of the two engines—up into the sky.

The rotorcraft leveled out, and both men let out audible sighs of relief. They weren't crashing—not yet. The view from the air was a breathtaking canopy of rolling hills, cypress and pine trees, and snow-capped mountains beneath a clear blue sky. But neither could give a shit about any of that. They'd survived the ascent, now it was time to rescue their family.

Using the GPS tracker on the detonator app as their guide, they flew over highways, passing farms and villas until Roland pointed to the map on the phone's screen.

"They're straight ahead of us," he said.

"Copy that."

And then they ran out of gas.

CHAPTER 84

As both engines sputtered and spat, Chris finally looked at the one part of the control panel he hadn't bothered to check: the fuel gauge.

"Shit," he said.

"What?"

"We're out of gas."

"*What?*"

"Yeah, I fucked up."

"You think?"

Chris steadied the chopper as it lost power and altitude.

"What are you going to do?" Roland asked.

"I don't know—land?"

• • •

A bearded terrorist in the passenger seat of the first Land Rover in the caravan heard the propellers. He lowered the side window and stuck out his head. A blue helicopter was hovering above them. It was much lower than it should have been, and black smoke was spewing from its engines.

Other drivers on the road noticed too, and as the chopper

dropped from the sky, they began to panic. It was instant gridlock—lots of honking and screaming in Italian. Some cars crashed, some went off-road in an attempt to avoid the incoming aircraft.

• • •

Chris and Roland were in a chaotic world of thumping propellors, whining engines, and flashing lights and pulsating beeps from a panic-stricken control panel. Chris noticed the Land Rovers continuing through the cluster-fuck of European cars. That was their target, unfazed by an impending helicopter crash—determined to complete their mission. Chris was going to land right in front of them. He clenched his teeth and prepared for a crash landing. Roland held onto the side of his seat. They dropped faster, less than fifty feet above the pavement.

On the ground, Alena, George, and Tricia heard the incoming chopper, and their eyes widened when they saw who was flying the doomed aircraft.

It got lower and lower—louder and louder.

There was a resounding thud followed by scraping metal as the helicopter crashed onto the highway. Its engines powered down, and the propellers stopped turning. There was smoke everywhere, but no fire, no explosion. Chris had done it again.

He smiled at Roland. "Told you I could do it."

But the Harvard man didn't respond. He was distracted. That was when Chris saw them. Four Middle Eastern men wearing suicide vests and carrying AK-47s had surrounded the helo. They were yelling something in Arabic. It sounded angry. Sounded like they were going to open fire at any moment.

Chris said, "We got this. Remember the plan."

"What plan?"

"Just follow my lead."

Chris slowly raised his hands and opened the door.

"This is why Trish makes our plans," Roland muttered to himself as he put his own hands up and exited the aircraft.

The terrorists used their rifles to force Chris and Roland to the rear of the helicopter. The three Defenders were parked a few feet behind them. *Alena, George, and Tricia are in one of those*, thought Chris. It was impossible to know which one because the windows were tinted.

Two terrorists stepped forward and proceeded to inspect Chris and Roland. They went through each pocket and patted them down from shoulders to ankles. It wasn't much different from what TSA performs on passengers before every commercial flight, only these guys had guns. Chris and Roland let it happen, staring forward in silence. Once the terrorists were satisfied their captives had no weapons on them, they stepped back. The last thing they would ever do on this earth.

Chris dropped to the ground and rolled against the legs of the man to his right. It took the skinny kid by surprise, and he was unable to raise his rifle fast enough. Chris took control of the Kalashnikov and immediately put it to use. He turned the selector to full auto and pressed the trigger, letting off a burst of lead into the four men that surrounded them. He stood up. The rifle in his hand was still smoking, and all four terrorists were lying dead on the pavement. Chris had killed everyone before Roland could register what to do next.

However, the gunshots had alerted the rest of the terrorists waiting in the Land Rovers. Six men in suicide vests exited the first two SUVs with their weapons drawn.

"Almawt lil'amirikiiyn!" one of them screamed.

Death to the Americans!

"*La ilaha illal-lah!*" screamed another.

There is no god but Allah!

But these weren't trained soldiers. They were boys with assault rifles, and they didn't stand a chance against former Special Forces operative Chris Harding.

• • •

Alena, George, and Tricia could hear everything. And so could the men in the front seat. Gunshots cracking through the air, penetrating steel and shattering glass. Screams in Arabic followed by bodies hitting the pavement. The Islamic extremists were losing the battle, but George, Tricia, and Alena were still wearing suicide vests that could be detonated at any moment. No matter how many Hamas and Hezbollah goons Chris killed, they would still be dead.

George was fed up. His arms were cuffed behind him, he was gagged, and he was wearing a vest filled with explosives. Worse still, his wife and unborn child were in the same predicament. Hands down the worst situation he'd ever been in. But the men in the front seat were in a tough spot too. They were tasked with guarding the prisoners, but at the same time a gunfight was underway, and they could hear their fellow "Freedom Fighters" dying at the hands of an American in a baseball cap. The mission given to them by their leader, ordained by Allah, was no longer possible. Could they still make it to heaven if they martyred themselves right there on the street, along with three more Americans?

The bearded man from the hollers of Kentucky was watching them, observing every detail of their expressions. The Jihadists looked at each other and nodded. The one in the passenger seat opened an app on his phone—an app designed to detonate explosive devices.

Not on my watch, George thought.

His snakeskin cowboy boots had been with him for twenty years, and they'd never let him down. He jammed the heel of his left boot against the center console in front of him. The plastic cracked, startling the terrorists who were mentally preparing to die. They both muttered something in Arabic. George did it again. He'd learned this trick from Chris. Upset your enemy so much that they put *themselves* in an unforgiving situation.

The man in the passenger seat turned around. He was about to say something when the heel of a boot collided with his jaw, instantly breaking the bone. Before the pain even registered, another kick made impact with his cheek. The skin burst open, and the bone splintered up to his eye socket. The terrorist fell backward, screaming in agony.

The man behind the wheel went for his rifle.

But George was faster.

He lunged forward and head-butted the guy, causing him to drop the Kalashnikov. George continued pushing his massive body over the center console into the front seating area, thrashing his way through the two stunned and injured terrorists. Unfortunately, George hadn't considered his next move. He was stuck.

Tricia had watched her husband's impromptu attack with trepidation. Now she was furious that he'd let his anger get the better of him—a year of training down the drain. Beside her, Alena was frozen in fear, unsure what to do.

And fear was the only thing any of them should have been feeling.

The driver caught his bearings, picked up his weapon, and

aimed it at George's head.

"Go to hell, you stupid American," he said in a thick accent.

Before he could pull the trigger, his brains were blown out the front of his forehead, spraying the contents of his skull over the front seat and console.

No one had noticed that the gunfire had stopped up ahead. The driver's side door was open, and Chris still had the AK-47 aimed at the dead Jihadist. The other man—the one with the broken jaw—put his hands up. Chris kept his weapon on him as he removed a knife from the dead man's pocket and used it to cut George loose.

Unfazed by the blood and brains that filled his long hair and beard, George set his sights on the terrorist with the broken jaw. Suddenly the man who was prepared to end his own life no longer wanted to die. Being killed by an unbeliever was not what he had in mind. No more virgins for him, no welcoming gates of heaven. Would he go to hell? He was only nineteen. He was still a virgin himself.

In broken English, he pleaded for his life. "Please, I beg you, don't—"

George took the terrorist's head in his bare hands and squeezed. His eyes went red. The veins in his neck popped out as his anger and strength increased. It happened fast. The skull cracked beneath his grip, and the man's head deflated like a balloon, squirting blood and gooey brain particles into George's crazed face.

Chris opened the back door and helped Alena and Tricia out of the vehicle, both in shock at what they'd just witnessed. The gags and zip-ties were removed, followed by the suicide vests, which were carefully placed back inside the SUV.

Alena wrapped her arms around Chris.

Tricia did the same to George.

Roland wished he could hug his girlfriend.

And there it was. Standing on the side of a highway on the outskirts of Rome, surrounded by dead bodies, a smoking helicopter, and a dozen abandoned Fiats, they'd thwarted an assassination attempt on the president and stopped the worst cyberattack in American history.

But that sense of accomplishment ended with the thumping sound of a helicopter approaching and a green Bell UH-1 "Huey" darkening the sky above them. Like the ones flown in Vietnam, it had a flat open space in the passenger area, void of doors, and was able to carry up to thirteen passengers. There were eleven men in the back wearing black tactical gear and armed with M4 rifles—United States private military contractors. As the chopper got lower, they were able to recognize the passengers in front: Dan Greenwood and FBI Director Steven House.

CHAPTER 85

From the Bell UH-1's cockpit, the A1 motorway looked like a scene out of a zombie apocalypse movie—cars scattered in every direction, abandoned by their drivers, and dead bodies covering the pavement next to three Land Rovers riddled with bullet holes. Greenwood pointed to five people standing beside one of the SUVs.

"That's them," he said.

House did a press check on his Glock 17—the standard issue sidearm felt cumbersome against his two-thousand-dollar suit pants—and confirmed the magazine was fully loaded with seventeen 9mm rounds.

"You're staying right here, Director," Greenwood said. "This could easily turn into an international shit show if we don't do it right. I make the arrest. They're all yours after that."

"Fine, but let my men contain the scene first. Last thing I need is you getting killed."

• • •

Chris watched the helo as it prepared to land. He'd planned for this possibility. Mostafa told him the FBI was on their way. That meant Greenwood. House was an added bonus.

"What the hell is House doing here?" Tricia asked.

The FBI director was a politician, not an operator. In fact, it was doubtful he'd ever spent a single day in the field. His world was boardrooms, offices, and restaurants. His presence in Italy meant he was scared, not just for his career but for his life. This was an opportunity. And Chris wasn't about to let it pass them by.

Once the chopper landed, they would be done for—outmanned and outgunned. Even the Harvard man's Irish luck would be unable to save them.

Use what God gave you.

His father's words echoed through Chris's mind.

There were three cars smashed together a couple of feet behind the third Land Rover. If they could just get there before Greenwood and House landed. Chris quickly detailed his plan to the others. It was a good one, even Tricia was impressed.

"Behind the Fiats," Chris said. "Go!"

Everyone ran to the wreck. Roland was still grasping his AK-47 like a child holding a doll, and George had picked up two rifles from among the carnage. But Tricia and Alena were unarmed. Once they were all crouched behind the cars, Chris took out the Glock 17 he'd relieved from Mostafa and gave it to Alena. As she took the weapon, their eyes met. Nothing was said; it was all in the eyes. They were making sure the other knew how they felt, in the high probability that they didn't make it out of this one alive.

George handed Tricia one of his rifles, a battered old AK covered in blood from its previous owner. She took the weapon, removed the mag, and reinserted it after confirming it was fully loaded. George's training was about to come in handy. And she was mad.

"This is for our baby girl," she said, kissing her husband.

NEW BEGINNING

The "Huey" landed in the grass several yards from the caravan of Defenders, and eleven private military contractors jumped out with their M4s pressed to their shoulders. Greenwood followed close behind, using his men as a shield. Harding, Anderson, and the hick from Kentucky were not to be underestimated. He'd made that mistake before—wouldn't make it again.

The PMCs passed the first Defender. The open field that surrounded the highway was empty. It was quiet, eerie almost—just a soft breeze rustling against the grass and the very distant sound of police sirens.

From behind the wall of Fiats, Chris watched—waiting for the right moment.

"Almost there," he whispered.

The contractors surrounded the second SUV in the caravan. The first man looked their way, and then said something into his radio.

"Now," Chris whispered to Roland.

The Harvard man pressed the green "detonate" button on the suicide vest detonator app.

There was a clicking sound. Greenwood's men looked at each other. One of them saw the suicide vest on a dead body beside his feet.

"Shit."

His last words.

The explosion was deafening. A cloud of fire burst into the air as every single vest went off at the same time—a dozen sticks of dynamite blasting through all three Defenders and propelling the contractors into the air. Some were instantly burned to a crisp, others were lifted twenty feet in the air before being dropped to the ground.

They were a dozen feet away, but the blast knocked Chris, Roland, Alena, George, and Tricia to the ground. Everything around them was on fire, and a cloud of black and gray smoke had engulfed the area like a sandstorm in the desert. Through the fog were more body parts, some on the pavement, some in the grass, all of them missing limbs. One man's large intestines was spewed out on the pavement beside what was left of his legs—a bloody tangle of shredded skin and bones.

Chris opened his eyes. His head was spinning—another concussion, no doubt. Roland's bullet wound had been reopened, and he couldn't get up. Alena and Tricia had a few cuts, probably concussed as well, and George was having a hard time sitting up. Perhaps he really did have back problems.

Tricia noticed Roland's gaping wound and rushed to his side.

"I'm okay," he said. "Just need a real doctor."

Alena stood guard, holding onto her Glock with both hands, while Chris and George grabbed their rifles and went to inspect the damage. The Land Rovers were nothing more than burnt frames with small fires still burning around them. There was a man whose top half had been blown to bits, leaving only his legs, pelvis, and pieces of his insides behind. Beside him was the bloodied head of another man, his green eyes still open. There were more bodies strewn over the grass beside the pavement, and beyond that—through the haze of smoke—they could make out the "Huey."

They counted eleven dead contractors. Chris tried not to think about what would have happened if the terrorists had succeeded. The innocent lives lost.

Focus on what's ahead.

Greenwood and House were not among the dead.

They were still out there somewhere.

NEW BEGINNING

Chris heard the thud of metal ripping into flesh before he heard the cracking sound of the M4. The bullet shot through George's chest, taking flesh and muscle with it. It hit him like a punch, and he instantly dropped his weapon and fell to the ground. Chris turned. Raised his rifle to fire. But before he could pull the trigger, another bullet penetrated his left thigh. He dropped to the ground, hard. Another shot. This one missed. Chris used his other leg to lift himself up, still grasping his rifle. He felt lightheaded. Blood was escaping his left thigh with a vengeance, which meant he only had minutes before lights out.

Fight.

Never give up.

The shooter appeared from out of the smoky fog, like a phantom, uninjured by the blast.

Dan Greenwood smiled as he approached Chris and George. Finally, he had gotten the better of these two bearded assholes.

He pointed his M4 at Chris, who was still holding his own weapon. "Don't be stupid. Drop that Russian piece of shit."

Chris ignored the command. He tightened his grip on the Kalashnikov. Started to raise it. But Greenwood's reflexes were faster, and he pulled the trigger first, sending a 55-grain bullet into Chris's right arm. He let go of the AK and slumped to the ground, panting, out of breath—and over forty years old.

"You just don't give up, do you?" Greenwood said, towered over Chris and aiming the gun directly at his heart.

Chris said nothing.

Greenwood continued, like a villain basking in the glory of his success. "I've fought a lot of men in my life. Killed many of them. But you—you've been quite a challenge. Under different circumstances, I would have recruited you."

"I'd never work for you."

"No, you wouldn't. You're too stubborn for your own good. This free country you're fighting for—it doesn't exist. Your fight is in vain, Mr. Harding. But no matter, I'm going to kill you. And after that I'll kill your friends, and I'll kill that pretty reporter you're so fond of. I'll kill your ex-wife, and I'll kill your daughter. And the world will move on as if none of you ever existed."

Those were the wrong words.

Every Goliath has a weakness. It's just up to David to find it, to exploit it. And it just so happened that Chris had one more trick up his sleeve.

He thrust his right foot into the air. Greenwood was just close enough. The impact was quick, and it was sudden. The tip of Chris's boot landed in the PMCs crotch, smashing his manhood. Greenwood recoiled in pain, and for a split second, his attention was not on his prisoner. It provided Chris the opening he needed. He grabbed the AK with his left hand and, using all the energy and strength he could muster, lifted the Soviet rifle to his shoulder and pressed the trigger.

Greenwood met his maker before he heard the shot. The bullet shattered the top part of his skull, taking a chunk of his brain with it. The impact propelled his body into the air, and he landed with a thud on the pavement as a pool of blood surrounded his deformed head.

Chris's energy was spent. He dropped the rifle and collapsed, stretching his body out against the pavement and staring up at the blue sky. Then he remembered George. He looked over at his friend lying beside him. He wasn't moving.

"George!" he heard Tricia scream from behind the smoking SUVs.

NEW BEGINNING

She came running through the rubble with her rifle held to her shoulder. Alena and Roland were right behind her, Alena's Glock leading the way. Tricia let go of her weapon and dropped to the ground beside her husband.

"George!" she screamed. Tears in her eyes. "George!" She shook his body.

Alena helped Chris up. He was in a daze—a brain fog—and was losing blood, fast.

"It's over," he panted.

Alena wrapped her arms around his neck and grabbed his face, staring into his blue eyes.

"You crazy, crazy man," she said.

Chris cracked a grin, but he couldn't smile; his friend was down. He looked over at his fallen brother. "Get up, you stupid redneck."

Tricia was crying and shaking him. The big man was soaked in his own blood. And he wasn't waking up.

Roland knelt beside George. "He needs CPR."

Alena pulled Tricia away as the Harvard man began compressions.

"One and two and—" Ribs cracked. He breathed into George's mouth. "One and two and—" More compressions. Another breath. Then, "One and two and—"

Coughing, wheezing, and George opened his eyes.

"Get the hell off me, Roland," he said, choking on each word.

But while CPR was being performed, and while Chris and George's wounds were being wrapped in torn shirts, a man in a blue suit was walking their way.

• • •

House had witnessed everything. At first, he was scared. The explosion decimated every one of Greenwood's men. Then Greenwood himself was killed. The FBI director had never seen so much carnage, and horror filled his eyes as he searched for a way out of his situation. Everyone was huddled around Chris and George. No one was paying attention. Had they forgotten about him? This was his chance.

He unholstered his Glock and climbed out of the helicopter, slowly walking toward the road. The smoke helped to camouflage him, and as he got closer, his hands tightened around the gun. Finger against the trigger. He'd trained for this. He would succeed. Start with the most dangerous one. He aimed the pistol at Chris's head.

House felt a sharp pain in his shoulder, followed by the cracking sound of a gun firing. He dropped his weapon and slumped to the ground, shock setting in as he watched blood escape the hole in his shoulder where the 9mm round had made impact. He then looked up and found himself staring down the barrel of a Glock 17.

Alena was still holding the pistol with both hands.

Just aim and shoot, she'd remembered as she pulled the trigger.

The FBI director writhed in agony on the ground. "You shot me."

"Shut up," Alena snapped, picking up his gun and kicking him in the stomach.

He groaned as his good arm went for his now bruised gut.

Alena returned to Chris's side. There was a shit-eating grin all over his face.

"That was sexy as hell," he said, lifting himself up to face her.

"I blame you."

"I taught you well."

"How many people did you kill today?"

"I lost count."

"Exactly. It's called restraint. House is still alive."

"For now."

Roland, George, and Tricia were busy celebrating George's return to life from the Harvard man's magical kiss, and Chris figured this was a good time to ravish the girl. If it had been a movie, the camera would have encircled them as he used his good arm to cradle Alena's cheek and then pull her close into a "John Wayne" kiss. Alena, taken aback by such a firm and confident display of affection, melted into his arms.

Their brief interlude was interrupted by incoming police sirens and a sea of blue and red lights from Rome's finest appearing on the horizon. Color drained from their faces.

"Please tell me you two have an exit strategy," Tricia said to Chris and Roland.

The Harvard man looked to Chris, who swallowed hard, unsure how to respond.

House smiled. His life was saved, and those goddam Woodhaven operatives would end up in an Italian prison by noon. He eyed the briefcase containing the AI tablet that was beside Roland. He could still activate Octavia. Still prevent his own demise.

But as the sirens grew louder, another sound emanated from the sky. Everyone looked up to see two U.S. Army Black Hawk helicopters coming in for a landing.

"Elgerson came through," said Chris, letting out a sigh of relief. "Just in time."

CHAPTER 86

Steven House opened his eyes. At first, he was confused. His last memories were a blur.

Soldiers surrounding him.

The butt of a rifle against his face.

Darkness.

Head spinning.

Staring out of a helicopter, mid-air.

A needle entering his arm.

Darkness.

He felt groggy, but as his eyes adjusted to being open, he realized where he was—alone in what appeared to be an old garage with plaster walls and a concrete floor, the stench of decay filling the air. He was hanging from the ceiling, his arms attached to two chains, his feet barely touching the floor. He was naked, and the bullet wound in his shoulder was caked with dried blood. It throbbed. But so did the rest of his body.

"Help, someone help!" he screamed.

There was the sound of footsteps outside the door, then it opened. House felt a sense of dread as he looked at the man standing in the doorway.

NEW BEGINNING

Chris Harding's face was riddled with cuts and bruises, and his beard and clothing were covered in dirt and blood. His legs were bandaged, as was his shoulder. He didn't appear to have a weapon. That was good. Or was it? House wasn't sure.

"Where the hell am I?" the FBI director demanded.

"Doesn't matter," Chris replied as he entered the room and closed the door.

"Get me out of these fucking things."

"You should work out more, Steven. You're a bit flabby."

"You'll never get away with this. I'm the director of the FBI for God's sake. You have no idea what—"

"I know quite a bit, actually." Chris stepped forward. "You betrayed us just like you betrayed your country. And innocent people died because of you." He got closer, just inches from his prisoner's face. "Some of them were my friends."

"I was only doing my job," House said. "I wanted none of that to happen. You have to believe me."

"Oh I believe you. You had no choice."

"Exactly." House felt a burst of energy. He could get out of this. "We're on the same side, you and me. There's a deal to be made here. You have the tablet that controls Octavia. You can stop the attack from happening. You'll be a hero. All of you will. I can corroborate everything. You'll receive pardons. You can return to your life."

"That's a pretty good deal. And what happens to you?"

"You need someone in my position. My office will open up so many doors for you."

"I'll bet. Like the island?"

House froze. "That's not, uh, I mean, I can—"

"I've seen the pictures. Those girls were fifteen, tops."

"They look older these days."

Chris took out his cell phone. "You're going to tell me exactly what I need to know, and then you're going to pray to God you survive prison. Because that's where you're going. And we both know what they do to perverts in prison."

House swallowed hard before nodding. Not the deal he'd hoped to make.

"Where is Al Kempe?" Chris said.

"I—I have no idea."

"Take a wild guess."

"Somewhere in Russia," House stammered.

"Actionable intel, Director. Don't waste my fucking time."

"He doesn't tell me everything."

"I wouldn't either."

"I don't know where he is. I'm telling the truth."

"We'll see about that," Chris said, crossing the room to a wooden bench against the wall.

House hadn't noticed the bench, or the metal tool box on top of it.

Chris opened the box and removed a pair of pliers. He shook his head, replaced the tool, and came out with a carpenter's hammer. He looked back at the FBI director who was watching him, hoping and praying this was all theatrics. The bearded man returned to House's side with the hammer in his left hand. He locked eyes with the naked man.

"Al Kempe," he said.

House was sweating bullets, his eyes darting between Chris and the hammer.

"I swear to God, I don't know."

"Wrong answer."

In one swift motion, Chris swung the hammer at House, angling the claw toward his chest. The sharp edge cut into the skin and extracted a healthy chunk of muscle tissue from just below the right breast. House screamed as fresh blood poured out of the wound.

"Al Kempe," Chris said again.

House hesitated. Chris did not. He swung the hammer once more, this time making impact with the director's midsection. The claw ripped through the belly, penetrating the large intestines, the bottom half of the stomach, the pancreas, and both kidneys, and sent a swath of blood across Chris's face and chest. House gasped, his body going into shock as vital fluids and shredded tissue poured out of the open cavity.

"Please, please," he said as he coughed up blood. "They'll kill me if I tell you."

Chris pointed the edge of the claw at House's penis.

"Next one goes here," he said.

"I'm losing a lot of blood."

"Answer the question and it all goes away."

House nodded. "Okay, okay. You knew too much. He was afraid of exposure. His company, Maritime, owns a condo in Saint Petersburg."

"Are you sure he's there now?"

"We spoke right after I landed in Rome. I trace all our calls. He was at the condo."

"Thank you. See, that wasn't so hard," Chris said, lowering the hammer to his side.

"I need medical attention."

Chris stared back in stony silence.

"You promised," House pleaded.

The hammer came back up.

"I said it would all go away. And it will."

House's eyes widened, the realization sinking in.

"I don't want to die. Please, I'm just a politician, a paper pusher." He choked up more blood. "I didn't even want to be involved. I was forced." Rapid breathing. Panic. Then, "Have mercy on me, *please*."

But there was no mercy in Chris's eyes, only retribution. He swung the claw with all the strength he could muster. It landed firmly between the edge of House's pubic bone and his penis. The blunt force of the metal edge severed the member, cutting straight through the urethra and landing in the scrotum. Pulsating blood pumped from the wound as the appendage dropped to the concrete floor.

House gasped, unable to breathe, or even process the pain, and by the time his brain registered what happened, he had lost consciousness—his soul on its way to hell.

• • •

Chris put on his aviator sunglasses as he exited the garage onto a narrow street in Vicenza that was lined with broken-down buildings. Roland was waiting for him behind the wheel of an open-top green Army Jeep. He noticed the fresh blood splattered across Chris's face and chest.

"I guess he talked," Roland said, firing up the engine.

"Sure did," Chris replied, climbing in the passenger side. He lit a cigarette. "Looks like we're headed back to Russia."

CHAPTER 87

Saint Petersburg, Russia

Formally known as Leningrad until the fall of the Soviet Union in 1991, Saint Petersburg is the seat of European culture in Russia, a plethora of breathtaking Imperial palaces constructed of white marble and gold. It was two days before Christmas, and snow was falling over the second-largest city in Russia. There were horse-drawn carriages, lavishly decorated Christmas trees, and glittering lights everywhere. It was here that Al Kempe had found refuge, and like Edward Snowden before him, he would likely never return to the United States. He'd been well compensated for his sacrifice. A three-bedroom condo with views of the Bloshaya Nevka and the Winter Palace, along with enough money to last a lifetime. The SVR would still find use for him. His knowledge of American policies was endless, making him the ultimate spy, a treasure chest filled with decades of classified information. It was enough to keep him necessary until old age took its toll. The NWO was another story. They dealt in the shadows, influencing a global army of invisible operatives, and did not accept failure.

Kempe arrived at his condo after a dinner of steak and potatoes washed down by three bourbons. His mind was heavy. He wondered what had happened to Octavia. If House had retrieved the tablet then he would have contacted him by now. It had been two days since they last spoke and still no news of the cyberattack. Had Chris Harding and his band of idiots actually succeeded? No, that was impossible.

He poured himself a Johnnie Walker Blue Label from a glass decanter on a bar beside the window. The city was beautiful this time of year. The lights, the snow—it was magical. He wanted to enjoy it. Had he made the right choice? America and its corporate greed was a dying empire. He lit a cigar, enjoying the taste of the rich tobacco against his lips. Yes, he'd made the right choice. He took a seat on the leather couch in the center of the room, resting his cigar on a glass ashtray on the coffee table. He felt relaxed, safe even. The building was outfitted with a state-of-the-art security system, and armed agents—courtesy of the SVR's counterpart, Russia's Federal Security Service, the FSB—patrolled each floor.

He turned on the TV that was mounted on the wall in front of him and leaned back against a mountain of throw pillows.

A blond Fox News reporter from the press corps was talking about her experience at the White House Briefing Room earlier that evening. News of the attempted assassination of the president had filled headlines over the past two days, and aerial footage of American private military contractors and Hamas militants slaughtered on the road to Rome suggested a covert CIA mission to thwart the terrorist attack.

Kempe stared at the screen, unfazed by what was now old news. He started to doze off, the white noise of the TV lulling him to sleep.

It couldn't have been more than five minutes before he opened his eyes. Something had startled him. He scanned the room. Nothing had changed. His cigar was still burning on the edge of the ashtray. His half-empty glass of bourbon was still on the table beside the couch. Snow was still falling outside. Everything was quiet but the muffled sound of traffic from the street below.

Wait, the TV.

He froze.

It had been turned off.

He felt a knot forming in his stomach as he turned his head to the left. That's when he saw him. A figure in dark clothes standing at the edge of the room. The figure came closer, the light from the window illuminating the face of Chris Harding.

"You look tired and weak, old man," Chris said as he removed a P365-AXG LEGION from the back of his jeans.

For the first time in his life, Kempe was speechless. He had a Colt Cobra .38 Special in a holster on his hip, but attempting to use it would be a death wish.

"You're probably trying to figure out how I got past your guards," Chris said.

"Hardly," Kempe replied. "This wouldn't be the first time you came to my home unannounced. I know the answer, but I have to ask. What do you want?"

Chris attached a suppressor to the barrel of his gun.

"That's what I thought," the old man said slowly.

He paused before carefully retrieving his cigar from the ashtray, along with the gold lighter beside it. He relit the Cuban tobacco, took one last puff, then stared back at his executioner as he resigned himself to his fate.

CHAPTER 88

Washington, D.C.

Robin Valencia left her office early, arriving home a few minutes past 4:00 p.m.—and not because it was Christmas Eve. The past few days had been one anxiety-ridden moment after another, and she needed an escape from the world. When President Douglas arrived safely at the G20 Summit, she knew something was wrong, and when Octavia failed to activate, she started to panic. House's cell phone went straight to voicemail, Kempe's number was out of service, and she had a dozen missed calls, two voicemails, and several text messages from Vice President Walter that she had ignored. She thought about calling Jean Mackler but decided it was too risky. There was no telling what had happened, or how exposed she was.

She lived in a two-bedroom luxury co-op at The Watergate on Virginia Avenue. The crushed gray vinyl floors, stainless steel appliances, and granite countertops were clean—pristine in every way—evidence of her hundred-hour work weeks. After ordering Chinese take-out from Uber Eats, Valencia poured herself a glass of wine and stepped out onto her balcony. The cold air felt good against her skin. She could see the lights of the capitol reflecting off the Potomac River. The seat of American power—a power she was to have harnessed. But what went wrong? She sipped her cabernet and wondered. Were the Woodhaven operatives more capable than Kempe had let on? If so, what did that mean for her? Politics was about pivoting, and if she'd learned one thing about navigating the swamp, it was to always be willing to jump ship and join the winning team if necessary. Whatever it took to ensure the country moved toward a more diverse and inclusive society.

Her thoughts were interrupted by the phone vibrating in her pocket. An unknown number was calling. Perhaps it was Kempe checking in, or House reporting good news. So she answered. The voice on the other end was deep. Void of emotion. She didn't recognize it.

"Congresswoman Robin Valencia?" the man said.

"Who is this?"

There was a pause. Then, "You know who I am."

An uneasy feeling crept into Valencia's gut. She couldn't place the voice. She searched her memory but knew she had never spoken to this man before.

She said, "What do you want?"

"I want you to know that your time is up. You're finished."

"It's against the law to threaten a member of Congress," she replied sharply.

"This isn't a threat. It's a fact."

Valencia went back inside, closing the sliding balcony door behind her. She leaned into the phone as if it would increase the volume of her voice. "Who the hell is this?"

Breathing on the other end. A static crack in the connection. Then, "My name is Chris Harding. And I know who you work for, what you did. What you tried to do. And we'll speak again when the time is right. If you're still alive." He disconnected the call.

Before Valencia could process what she'd just been told, her front door was kicked in. Six federal agents wearing black tactical gear and armed with assault rifles stormed into the apartment. She screamed. She dropped her phone. Dropped her glass of wine. It shattered on the floor. Her mind was racing. Was this really happening? She stepped back, eyes widening in fear. But that fear quickly became indignation.

She said, "I am a United States congresswoman. You do not have the—"

One of the men grabbed her and violently thrust her to the floor. Another pinned his leg against the back of her neck, while the first guy slammed her arms together behind her. She felt cold steel as a pair of handcuffs were fastened around her wrists.

"This is unlawful. I demand to know my charges," she ordered.

But the men said nothing. She heard the sound of police sirens in the distance. They were getting louder. Even with the balcony door closed, they seemed like they were right outside her apartment. One of the men nodded at the other as if the sirens were their cue. Valencia was lifted up and her arms were grasped by two men, one on each side. Another came forward with a black cloth sack. Valencia stared in disbelief.

"No!" she screamed. Then in a timid voice, "This isn't fair."

The bag went over her head. Complete darkness.

CHAPTER 89

A BEAUTIFUL BLOND Fox News reporter stood in front of the White House. It was Christmas Day, and she was reporting the biggest story of the year, one that would go down as the most expansive federal government upheaval in history.

"Vice President Kim Walter resigned this morning after incriminating evidence surfaced connecting her to the assassination attempt on President David Douglas four days ago in Rome. She is also believed to have colluded with California Representative Robin Valencia on a conspiracy to push forward legislation that would give the federal government complete control over private-sector businesses. The catalyst used to power what many in Washington are now referring to as a 'Communist Occupation Bill' was an attempted cyberattack on our financial institutions by popular social media app, Nysta. If successful, it would have stolen billions of dollars from American bank, investment, and retirement accounts. And, in a shocking turn of events, it was the cybersecurity firm responsible for managing Nysta's data, Auspex Technology, who developed the artificial intelligence-powered computer responsible for carrying out this attack. The vice president has been indicted. So has Congresswoman Valencia. However, when federal and local police arrived at the congresswoman's home last night to serve the indictment, she

was not there. Sources tell us that she has not been heard from since, and a search for her whereabouts is currently underway."

• • •

A few blocks away, in front of the J. Edgar Hoover Building, a striking brunette correspondent for CNN continued the same story.

"FBI Director Steven House was found dead yesterday inside an abandoned garage in Vicenza, Italy. He was believed to have been tortured and killed by the very men he hired to carry out what many are now calling a 'democratic coup.' Disturbing evidence has also come to light connecting him to Little Saint James in the U.S. Virgin Islands, known as 'Epstein Island,' and some believe his sexual deviance was used as blackmail to coerce him into orchestrating this political attack."

• • •

A silver-haired CNBC news anchor in a blue suit continued the coverage from the studio with a backdrop of New York City behind him.

"Nysta COO Barry Allen and Auspex CEO Jean Mackler were both arrested today for their involvement in the attack."

Footage of Mackler being arrested at the Dallas Airport as he exited his private jet appeared on the screen, followed by images of Allen being taken in handcuffs from his home in San Francisco while his family watched in horror.

• • •

The blond Fox News reporter finished her story in front of the White House.

"The sweep of indictments this morning included more than a dozen

members of Congress who had agreed to a bribe in exchange for their vote on Valencia's new bill—bribes to be paid for with money stolen in the Nysta cyberattack. Their involvement was discovered during a covert CIA operation that remains classified. New York Times *journalist Alena Moore broke the story. Her explosive report brought to light a global conspiracy that would have forced Congress to pass Valencia's controversial bill, the United States Corporation Oversight Act, as a solution to a financial collapse brought on by the cyberattack. While Moore alludes to a collaboration between China and Russia in developing the technology and carrying out the attack, leaders from both countries have denied responsibility, stating that this was the work of American leaders with their own financial and political agendas."*

・・・

The bartender pulled the tap handle, filling a frosted pint glass with 21st Amendment West Coast IPA. He shut off the tap as soon as the foam hit the top and began to cascade down the side of the glass. The freshly poured beer was then placed on top of a napkin on the bar. Chris lifted the glass to his mouth and took a sip.

"Oh, that's good," he said with a grin.

Roland, George, and Tricia were beside him, Roland with a Deschutes Fresh Haze IPA, George with his version of a "craft" beer—a Corona with lime—and Tricia with a Diet Coke; no alcohol for her until the baby came in the spring.

McClellan's Retreat was a cozy bar on Florida Avenue NW between Washington's Kalorama and Dupont Circle neighborhoods. It was named after Civil War General George B. McClellan and featured exposed brick walls and red-backed bar stools. The crew had snagged five of those stools just in time for the evening rush. It was starting to get busy as people snuck away from Christmas gatherings to have a drink and unwind after an entire day spent with extended family.

As the three men sipped their brews and the lady sipped her soda, they watched the blond Fox News reporter in front of the White House on the TV mounted behind the bar. Regardless of how the media portrayed the situation, Chris knew the bad guys had gotten what they deserved. The threat had been neutralized, but more importantly, he'd kept the promise he made to Laura Wilson and ensured those responsible for her husband's death paid for their sins. It had come at a cost, though. Chris had veered past a line he had never crossed before—becoming an executioner, an angel of death to those in his path. Had he damned his soul in the process? Become the very thing he was fighting to destroy? Would his daughter forgive him if she one day discovered the things he had done?

Aaron Elgerson had saved their asses. After transporting them back to Camp Ederle, he employed the help of an old CIA buddy to spin the optics. Everything was labeled a covert CIA operation, classified with no questions asked, and the tablet controlling Octavia was found "mysteriously" destroyed. The AI computer itself was seized by the FBI's National Cyber Investigative Joint Task Force, and the Nysta app was permanently shut down and all of its data deleted. And it was Elgerson's CIA guy who tipped off the Anderson team about Robin Valencia's impending arrest.

"You never heard this from me, but she won't be processed," he had said.

"So she's going to a CIA black site," Chris had replied.

"No such thing. But if there was, you're damn straight that's where she's going. No matter how much evidence we have against her, the public outrage over arresting a politician of her caliber would be catastrophic. She'd never see the inside of a jail cell."

And yet again, Alena's mind had been blown. But this time she wasn't concerned with the human rights violation. Robin Valencia deserved everything that was coming her way.

The FBI's internal investigation into Steven House had uncovered even more incriminating evidence about Woodhaven than Seth Wilson's file indicated. House had a safe in his office that contained reports on every Woodhaven operation since its inception in 2017. As agents of Woodhaven, Chris, Roland, Terry, George, and Tricia had thought they were investigating the NWO. In reality, every op—every piece of evidence that came their way—was to further Russian intelligence. That information, along with the contents of Wilson's file, was enough to convince President Douglas that they were not domestic terrorists but heroes who had not only rescued the country but had saved his life. Under his directive, the Woodhaven file had been permanently sealed, including their employment record with Russian spy, Al Kempe. Chris, Roland, George, and Tricia were given fresh identities—Chris was cleared of murder charges in Colorado—and they were now free to live their lives without fear of prosecution for any "crimes" they may have committed. Alena was given the cover of an investigative journalist working in tandem with the CIA on an exclusive story. As compensation for the FBI's betrayal and as a thank-you for their service, they were each awarded a taxable payment of $25,000.

While at Camp Ederle, Elgerson's CIA man had said, "The public cannot know about the NWO—it plays into an already popular theory that the United States is controlled by the Deep State. Of course, that doesn't mean we won't investigate. In fact, we'd like you to head up a new task force. Get to the bottom of this global organization hell-bent on destroying our country."

It was strangely similar to the offer the Anderson team had received when they joined Woodhaven. Their answer was a resounding no. They were through working with the federal government. The CIA man understood and extended an open door if they should ever need anything. But that didn't mean they were finished with the NWO. Within hours of returning to Camp Ederle, Alena flew back to New York. She had a story to complete, while the Anderson team had unfinished business to conduct in Vicenza and Saint Petersburg.

George and Tricia were starting a family and were no longer interested in chasing bad guys. They did, however, provide communication support and surveillance while Chris and Roland traveled to Russia. It was Roland who disarmed Kempe's security system, giving Chris the green light to kill the seven FSB agents guarding the Russian spy. George and Tricia would now be heading back to Kentucky. They wanted their little girl born into tranquility. The compound was their safe haven, and it was where they could finally live out their lives in peace, away from the ever-watchful eyes of the federal government.

Chris and Roland wanted the same thing—a new beginning, a life spent with those they loved. For Roland, that was with a beautiful woman in Kentucky who saw something in him no one ever had. And for Chris, that meant finding love again and, perhaps, one day being the father to Claire he longed to be. But history had shown that getting close to others was a death sentence. Even with false identities. It was time to cut off the head of the snake and destroy the New World Order once and for all. Only this time, they would do it on their own terms.

Unlike House, Al Kempe had died honorably, having known the risks of the game. He was in it for money, not ideology, and preferred a quick and painless death. Before two 9mm rounds entered his chest and stole his last breath, he gave up his NWO contact—a man code-named The Watchmaker, whose true identity was unknown, even to Kempe. He was not on any country's intelligence database, had no criminal record, no digital footprint of any kind, and according to Kempe, operated in the old way—through secret drops, handwritten letters in code, and self-destructing recording devices. It wasn't much to go on, but it was a start. The Watchmaker was responsible for every NWO operation since at least the early 1990s. Finding him was the first step in taking them down.

• • •

Chris stepped outside the bar and lit a cigarette. It was cold. Snow was falling. And in the distance he thought he heard carolers singing.

"Could I have one?"

He turned. Alena was standing there in a black peacoat, a red scarf around her neck. He hadn't seen her in four days.

"You don't smoke," he said, cracking a smile.

"I've had a few over the years," she said. "I am a writer, after all. I just don't make a habit of it—unlike someone I know."

Chris handed her a cigarette from the pack of Camel Blues. Alena put it between her lips and leaned forward, allowing him to light it for her.

"Read your story," he said. "I was impressed."

"Thank you," she replied, taking a drag. "My editor loved it too. He even published it despite the fact our biggest advertiser is, well was, Auspex Technology."

"Their stock took a massive hit yesterday."

"Yeah, ninety percent—billions lost. Even if Jean Mackler

makes it out of prison, which is doubtful, his career is over."

"You took down one of the richest men in the world. Using words."

"I guess I did." Alena smiled. "And I got my own column. I can finally write exactly what I want—no oversight."

"You earned it."

"I turned it down."

"You what?"

She nodded. "I know."

"Isn't that what you've been working toward all these years?"

"It's exactly what I've been working toward. I don't know, I just—it feels wrong profiting from someone else's pain. Too many people were hurt. Too many people died. I know you're used to it, but I'm not."

"I'm not used to it either."

"Sorry, I didn't mean it like that. What I meant to say was, I learned from this experience. Life is short. It can be gone just like that, and I don't want to waste it. I want to cherish it. Spend it with those I care about, not chasing a career." She paused. "I quit the newspaper. Henry, my editor, boy was he upset—begged me to stay. But in the end, he understood."

"What are you going to do?"

"Amy woke up from her coma. It's going to be a long road, but I want to be there for her. Rebuild that friendship."

Chris stared at her. Those big brown eyes. He was falling in love with her, smoking cigarettes on the sidewalk in the snow.

"I want that too," he said.

"Want what?"

"What you said about not wasting your life—I want that. And uh…" *Don't say it. She's going to freak out.* "I want to spend it with the person I care about."

Alena stared back at him, processing what he'd just said.

"In case I wasn't clear, that person—it's you," he stammered.

Too much! Too much!

She looked into his eyes. She'd never seen him so vulnerable. She stepped closer, blowing the smoke out the side of her mouth, and kissed him. Then she said, "When you get back from doing whatever it is you have to do, I'll be here."

He smiled. "We'll get an IPA."

She laughed. "We'll do more than get an IPA."

• • •

Chris and Alena joined the group at the bar. Alena ordered the same IPA as Chris—a detail everyone noticed—and then took a stool beside him. As soon as her beer arrived, George raised his glass.

"I want to make a toast," he announced.

They all raised their glasses as well and faced the bearded man. Like Chris, he wasn't one for big speeches, or words for that matter, but today was a celebration.

"To those who couldn't be with us here today," he said. "To Terry—who, even though he was a Texan, became like a brother to me."

"To Terry," they all echoed.

"To Steven House, who got his penis chopped off."

"George," Tricia scolded.

Alena raised an eyebrow at Chris. He shrugged.

George continued. "To Natalya Palmer, the super hot spy who came over from the dark side to save our asses. To Adam Conner—our old boss—who, well, he was a moron, but he died serving his country. To Frank and Susie Boone, to Seth Wilson, and to every innocent life lost because of the evil in this world—may your souls find peace."

Chris nearly choked at George's sudden poetic use of language.

"He reads that Kindle every day," Tricia whispered to him.

Everyone cheered and took massive gulps of their drinks.

"I'm not done," George said, cutting them off mid-gulp. "I, uh—I'm scared. As you all know, I'm about to become a father, and to be honest, I have no idea how the hell I'm gonna do it." He smiled at Tricia. "Thank you for going on this adventure with me. To my ride-or-die, the sweetest piece of ass I ever had."

"Seriously, George!" Tricia exclaimed.

"Sorry," he stammered. "Here's to the most beautiful woman in the world—my chocolate princess."

Tricia put her hand over her face in shame.

Now George addressed Chris and Roland. "Don't get yourselves killed out there. If y'all end up in a pinch, you know who to call." He wasn't sure what to say next, so he raised his half-full pint of beer and said, "Merry Christmas."

And so they drank and talked and ordered deep-fried food, and for a moment, all was right with the world. But the enemy was still out there, and Chris Harding's fight with the NWO had only just begun.

EPILOGUE

Berlin, Germany

Fritz Geissler woke up early. He was a small, unassuming man in his late seventies with pale white skin, a round face, and white hair. He checked his gold pocket watch on the bedside table, confirming the time: exactly 5:30 a.m. His life was one of consistency, and time was his most valuable asset. It was also the trade of his profession. The small apartment was above his watchmaking shop a few blocks from the site of the old Reich Security Main Office where Heinrich Himmler had once served Adolf Hitler as the Reichsführer of the Schutzstaffel, the Nazis' elite paramilitary unit known as the SS. The war was lost by the time Geissler was born in Brazil in 1947. But for his father, a former member of the Gestapo, the war had never ended, and from an early age, young Geissler was taught to hate America.

To defeat one's enemy requires the ability to think the way they do. So in 1965, when he was eighteen years old, Geissler moved to the United States to study economics at Harvard University, eventually graduating with a master's degree in 1971. It was while working on Wall Street in the mid-1970s that Geissler's opportunity finally came. His recruitment into the New World Order was unlike anything he'd experienced before, requiring a mastery of conflicting disciplines—mathematics, creative writing, and political science, combined with spycraft and espionage, all while maintaining the front of a law-abiding citizen. In 1982, after seven years of preparation, Geissler was murdered outside his New York City apartment. And thus began his new life, his new identity—his chance to fulfill the destiny of his Aryan race.

Geissler dressed for the day, made himself a cup of black coffee, and sat down at the kitchen table to read the morning newspaper. Its crisp pages and black ink that smeared with touch were staples of his morning routine. The internet was not for reading the news. And besides, he didn't own a computer or a cell phone. A man in his position could never be too careful.

He sipped his coffee and inspected the day's headlines. The front page was plastered with news from the United States. It was the day after Christmas, and America had just finished its glutinous display of rich food and overspending, all in the name of a God they would ignore for the next twelve months. He'd failed. Not just at orchestrating the cyberattack but at launching a third world war the year before. There had always been bumps along the road—unforeseen circumstances—but this was different; someone was intentionally sabotaging his efforts.

He turned to the last page. It was the crossword puzzle section, and someone had already penciled in the answers. Only they weren't answers; they were code. The old spy read the message, deciphering its meaning and letting it stew in his mind. Two words.

NEW BEGINNING

The name was unfamiliar to him, but it was the name of the man responsible for terminating his American asset and thwarting the most important operation of his career.

Two words.

Chris Harding.

ACKNOWLEDGMENTS

Writing is hard. It's a never-ending struggle to make something from nothing—and then fix the problems you create for yourself in the process—but that *something* comes from one place: the imagination. And I've always had a prolific one. I'm like an AI computer, soaking up everything around me and storing it away somewhere deep inside my consciousness, so deep that I forget it's even there. That is, until it makes its way onto the pages of the stories I tell.

This was especially true for this novel. People, places, moments in my life—things I'd all but forgotten—appeared out of nowhere, in scenes, in characters. Slices of realism intertwined with fiction. And that's where the theme of this book was born. The idea that we can start over. Be it a new job, new relationships—a new life. It's a second chance at redemption. And it's funny because I had no idea that was the story I wanted to tell until I was finished. But that's the beauty of art; it takes on a life of its own, using the artist's databank of memories, feelings, desires, and goals to create something brand new that, hopefully, resonates with an audience. In this case, you. And it was always you, **Dear Reader**. You purchased this book. You allowed me into your life, into your imagination. You made the world of Chris Harding possible.

ACKNOWLEDGEMENTS

I'm obsessed with movies and books, and I'd be remiss if I didn't list the authors and filmmakers who influenced *New Beginning*.

Jack Carr's *The Terminal List* series, specifically *The Devil's Hand* and *Only the Dead*. **Lee Child's** *A Wanted Man*—also the Amazon Prime series *Reacher*, which was based on his novels. *Mission: Impossible - Dead Reckoning Part One*, starring the ultimate action hero, **Tom Cruise**, and *The Night Agent* on Netflix, which was adapted from the bestselling novel by **Matthew Quirk**. Every picture written by, directed by, or starring **Sylvester Stallone**. His work ethic and drive are constant reminders that, with enough effort, anything can be achieved. And if you've ever wondered where Chris Harding's penchant for violent extermination of the bad guys comes from, now you know.

So many people in my life contributed to this project—in one way or another, some directly, some not so much, but all equally important—that it would be impossible to list them all here. But I'll try my best.

First, I want to thank my parents **Billy and Veronica Walker** for homeschooling me through much of my early education. They had the foresight and wisdom to provide me that unique experience. An experience that gave me the ability, and desire, to disregard the man in the suit and follow my own path. To live life on my own terms. And to never stop learning. Thank you, Mom, for always reading my early drafts and offering invaluable notes, as well as motherly praise when needed. In case you were wondering, my father did indeed make a cameo in this book. He really is a barber. And he owns the **Lansdowne Barber Shop** in Lexington, Kentucky. As far as brokering information for spies—to my knowledge, that part is fiction. But then, if it were true, would he have

ACKNOWLEDGEMENTS

told me? Thank you, Dad, for always supporting my endeavors, no matter what they are. Also—thank you for selling so many copies of *Disarm* to your customers. More cases of books are on their way.

Every project I undertake, whether it a book or a screenplay, would not be possible without **Mark and Shannon Hartman**. You've created a one-of-a-kind place at **Priscilla's Coffee Shop** in Toluca Lake, California. It's my favorite spot in town and the only way to start my morning. On any given day that's where you'll find me—perched at one of the tables with a stack of books, drinking iced coffee and writing my latest novel.

To the **Priscilla's Coffee Shop Staff**: You're the real deal, the best there is. Writing is a lonely profession, and quietly typing away among you makes that solitude tolerable.

To **Mary Amerson**, for your daily dose of happiness. When I have writer's block—which is often—your cheerful smile brightens my day. Thank you, always.

To my little sister, **Lacey Nguyen**, who always reads early drafts of my work. Thank you for supporting your crazy big brother.

To my niece, **Addie Nguyen**, a fellow author and creative soul. Your enthusiasm for life inspires me to keep doing what I do. I love you so much.

To my best friend, **Chris Desmond**, whose advice on weapons and gear was invaluable during the creation of this novel. Hopefully I got it right. One day we'll make our first million. Until then, thank you for being the brother I never had. Also—keep sending awesome gun pics.

To **Mary, Val, and Julie** at **Books and Moods**: Thank you for designing such kick-ass covers for my books. You do amazing work, and it's an honor to collaborate with you.

ACKNOWLEDGEMENTS

To **Luke Fontneau** at **SilverLining Pictures**: Thank you for being such a positive influence on my work. The film business is a brutal one, and having a friend and colleague like you makes navigating the swamp easier. And it doesn't hurt that we have the same first name.

To **Grisel Hernandez**, who called me a wizard because I make up stories. Our long conversations about life and the future influenced the pages within this book. Thank you for your friendship.

To **Santiago Carpio**: Thank you for the *Disarm* hat. I feel a merch business coming on.

To **Diego Gonzalez**, who was the first person in the world to buy *Disarm*.

To **Marco Samaan**, for pushing me to think like an entrepreneur.

To one of my favorite people: **Alyssa Bustamante**. Thank you for reading everything I write—even stealing pages to use in your acting classes.

To the men and women in the military, to the politicians, to the government agency people (the good ones) fighting to keep our democracy alive. This book is a work of fiction, but the fight to destroy freedom is real. And our enemies will not stop until we are destroyed.

And finally, to my development editor, manager, and life partner—the love of my life, **Camila Carpio**. It was once said, and it's true, that there's a "Camila" in everything I write. My love, you're the one who inspired me to begin this journey in the first place. Who told me to self-publish *Disarm* when I was unhappy with traditional publishing offers. And who motivates me every single day to get up, and keep at it. Living with a writer can't be easy. But you stand by me no matter what, embodying the true definition of

ACKNOWLEDGEMENTS

a ride-or-die. You're the most talented and beautiful woman I've ever known, and you could have been with anyone, yet you chose me. So thank you. Thank you for sharing your life with me. For allowing me to go off and write, alone, every single day. For reading every draft—the good, the bad, and the shit—providing honest feedback, and letting me know when something doesn't work, or in fact does work and to never change it. But most of all, thank you for being my girl.

ABOUT THE AUTHOR

Lukas Walker is the author of *Disarm*. He was born and raised in Lexington, Kentucky and lives in Los Angeles with his fiancée. You can follow him on Instagram, Facebook, and TikTok at LukasWalkerAuthor.

If you enjoyed this book, please consider leaving a review on either Amazon or Goodreads.

Made in the USA
Middletown, DE
03 November 2024